Do No Harm

BOOK ONE
OF THE
THE HEIR OF PEACE

M.B. Hampshire

M.B. HAMPSHIRE

Dedication

To my God who made all this possible, and to my brother, Ezekiel, the white rabbit himself. He gave me one—and only one—critique the entire time he read my work, and that would be, "It's good." Thanks a lot for such enlightening constructive criticism, Ezekiel.

Copyright ©2024 by M.B. Hampshire

All rights reserved.

ISBN: 979-8-9920099-0-3 (Paperback)
ISBN: 979-8-9920099-1-0 (Hardback)
ISBN: 979-8-9920099-2-7 (eBook)

No part of this publication may be reproduced, distributed, or transmitted in any form or by any means, including photocopying, recording, or other electronic or mechanical methods, without the prior written permission of the publisher, except as permitted by U.S. copyright law. For permission requests, contact the author at author.mbhampshire@gmail.com.

The story, all names, characters, and incidents portrayed in this production are fictitious. No identification with actual persons (living or deceased), places, buildings, and products is intended or should be inferred.

Book Cover and Illustrations by M.B. Hampshire.
Book Layout by Megan Lamb.

Connect with the author!
Website: mbhampshire.com
Email: author.mbhampshire@gmail.com
Instagram: @mb_the_author

Table of Contents

Map 1

The Treaty of Idella 3

Prolgue 4

Letter 7

Chapter 1   Unfortunate News 9

Chapter 2   A Ludicrous and Lengthy Chat 24

Chapter 3   Unwanted Answers 39

Chapter 4   Burning Ties 53

Chapter 5   Rekindling the Coward 62

Letter 66

Chapter 6   Threatening are the Shoes that Travel the World 68

Chapter 7   Dreaming of a Nightmare 79

Chapter 8   A Pointed Conversation 91

Chapter 9   Suppression? 98

Chapter 10   From Dust to Dust 112

Chapter 11   The Coward's Company 125

Letter 132

Chapter 12   The Child 134

Chapter 13   The Weaver 146

Chapter 14   The Voice Inside the Blade 160

Chapter 15   Robin 173

Chapter 16   A Rhythm Lost 188

	Letter	192
Chapter 17	Merry Woodsmen	194
Chapter 18	House of Suspicion	207
Chapter 19	Making Friends	220
Chapter 20	The Start of Something Dark	237
Chapter 21	Batch of Shadows	248
	Letter	259
Chapter 22	Lying Between the Lines	261
Chapter 23	Farewell Future, See Me Now in the Shadow of Past	279
Chapter 24	Twisted Justice	295
Chapter 25	The Hated Man's End	308
Chapter 26	A Healer's Decision	320
	Letter	329
	Acknowledgements	333
	Pronunciations	334
	Plant Catalog and Miscellaneous Descriptions	335

Map Key

△ - Capital
☐ - City/Village
○ - Specific Location
✕ - Port
⊠ - Port Town/Village
- - - - - Reach of Roshan Peaks
═════ - Drastic Cliff
═ ═ ═ - River

Map

The Treaty of Idella

Dated: 0130fm (following massacre)
In the third month of summer.

Preamble

In light of recent necessities it has been seen fit for the kingdoms of Avalon and Logres to strike an accord with the sovereign kingdom of the Sher Wood, in order that an agreement should be made, regarding the flow of trade between lands. Due to the rise in overland trade required from the constant supply trains supporting each respective kingdom, and from the sporadic attitude of the ungovernable waters surrounding each, it is proposed that a portion of land be paved through Sher. This land would be neutral ground with which the citizens of each included kingdom shall be able to equally travel to and from, without subjecting themselves to the Sher laws therein.

Article VII

The sovereign kingdom of Sher withholds the right to keep all borders closed for any such length as the governing monarch sees fit, including the right to enforce any and all laws and consequences for any outside party breaking this agreement. Within such neutral ground as the kingdoms see fit, all Sher laws will be absolved, however, the kingdom of Sher retains ownership of the neutral land. Should any participant of the following agreement be caught on Sher's sacred ground, Sher reserves the right to return the neutral ground back to its original state, and the pass between shall once more be subject to all regulations from the Myth government of the Sher Wood.

King Uther Pendragon   *Mayor Faton*

King Daehue Penthellion

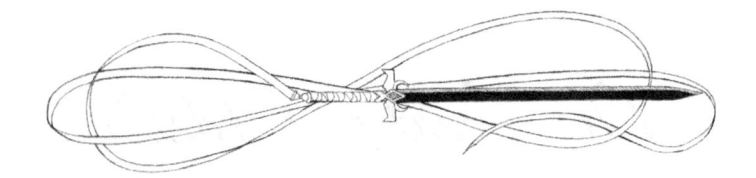

Prologue

The forest was dark that day, and utterly quiet. The browns of the thick tree trunks blurred together as rain snaked its way through the canopy, and all the creatures, both friend and foe, hid from the murk. Even the squirrels, who normally cared nothing for the troubles of others, stayed out of sight and away from the mud coating the forest floor. Only the soldiers moved on that day, stopping at every treehouse, stump, cabin, and cave. They might have stopped the downpour under different circumstances, or directed it away from their path, but not then. With every ivirian and Faun they collected, the deluge seemed more and more appropriate. Even the mud coating their shoes felt necessary.

After stopping at a small wooden cottage, the soldiers made their way to the next house. The home was made out of a bent tree trunk, curved so that it looked like a wave. They might have passed by if not for the small tower built into it, proclaiming it as a house. The sergeant in charge sighed, calling for the company to halt. Even before he made it to the fence of the home, the door was opening. A young ivirian came out, his wings drooping as he shouldered a heavy looking pack. The sergeant straightened as he met the child's gaze.

"Daleon, son of Cavair?" the sergeant asked. The iviro didn't bother to yell from his position, only nodding as he moved forward.

"Wait!" All of the soldiers tensed as a girl burst out of the trunk. She collided with the ivirian, sending them both staggering backwards.

The sergeant sighed. He had been briefed about this house already. "Move out," he replied. A soldier glanced at the two, but the sergeant just shook his head. This was one fight that did not need to happen. "He'll join us soon."

As the group marched away, the young ivirian looked down at his sister. "What are you doing?"

The girl, two years his junior, glared up at the rain, which splashed against her face. "I have to come!"

Her brother smiled down at her. "No way. I go because you need to be protected. How can I accomplish that if you're there too? Besides, this is the only way that I can prove I'm stronger than you." His joke didn't lighten the mood. In fact, she hardly noticed it.

"You don't have to do this," she told him, her bare feet sinking deeper in the wet ground. "I need to protect you. What if you get hurt, and I'm not there? What will you do?"

The iviro, Daleon, placed a hand on her shoulder. "I'll go to a doctor."

"Sands! You know what I mean." She glared up at him.

"Listen, Lyn." Daleon closed his eyes. "It's my duty to protect my family and my kingdom. But while I'm gone, you have to protect Mother and Father. I can't do it while I'm at sea, understand? You have to promise me that you will do what's right."

Lyn took a deep breath. A large tremor rolled across her body, from her head to her feet, until all the shaking had deserted her. There was no point in arguing further and continuing would only drive the hopeless fear deeper inside her.

"I'll do it." She pulled back, stepping onto the stone porch in front of the house. "But I promise that I'll follow you. As soon as I can, I will meet you at the front lines."

"Lyn!" Daleon covered his face with a hand. "You can't make promises you know you won't keep."

"This one I will," she said firmly. "I'll find a way."

He dropped his hand, a sign to her and to himself that he had given up. Now that she made the vow, there was no stopping her, no matter what he said. At least she wasn't trying to hinder his departure any longer. Daleon forced a small smile, hiding the exhaustion behind his teeth. They both knew that the war could last until she was eighteen, but *surely* the hope was that it would end before then. A prolonged fight could mean that Sher would not only be forced to give up more citizens, but face the thought of those given dying in a fight they had not caused. If the humans persisted in fighting, eventually his own kingdom would have to do more than guard their borders.

Daleon sighed. He rubbed the side of his head, eyes darting off to the left. Standing a short distance away, partially covered in shadows, was the outline of a soldier. The ivira was waiting, her posture tense. She was there to make sure he didn't run.

With yet another sigh, Daleon glanced back at his sister. Resignation steadied him as he said, "I'll see you then."

My dear Ivory Bishop,

Since you left I have found every attempt at assistance to be futile. Every scholar I choose seems to lack in one manner or the other, despite insisting on their qualifications. They never learn that I disapprove of ignorant workers, so the result is a decrease in the amount of truly 'intelligent' people in the world. As such is the case, I have been forced to send my thoughts without any real observations regarding its contents, or alterations to make it... smoother. Therefore, even though this won't reach you in advance of my sending the original, I have elected to send you some of its contents, as I have done previously. You will find those contents attached to this letter.

Regarding other issues, I do assume you are keeping up to date with present affairs, but there are additional happenings that you must be informed of, which are not common knowledge. Firstly, the killer of our dear acquaintance turned out to be laughably easy to find, and has been dealt with before the penning of this page. I would not have bothered if I hadn't been prodded to waste my time, but after seeing him I was glad. As for his employer, that is a more complicated matter. I find myself now faced with a just reason for all my actions, an actual excuse for any move I make. How ironic is it that we can plead justified for any and all grievances caused by our response?

But as to dealing with the employer, that will prove harder than we anticipated. The price on that fox's head is too high to stroll in and take without terrible repercussions. I expect an extra half-year to be added onto our plan, assuming the rumors I've heard are false. They are the main reason I have sent word so quickly after your last letter. Our spies on the Onyx board have told me that there is one on the board who possesses extreme power, enough to ruin our plans. I have yet to prove this, but you should be wary, in case we have to prolong our movements.

Aside from that, I would like to know how you fare? You spoke little of it in your letter, which made me concerned. I would hate for idleness to reach you after all these years. But regardless, I see that we will soon be reunited. Perhaps you can tell me what you have left out then?

Farewell,

Ivory Knight

1

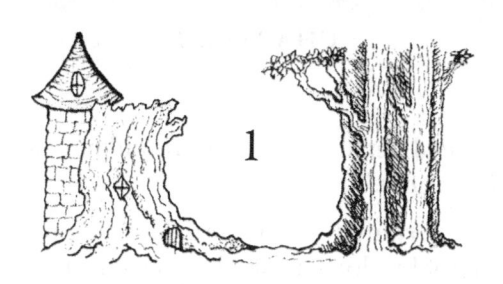

Unfortunate News

The sun started its journey upwards over Sher. Light brushed its hand over oaks and maples, dipping the tips of its fingers through many branches which formed the canopy. Inside the forest blew a quiet breeze between scattered tree trunks. It rustled leaves and tickled the noses of the deer waking up. Many inhabitants were still asleep, but just as many were awake. The soldiers on duty felt the same airy chill as the ivirian causing a loud racket at the front door of a treehouse.

The home was made from a large, old, rust colored tree that curved like a rising wave. At its side there was a stone tower with a window planted directly in the middle of its plum roof. It sat in the center of an artificial clearing, but the inhabitants had not left the space unused. An enormous garden spread out in a half circle around the tower and trunk, filled with different herbs, flowers, and vegetables. It was from the garden that ivy spread up and over the house. There was also a small section dedicated to geese, but it was smaller, and a tiny house took up most of its room. The birds inside the space were squawking at the ivirian, trying to make him stop the horrible noise.

"Where is the owner of this house?" he barked, his black eyes twitching in annoyance. He had been there for at least five minutes, *trying* to get the attention of the owners.

"That would be me."

The old ivirian turned to see a human—no, an elestiel—with a basket of eggs standing in front of him. She was at least eighteen, as the ages of humans and their half-breed cousins are easy to guess. Coppery hair fell just above her elbows and, he sneered, she had those horrid golden eyes that marked her kind.

It only took him a moment to pull out his sword, his wings itching to extend. "What are you doing in this forest?" he growled.

CHAPTER 1

The elestiel pulled her shawl tighter around her shoulders, looking unperturbed. "I live here."

"No elestiel is permitted to be here," he snapped. "Speak truth, scum, or you will not live longer than it takes for my sword to fall."

She sighed and held out her arm, pulling the gown's sleeve up until it showed a black tattoo inked on her skin. The design was a lozenge with a maple leaf in the middle, and thorns spread out underneath it. It was the crest of Sher's government.

"How did you get that?"

She shook her head at him. "I'm a legal citizen. They put this on me when it became official. Surely you're not going to disbelieve the crest that *only* the Mayor has access to, right?"

"Of course not." The ivirian shoved his sword back into its scabbard with gusto. Even with her assurance, he eyed her suspiciously. Now that he was paying attention, he could see not just golden eyes, but pointed ears as well. It meant that she was part elf, as well as elestiel. Truly disgusting.

The girl seemed to understand his reaction, and hefted her basket up. "What is it you need from me?"

She watched as he straightened, spitting once on the ground before pulling out a piece of paper from a pouch on his hip. Realization dawned upon her as she took in his appearance. The scapular he wore was black and clasped around his neck, his billowing pants slit down the sides. Around the bicep of his left arm there was a silver token with two stars set within a lozenge. Together they meant one thing.

"I'm searching for a man named Merlin." The ivirian walked closer to her, holding up his paper so close to her face that it was a breath away from touching her nose. "Have you seen him?"

She didn't need to look at it to know that it was a human man with a long white beard, a pointed hat, and stars covering his robes. The image was a popular design for him. Instead of saying this she stuck her head out from behind the parchment. "Why are you looking for Merlin?" Her eyes strayed to the token once more. "Are you... arresting him?"

"Ha!" He pulled the paper away and shoved it back into the pouch. "You do know where he is! Tell me!"

"Look sir—" she started.

"Sheriff, Sheriff Rainault." He put both arms behind his back. "I have come from the capital in search of his help, so I would have you give it to me before I decide to take it by force."

Rather than answer, the elestiel walked around the ivirian, making sure to avoid his bat-like wings in the process. She stopped at her front door, and *then* spoke. "I am Merlin, but I won't help you. So just leave." She watched as surprise appeared on Rainault's square face, a feature not normal for round-faced ivirians.

"You lie," he told her. "I was told he was a man—"

"With a white beard and blue clothes, yes, I know." Merlin shook her head. "I don't know where that started, but it is not true."

"But, but..." the Sheriff spluttered. "If it is you, then you have to help me! I have a disease, there is no cure other than the power you possess. Please, heal me. No one else can!"

Her eyes skimmed over him dismissively. One moment he had been ready to kill her and the next he was begging to be healed. The sheriff probably *still* wanted to kill her, but his health was more important to him. "No, I won't. Sorry, but your money would be better used someplace else. Along with whatever time you have left."

"I can pay!" Rainault shoved his hands in his pouch again, probably pulling out bronze coins. His voice displayed anxiety, but his eyes held confidence. He believed that she would heal him, just because of his money.

"It doesn't matter what you try to pay me." She put one hand on the doorknob. "I won't accept it."

Rainault's gray skin paled as the click of her door sounded. He froze with his fist full of coins. "What manner of healer are you," he gasped, "to deny a sick iviro healing?"

"Forgive me for speaking plainly, but it's because I don't like you." Merlin turned back. "You're rude to me and probably other people as well. Your manners don't exist, and your eyes look pompous."

"But," his shoulders drooped, "but everyone says you are benevolent and kind. How could you not heal me? Don't you know I'll die?"

Merlin looked at him sadly, feeling the remains of her good mood plummet further. He really was sick, she could feel it and see it. Ivirian

CHAPTER 1

bones should be hollow, but his bones had tiny cracks running along the inside of them, and through the cracks were leaking incredibly small amounts of marrow at a steady rate. The leakage was small enough that he wouldn't be in danger for another month or so, but he would eventually die from it.

His wings were the most visibly damaged, as the bones running along the top were leaking into the membrane. What once was colored like the night sky was marred by murky gray spreading through the patterns. The only thing keeping him alive appeared to be an increase in his blood production, which was helping make up for the loss of marrow. However, the excess was also making the leakage worse. Doubtless he was using an herb called ridane for his blood. Regardless of that, Merlin knew which illness plagued him; Talin's Disease.

Sighing, she told him, "You've brought this on yourself. I will not heal you. Go back to Nottingham." Sheriff Rainault's mouth dropped open in disbelief as she stepped into her house and shut the door.

Inside, Merlin rested her head against the closed door, listening for his departure. For a few moments it was silent, and then a stream of curses poured out of the sheriff. She listened silently to his gravelly screams through the wood until he finished off his visit with an angry kick that rattled the door violently. The act triggered another curse, but she could tell it was directed at himself, not her. A solid door like the one they owned would be painful to kick with any force.

When he had completely left the vicinity, Merlin pushed herself away from the entrance. Though slightly rattled, she needed to finish putting her fresh eggs into the family cellar and lighting the candles around the house. She made her way around the main floor, lighting each pillar of wax in the living room, kitchen, and stairwell. As she made her way up the tower, she paused only briefly at the door to the second bedroom. Merlin stood just long enough for pain to rise in her heart, and then she continued her way up.

Afterward she went back into the kitchen to prepare herself food, only to find a bowl of scrambled eggs sitting on their dining table. She missed it and the card when she put the golden eggs away.

The small paper said: *Have a good day dear, we'll see you in a few months. Remember to send us word if you get a response.*

Smiling to herself, Merlin procured a spoon and bowl. Just as she was planning to sit, the kitchen window began rattling excessively. Displayed behind the glass sat a cat with bright emerald eyes and glossy black fur, pawing at the pane. Merlin sighed to herself and opened the window, letting the animal in before she shut the opening.

"Good morning!" it announced, landing on the counter and then hopping to the table. "I see you already have a meal prepared for me, how nice."

"Ack! Wait!" Merlin launched herself at the table, grabbing the cat before she could stick her paw in the bowl of eggs. "That's my food, Gwen!"

The cat glared at Merlin, letting her entire body go limp, and subsequently doubling the weight. "What did I say about grabbing me?" Gwen hissed. "Just because I'm smaller doesn't mean you get to treat me like it!" Merlin looked down, but before she could say anything, Gwen bit her hand.

"Ow!" Merlin dropped the cat, cradling her hand. "Guinevere!" The cat landed on all fours, sticking out her tongue as she scrunched up to pounce yet again. Merlin's eyes widened, and she quickly grabbed the cat, mid leap. "Cut it out!" she commanded. "I'll give you some, but let me get it first!"

Gwen yowled, squirming in Merlin's hands as the girl set the cat down on the bench opposite the one Merlin had been on. "Hmph!" Gwen plopped her head down on the table with a loud thump, glaring at Merlin as she scooped food into two bowls. "I suppose your mother left this?" she grumbled.

Merlin smirked. "Yes, Mother and Father left earlier, so unfortunately you won't get to say goodbye."

"That's fine." Merlin sat Gwen's plate down, finally starting on her own meal. Gwen scooped a pawful of eggs in her claws, stuffing it inside her mouth. She asked through the food, "Where are they going now?"

"Logres." Merlin rolled her eyes. "They have extra herbs to sell this year, and the pass is hard to get through now, so it will probably take them longer to get back."

Gwen swallowed. "Good thing they got permission to go." She blinked. "By the way, who was that screaming guy outside? He didn't sound very pleasant."

CHAPTER 1

"Oh that, he was a sheriff from Nottingham. He wanted me to heal him, and for good reason." Merlin made an ugly expression. "He reeked of illness."

"And you didn't help him?" Gwen narrowed her eyes as she slowly put another pawful of food in her mouth.

Merlin sighed. "No, I didn't. He was rude, and he has Talin's Disease."

"Ah. I guess he had it coming." Gwen shook her head. "That would be why he sounded so angry."

"Exactly." Merlin set her spoon down again. "I can't justify healing that, and even if I did, it would take too long. I'm nervous already, adding something that would make us late would not help."

The cat nodded. "Yes, yes, you are correct. But don't worry Merlin, everything will be fine."

"You're right," Merlin stood. "Stay here while I get dressed, then we can go."

"Aw." Gwen rested her head on her paw, a mischievous look appearing in her eyes. "But I thought you wanted to travel in your nightgown? The shawl gives it a nice touch."

Merlin glared at Gwen. "Oh, very funny. Not all of us can just walk around in fur. Wait here!"

~·~·~·~

It didn't take long for Merlin to pull on the various garments needed for the day. Human women generally wore dresses—or so Merlin had been told—but she preferred the more functional olive riding pants. Not that she did much riding. Aside from that, she wore just a cotton under shirt and a black vest that laced up the front. Really her cape was the only remarkable cloth she wore. It was the color of a nightshade petal, the darkest part. It ended just below her waist and it had a hood that covered her face on all sides. What made it special was that the thread had been spliced together with terebinth wood, a special tree that was impervious to nearly everything. The plant was extremely hard to come by, what with the war around them, but her mother had managed to acquire some just for Merlin.

Coming back to her senses, she pulled on a satchel and hurried down the tower stairs. Gwen was probably getting bored, and a bored cat spelled both destruction and chaos. When she got to the bottom of the stairs, Gwen was waiting, her tail swishing back and forth. "Are you ready?"

"Yes."

"No."

Merlin blinked at the cat. "No?"

Gwen sighed in exasperation, placing a paw on her head. "Are you going to walk around with your hair flying all over the place? Or are you going to tie it?"

"Goodness." Merlin went over to the side table, picking up a leather string that was draped over it. "Thanks, *Mom*." she said sarcastically. Gwen spit her tongue out as Merlin pulled her hair into a loose ponytail. The cat was right, unfortunately. Her hair tended to tangle into impenetrable knots when left down. That, and shrouding her ears, even partially, was necessary for venturing outdoors.

"Now can we go?" Merlin drawled.

"Yes, yes." Gwen leapt forward, coming to a screeching halt at the closed door. She turned and looked blankly at Merlin. Her gaze clearly meant that it was Merlin's fault she had been stopped.

The elestiel rolled her eyes, quickly fixing 'her' error by opening the door. Outside, the sun had climbed higher in the sky, and a comfortable warmth had fallen upon the forest. Merlin smiled as a white rabbit hopped across her lawn and into a hole. The opening disappeared once the bunny had been fully swallowed. Usually prey avoided their clearing since the ground was flat and empty. The lack of bumps in the dirt was again thanks to her mother, an ivira belonging to the Growth Order.

Gwen laughed and sprinted down the path of the house, into the woods. Merlin shook her head, following the cat outside of the fenced in square that guarded her home. As soon as she left the clearing, the atmosphere of the forest changed, growing darker from the number of trees. The Sher Wood was a kingdom completely made up of forest, mountains, and more forest. What separated Sher's trees from other woods was the size. The trunks of the trees were enormous in diameter, and most of the roots were so far deep in the ground that no one could dig them up. Although, some rebellious roots were above the ground, winding around neighboring trees and making tunnels over paths. Everything was covered with moss as well, or ferns hanging from branches twenty feet from the ground. There were flowers too, blooming in hidden patches all around the forest floor.

Merlin ducked underneath a root that had grown over the path, only to make a sudden dive to the ground as Gwen sprung off the wood. The cat landed next to Merlin.

Her green eyes danced with excitement. "We're never going to get there if you're lying on the ground."

"Oh haha." Merlin pushed herself up onto her elbows. "Watch where you're jumping next time." Gwen ignored her and sprinted a little further down the path. Merlin moved to follow when she realized that she had fallen right next to a small patch of little white flowers with round petals. The stems were a bright yellow that twisted in interlocking tangles of leaves and roots.

"Ha!" she exclaimed. "Gwen, there's lulac!"

The cat slowed from her fast run to look back at Merlin. "Maybe it's a sign," she called.

"You may be right." Merlin agreed as she carefully pulled the imbued plant out of the dirt. The flowers were pretty enough, but the roots were used for calming incensed individuals, and would sell for at least four bronze coins. At the very least lulacs were rare, and seeing them was a sign of good luck. She needed that reassurance, what with where she was going, and what she was hoping for.

"Merlin?" She looked back up at the cat, who gestured with her paw. "Are you coming?"

"Right, I am!" It only took a few seconds for Merlin to secure the roots in a small pouch before she returned to an upright position. There was no use in agitation... yet.

After an hour of walking through the forest without seeing anyone but a couple of deer and squirrels, they finally arrived at their destination. Behind a wall of weeping willows, still lily pads sat on the surface of an emerald pond so green that its edges faded into the ground completely. Moss grew from the center and spread out in honeycombs around cattails which dipped their heads in a steep bow. An enormous dome of leaves rose up from a great oak tree sitting peacefully in the center of the pond. Hanging from its branches were dozens of bird houses, each intricately made. Some were shaped like short fat mushrooms with white tops, others were shaped like tree nooks. There were unfamiliar designs as well: square buildings with pointed roofs and windows lined in trim.

Flying in and out of the houses were blue jays, robins, cardinals, and other birds Merlin didn't recognize. In their beaks they carried white envelopes of various sizes and numbers, and in their claws they held strings wrapped around parcels. The birds lugged their items high up into the tree beyond where Merlin could see, but she knew where they were headed. There was an opening at the top where birds dropped their packages or could dive through and bring their envelopes personally.

Merlin gave a contented sigh at the same time as Gwen. She glanced down at the cat, who was staring up at blue jays in the tree with a desiring expression. "No Gwen, you cannot eat them."

"Fine." Gwen shook her head, hopping onto Merlin's waist before climbing to a perch on her shoulder.

"Ow!" Merlin exclaimed as she wobbled. "What is wrong with you?"

Gwen pointed a claw at the pond. "It's water."

Exasperated, she rolled her eyes. "There's a bridge!" Merlin waved emphatically at a moss-covered bridge. The dark wood spanned from one side of the pond to a deck around the oak tree. "You know that!"

"But last time I slipped and fell in!" Gwen whined. "I was green for a month!"

Merlin ignored her and felt her pants for any holes. "Your claws are going to rip my clothes!"

Gwen growled and put both her paws on Merlin's head. "Stop complaining and let's *go*!" On the last word, the cat shoved forward so forcefully that Merlin took three dangerously imbalanced steps towards what appeared to be the edge of the pond.

"Eek!" They both squealed as Merlin corrected herself, nearly sending the cat flying off. The birds above chirped at them, squeaking in what was clearly laughter.

Merlin glared at the tree house, before straightening her back, and marching forward. Her feet carried her across the mossy walkway right up to a door that had been chiseled into the tree trunk. On either side of it hung potted plants that draped over the edge of their container. Gray flowers resembling lilies dangled from the green stems, a dim version

CHAPTER 1

of themselves outside of nighttime. When the moon rose in the sky, the moonlit flowers would glow like starlight. It was a beautiful sight, and an efficient way of lighting the office.

With wood creaking underneath her feet, Merlin pulled open the hefty door. Above her head a small bell chimed, and the smell of paper and leather greeted her.

The inside of the tree was really a series of large circular rooms stacked on top of each other with wooden slides and shafts running between floors. A large basket was sitting on the far side of the room with three such beams ending above it. A couple letters were sliding down the wood as Merlin left the front door partially open, landing with little taps inside the basket. By it sat a desk and high chair, with open slots spanning the entire wall behind it. Each slot had at least one piece of mail sitting inside it. Around the desk and over most of the floor were stacks of letters and packages, each with a line through their seal. There were a couple journals strewn about as well, but not enough to warrant picking up.

Merlin picked her way through the piles carefully, using the light of the mounted candles to avoid stepping on anything too valuable. When she reached the desk, she had to peer over the top of it to see a slouched gnome laying against the wood. His red cap was pulled low over his face, and a brown sweater hung over the back of the chair.

"Um, Myrtle?" Merlin said gently. When the gnome didn't wake up, she spoke louder, "Myrtle!"

Gwen hopped off her shoulder, landing with a thump on the tip of the slanted desk. *That* woke Myrtle. He shot up in his seat, looking back and forth through the cap. He had black letters smudged on his round cheek, though miraculously nothing on his short white beard. When he turned, his elbow knocked his thin glasses off the desk.

"What? Who—" He stopped shaking and reached up. "Oh, confound it all!" Myrtle pushed up his hat so that he could see.

Merlin grinned at the elderly gnome. "Good afternoon."

"Ah, Merlin. It's just you." Myrtle rubbed his cheek, advantageously rubbing the ink off in the process. "Thought it was the inspector, he's supposed to be here you know."

"Yes, you mentioned it last time." In fact he mentioned it *every* time she was there. "I'm sure he'll get here eventually."

"Hmph." Myrtle snorted disdainfully. "He better, I'm ready to retire."

Merlin nodded as sympathetically as she could. The government had promised him a replacement twenty years ago, and they still hadn't sent him an inspector to approve the transfer. Gwen made a coughing noise which drew Merlin's attention from the gnome. The cat was jerking her head towards a square on the back wall which was filled with black letters. Her throat caught at the reminder.

"So... Myrtle." Merlin turned back. "Do you have a letter for me?"

He blinked at her incomprehensibly. "Didn't I get it delivered to you last week?"

"Yes, but I'm not looking for one from Dal, it should be from the government." Merlin nodded to the official black envelopes.

"Oh, so not one from your brother..." Myrtle's eyes got a faraway look as he swiveled his chair around. "Then you'll be wanting... What is this?" He pulled out a regular letter from within a cabinet. Myrtle let out a shrill whistle and glared. From the post office's winding staircase flew a little black sparrow with a red head. It landed on the desk by Gwen. The cat's head snapped towards the animal, but Merlin had already put a restraining hand on her.

"Do you see this?" Myrtle held up the letter, and Merlin could see a streak of dirt across the corner of it. "Sloppy delivery. You're a bird! How can you get dirt on this if it's in the air?" He stared pointedly at the bird.

It chirped at him halfheartedly.

"I don't want excuses." Myrtle sat the letter on the flat tip of his desk, and nodded to it. "Go apologize to Miss Locks right now. You're going to get my office destroyed by bears at this rate." The sparrow made one last sad noise before flapping off the desk, the letter in its beak. Grumbling to himself about more sloppy deliveries, the gnome swiveled in his chair again.

"Uh, Myrtle?" Merlin let go of Gwen. "Did you find a letter for me?"

"Oh that," Myrtle reached up to a top cabinet. "You'll be wanting the one we got yesterday." Gwen gave Merlin a superior look, which she ignored. Her attention was focused sharply on Myrtle's search for the letter.

Her skin tingled.

CHAPTER 1

Her breath was shallow.

It was years of practicing self-control that held her back from jumping over the desk and finding the letter herself.

"Here we are." Myrtle spun around, holding out a sleek black envelope with an orange seal. "You don't have to pay for this since it's an official notice."

Merlin swallowed, taking the letter from him with both hands. Its seemingly smooth surface was actually rough in her hands, and when she slid her thumb underneath the seal, the wax bent in half. Inside there was a single sheet of paper folded into three segments.

To: Merlin Lynwood, daughter of Cavair Lynwood
From: Sher Armed Forces Naval Division
[Time sent: 1:15 pm]

We have received your request form and have looked over your specific abilities and qualifications. Please be assured that we thoroughly thought through your position. However, while the kingdom of Sher greatly appreciates your willingness to serve, we must regretfully decline your acceptance into the military. Due to cultural divisions, it would be deleterious to include you in the new recruits. Many of our brethren would be dismayed at your appearance, and would not be willing to accept your medicinal assistance.

Please rest assured that your family will continue to be protected. If you would still like to support our forces, any food that can be donated would be a great service, as well as any materials and monetary support...

Her eyes blurred to the point of blindness, leaving no room for her to finish reading. The letter slipped from her fingers, dropping to the paper covered ground. A splash of black amid the white. It made a resounding thump that echoed in her ears over and over again. *We must decline your acceptance into the military.* Trembling, Merlin tried to breathe deeply, but her lungs could only hold small amounts of air.

Her heart was beating rapidly in her chest, she knew she needed to calm down.

"Merlin!" Gwen's face appeared in front of her. The cat's expression held nothing but concern. "What is it?!" Merlin couldn't say anything, she couldn't do anything except turn her head to stare at the black spot on the ground.

"What's wrong with her?" cried Myrtle.

Her vision was beginning to darken.

"I'm sorry Merlin." That was all the warning she got before the cat smacked her across the face.

Merlin recoiled, blinking rapidly as pain swelled in her cheek. She gasped, shaking her head. "I—I'm sorry." Her eyes began to tear up, but Merlin rubbed the liquid away.

Myrtle was giving her a look as if she was an injured puppy. "There, there," he said, patting her shoulder. "Whatever it is, I'm sure you'll be all right." He was trying to sound comforting, but it made Merlin feel worse.

"Merlin." The cat was glaring at her intensely. "What was in there? They didn't..."

"They... they declined my submission." Merlin spoke slowly. She didn't want to believe it. She wanted to pretend that the letter was for someone else.

"What?" Gwen's voice pitched higher. "But how is that possible?"

Merlin waved at the envelope. "Cultural differences based on my appearance."

Gwen pounced on the envelope, sticking her claws into it. "What does that even mean? So just because you have pale skin you can't join them? Or is it your ears?"

Myrtle cleared his throat, and the two turned to look at him. He stroked his beard thoughtfully. "Now, I've been a postman for forty years, a jolly one despite my attempts to retire. In recent years I have unfortunately delivered countless armed notices, and after that much time looking at letters, you start to understand the sender." Merlin tilted her head and Myrtle continued, "I'd say that they are talking about your ancestry."

"My... ancestry?" She looked down at her hands. Her parents were ivirians, there was nothing strange about that. Her grandfather was an ivirian, her brother was too. So what...

That's when it hit her. Myrtle wasn't talking about her parent's ancestors, he meant her birth parents.

Myrtle sighed, his voice coming out tinny. "It's not surprising, given the war going on. Golden eyes tend to be a sore spot for everyone, not to mention they incite fear. I'm sorry, Merlin." He gently reached out and patted her shoulder again.

Gwen hissed. "Well they don't make everyone scared! Come on Merlin, let's go." The cat picked up the letter with her mouth, marching towards the slightly open door. Her movement snapped Merlin out of her daze, and she was able to thank Myrtle decently before hurrying out of the office.

Outside Gwen already made it across the bridge, the horrid letter discarded on the ground. The cat was releasing all her anger on a small mushroom by ripping it to shreds with her claws. Gwen yowled and hissed as she stomped on it again.

"Guinevere!" Merlin rushed forward. "Stop! What if that's someone's house?!" Gwen stopped her hissing, and glanced down at the fungi.

"It's not. I checked," she replied, sounding less than sure. The birds in the tree started to laugh again. Merlin glared up at them in time to see a stork fly into the tree. A sudden feeling of tears readying to burst came as the bird passed her. Storks were used for government letters only, which probably meant another black envelope—also used only by the government—had been delivered. The girl swallowed down the raging emotions before any tears could be shed. Instead Merlin turned to the remains, kneeling down to gently inspect the pieces.

Merlin exhaled in relief, letting part of the mushroom drop. "All right, it's just a normal mushroom." She opened one eye to stare coldly at her friend. "You were lucky this time. But I can't tell you right away if this is poisonous, so we'll have to wait and see."

Gwen pouted. "Don't worry about me, Merlin. Let's just go home. I know the news was... not good."

Merlin pursed her lips, subconsciously picking up the battered letter. "Gwen, I just... I promised him I'd go." Her chest heaved, feeling like a boulder had been placed on top of it.

The cat nodded, stepping over to her. "I know. Listen, we can talk about it more at home. I don't think it would be good for Myrtle if you start crying in front of his post office."

"I won't cry." Merlin assured. She got up and began making her way back up the path without any more objection. They walked silently for some time, neither sure what to say. A brush of warmth blew through the trees, cinders riding the wind. Merlin skirted to a stop, watching the ashes twirl in the air. A puff of black smoke accompanied the chars, and the smell of burnt oak flooded Merlin's nose.

"What—?" Gwen started, coughing when a cloud blew in her face.

Merlin inhaled sharply, and shot off the path, following the acidic smell of charcoal. She charged through tall patches of grass and ducked under a branch, coming to a complete stop so abruptly that Gwen collided with her leg.

In front of them sat piles of blackened oak trees and smoking spruce carcasses. Scattered stones steamed on the ground, and half mutilated trunks crumbled with every gust of tortured air. Ash fell like rain around the clearing, and the putrid smell of decaying ivy entwined itself over everything.

"What happened?" Gwen choked. The cat could hardly move without stirring up more black dust. Merlin opened her mouth to speak, but her attention caught on something. Closer to the edge of the desolation was a pile of burnt wood, and it appeared to be shuddering. Her eyes narrowed. She tentatively moved forward, edging around the hot area. The cat followed her silently until they reached the pile. Now that they were nearer, Merlin could tell that it was not shuddering, it was moving up and down. She exchanged glances with Gwen before grabbing a rough stick. Merlin clenched it tightly as she stuck it between two logs and pushed.

Gwen gasped. "T-that's—"

"A human." Merlin finished, staring down at the unconscious man.

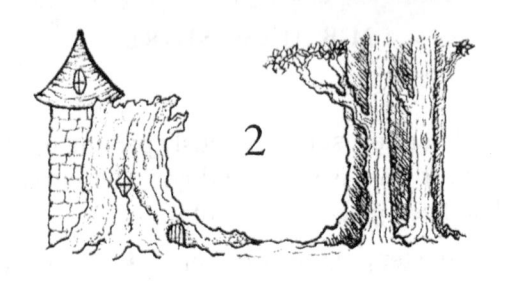

A Ludicrous and Lengthy Chat

His hair was short and silver, at least the parts that weren't covered in ash. Black smudges covered his face, his shoes were completely gone, and the lower pant legs of his trousers were tattered. If that wasn't enough, the right sleeve and shoulder of his undershirt and tunic had also been blown off to reveal fresh red cuts. There was one particularly large gash that ran across four old scars. Merlin narrowed her eyes, focusing on the internal damage. She sensed that the largest injury was just above his lung, four ribs were cracked on the left, and two on the right. There were other injuries, but nothing life threatening.

She crouched down and shoved off the remaining twigs and brush from him. Gwen was moving slowly towards her, eyeing the boy dubiously. "He's alive." Merlin informed her.

Gwen heaved a sigh of relief. "Thank goodness." Her pace increased, and the cat was soon sitting next to Merlin. "Why do you think he's here?"

"I don't know." Merlin frowned. There was a chance he was Avalonian, but he could just as easily be a spy from Logres that was supposed to enter Avalon. The odds of that were slim. Merlin glared at him. "He must be very foolish to be here."

Gwen tilted her head. "If someone finds him, they'll kill him."

Merlin snorted. "It would be no more than he deserves. Humans don't belong in Sher. He's going to make the war worse."

"You might be right," the cat agreed. "But we can't leave him here"

"Why not?" Merlin looked up at her. "It's his own fault for coming into the forest."

"Well, I think we should help him." Gwen said, ignoring her censure. "Maybe he didn't mean to be here."

"I doubt that." Merlin muttered, leaning over the man. "We're not close enough to the border for any stragglers to be here." She gently placed her finger on one of his eyelids, lifting it up to peer at his pupils. Merlin gasped, drawing back her hand. "Forget what I said. He's not human."

Gwen jumped. "What? What do you mean?"

Merlin pointed at his face. "His eyes are gold." If Gwen's face could pale, it would have then. Golden eyes could only mean one thing, that boy was an elestiel—a human who had access to the Rideon, the source of power that hung over the entire world. It was from the Rideon that Merlin drew her own power, as well as making her stronger and faster than the average human.

"We should find a soldier," started Merlin dubiously.

"No!" Gwen shook her head violently. "If you do that they'll report it to the Mayor!"

The cat was right. Anyone would think that she was with the elestiel, even if she reported him. The mayor would certainly revoke her citizenship.

"We'll have to bring him with us then." Merlin grimaced. From the ground the man groaned loudly, and Merlin quickly picked up his arm. Another pained moan escaped him, but Merlin continued to pull him up, maneuvering him so that his weight was leaning on her.

Gwen walked up, one paw stopped mid-step. "Is he heavy?"

Merlin gave her own groan. "Let's just go."

It took twice as long as it normally would to get home, what with the extra weight of another person slowing Merlin down. Gwen made repeated apologies for not being able to help, but there was nothing she could feasibly do. The cat got her chance to be of assistance when they arrived at the house, making a remarkable jump to open the door.

"Can you get a towel?" Merlin asked, puffing as she made her way into the living room.

"One moment!" Gwen appeared, dragging a cloth in her mouth. She dropped it in the middle of the room, pulling both sides out to make it smooth. Merlin tried to gently set the boy down on it, but winced when his head thumped against the ground.

"Right. Water, cloth, clothes, and…" Her muttering died out as she retrieved each item from the various corners of the house. She set a bowl of water next to the boy and plunged the cloth inside it before she began scrubbing at his face. The black came off his skin easily, displaying its actual shade, a bronze russet that reminded her of a toasted almond.

Gwen leaned over the boy, peering at his now clean face. "He's kind of handsome."

"Seriously?" Merlin rolled her eyes as she set down the cloth. "He's here, bleeding, and you're thinking about his appearance." She grabbed his left sleeve, tearing it into little pieces.

"There isn't anything else I can do." Gwen defended. "Besides, you know it's true."

Merlin glanced at his face again, wiping the cuts on his arm. His jaw had a sharp line to it, and there *was* a certain appeal to his somewhat softer overall appearance. She could also see now he had a few strands of hair that looked like actual silver, which was a rather unusual shade for an elestiel. Begrudgingly she said, "I suppose."

She rolled her eyes, turning her attention back to her work. His left arm had just as many old scars as the right did, all varying in age. Some looked sort of new, others were several years old. What could he have been doing to receive so many deep cuts?

With a sigh, Merlin set the boy's arm back down. "All right, step back. I'm going to heal him now." Gwen obeyed, leaping up to the brown settee and curling into a ball.

With the cat out of the way, Merlin was safely able to continue. She extended her right hand out over the boy and flexed her fingers. A buzz ran along her skin as golden flecks of light similar to embers appeared suspended in the air. In a circle she directed her hand, making a smaller loop inside the first. Her signet, the key to unlocking her gift, was formed.

As soon as she connected the second circle, Merlin's senses were plunged into the unbridled power of the Rideon. It stuck to her skin, her clothing, her hair, and yet somehow it flowed freely in the air. Heavy currents of energy swayed in continual movement around her, a solid weight that pressed down and lifted Merlin up at the same time. The power was a vast ocean that neither grew nor shrank, was neither wet nor dry.

Connecting with the power had been overwhelming the first time, but now she could control the outflow of power coming from her. Only the tiniest sliver escaped her grip when she worked her gift. Taking a deep, steadying breath, Merlin put one hand on the boy's shoulder. Her mind began taking in the state of the injuries—inaccuracies—of his current health, focusing on the broken bones, the cuts, the bruises. When Merlin found all the fresh wounds, she began mentally pushing power into the boy. She wove the skin back together, and mended the bones that snapped.

Time passed slowly as she worked without comprehension of her surroundings. Her eyes were open but her vision held only the healing. After an hour passed, she cut off her connection to the Rideon. Awareness came back to her in the form of sore joints and dry eyes.

"Is he all right?" Gwen asked from her curled up spot on the sofa.

Merlin stood, smiling slightly. "Yes, but it will take a bit before he wakes up. So get off the couch, I'm going to move him." She looped her arms underneath the elestiel's shoulders and hoisted him up. As soon as he was there however, Merlin felt dismayed. His clothes were still covered in ash, and the poor furniture was suffering from it.

"I guess I'll go find him some clothes." Merlin glanced at the window. "Maybe you could watch the yard?"

Gwen purred. "I'll do it." The cat sauntered over to the wall, hopping to the windowsill like she had always planned on sitting there. Merlin shook her head and turned around. She made her way through the house, entering the section connected to the tower. The wooden steps creaked as she went up, stopping at the entrance of the farthest room. The tower itself had only one living area, but the stairs had doors connected to the other rooms in the high parts of the tree trunk.

Merlin froze as she stood in front of the entrance, her hands hanging by her side. The curtain of distraction that the injured boy provided was drawn away before she had time to grab hold of it once more. Her hand shook as she raised it, her fingers brushing against the handle.

CHAPTER 2

Another moment passed, and she grasped the knob. A soft click sounded as she twisted the iron, the door swinging open.

There was less dust than she expected.

The room was clean and blank, a stale light filtered through the window on the far wall. Merlin bit her lip, stepping farther in. Her feet met a woven surface, the beige rug that was spread across the floor. The smallest puff of sound erupted from the weave, but Merlin didn't pay attention to it. Her gaze was drawn to the old desk on the left, and it pulled her inward. A blank piece of paper sat in the middle of the surface, its edges beginning to roll in on itself. A limp quill was placed at the top of the page, and a small collection of pouches lined the back of the desk. Merlin didn't have to open them to know they held dried out herbs. Useless plants that could do nothing now.

Her throat caught as her eyes fell on a small paper tied to rough wood. Merlin breathed raggedly, hesitantly picking up the picture. The drawing itself was not very good, just a quick sketch of three people. Merlin backed up and sat on one of the low post beds, creating wrinkles in the once smooth blankets. She had drawn the picture when she was five years old, sketching three scrawny figures side by side. One was very small, and the other had four prominent wings that spread out through most of the paper. The third figure had been drawn lightly, and was barely visible. Her brother had laughed when he saw the drawing, rustling her hair as he took it. She could still hear him making fun of her terrible drawing.

Merlin set the frame down on one side and laid back on the bed. She could faintly smell Daleon's scent in the room, an earthy, maple smell. That's when Merlin started crying. All the emotions she had locked up after reading that letter now had nothing to keep them back. She pulled herself upwards as tears poured down her cheeks. Her hands shook and she covered her face, hunching forward. The room was so quiet her own sniffling echoed in her ears.

"I-I tried, brother." Merlin whimpered, unable to keep the thoughts inside. "I promised I would follow you, but I can't make it. I failed you." It had been two long years since he left, and never once had she forgotten their last conversation. "What am I supposed to do?" she asked the room, as if the collection of his belongings could summon his answer. When no response came, Merlin picked up the picture, staring at the mini-Daleon.

"It can't happen again, can it?" she asked desperately, panting from the rush of emotion. How many times was this going to happen? How many times would the government deny her the right to protect her family? Merlin hugged the picture tightly, withholding another round of breathless sobs. Her heart squeezed, and then wrenched as her thoughts turned sharply against her brother. She pulled back the picture and glared at the thin ivirian. Had he known this would happen? Many letters had been sent between them in the past two years, and she could pull from almost any of them sentences which warned her away from the front lines.

His silly principles had made him leave with no fight, and it was those same feelings that she now attributed his telling her that the troops were steadily growing to hate humans and elestiels. But was he really telling her not to join the navy?

"And if so," she continued aloud, "why didn't you stop me before? Don't you know, elves can't break their promises?"

The silence that met her quenched any remaining tears. She felt utterly drained. Her eyes dried out and grit coated the underside of her eyelids. Even her tongue felt as though sand had cocooned its entirety.

Merlin stood, leaving the picture on the bed. Like a coin flipped through the air, her sadness morphed into cold determination. Her hands worked on their own as she opened his wardrobe and pulled out clothing. Daleon had good reasons to fight, but she had her own volitions that were just as important. The military could try to stop her, Daleon could warn her against it, but somehow she would find a way to get to the front lines. First she had to take care of the elestiel downstairs, and then she would deal with traveling.

While she worked, leftover tears tried to blur her eyes, making it impossible to determine if she was pulling out the correct garments. When it seemed like she had a good enough selection of clothing, she closed the wardrobe with a loud smack. The dried streaks of tears on her cheeks cracked as she frowned at Daleon's desk. There was an item she hadn't noticed sitting on the right side. It was a black string bracelet with a single charm in the shape of a sword. Her hand had already grabbed it before Merlin could process whether or not she should.

Likewise her feet followed suit, taking her out of the lifeless room, down to the base of the stairs without any reference to her own desire. She managed to stop at the tower door, trying to force a normal expres-

CHAPTER 2

sion. There would be no avoiding a lengthy conversation if she worried Gwen, and that was the last task she wanted to deal with. With the cat on her mind, Merlin heard a loud hiss from the other room. She dashed towards the noise, thrusting open the tower door.

Gwen was poised on the top of the sofa, her fur standing on end. The man, who *had* been unconscious, was now backed into the farthest corner of the room. His eyes widened at Merlin when she entered, one hand around his waist. She met his gaze for only a second as Gwen hissed again.

"What is going on?" Merlin demanded, pointing her glare at the cat.

Gwen didn't turn as she answered. "He woke up, that's what."

"*Jana,*" the man said. His voice drew their attention, sounding wistful. "*Ceva velo lutien?*"

Gwen hissed again. "What did you say?"

"Calm down." Merlin directed, waving her free hand at the cat. She glared at the man. "Can you speak in Allmens tongue?"

"Yes," he responded suspiciously, eyeing her like he would need to fight.

Merlin set the pile of clothes on the couch's top. "Good. Then your explanation will be much easier to understand. Take these clothes and head towards the tower, there should be a room you can use to change in. I assume you'd rather not stay in those rags." She nodded to his burnt and ripped up ensemble.

"Who *are* you?" he asked, scanning Merlin from the tip of her boots to the top of her head. His accented voice seemed to draw out the vowels of his words, accentuating his confusion. There was no denying it, he was Avalonian.

"Who are *you*?" Merlin countered, crossing her arms. "And why is an elestiel roaming through Sher?"

"You're an elestiel." He sort of nodded as he spoke, like he was trying to gesture but didn't want to at the same time.

"How astute," she said flatly. Cocking her head to the side, Merlin widened her eyes. "I have permission to be here. You don't. So explain before I kick you out. You should be glad I didn't kill you."

He squinted. "Why did you help me?"

Merlin jerked her thumb at Gwen. "She asked me to. I do hope you have coins to pay for my assistance. Your satchel appears to have been missed by the fire."

"You can't expect me to pay." His posture unbent slightly, seeming more aggravated. "I was unconscious! I didn't ask you for help."

"That's a good point." Merlin turned to the cat, pushed slightly by her desire to appear normal. "Guess you'll have to pay."

Gwen coughed. "Put it on my tab."

Merlin turned back to the man, noting that he was still plastered to the wall. "Well? Are you going to change or not?"

"I'm not going to pay for those clothes," he stated, still frozen in place.

She frowned. "I don't expect you to." Merlin didn't wait for him to respond, signaling with her eyes for Gwen to watch him. She gripped the bracelet in her hand and walked straight into the kitchen. Once inside she set her brother's bracelet down, mechanically moving towards the pantry. Something told her that the rest of her afternoon would be taken up with dealing with the elestiel, and if that was the case, she would only do it with a cup of tea in hand.

Off-handedly, she frowned at the coffee container sitting by the tea leaves. She would rather drink that any day, but tea was much cheaper and easier to acquire. It was still disappointing to grab the glass jar of peppermint leaves and carry them out of the pantry. The plant looked limp when she sprinkled it in each teacup, falling to the bottom of the dish quickly. Merlin brushed aside a few wisps of hair as she grasped the iron kettle that was sitting on the main table. The water inside sloshed as Merlin hooked it above the fireplace. Moments later she had increased the wood inside, the ever-burning flames heightening in warmth.

Someone cleared their throat, and Merlin turned around, her heart squeezing at the sight of him. He stood in the doorway of the room, looking down at the fabric hanging just above his knees. Somehow he had managed to clean the black from his hair, brushing the longest strands to the right side of his head. Merlin's attention was not on his face though, her eyes were staring at the clothes. The dark green tunic fit him better than it had fit Daleon, the wide short sleeves leaving room for the billowing undershirt to be pulled through. Two of her brother's brown belts were clasped around his waist, the unburnt

CHAPTER 2

satchel hanging from one. He was even wearing Daleon's two leather vambraces—the armguards her brother wore while their father taught him how to handle a sword.

Why in the world had she given those clothes to the boy? They didn't belong to him. Merlin's brain screamed at her to tell him to take off the clothes and just wear the burnt ones, but she clamped down on the urge.

The man was now giving her a strange look, his golden eyes narrowed. Merlin cleared her own throat, waving awkwardly at the table in the middle of the room. It was unnerving to see her eyes in the face of another person.

"Sit down," she managed to say, grabbing both teacups and setting them down.

He moved cautiously towards her, sitting with one leg poised away from the bench, like he thought he would need to flee. "Thank you for the clothes."

"I'm not sure you're welcome." Merlin sat, pursing her lips. Now that he was closer, she could tell that his eyes were more orange than her own. "What is your name?"

He scanned the room as he answered. "You may call me Lancelot." He directed his eyes to look at her, sizing her up again. "What is your name?"

She smirked, drawing a circle on the table absently. "My name is Merlin."

His eyebrows shot up at her name, and he leaned closer across the table eagerly. "It was said you were a man of lost wits."

"Hmph." Merlin leaned backwards so as to keep the distance between them. "I am not some old geezer! I'm tired, that's what I am! Tired of everyone thinking I'm some batty cricket that heals anything that moves." She shut her mouth in an attempt to stem the flow of her irritated words.

"My apologies," he laughed unapologetically. "I meant no disrespect. I'm actually glad you found me. I've been searching for you."

"Me?" Surprised, Merlin raised an eyebrow. Elohim must have had a hand in guiding Lancelot for her to have found him the way she did. Yet, regardless of whether or not the deity participated in their meeting, Merlin still needed to make herself clear. "I don't leave the forest if that's what you're asking for. I know you're not sick, which means you have a family member who is. Besides the fact that I don't make house calls anymore, I could never go to Avalon."

He waved a hand. "You misunderstood me. Your healing might come in handy later, but that has nothing to do with my immediate request."

Her surprise was nearly palpable. "What do you need me for, then?" she asked slowly, unsure if she really wanted to know the answer.

She watched Lancelot sit straight again, lacing his fingers together. A dashing smile spread across his face, the kind which Merlin immediately knew held trouble behind it. "Put bluntly, you must help me end the war."

"What?" Merlin exclaimed.

"You heard me."

"I did not!" Merlin snapped. "Because you would have to be *completely* senseless to say what I think you just said."

"Not from my perspective," he said simply.

Behind them the kettle began shrieking its high-pitched whistle. Neither of them moved to retrieve it. Instead Merlin covered her mouth with a hand, tilting her head. "I thought I healed you, but even I can make a mistake. *Clearly* there is something wrong with your head."

"I assure you, my head is fine." Lancelot began rustling through his satchel. "If you'll pour the water, I'll explain in further detail why I've come." He paused in his search to stare at her.

Merlin huffed. "Fine." There was in her mind the option of tossing the witless man out of her home, but she withheld that action for a later time. It didn't stop her, however, from muttering under her breath as she filled both cups. "What in the great northern woods of Norestere does he expect me to do?"

The wooden cups steamed as she turned around, heating her fingers to a painful temperature before she set them down. Lancelot thanked her and took his cup. From his small satchel he'd produced a book far too big to have fit inside it, and set the navy cover on the table.

"Let me properly introduce myself," he said after a sip of tea. "I am Sir Lancelot, a knight of Avalon."

"A knight, huh?" Merlin was unimpressed *and* disgusted. "That's not surprising."

He raised an eyebrow. "Oh?"

Merlin ran her finger around the lip of her cup. "You're an elestiel. Don't the human kingdoms require knights to be an elestiel?"

It may have been her imagination, but she thought she saw the knight twitch. It was just a small quiver, barely even noticeable. The knight shifted in his seat. "Most of the army is made up of humans, but yes, the higher-ranking soldiers are elestiels." He tapped the table absently.

"I thought so." Merlin sighed. "*Please*, don't let my question stop you from explaining. I'm *ever* so curious as to your plan to *end* the war."

Exasperated, Lancelot crossed his arms over his chest. The wood beneath him creaked and groaned. "You're very rude."

Merlin took a large sip of her tea before deigning to respond. "And you are presumptuous. Shall we carry on insults or would you prefer to actually explain your plan to me?"

"*E'pyl evera, chuva,*" Lancelot muttered, slipping back into irritated Avalonian.

Merlin didn't understand what he was saying, but she could hear his annoyed tone just fine. It brought a smirk to her lips as she took another sip of her tea, keeping eye contact with the ruffled knight.

He caught the look and sighed. "Very well. First, how much do you know about this war?"

Merlin set her cup down. "How much?" She gave a short laugh. "As much as anyone knows. Logres laid siege on the trade ships of Avalon after you all killed their king, and successfully plunged the rest of us into war."

"We did *not* kill their king." Lancelot said firmly. "It was never proven that we had anything to do with it. They blame us without reason. If the Regent could see sense, then maybe peace would be reached."

"Hm, maybe he's hostile because it was his father who was killed." Merlin pointed out innocently. "Maybe if your king would admit that it was him, and pay the dues from that, there would be peace."

"My king did no such thing." Lancelot balled his visible hand into a fist. "But arguing over the cause is not going to bring clarity. As it is now, the only way to stop this fight is for one of the rulers to step down."

"And I presume that you would like the Gressan Regent to be the one to step down?" Merlin shook her head.

"Should my king step down, nothing would change. Another would take his place with intentions worse than his own." Lancelot insisted. "This war will only stop when the Regent is replaced, or agrees to a peace treaty."

"I find it hard to believe that the Regent would agree to either. As I said before, his *father* was killed."

Lancelot gave her a look of pure annoyance held by a thin thread of self-control. "Have you heard of the Last Pendragon?" he asked.

Merlin frowned and squeezed her cup. "Not the one sitting on the throne of Logres?"

He sighed. "Before that there was another heir, Arthur Pendragon. On the night he was born King Uther and his wife perished in a fire. It was said that the prince died that night, but I have reason to believe he is alive. He can stop the war. All I need is for you to come with me."

"Ha." Merlin set her cup down slowly, folding her hands in her lap. Obviously his mind held no sense or reason—to a degree worse than she first thought—but the severity was simply amazing. Whatever ailed him should be studied by physicians. "Listen," Merlin started. "As I said, I thought I did a good job, but I *have* made mistakes before. Since I'm a nice person, I'll look over your head again."

"I am *not* ill!" Lancelot smacked the book on the table. He pushed it towards her. "This is my proof. Read it and believe me."

His insistence made Merlin's skin prickle indignantly. Had her curiosity not been tempted prior, she would have finally resolved to toss the knight out of her kitchen. It took her a moment to contain her irritation before she pulled the book across the table. Its gilt title was set in scrawled lettering that read, *Ginora's Prophetic Suggestions*. Merlin flicked her gaze momentarily back to Lancelot, who raised both eyebrows as if to ask why she was hesitating.

Merlin sighed and slipped her fingers underneath the hard cover. "It's blank," she observed after flipping through several empty pages. "Your invisible proof is quite convincing."

He sat back, marveling at her with an open mouth. "I spoke with several people who assured me you were very kind, how is it that you're so altered a person?"

CHAPTER 2

Merlin raised both hands. "I draw a line at helping senseless knights attack the opposing kingdom, not to mention I dislike nobles. Really your entire presence offends me."

He snorted, gesturing to the book. "It's fortunate then, that I am not some insane knight whom you can't believe. I'm sure you can ignore my occupation in order for us to work together." Lancelot cleared his throat. "How do I stop this war?"

Merlin was about to comment on his craziness again, when before her eyes words appeared on the blank pages. Her mouth dropped open as she registered the sentence.

As I said before; ARTHUR MUST SEE MERLIN. Are you illiterate?

Merlin goggled at the page. "What is this?"

"This book holds the spirit of Ginora, an elven enchantress." Lancelot gloated. He was grinning with all the superiority that proving oneself provides. "Apparently she was in search of the answer to everything, and in the process of hunting for it, she was trapped within the book. Now she can answer anything, but do nothing."

Merlin twisted her mouth into a frown. "How do you know all this?"

He shrugged. "It was all on the plaque."

"A plaque?" she repeated. "Did you steal this?"

"That's besides the point." He waved her words aside. "As you can see, I have proof."

"And how exactly did you get an elvish book?" Merlin wasn't quite sure of how she felt about a book with an elf inside it, but that was the least of her concerns. "Most elvish literature was taken with them to Norestere when they immigrated."

Lancelot made a calming gesture. "The book was made before the Massacre alongside an Avalonian philosopher. He claimed the book when Ginora was lost inside it."

"Whatever the case, how can I trust it? You could make it say something to trick me." Merlin pointed out. "Besides, I'm sure I'm not the only Merlin in this world. For that matter, there are probably more Arthurs too."

"That's true," Lancelot crossed his arms. "But I am fairly certain you're the one." He looked back at the book. "Is this the Merlin that Arthur Pendragon needs?"

It took a moment before the words on the page changed to, *Yes*. Lancelot nodded, his eyes determined.

Merlin felt a small wave of anxiety replace the anger in her stomach. "That still doesn't matter. I cannot number the problems riddled in your plan."

"Ask it yourself then." Lancelot's voice became stern, dropping the humor. "If you can think of a question that will either prove, or disprove what I'm saying, then ask. But be wary, you can only ask two questions per person, per day."

She blinked, looking back at the book. He had already asked his two questions, which meant she had to be the one to ask. Except, how could she? It was such a ridiculous proposition in all regards, and there was no guarantee the book was telling the truth. It would have to be something she could prove, then. Something that the knight didn't know.

"Who are my parents?" she asked.

The book rustled, the words swapping. *Your parents are Cavair Lynwood and Philene Lynwood. Don't bother trying to find the other ones, I am not a genealogy.*

"Other ones?" Lancelot asked at the same time as Merlin spoke.

"What does it mean, it won't tell me? Is that possible?"

"Yes," he held up both hands. "It sometimes won't tell me things, I guess because us lower beings aren't supposed to have all the information. That's what it said, anyway. Now, other ones?"

Merlin sighed, sitting back on the bench. "I'm adopted. It's telling me not to ask about my birth parents." She frowned at the book. When she was younger she had been curious, but now she had no desire for an answer to that question. Surely the book understood that.

"Well, regardless of your birth, my point is simple." Lancelot started speaking again, but his tone was slightly more gentle than before. "This war must end, and the only way for that to be accomplished is if you and I find Arthur. He needs to see you, for whatever reason. Come with me to Norestere. I swear to protect you as we travel." His eyes widened eagerly, waiting for her answer.

The look reminded Merlin of the expression the sheriff had worn earlier that morning. The only difference was that Lancelot was not fully convinced she would say yes. He was trying to appear open, but she still hardly knew anything about him. There was mystery clinging to him that she did not understand. Yet, the real problem was not that his plan was ludicrous—it was that she already had somewhere to be.

"I... need to think this over." Merlin told him, glancing out the kitchen window. The forest was growing darker with the setting sun. "You may stay here tonight, and I will give you an answer tomorrow."

"Very well." Lancelot stood, then looked uncomfortable. "Do you have a needle and thread I might borrow?"

She leaned back, surprised. "What do you need it for?"

"There are two large holes in these shirts," Lancelot explained.

"Oh, I see." Merlin grinned. "I didn't realize nobles could sew."

He gave her a charming smile. "It's an excellent way to stop bleeding injuries."

It reminded her of the cuts on his arms, which prompted her to say seriously, "Speaking of which, you may be fatigued currently. That's because I had to use your energy to heal you. I took care of your fresh wounds, but left the um, other scars."

His eyes slid down to his arms where his scars were hidden beneath his sleeves, then back up to her. "Thank you."

"Mm, you're sort of welcome." Merlin cocked her head, snuffing out the tiniest bit of curiosity. "How exactly did you end up so injured?"

His dark skin reddened faintly. "The last thing I remember was stepping through a patch of red flowers, and then nothing."

"Oh." Merlin hid her smile. "You must have stepped on a Dragon Blossom. They burst into flames when they aren't handled correctly." Watching Lancelot's face pale helped lighten the stress in Merlin's mind, just a bit.

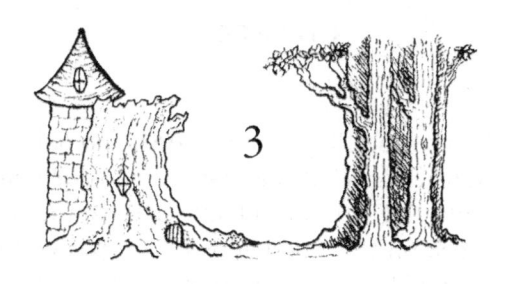

Unwanted Answers

M

"I'm sure he has his reasons," Gwen told her. The cat lay on the foot of Merlin's bed, paws dangling off the side. The room was lit dimly from several candles and a lamp which hung from a hook on the ceiling. Inside the black iron sat a single white lotus that glowed brightly, and would continue glowing as long as Merlin took care of it.

"Undoubtedly he does." Merlin grabbed a folded blanket along with a gray pillow. "But that doesn't make his plan any better."

Gwen's tail swished. "I think you should go with him. The military might not need you, but he does. Who knows, maybe you could even end the war."

"End the war?" Merlin set the stack of bedding on her desk and paused. Her fingers fidgeted with the folded blanket, flattening the wrinkles and tugging at the corners. If only ending the war was as simple as that small action. Just a couple tugs to straighten each kingdom out. But life was not that simple, no matter how the knight tried to phrase it. "I can't do that, and neither can he." Merlin dragged her fingertips across her forehead and down her nose, applying pressure as she went.

Guinevere yawned while hopping off the bed. She held her head high and stared pointedly at Merlin. "They said no to you, Merlin. If you can't help the soldiers, then you should consider what you can actually accomplish. Don't the citizens deserve their family back?" With those final words, the cat sniffed once and marched out of the room, silently descending the stairs of the house.

Merlin sighed as she turned back to her desk, spotting a silver gleam next to the blanket. Gently, she lifted up the charm she had taken from her brother's room. The metal sword was cool between her fingers, and sharp at its end. What was she going to do? Follow the knight on a precarious quest? Or find a reliable path to the front lines? She set the bracelet back on the wooden desk and picked up the bedding instead. It was soft and heavy in her arms, bending into her hold as she made her way from the top of the treehouse to the bottom of the tower.

Lancelot was sitting on the couch in the living room, pulling a needle through the back of his tunic. The undershirt he was wearing already had the wing openings sewn together in straight seams all the way up to the neckline, closing the back together so that it was not flapping open. His attention appeared to be wholly snared by his task.

"Your stitches are straighter than mine." Merlin noted, setting her pile on the end of the couch.

He looked up without surprise, so maybe he had heard her enter. "Practice, and necessity."

Merlin peered at him, as if looking could make her understand him. "Necessity?"

Lancelot nodded, returning to his work. He stuck the needle through the thick green fabric with precise force. "Thank you for the lodging, I haven't slept in a building in quite some time."

Merlin blew a strand of hair from her face. "You could have slept in a bed if you wanted."

"This is fine." He tugged the needle and thread upwards. "I'd rather not pay for a room, so the couch suits me."

She was tempted to tell him she would charge for the couch anyway, but Merlin decided not to. Even if he had taken a bed she wouldn't have charged him. "All right then," Merlin moved to leave the room, but she stopped in front of the stairwell door. She could see Gwen in the kitchen, curled up on a small bed by the fireplace.

He must have his reasons.

"Lancelot," Merlin put a hand on the doorframe while she turned, leaning on the smooth wood. The knight paused in his sewing so that he could look back at her. Merlin tapped the frame with a finger, creating little thumping sounds as she grasped for the right words. "Why are you doing this?" She decided on the straightforward route. "It's not your responsibility to end the war."

Her question seemed to trigger something inside the knight, his eyes growing cloudy. His expression tightened, and Merlin got the feeling that his mind was no longer on her question. It was far away, in a memory, an idea spurred onward by her words. She stayed quiet while he thought, unwilling to hurry his answer. Eventually he did speak, but his voice was distracted.

"If I don't do something, who will?" he asked seriously. "War is carried on the backs of those willing to fight for it, but I see no one bearing the weight of peace. When did bloodshed become our *only* answer?"

Merlin frowned. "But you're just a knight, shouldn't the king do something about it?"

His expression cleared and he met her gaze. "Why would a king fight for anything less than victory?"

"Are they not the same? Peace and victory?"

Lancelot shook his head. "No, I don't believe they are."

For another moment Merlin waited, but he said nothing more. He simply frowned, eyebrows scrunched together. Merlin left him there after a halfhearted goodnight, returning to her room. She shut the oak door and locked it with a soft click from the iron handle.

Many routine preparations later, she lay in bed, eyes squeezed shut. Exhaustion was sitting upon her like a heavy blanket, yet her mind still held many thoughts that needed addressing. Before her stood two options; one to go with the knight, and the other to stay and try to join the army despite their denial. She pulled her warm sheets further up over her face. Her thoughts tumbled from plan to plan. Should she go with Lancelot? Or was her path bound for the front lines? Surely she should go to her brother...

The warring in her mind carried on even as she drifted into the dark halls of sleep.

Wet soil squished under her boots, its humid smell filling her nose. There was something rancid in the wind as she ran, pushing through wet bramble that blocked her way. Someone was shouting her name behind her, but the voice was faint and muffled. Even so, she knew who called her. She broke out of the bushes onto a flat path, dodging around an ivirian's bug-like wings.

CHAPTER 3

Ahead of her she could see trees molded into a hasty dome with an arch as its front door. There were two guards standing at the entrance, along with a small crowd of noisy people. She could hear them complaining, begging, speculating as to what it was like inside. It was all frivolous commentary that only the unaffected could make. Why they were here and not somewhere else, avoiding the drizzle of rain and the crying of mothers, she didn't know.

"Watch it, child!" an ivirian with dull green skin snapped at her as she pushed past the ivira. "You can't be over there!"

Hands reached out to grab her, but she ducked underneath them. Her copper hair fell in front of her eyes, mud splattered on her skirt. A large drop of rain crashed onto her head as she collided with the crowd. Someone gasped next to her. Another jumped from surprise.

"Let me through!" she screamed, pushing forward against the press of bodies. "Move!" She kicked, punched, and charged past the ivirians, landing in the soggy ground in front of the guards.

They both looked down at her, one clenched his spear, the other simply widened his eyes. Each had an iron token strapped around their left arm, and metal clips adorned their long hair. These were the ones in charge of the door. They had to be.

"Let me in, please!" She pulled herself up, her clothes drenched in cold sludge that dripped from their edges, and down the sides of her face. "I need to get in!"

One guard bent down to her height. "No one can go in now, little elf. It's sectioned off to prevent the disease from spreading."

"No, you have to let me in!" she cried. "I have to save him! Let me save him!"

The guard rose. "There is no entry at this time. Go home, pray to Elohim that this may pass."

"No." She squeezed her dirty knuckles till they were white. The air was growing harder to breathe in by the minute. "No!" Her feet moved quicker than they had ever before as she dashed past the guard, smacking into the closed door with all her strength. It barely even shook at her measly force. Tears began falling from her eyes faster than any rain from the sky. She threw her tiny fists against the wood, pounding it with loud smacks.

"Stop!" She heard the guard coming behind her, arms wrapped around her waist, pulling her back from the entrance.

"No, you have to let me go!" she shrieked. "I can heal him, I can save him!"

"Merlin!" Two voices—each sounding horrified—called out her name.

The guard holding her growled as she flung her arms and legs out violently. "Get this child under control!" he barked as he transferred Merlin into someone else's hold.

"I'm sorry," said a young male voice.

She couldn't see the first speaker, but the second was the person holding her. "Merlin, you must calm down. We can explain, then they'll let us in!"

"They need to let me in, now!" Merlin struggled against her brother's hold. "Let me go, Daleon!"

Merlin snapped up in her bed, panting so quickly that she was choking on air. Sweat dripped down her nose bridge and back—her hair was a tangled mess. From her room's window small streams of light were starting to poke through the glass and reach towards her bed. The sun was dawning, and she could hardly acknowledge it. Her heart felt as though it would beat right out of her chest and just keep thrumming faster and faster. Merlin's shaking hand tried adjusting the satin nightgown on her shoulders, anything to take her mind off the dream, the memory.

It was so vivid. As if she was still stuck in that moment, reliving the fear and anxiety, helpless to fight against it.

How could she have forgotten—even briefly—what happened that day? How could she have been tempted into doing anything other than securing the safety of her brother? She needed to be in the north, ready to save her brother should the time come for Sher to join the war.

Slowly, her breath steadied, and Merlin was able to rise from her bed. She knew what she needed to do now. Her feet carried her across the hardwood floor to her desk, where a flat piece of parchment was already placed on it. A small pot of ink sat next to it along with a quill. As she sat, a plan formed in her mind, each piece coming together like a numbered puzzle. Merlin began to write, filling her room with small

CHAPTER 3

scratching sounds. Dawn had long since passed by the time Merlin finished her letter, sitting it face up on her desk. Her parents would see it when they got back, and they would know she had made it north, to the Port of Sal Azure.

L

When he opened his eyes, there was a cat staring down into them. He jumped up, the cat bouncing off him to the floor. For a moment he couldn't remember where he was. The smell of cinnamon and oak hovered in the room, over chairs, tables, and even around unlit candles. The only light came from windows around the living room. He was sitting on a green couch, a gray blanket covering his legs.

Ah, that's it. He rubbed his temples as he remembered where he was, and the events of the previous day. Lancelot was still tired from Merlin's healing, and his side ached where pain should have been.

"Hmph."

He looked down at the cat, who was glaring at him in an irritated fashion. "Good morning..." Lancelot paused uncomfortably. He couldn't remember her name, was it Jen?

The cat sighed and hopped up onto the couch. "Gwen. My name is Gwen."

"Ah," He ran a hand through his hair, folding his legs beneath him so that the cat would not be bothered by them. "Sorry, I'll remember that now."

"You'd better." Gwen rolled her eyes. "Especially if she agrees to go with you."

"Will she?" Lancelot asked cautiously.

"If she listens to me." The cat rubbed behind her ear. "It would be good for her to go. She's never left the forest, believe it or not."

"I see," he nodded. No wonder she seemed unaware of the war. Obviously news of current events had not reached her. Maybe he should tell her? If she knew all that was happening, perhaps it would convince her to come with him.

Gwen cleared her throat, drawing his attention back to her. "I do have a request."

He looked uneasily at her. "Oh?"

"Yes." The cat's tail swished. "I want information. Everything you have."

Lancelot's chest tightened. "What?"

"My dear, *intelligent* friend forgot to ask you some important questions." Gwen's eyes lit up, and she pointed her tail at a coffee table to the left. His book was sitting with its pages flipped open. "I tried asking that, but apparently I can only ask it two questions." Gwen observed.

"That's correct." Lancelot reached over and shut the book. He didn't like where this was going.

"Yes, so now you have to answer my question in its stead." Gwen collapsed on the sofa, eyes narrowing. "For example, I would like to know how you passed through Akiva's Wall."

A nervous laugh escaped him as he eyed the cat. Aside from the strange feeling he got while talking to the animal, he could feel the suspicion that lay behind her eyes. "Merlin didn't bother asking me that."

"That's because she was busy dealing with your proposition. I am not."

"Well," The knight felt his heart skip a beat. "There was a hole."

"A hole?" Gwen repeated dryly. The cat looked unamused.

He pressed his mouth together tightly, not wanting to add anything further. Sher was surrounded by an unending wall of iron spiked tree roots, making it nearly impossible for a large group to get through. That was without considering the death traps conjured by the Ivirian Orders inside the wall. It was amazing that he had survived. Too amazing.

The cat tilted her head, whiskers twitching. "Well, I suppose if you don't want to tell me, I'll just have to figure it out myself."

Lancelot frowned at the cat, already feeling a shadow of foreboding come over him. "Is it really necessary for you to know?"

"Yes, it is." Gwen's tail flopped down to the couch. "Merlin's parents found me years ago and took me in, all the Lynwood's welcomed me. I don't want her traveling with someone suspicious and worrying her parents."

Lancelot looked down at the cat, glad that his skin was dark enough to hide most of his ashamed flush. She had a point, despite his resistance to explain exactly how he got in. But maybe she and Merlin both deserved his full honesty. Before he could say anything a thumping sound came from the house. He and Gwen twisted their heads around. Seconds later Merlin appeared, wearing almost the same thing she had worn the day before. The only difference was that her pants were a slightly darker green. That and her hair was let down.

Lancelot's eyebrows raised as he saw that her ears were pointed. "You're an elf?" he gawked.

"Good morning." Merlin's expression soured. "And yes, half-elf."

"Merlin!" Gwen sprung up onto the couch and leapt at the girl. "He was just about to tell me!"

The girl moved to the left, letting the cat fly past her, a betrayed look in the animal's eyes. "Moving on, I have made a decision." She walked closer, sitting on a chair in front of him. He watched as she clasped her hands. "I can give you my answer now, or while I make breakfast. Which do you prefer?"

His stomach rumbled at the mention of food, but he waited, asking warily, "Will I have to pay for it?"

"Shining Silver Sands!" Merlin stood up briskly, her voice full of annoyance. "I don't make guests pay for everything! Come into the kitchen if you want something edible to eat."

As she left, Lancelot murmured, "As opposed to what, something inedible?"

Gwen chortled, appearing by his leg. "Come on, let's go make sure she doesn't feed you wood shavings."

"Is she likely to do that?" he asked. Lancelot did not receive an answer and was forced to follow the still laughing cat. Soon he found himself in the same seat from the night before, watching as the half-elf elestiel cracked golden eggs in a skillet. Lancelot blinked at it, then at the girl. Before he could ask, Merlin began speaking.

"Listen, your quest is honorable, and had I been like minded, I would probably say yes to you." Lancelot felt his mood plummeting. "But unfortunately I am *not* like you, I have somewhere else to be, and something more important to do. It takes precedence over your request." He could tell she was trying to be gentle, but her words were still harsh.

"What could be more important than saving thousands of lives?" Lancelot squeezed his fist tightly, but kept his voice steady.

She sighed, scraping at the eggs in the pan mindlessly. The fire crackled. Merlin seemed to be debating something, visibly struggling over the decision.

"Explain, Merlin."

Lancelot glanced at the cat. Only her head could be seen above the table, and she was glaring ferociously.

Merlin coughed. Lancelot watched as she scraped the eggs into one big bowl, and carried it to the table. When she sat down, she began dishing out the food, frowning at the table. The knight crossed his arms, unwilling to eat until she explained. His stomach betrayed him however, and growled loudly. Gwen paused in her glare to hop onto the table, sniffing at her own bowl.

After what seemed like forever, Merlin sighed. She looked at Lancelot directly, and crossed her own arms. "My brother was drafted for the war, I need to go to him."

"Merlin!" Gwen exclaimed.

The elestiel held up her hand, silencing the cat immediately. "He's my brother, Gwen. I have to be there in case... in case something happens."

"Is he powerless?" Lancelot asked, trying to keep a handle on his disbelief. "What frailty ails him that you put his life above thousands?"

Merlin scowled. "My brother is not weak. But even the strongest ivirian can fall by the sword. I don't trust any healer other than myself to save him."

Lancelot gritted his teeth and clenched his fists. "You're sacrificing countless humans just to save the life of a brother who doesn't need protection?"

"We may not be active in *your* war," Merlin snapped, "but there is danger for anyone on the water. He may not need me now, but should the time come when he's injured, I *must* be there."

Lancelot stood up, years of practice holding back his anger. He was going to have to find Arthur by himself, somehow. "You may be willing to sacrifice the soldiers, but I am not. Excuse me while I find a different Merlin."

"Sit down!" Merlin ordered, threatening him with her fork. "May I remind you that I am not Avalonian, and I am not Gressan either.

Sher takes no part in your war, so neither do I." He opened his mouth to snap again, but she stopped him. "I will, however, travel with you."

"What?" Gwen jumped in surprise, the cat's whole body flying backwards off the table.

"Coming with me is the same thing as helping me," Lancelot said carefully.

"No," Merlin took a bite of her food. "I'm going to travel with you until we hit The Great Way. See, I promised my brother years ago that I would join him, and elves can never break their promises. That is the other reason why I cannot join you."

"Surely he would understand," Lancelot tried again.

Her face darkened. "You know nothing of elves, apparently. Should we ever break a promise, something bad happens to us. The severity is based on the promise. Breaking the one I made might kill me."

Gwen cleared her throat loudly. "Are you going to eat that?" She pointed at Lancelot's bowl. He huffed and plopped down on the bench, scooping a large spoon of eggs into his mouth. Unsurprisingly, the golden eggs were better than regular chicken eggs.

"You could have just said no," Gwen muttered.

Lancelot ignored her and took another bite. Had a traveling companion been his goal, Merlin's proposition would have been fine, but that was not his goal, he needed her for more than just guidance. He squeezed his spoon. Maybe he could convince her as they walked? What other option did he have?

"I'll agree on one condition," the knight told her. "You have to think about joining me. You can give me your final answer at the pass."

She gave him a suspicious look. "That's it?"

Lancelot raised his hands. "Do you agree?"

Merlin looked to Gwen, who gave a short nod, before she said, "Deal."

"Good." He straightened. "Then I swear to keep you safe as we travel." She looked uncomfortable with his declaration, but at least she didn't contest it. A knight's oath was too important to be taken lightly.

Gwen stepped over her bowl, placed one paw on Lancelot's shoulder and looked directly at him. "Don't worry, I will come too. Thank you for asking." Merlin laughed while Lancelot only smiled.

A loud crash startled all three of them, making them jump up from their seats. There was another loud sound, and this time Lancelot recognized it as a heavy knock. Guinevere hissed and leapt from the table to the only window, peeking through it.

"Merlin, it's that iviro again. It looks like he brought friends this time."

Lancelot opened his mouth, but Merlin waved him off. "Don't say anything!" She rushed around the furniture, grabbing his arm. Before he could ask anything, she pushed him into a small circular room with stairs going upward—the tower. Merlin's face looked both nervous and annoyed as she darted back. "Do not come out, understand?" The urgency was clear even with her lowered voice. "*Understand?*"

He blinked, shaking his head. "Yes!" As soon as the word left his mouth Merlin slammed the door shut in his face.

M

The banging continued to get louder and more forceful as Merlin hurried towards the noise. She hoped the knight would stay put. His presence would only make things worse. There was another enormous bang when she reached the front door. Not pausing to take a breath, Merlin threw open the entrance, and was instantly pushed aside.

"Excuse—" the shout caught in her throat. Merlin stared in horror, backing away from the intruders so quickly she tripped on a chair. Five pairs of talons scraped across the wood flooring, screeching as the owners made their way forward. Leathery black capes hung on their shoulders, the edges of the fabric burnt and torn. Black hoods were pulled low over their faces, showing only a bright silver beak. Swords hung at their sides, and sharp, claw-like nails stuck out from their black fingertips.

The sound of slow footsteps accompanied one last figure walking in. He looked the same as he had before, all squares and cruel eyes. Rainault's wings fluttered behind him as he stopped in front of the group. Nausea swirled in Merlin's stomach before his first step had fallen. The core on his inside had grown even more putrid, and she could feel the illness coiling around the rest of him like a noose. Even his wings had grown in their monotonous color. Merlin swallowed hard, her hands beginning to shake.

The sheriff cleared his throat, snapping Merlin's attention back to him. She glared, finding her voice. "You fool! Why are they here? I've done nothing wrong!"

Rainault tilted his head. "Is that what you think?" His voice was at odds with his tense appearance, all silky and smooth. Merlin hadn't noticed the other day, but it was rather annoying.

"It is not against the law to refuse healing. It's my right!" She clenched her fist. "You have no grounds to be here. Get out of my house, now!"

The sheriff shrugged, waving at his companions. Merlin inhaled sharply as all five reached up and pulled back their hoods. Black feathers tumbled out of the fabric, just as Merlin knew they would. She trembled as she saw the blindfolds tied tightly around their avian heads.

Rainault smiled, pushing back his black hair. "As you can see, ordering me around is not going to increase your lifespan."

"Ha!" The interruption came out as a blurt. "My lifespan? You brought Cockatrices here! Five of them! We're both going to die!"

Cockatrice, the most dangerous creature in all of Sher. The birdlike creatures came from a small clan that trained them through birth, and rebirth, every time one of them died. Merlin heard they kept their eyes covered because anyone who looked into them would die, and thus end the fight too quickly. Such creatures were left with only a dark existence, to be used for violence and harm.

"Oh, they won't kill me." Rainault walked over to the couch and sat down. He eyed the blanket that Lancelot had used. "Visitor?"

"Get to the point!" Merlin sneered. "I still won't heal you, if that's why you're here."

His calm face crinkled. "You will heal me, whether it's done willingly or not." He stood, fingering the hem of the blanket. Merlin's skin crawled. "However, that is not the only reason I'm here." He waved two fingers at the Cockatrice, and two of them responded. They both turned around, marching further into the house. Merlin cringed as their three talons carved into the ground.

Please don't find him, please don't find him, she pleaded. Both Cockatrices came out of the tower dragging Lancelot. He was attempting to walk properly, but they weren't giving him any time. Merlin felt her insides scream as a glaring Lancelot was pushed next to her.

"What is going on?" he whispered, putting one hand on his bag.

Merlin sighed, speaking through her teeth. "We're about to die, that's what."

Rainault stared for a second at Lancelot, a strange look on his face. It only lasted a second and then he began, "So, what was that about not committing a crime?" Rainault waved the blanket at them. "It's against the law to harbor an unregistered human. What's more, he's an enemy elestiel. Of all the people here, you should know the government's attitude towards your kind."

She flinched. "I don't know what you're talking about."

The ivirian smirked. "I'm sure you don't. That's beside the point anyway. Now, you will heal me immediately, or I will kill this boy and then you."

"*Empa?*" Lancelot exclaimed in Avalonian.

"Be quiet." she muttered. Gwen appeared behind the group, proceeding to try and signal Merlin with her eyes. It was not working. "You can kill him, sheriff. I don't have any ties with him." she said loudly.

Lance shot her an offended look. "Um, no?"

Rainault tilted his head. "You really are compassionless. I almost pity him."

"*Ankho'valili!*" Lancelot sounded outraged, which betrayed his calm expression.

"I said be quiet!" Merlin turned and glared at him. "You do realize you have no right to say anything, or even be here? So be silent!" She turned quickly, not wanting to see any hurt that might be on his face. Even if the sentiment was fake, the words were not.

One Cockatrice made a cawing, hissing sound. Rainault grinned. "Fine. I'll kill you both. But first, heal me now! I can at least promise your family's safety." As he spoke, the cat silently crept along the edge of the room, passing the monsters in blindfolds. Gwen caught Merlin's eye again. She lifted one paw and shook it gently. For a moment Merlin didn't understand, until she felt the brush of something on her wrist. Her brother's bracelet! She had completely forgotten that she had put

CHAPTER 3

it on. The cool sword charm was pressing against her wrist as Rainault talked. Merlin blinked, he was still speaking?

"Wouldn't want them all dead because of you." He sounded as if he had been trying to chastise her. Merlin flushed slightly, scolding herself for not paying attention.

Gwen scrunched herself tightly into a ball, her direction aimed at one of the Cockatrices. Merlin made sure her eyes were focused on the ivirian while she responded. "Everything you say is the exact same thing. Heal me, I'll kill you, I'll kill all your family. Either get on with it, or leave. I know you have Talin's disease, and that only comes from abusing the Rideon. You don't deserve any healing."

The hissing Cockatrice stepped forward, but Rainault held up a hand. He stepped forward, shifting the position of his hand so that his palm was facing out. The ivirian's other hand came up, setting down a small, sanded piece of wood. Merlin gulped as she recognized it, and that filled her with dread. It was a military sanctioned Ignition Stone, made from terebinth wood, which could only mean one thing.

Her heartbeat sped up as Rainault tapped the wood three times with his thumb. His connection to the Rideon grew as it unlocked with the last tap of his signet. In response, the flames on the candles around the room rose from their wicks, floating over to the base of his hand. All her muscles tensed as the lights began dancing around his fingers. There was no doubt now. He was of the Purge Order.

4

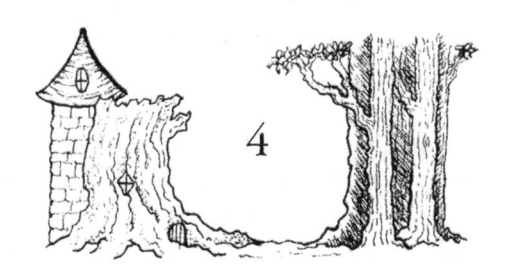

Burning Ties

M

Orange curls of light spun around the ivirian's hand, growing larger as he laughed. Merlin's expression must have shown the horror she felt, because Rainault continued to cackle. Already smoke was building up inside the room, soaking into the wooden walls, the maple flooring. How long would it take for a single flame to latch on to the sofa next to him, the chair by her side, or the intricate arches holding up the ceiling? There was more than enough kindling in her home to start a devastating fire.

For one moment—while the fire grew and the ivirian laughed—everyone seemed to freeze. As if the whole group was taking a breath, calming themselves and their tight muscles. The moment didn't last long. The swirling fire froze above Rainault's hand, compressing itself into a tight ball. Merlin tried to move away, edging to the left until the arm of a chair dug into her thigh. Her eyes whipped over to Rainault. Light was reflected in his hateful eyes as he drew back his hand and threw.

Merlin raised her hands, trying to protect her face. Heat rose suddenly around her, no doubt the first experience of what burning would feel like. Her lungs heaved up and down for two seconds, and then, slowly, she lowered her arms. The fire hadn't connected with her, hadn't consumed her. But why? She inhaled sharply, swallowing some of the smoke that built up around them.

Lancelot stood in front of her, holding up his left hand. The fire was stopped just in front of his palm, flickering in place. Merlin pressed her hand over her mouth and nose, staring at the knight in shock. Had he made his signet without her seeing it? Was that even possible with them standing so near to each other?

CHAPTER 4

Quick moments passed before Rainault let out a guttural scream. "Get them both, now!" All five Cockatrices surged forward, skillfully unsheathing their longswords. At the same time Guinevere sprang into motion, ricocheting off a bird and landing on the side table. The cat hissed in triumph and leaned down, biting something that sat on the wood. One of the Cockatrices cawed angrily and turned towards the feline, hefting its sword up to strike Gwen. The cat leapt off the furniture as the bird swung down with such force that the table was sliced in half.

The other four attackers charged in a line, straight at Lancelot. Merlin pressed herself against the wall, but the knight stood his ground. He twisted his hand to the side as if he was offering something to the birds, and the flames responded. It split apart into four separate beams of bright light, crackling and snapping uncontrollably. With a shriek the birds tried to dodge around the fire, but just as they took a step forward, a burning claw of heat reached out from within the pillars and clasped the attackers. Four identical screams of pain ripped through the room, only to give way before a fifth, guttural cry.

Rainault snarled as he pushed aside two burning Cockatrices, fire leaping onto his clothes and hair. Merlin's body trembled as the ivirian swung out his hands, flame rising off the sleeves of his allies. Lancelot's control faltered, and great tongues of fire broke free, flying to the walls of the house. Rainault was trying to *destroy* her home.

Rainault was trying to destroy her *parents'* home.

Merlin let out her own cry, and flicked her wrist. Immediately the charm on her bracelet began to grow, getting larger and heavier until she had a perfectly balanced sword in her hand. She lunged around Lancelot, slashing the sword down directly at Rainault's throat. The ivirian's filthy core flashed inside him as he grabbed the sword. Merlin gritted her teeth, pushing the silver blade down harder against his hand. Blood began trickling along his palm, dripping to the floor.

The taste of metal coated the inside of Merlin's mouth as she growled, smoke filling her nose. A drop of sweat ran down her forehead. When had it gotten so hot? Her vision was now tinted red, but all she could do was keep driving the sword farther and farther down.

Rainault stared up at her, gritting his teeth. He glanced to the side, drawing her eyes with him. Flames now crawled along the ceiling, licking the walls to set them ablaze. The ivirian looked back at her. He reached up and grabbed the sword with his other hand, his pupils shrinking to slits. Merlin gasped as he started to succeed in moving the sword away.

"There's no escape here!" he rasped, his voice cracking as he let out a piercing laugh. "You can die with me!" Something fell in the room, maybe a beam from the ceiling? Merlin didn't know, she couldn't tell. It was getting so hot that her eyes stung from staying open. Was she really going to die here?

"Oupht ouf thfe wmay!!" Merlin snapped to attention in time to see Gwen jump onto Rainault's face, book in mouth, and then shoot past her. She had no time to react as another person came hurtling by. Arms wrapped around her waist as Lancelot dragged Merlin away from the ivirian. Rainault screamed as her blade sliced out of his grasp.

"What are you doing?" Merlin wailed. Her world spun and morphed from red to startling light. The sudden absence of heat and smoke sent relief throughout her lungs, but that did nothing to calm her. She was facing the house, her childhood home, and it was only Lancelot's firm hold on her that was keeping her from running back inside. "Let me go!" she shouted, turning to glare at him. His face was smudged with ash, but he looked only determined.

"No!" If it was even possible, he tightened his grasp around her. Merlin turned back to the house, her eyes beginning to tear up. The fire was spreading from the living room, lighting up the tower in ways no common hearth ever could. A large clump of the main house buckled and collapsed in on itself, sending embers into the air. Merlin's knees gave out and she fell, pulling Lancelot with her. She didn't care if it offended him, she just knelt there watching as the smoldering flames consumed her home. It hardly seemed possible that her house—which was pristine that morning—could be blackening past recognition. Her mother's fabrics were still waiting to be finished in the parlor, and her father had many unread books sitting in his study. So many memories, keepsakes, and important items lived there, all now dissolving into black rain falling upon the grass.

"Merlin," Lancelot's voice was urgent. He still held her in place, but his grip had lightened till she barely noticed it. "I'm sorry, but we need to leave."

"No, I..." Merlin stopped, her eyes widening. Out of the roof of the building rose three Cockatrice, propelled by what she had assumed were capes. Now she could see that they were actually enormous, black wings, which dripped fire onto their arms and feet. As they rose, chunks of wood and embers fell off their shoulders and heads, and patches of their feathers burnt away to reveal seared flesh.

Lancelot gasped. "We're leaving, now!"

Merlin wanted to protest, but she couldn't, not while the creatures shrieked as their own skin melted off. She tried to swallow, tried to move, but Merlin's limbs refused. She was stuck to the ground, stuck to her home, stuck to her fear. How could she have let her parents' home be destroyed? Merlin heard Lancelot call her name, his arms releasing her only to grab her shoulders and shake.

"*Ankho'valili!*" He let go of her again, but this time he pried his arm underneath her legs, one hand on her back. Merlin coughed in surprise as he picked her up.

"What are you doing?!"

It was the second time she'd asked him that, but this time he just ignored her, spinning around so that she could no longer see her house.

Merlin shook her head, trying to snap out of the fog that had taken over her mind. How fast was the knight running? How strong must he be to carry her? Merlin shifted her head, watching as the tree's rushed by them. They were hurrying down the path, but it was only a matter of time before they would be caught again.

No! Merlin squeezed her eyes shut. She needed to help Lancelot, not continue crying over her house. There would be time to mourn later. "Turn left!" she ordered, snapping open her eyes. Immediately Lancelot turned, dodging a tree and plunging them into deeper forest. Twigs snapped as the knight continued running, leaping over tree roots and trunks.

The Cockatrices behind them cawed, their wings flapping loudly. Merlin bit down on her tongue to keep from growling. How were those creatures following them through the trees? She felt Lancelot's grip shift as he started to look back.

"Don't!" Merlin reached up and put her arms around his neck, trying to keep him from looking. No doubt those birds were angry enough to discard the blindfolds. "Their sight is deadly!"

"Excellent." he grumbled, sounding winded. A small pang of guilt pinched at Merlin, but she set it aside. There was no way she could keep up with Lancelot on her own, so carrying her was the only option.

Wait a moment. She looked at his face, narrowing her eyes. "Can you wield fire?"

He glanced down at her before maneuvering around another tree. "Not while carrying you. Besides, this is a forest! I might start something I can't control!"

There was another loud caw, and suddenly one of the birds was flying right next to them. Merlin yelped, flicking out her wrist to summon the sword once again. Her eyes closed automatically as she stabbed forward. The blade connected with something soft for a moment before it was pulled out, a squelching noise accompanying the move. Lancelot made a relieved sound while Merlin cracked open her eyelids. The bird was gone and the blade was stained with black blood. A small bit of triumph worked its way into Merlin, bolstering her resolve.

"Lancelot, stop!"

He ignored her command. "If I stop, they'll catch us!"

Merlin gritted her teeth and grabbed a small clump of his hair. "I said stop!" She yanked at the hair. Lancelot yelped and skidded to a stop, stumbling over branches as he froze.

"What was that?!" he yelled, turning to glare at her.

"I said stop!" Merlin repeated, releasing the section. "Now put me down, quickly!" He rolled his eyes, but at least he put her down at the same time. Behind them they heard a clear screeching sound, not unlike the noise a hawk makes when it catches its prey. Merlin quickly scanned the trees by her, ducking behind one. When Lancelot didn't follow, she grabbed his arm and pulled.

"Hiding isn't going to work!" he hissed. "They're almost upon us!"

"I know that!" Merlin squeezed her sword hilt. "So go over there and burn them!"

Lancelot's expression changed to a look of longsuffering. "I already said I couldn't do that!"

Merlin felt ready to push him out from behind the tree. "It's fine! If you hit a tree, the Growth Ivirians will just regrow it! So go!"

"I need wood to start a fire!"

Merlin bent down and picked up a stick, angrily handing it to him. "There, now go!" He looked confused, but finally he didn't argue, instead squeezing the twig he'd been given. A small flame sprung to life on his opposite palm, growing larger as the stick blackened and fell apart. Merlin watched as the knight closed both eyes and pushed himself out from behind the tree. Another round of cawing erupted as he lifted his arm and pointed forward. The smell of ash rose in the air as a bright flash of blue light spread across the trees. Merlin gaped at the blue fire shooting from Lancelot's finger. Heat blew in every direction, scorching the surrounding wood and instantly lighting it. Merlin had to scramble back as the temperature increased, stinging her eyes and cheeks.

She covered her face with her hands to keep the heat from her eyes. Piercing shrieks of pure agony rose from the direction of the creatures, the wailing getting louder. Merlin squeezed her eyes shut even harder, shifting her hands so that they covered her ears. The noise felt awful, as if it was threatening to shred her hearing into a million little pieces, and all the while heat poked needles into her uncovered skin.

The torment of flames did not stop until the screaming died completely.

Slowly, she lowered her hands from her ears and peeked open her eyes. Merlin's legs trembled as she tried to turn. A giant hallway of smoking trees replaced their original path, stretching out far but narrow in size. Lancelot was standing right where he had been, his arm still held up. Fire danced around him in small patches sprinkled throughout the wreckage. Merlin didn't look for the Cockatrice, she knew they would be dead. Instead, she walked to Lancelot, wobbling slightly. When she made it over to him she could see that he was also shaking. Gently she pushed his arm down.

"Good job," she told him, trying not to sound horrified. Her stomach wanted to heave from the smell and sight of destruction. Merlin clamped her mouth shut, pushing her repulsion down. There were more pressing matters to deal with. Lancelot was not burnt, but his face and hand were an unhealthy red, and his breathing was erratic.

His legs gave out abruptly, and he fell into a crouch. She knelt by him as he winced in pain. "Did I... get them all?"

"Yes, you did." Merlin sat down, taking a deep breath. "You also burnt a lot of the forest as well." She knew he would have given her an annoyed look if he wasn't injured. Merlin reached up and rubbed her forehead, forgetting momentarily that her hands felt drier than her mother's biscuits. She hissed at the stinging.

"I don't suppose," Lancelot started, "you can take care of burns?"

Merlin looked at him, noting that his eyes were still closed. "Give me a moment." After two more breaths she stood. "Once I'm done, we need to leave."

He nodded, face still slack. "What about the cat?"

Merlin froze. Where was Gwen? All she remembered was the cat jumping past her. Something heavy fell on Merlin's head, bouncing off and falling to the ground.

"Ow." she grumbled, looking down at the book that was lying on the grass. That was when another heavy object fell on top of her, landing on her back this time before heading to the ground. Merlin wanted to rub her head, but her hands hurt to move.

"Thank you for asking, but I'm right here, Lance." The cat sat down next to the book, looking pleased.

"Gwen!" Merlin smiled and then winced. "I'm glad you're here."

"Me too," the cat agreed. "And let me tell you, it was not easy. I was nearly charred just now."

"I'm glad you weren't." Merlin said as she began creating the golden circle of her signet. When she connected the two ends together, she sat down next to Lancelot. "All right Lance, I'm going to heal you now."

He flinched. "Don't call me Lance." She ignored him and made the last tiny circle. Merlin felt the Rideon wash over the two of them like a cool spring as she worked. Not five minutes later they were both spotlessly healthy.

Lancelot opened his eyes, blinking rapidly at the wreckage around them. "You're sure this can be fixed?"

Merlin didn't say anything, leaning back on her toes. Now that she had caught her breath, the image of her home was searing itself onto her eyes. A wash of guilt flooded over her as the memory repeated. How was she going to explain it to her parents? Sands, her parents! They would be gone for a few months, yes, but when they got back, where would they live? Everything had been in there: records, food, clothing, valuables. It had all just burnt down. Not to mention the note explaining her absence had been there too. Merlin clenched her fist tightly, feeling the bracelet swing against her wrist. The sword must have automatically changed back into charm form.

CHAPTER 4

Merlin gritted her teeth. *Rainault.* It was all his fault. Everything was gone because of him. Her hands shook from the sudden swelling of anger that was growing inside her. The image of her home was replaced with his taunting eyes, triumphant even as he burned.

"Lancelot," Merlin started, trying to control the fury. "Did you see Rainault leave the house?" She forced herself to look at him, and his expression seemed understanding.

"No, Merlin." He picked up the book that Guinevere had saved. "I don't think he'll be coming out of there alive."

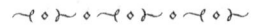

G

The cat eyed Merlin as she trembled. It wasn't the first time she had seen her so angry, but it was the first time Gwen sensed hate in her eyes. She sat back on her paws, tilting her head. "Merlin, a squad will be here soon. We should get moving."

Her friend looked down at her, Merlin's copper hair falling across her face. "Gwen, I can't, my parents' home..."

"There isn't anything you can do about that." Gwen pointed out. The knight looked like he wanted to speak, but Gwen gave him a small shake of her head. He closed his mouth immediately, while she looked back at Merlin. "If we stay here, or go back, we will all be taken to jail, or killed for harboring an unregistered elestiel. We need to leave."

Merlin looked like she wanted to argue, but slowly she nodded. "Fine."

"Where are we going?" Lancelot asked, and Gwen glared at him.

"North, like we agreed."

Lancelot glanced at Merlin before speaking again. "Not that I don't want to get there, but we have no supplies. Like water... or food."

The cat sighed. He was right. They would have procured the food from Merlin's house, but that was no longer an option. Now supplies had to come from somewhere else, and they would need a place to stay for the night as well. Gwen's whiskers twitched as she peered around the forest. She knew Merlin would need somewhere to calm down, which left only one place that met all the requirements. It was close, they both knew the owner, and they would not immediately be turned in to the authorities.

"All right, in that case, we'll go someplace else." Gwen announced. Both elestiels looked at her. "We'll go there now, and stock up on supplies. So please, let's go."

Lancelot nodded, standing up and brushing off ash. When Merlin didn't immediately stand, the cat walked the last few steps over to her and crouched. Gwen's tail flicked to the side as she made Merlin look at her. "We can figure this out later. For now we need to leave. All right?"

Merlin blinked, then stood, still clenching her fists. "I'm fine." She wheeled around and started walking briskly up the burnt path.

Gwen turned to the knight. "We should follow her." Lancelot put up no fight as they did precisely that.

As they walked around the ash covered ground, smoke drifted up through the trees and heat pulsed along the forest. The temperature tugged at Gwen as she returned to peering at the trees. She had heard something out there, something that did not sound like a forest animal. She could feel it, too—the cold press of eyes watching them from the shadows, hidden within the trees. Her claws began to ache with the need to prove herself wrong, but she ignored it. There was no time to waste on her suspicions. Not yet, at least.

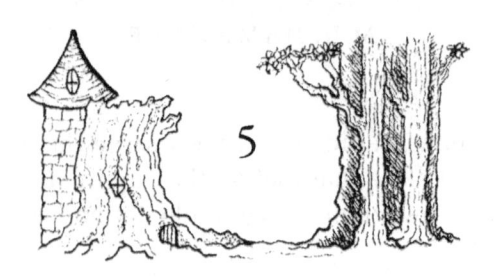

Rekindling the Coward

R

Dirt clung to the inside of his nails as he clawed the ground, pulling roots and insects up from the earth. Ants swarmed out of their home and over his face, his legs, his back. Their legs sent thousands of sharp, tormenting stings pulsing into his skin. He had no voice left with which to utter pained wails, and no strength to remove the horrid little insects as they bit into his raw pink flesh. Even the grass under his stomach speared him with their tips. Air blew against his sticky, stinging back, and small pebbles embedded themselves in the wet absence of skin. Blood was mixing with metal, mixing with cinders in his mouth. Weakness overtook his desperate attempts to blindly pull himself forward.

For his eyes held no sight, and his ears heard no sound.

All Rainault could do was *feel*.

Trembling, he let his head fall to the ground. At last he would die. Not from the disease, not from an enemy. Peace at last would greet him, and take all his troubles away. Then, and only then, could he fly again. Through green meadows and over streams, past clouds and an endless sea. He would be unified with the Rideon.

Rainault felt himself drifting away, heading towards the afterlife he had been told would not accept him. He was dimly aware of his eyes closing, when suddenly bright orange light flooded the world. Icy pain rippled across his body, rolling in waves of throbbing frigidness. Shrieks erupted from the depths of his lungs, pulled as if a hand had reached in and ripped it out of him.

"Stop!" he screamed, writhing and squirming on the ground, which only made his pain worse. What cruel punishment was this, to be set ablaze a second time? "Please!"

Begging took the breath out of his lungs, and he was forced to stop and gasp. Dizziness made his eyes swim, but the pain—as intense as it had been—was already fading away. What happened to him? Rainault took a deep breath, and threw himself onto his back with a cough. His eyes were clear, he could see trees and bits of bright blue. The sky that he could never enter. Rainault closed his eyes, wishing he'd died.

"Why?" he asked the forest even though he knew it could never answer. Instead Rainault began resigning himself to rise, until he heard the hissing. Quiet at first, the echoing sound rolled around the surrounding woods, rattling and spitting from every direction. His body shook with instinctual fear as the air around him seemed to turn a hundred times more thick. Pressure built in his chest and lungs. His head jerked as a thin, green string slithered up the side of his cheek. Rainault gasped, forcing his quivering eyes to look straight at it. A tiny green snake lay on his cheek, its little red tongue curling out from the jaws of its pointed head.

"You failed." The voice that came out of it reverberated as if hundreds of the same voice were speaking. "You had one job, and you *failed.*" The male voice was still, not a stutter amidst the endless echoes.

Rainault whimpered. "It wasn't my fault! There was a boy!"

The snake opened its mouth wide, almost like a smile. "Fool." Before Rainault could say more, the snake suddenly stuck straight up, wriggling until it abruptly stopped. Rainault stared, breathing rapidly as the blade of grass swayed back and forth. What happened? Should he run? A gloved hand appeared and latched onto the remains of Rainault's tunic. His teeth rattled as he was slammed against a tree, the breath knocked out of him.

The person before him was tall and clearly strong. A black hood was pulled over the man's head, and only shadows could be seen under it. Rainault felt his ribs beginning to bend as the man continued pressing him harder against the tree. He grabbed the guy's arm, trying uselessly to push back. Around them the hissing grew louder, and the ground began to sway, each piece of grass joining the tune. Rainault saw several reach up their heads and blow tiny sparks of fire.

The man reached up with his second hand, closing around Rainault's throat and squeezing. "You really are a charred moth," the voices called out. "Skinned by an elestiel without offensive power. Left to face death like the coward you are." The hand tightened.

CHAPTER 5

Rainault coughed, trying to force the air down. "I... was unprepared." he croaked out each word. "For..give me!"

The hand holding him against the tree released his clothing. The full weight of his body was now held up by only one hand, the extra weight like a noose. "Forgive you? You're sorry?" The man squeezed tighter as the hissing increased, and the voice became wistful. "Should I skin your seared flesh to prove your failure to your corpse? Or would you rather I pull out your teeth, and rip out your nails that you may live and know my anger?" Ringing was starting in Rainault's ears, but still he tried for more air. "Well?!" the voices screamed.

"No, sir!" he choked out.

The hooded man pulled the ivirian backward and threw him to the side. Rainault rolled, every rock and branch poking into him. He collided with yet another trunk, groaning as his world spun. His skin crawled, hands pushing against the ground as he tried to sit up. The grass wrapped itself around his fingers, but he pulled away, adjusting his back so he could sit straight.

Several feet away crouched the hooded man, his arms resting atop his knees. The grass around him slithered and writhed, clinging to his leather boots and loose black tunic. More tiny puffs of fire blew out of the farthest snakes in the clearing.

What had Rainault done to himself? He should *never* have made that bargain. Regret began scrubbing itself into every fiber of his being.

"P-please, my lord, spare me." Rainault begged. "I never meant to fail."

The man remained motionless, but the voice echoed around Rainault. "You might have had an honorable death, but cowards who beg deserve no such honor." Tears began streaming down the ivirian's cheeks. "Still, you are not completely without use."

A small, almost nonexistent hope came to life inside Rainault. "You mean, you won't kill me?"

"No." The hooded man lowered a hand, letting several snakes rub against his palm, and curl around his fingers. "You will die either by me, or by your disease, but you will certainly die. It's your choice how soon." The hope died. "Go now and accomplish your task. I want her ears served on a platter. And keep this in mind, *sheriff*; the next time your health requires me to save you, I won't."

The man stood, but Rainault made himself shoot forward, falling on his hands and knees. "Wait, sir, please! If you healed me, then is my disease gone? Can I live any longer?"

Rainault waited, but the man didn't even turn, he just kept walking farther away. "Your sickness can only be cured by the woman, as I said before." He began to disappear into the shadows of the forest. "Stop groveling and *worm* your way back into health." Those were his last words as he left Rainault's sight, the hissing grass falling silent behind him.

Dearest Ivory Knight,

I have read your demands, and they seem reasonable. But you've never needed my approval to show how your words were censored. Instead of editing, I laugh with every letter you send. If that was the plan all along, then consider it fulfilled.

You say you were prodded to find the culprit, but I know that it wasn't I who begged. Why bother finding someone who simply cleared away our trash? I would have hunted them down myself, had it been worth the effort. So tell me, who is it that would dare to nag you about such things? I will take care of them immediately. Even if you found something useful, a clean conscience doesn't demand respect. Although, it is amusing to think our earlier hunches were correct concerning the person who wanted our 'dear' acquaintance dead.

Moving from that, thank you for the warning. I suspect I already know of this Onyx weapon, but since I'm not sure, I will hold off on giving you my suspicions. Now finally, I come to the main reason that I, myself, wrote to you.

Our Marble Pawn is moving along well, though further down the road it could become difficult. From what I've seen, the government might become a rather large hindrance. Furthermore, a Marble Rook has appeared, claiming to search for another of our 'dear acquaintances. With this addition to their group, I am never short on something with which to be amused about.

But before I continue let me explain the lack of information in my last letter. There is no need for you to question me: I simply ran out of time when writing. It's hard to write for long while keeping an eye on them. I was nearly caught by a squirrel the other day while I wrote the first part of this. As of now, I have the time to explain further the routes and several observations I collected during my time in this forest.

Withall that being said, please refrain from questioning me when you know there's no need. I've proven my loyalty in more ways than one, including some that cannot be repeated on paper. Moreover, I expect that Ivory Rook has already confirmed my actions to you, so you must find some enjoyment in continuously testing my intentions.

Now, on to the dull politics which so drives this world...

Ivory Bishop

Chapter 6

Threatening are the Shoes that Travel the World

As they followed Sher's official thoroughfare, the Mason Line, Gwen's feeling of being followed faded away. The cat's hair slowly fell alongside her suspicion, but she kept it in her mind, just to be safe. Around them the trees grew apart, thinning as they began to climb a hill that could have been called a small mountain. From the bottom it was daunting, from the middle it was annoying. Little weeds grew between the large stones of the path, their leaves covered in spiky thistles. Those with boots would have no problem walking through, but Gwen had no such protection. There was even a continuous cloud of dry dirt that clung to her fur far worse than ash.

The cat whined as she stepped on a large leaf. Her paw throbbed as she lifted it, several barbs sticking into the pads. "Here." She looked up to see Lancelot crouching. He held out his hand, and Gwen reluctantly offered her paw. Gently, he proceeded to pull the barb out.

"Thank you." Gwen mumbled. She glanced at Merlin, who was still walking ahead.

Lancelot followed her gaze. "It's as if she's being pulled along by a string."

"Well, her house did just burn down." Gwen flexed her paw before setting it carefully on the ground. "It's surprising she didn't go back and dig through the rubble to make sure he was dead."

"Would she really have done that?" Lancelot asked as they started walking again.

"Yes." Gwen dodged another weed. "Wouldn't you?"

He frowned. "Maybe... But if he were alive, he would need to be arrested. That is the correct response."

Gwen looked at the back of Merlin's head, considering. "I guess that's the difference between you two." Gwen knew her friend was probably blaming herself even as they walked, but there wasn't anything anyone could do about it. Merlin would have to find some way of moving forward, and whichever way that happened was up to her. Gwen looked back at Lancelot. "I was wondering, you shoved a book in that satchel, which one *could* say is very small. It's an imbued item isn't it?"

They moved around a boulder and Lancelot put one hand on the bag. "Yes."

"A book and a bag. Did you steal them both?" she asked him rather bluntly.

He let out a short laugh. "Maybe."

Gwen narrowed her gaze at the guy. It was no secret to her that those items were rare in human lands, as an imbued item could only be created after years of exposure to the Rideon. Inside Sher there were many imbued plants, but only because of the sheer amount of myths spilling the Rideon all over. Human kingdoms did not have enough elestiels to create imbued items, so how did Lancelot have *two*? All Gwen could guess was that the satchel was very old, as well as the book it contained.

"Where exactly did you get two of them?"

At that moment they made it to the top of the large hill, so her question went unanswered. Merlin stopped and was standing staring out at the landscape before her. Gwen and Lancelot paused on either side of her, viewing the world around them.

Rolling hills of bright green spread out beneath them, and large mountains could be seen in the distance, covered in dark green trees. A blanket of colorful foliage made large splotches on the land, and a ravine sat to the right. The cliffs of the jagged line made it appear to be a scar on the earth. Gwen looked up at the sky above them, taking in the bright vividity of the cloudless blue. Even with a gust of chilly wind, she had to admit it was gorgeous. Lancelot commented as much, while he too stared.

The cat looked down from the sky, and noticed a tear rolling down Merlin's cheek. She turned her head to where the girl was looking, and saw a trail of black rising in the distance. They were far from it, but the location was doubtlessly her house. Gwen sighed.

CHAPTER 6

"Come on guys, the climb down is always easier." Gwen gave the steep ground a wary glare. "Besides, it will be nearly nightfall before we get down."

"Are we close to the place you mentioned?" asked Lancelot. "It would be dangerous to travel in the dark."

"It's at the base of the hill." They both looked at Merlin, whose voice sounded dry. She glared and quickly brushed the tear from her face before pushing past them. Her movement triggered both to follow.

Gwen's estimation of time was mostly correct. While they climbed down, the cat lost her footing and started tumbling down the mountain in a dangerous direction. It cost both elestiels a bit of time retrieving the cat, which made their walk longer. They even had to stop again so Lancelot could detangle a rabbit from a bush. Subsequently, the sun was setting by the time they made it to the bottom. Gwen gave a relieved sigh as the spiky weeds disappeared at the mountain's base.

"So, where is the place you spoke of?" Lancelot asked.

"Give me a moment." Gwen wiggled her sore paws. She twisted her neck back and forth, feeling a relieving pop. "All right. Open sesame!"

Lancelot's jaw dropped as a clump of trees to their right blurred and faded. In its place sat a large brown boot with a murky green beanstalk sitting behind it. Gwen smirked at him, remembering the first time she'd seen it. The boot made them all feel tiny. Four windows lined the front side of its leg, with moss growing along the edges of its sole. Directly between the front and back of the shoe's arch sat a smooth wooden door covered in tiny scratches. A cobblestone path led up to it, swept perfectly, which was no easy achievement with all the dirt. In fact, rocks and grit were more common than patches of grass. There was also a stall by the end of the boot, with a striped canopy providing a roof over a table and chair.

Even larger than the shoe, the beanstalk grew upward into the canopy of trees, its leaves sprouting from either side. Pale green sap filled the inside of its translucent outer shell, made yellow in the fading sun. Gwen knew from memory that there were hard ridges across the top of the stalk in a jagged line from being hacked at. She marveled for the fiftieth time at the plant's incapacity to grow back to its original height, so unlike any other plant in the forest.

When she decided she was finished looking, Gwen straightened her back and marched towards the door. "Come on then, we should get inside before it disappears again." Her words did the trick, and both companions followed her up to the house. Merlin opened the door when they got there, not waiting to knock. The cat hopped through the door first, dodging around a half suit of armor, propped in the door. She hissed at all the tables lining the rectangular room, their tops and underneath covered in piles of objects, from books and kitchen pans to shields and spearheads.

"Gwen." Merlin's tone was meant to be warning, but Guinevere simply ignored her.

"I told him last time to not leave stuff lying around the entrance!" she grumbled. Her fur was slowly lowering, but even so, Gwen jumped onto a table of books, pushing it aside as she landed. The top book wobbled and fell with a loud clatter. Gwen huffed and raised her head, yelling, "Jack!"

There were stairs leading up the leg of the shoe, and seconds after she yelled they could all hear the stairs begin squeaking. A familiar rusty voice started yelling down the stairs as he made his way down. "Oi! Hold your horses, I'm coming. Gee, what nice customers I have, I tell ya." He came down the stairs, glaring at them all.

The cat grinned. "Hi Jack."

L

He was short, no more than four feet tall with vibrant red hair brushed over his head and wrapped around his chin in a trimmed rectangle. Jack wore a faded green sweater that fell to his knees, and two shiny black shoes on each foot. His eyes were narrowed, and his round nose scrunched when he saw them. Jack pointed a polished cane at the three of them as he took the last step down to their level.

"Oh no, not you." The floor groaned under the new pressure. "I'm not listening to another one of your crazy ideas. Nearly burnt down my shop last time." Jack's voice rolled over the words and stressed the sounds of the hard *i*'s and *r*'s in his speech. Lancelot felt like he should have been surprised, but after the shoe house, he didn't have much surprise left in him.

CHAPTER 6

Gwen shrugged at Jack, then beamed at Lancelot. "This is Jack, he's a leprechaun, so don't leave anything valuable around, and don't trust a thing he says unless you're paying for it."

"Ha!" Jack headed towards them, his cane making small taps against the floor. "Fifteen years of dedicated service, and you say you don't trust me. Hmph!" He stopped by Merlin and looked at her directly. "What's up with you? Cat got your tongue? A hello might be nice."

"Hello, Jack." Merlin complied.

"I most certainly do not have her tongue." Gwen growled. She jumped from the table onto Merlin's shoulder. "That is disgusting."

Merlin's expression turned to surprise and she began to teeter to the side from the shift in balance. Lancelot quickly put a hand on her shoulder, steadying her before anything unfortunate could happen.

"Um, sir," Lancelot started, pulling away from Merlin as she gave him a distracted nod of thanks.

"No 'sir' here." Jack grumbled. He moved away from them to the end of the shoe, where a chimney sat. Clear tapping sounds came from the wooden panels lining the floor, stopping only when Jack sat in a chair surrounded by more junk. It was amazing that none of the goods had caught on fire. "Just call me Jack."

Lancelot twisted his mouth. "Jack, we've come for supplies and possibly accommodations for sleep. Can you help us?"

Jack's eyes slid to Merlin, who had withdrawn into herself again, staring blankly at the floor. "What's wrong with her?" he asked with a squint. The knight flinched and opened his mouth, but no sound came out. What should he say? Was it right for him to say anything at all? Merlin wasn't providing any form of help, she didn't even acknowledge his question. Lancelot knew from the short time he spent with her that her silence was uncharacteristic.

Gwen hopped off Merlin's shoulder, and put a paw on her boot. "We'll be gone soon." she assured him. "I've never known you to turn away customers, Jack."

"Is that what you are?" he snorted. "Does that mean you're going to pay?"

"Of course!" Gwen chirped, beginning to push Merlin towards the stairs.

Lancelot raised an eyebrow. As far as he knew, he was the only one carrying money on his person. There hadn't been time for Merlin to retrieve any funds amidst the blaze.

Jack stroked his beard, clearly thinking carefully. The leprechaun pulled out a pipe from the table closest to him. He stuck it in the fire and pulled it back out, sucking in a few breaths before blowing out smoke rings. Slowly, he lowered the pipe and held out a hand. "You can pay me upfront for the bed, and then again when you select the supplies."

Gwen laughed hesitantly by the stairwell. "I don't suppose you'll take a trustworthy I owe you?"

Jack stared at them with a vast lack of amusement.

"I can pay." Lancelot volunteered, sighing to himself as he began fiddling with his bag.

"Great!" the cat sang out unabashedly. "Then Merlin and I will head upstairs while you deal with this.

Jack blew out another smoke ring. "I want explanations, Guinevere."

She bowed slightly, then sauntered to the stairs, Merlin in tow. "Don't worry, Lance will explain!" She sang as they disappeared up the stairs.

The knight floundered momentarily, trying not to overreact. Except that both of them just *left* him alone with a leprechaun in his boot house that only appeared when someone said, "*open sesame.*" Maybe they weren't that close, but at least Gwen should have stayed. He sighed. Merlin probably needed Gwen more than he did.

"How much is the stay here?" Lancelot asked, trying to not sound uncomfortable.

"Three silver coins, each." Jack tapped the cane on the ground.

Lancelot had just pulled out his coin purse, but now he paused. "That's outrageous."

"Would ya like me to raise the price?"

"No, no." Hurriedly he pulled out the coins, each a shiny silver. "Thank you for your accommodations."

"Heh, accommodations, sure." Jack set down the still steaming pipe, leaning on his cane instead. His gaze turned sharp. "Explain what happened to Merlin, now."

CHAPTER 6

"Well," Lancelot ran a hand through his hair. "I'm not entirely sure of the details, but an ivirian appeared at her home yesterday morning, with the intent to kill her, I believe. There was a fight in the house, which led to a fire, and now the house is gone." That about summed up what Lancelot actually understood.

A vein popped out on Jack's forehead. "That's why you all reek of smoke."

"That is correct, yes." Lancelot stepped closer to the fire, observing a covered chair across from Jack. "I'm not sure why he was so aggressive, but I believe it had something to do with her not healing him." He carefully began uncovering the chair.

"That sounds like something she would do, stubborn fool." Jack thumped his cane on the ground emphatically. "But tell me why you are here. I've been a tradesman my whole life, and I have never seen you in this forest before. You don't belong here."

"I'm not trying to *stay* here." Lancelot told him as he finally sat down. With what he'd seen, he knew the leprechaun would want nothing but the truth. "I need Merlin's help to stop this war."

"And how could she do that?" Jack's skepticism was nearly palpable.

"She..." The knight hesitated. "I'm trying to find the missing prince of Logres, Prince Arthur. I have good reason to believe he's alive, and he needs to see Merlin for whatever reason."

Jack didn't laugh or even bat an eye at his reason, he just picked back up his pipe from the side table. Smoke curled in the air, rising in ringlets and curving waves. Heat rolled off the fireplace and sent orange light throughout the room. Outside there were thousands of crickets clicking from the grass, ringing their chirping bells in a discordant harmony that penetrated the boot's walls.

Jack grunted and pulled his pipe out from between his lips. "That is the *only* reason you are here?"

Lancelot blinked at him. "What other reason would I have?"

"Information gathering, I suppose." Jack drummed his fingers on his knee. "You are... a knight after all." Narrowing his eyes, Lancelot leaned forward. Jack's tone was dangerous, he could feel it.

"Avalon is not trying to enter into war with Sher." Lancelot affirmed. "There is no reason to send any form of spy into this forest. What I do is of my own volition."

Jack mimicked his posture, glaring intently at him. "And you have the status to do as you please?"

"I have the sense to."

"Do you?" Jack sat back, crossing his arms. "You know, I've been to Avalon before, and I'm fairly certain that a knight's duty is to follow their patrons. But you don't seem to be doing that. Or is your kingdom no longer bent on displaying strength through force?"

Lancelot's gut twisted. "I didn't leave on the best of terms, if that is what you are wondering." He let his hands slip down, and he gripped the chair's seat. In a quieter voice he muttered, "And my kingdom is much as it ever was."

The fire snapped, shooting a tiny ember up into the chimney. Jack grunted and raised his hand, pulling something shiny from beneath his shirt. It was a long chain with a circular pendant made from silver. Lancelot couldn't see the design well in the dim light, but he knew what was hammered there. Three bluebell flowers on a stem wrapped by a ribbon, with two notches on either bend of the stem.

He stood, wishing he had a sword to draw. "That doesn't belong to you."

Jack returned the token beneath his shirt and sneered. "We're not in Avalon now, boy. It belongs to me until I use it. I've only shown you now because I suspected you would recognize it."

"*E skir! E tokata vero!**" Lancelot snapped.

Jack looked unimpressed. "Have the guts to insult me in a language I understand. My knowledge of Avalonian is minimal."

The knight took a deep breath, "Regardless of our current location, it is still not yours. How did you even get it?"

"I found it." The leprechaun stroked his beard. "I had a wagon in the capitol, next to a noble's house. I saw it fall when a certain visitor left that house. Thought I'd keep it," he smirked. "Just in case." Lancelot's gut twisted. The look Jack was giving him spoke of knowledge the knight hoped no one would have.

"What do you want from me?" he asked, holding back all his anger by mere threads of self-control. It did him no good to lose his temper, and insulting Jack would land him nowhere.

---

* *Closely translated to: You monster (Or more likely devil), you cruel dog/mut.*

"I want you to leave." Jack said bluntly. "I don't trust you to be within a league of either of them. Avalon is getting too desperate after the queen's..." He didn't need to finish his sentence.

Lancelot flinched, and sat back down in his chair. "I'm afraid I cannot do that. I swore to protect Merlin as she traveled, so I won't be leaving, even if it means sleeping outside." Jack raised an eyebrow, prompting a slight flush to appear across Lancelot's cheeks. "And I need her to stop this war. Above all else, that is why I must stay."

"Hmph." Jack returned to his pipe, smoking with a deepening scowl. Flames reflected in his cold, discerning eyes. He was weighing Lancelot's words. The knight felt like he was sitting on a scale dipping between credible and insufficient.

After several moments of painstaking silence, Jack finally spoke. "If you do anything I deem wrong, I will throw you out and have a very long talk with Merlin about *why* you can't stay. And trust me, I will not leave out *anything*."

Lancelot crossed his arms over his chest. "Why are you letting me stay?" He let his suspicion lace his words and tone, making it quite clear.

Jack stood up, which was not as grand as when Lancelot had—what with the height difference—and tapped his cane on the floor. "That's my business and decision. Neither of which belongs to you."

He began walking away, leaving Lancelot alone by the fire. The knight watched him hobble forward, sifting through muddled emotions. More than exhaustion from the walk and fight, he was feeling vulnerable. No sword, no ally, no armor. Here he was in dangerous territory, trying so desperately to put an end to all the bloodshed, and he had no one on his side. Not that he had many people helping him in Avalon either.

A shiver ran up his spine. He needed a weapon, something that could help him protect himself. "Are your swords for sale?" Lancelot asked suddenly, rising quickly.

Jack twisted around. "You think I'm giving you a sword?"

"Selling me one, actually." The knight hurried to a table filled with sheathed blades.

"You're not doing very much to seem less dangerous, are you?" Jack grumbled as he walked over to Lancelot. He glanced from the swords to Lancelot, and then back at the swords. Jack let out a loud sigh, and waved his hand. "Fine, pick one out and I'll tell you how much it is." Jack instructed.

"*Sveit.**" Lancelot thanked him, casting his eyes down at the stacks of weapons. There were broadswords, longswords, arming swords, daggers and throwing knives. The variety applied to the quality as well, some looking ancient, while others appeared newly made. He had only glanced over the pile before something strange caught his eye. There was a ribbon hanging from one of the swords, shining like a stream of pearlescent starlight that shimmered unnaturally. It was attached to the end of a silver pommel on a black leather grip. Lancelot unburied the weapon carefully. The hilt was intricate, with two curved spikes rising on either side of the sheathed blade, and two facing down towards the grip. It had two rounded spikes sticking out horizontally, and in the center lay two lozenges set within each other. The entire hilt was made from dark silver, which split the leather grip in the middle to divide for both hands.

Carefully, Lancelot picked up the sword, and pulled it out of the leather sheath. Black steel greeted him, sleek and sharp along the edges and at the tip. Gold lettering ran up the middle of the sword, but Lancelot didn't recognize the language. What interested him was the ribbon that dangled off it, and the unusual appearance of the sword itself.

He fingered the trailing fabric, inspecting the strange enigma carefully. "Interesting..." Lancelot mumbled. After a moment he began wrapping the fabric in a loose loop. When he was finished, the silky rope hung from the end of the sword, tied together firmly. Twisting around he found Jack still standing behind him, watching intently.

"That is an interesting choice." he said gruffly, like he didn't want to speak more than he had too. "Its name is Solaris, and it has seen many owners."

Lancelot glanced down at the sword. "Were they killed?"

"Some," Jack patted the sheath. "A few even by this sword. I was told that it had taken so many lives, the blade should be red. That its owner hears the whispers of its victims' final cries, carried and preserved inside the steel. Do you really want such a dirty blade, *sir* Lancelot?" He stressed the title, intent clear.

The knight squeezed the grip. "How much?"

---

* *Sveit translates to thank you in Avalonian.*

CHAPTER 6

"Fifteen bronze or six silver coins up front." Jack paused, then shook his head. "But for you, I'd like seven silvers."

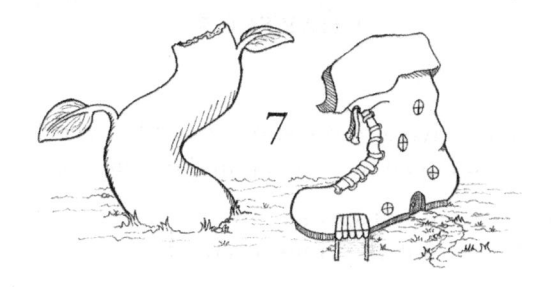

Dreaming of a Nightmare

M

The walls and floor were the same rusty wood as the ceiling, and a beige rug sat in the middle of the windowless room. A single bed sat in the farthest corner, simple cotton sheets spread out over it, and a limp pillow rested against the wall. There was nothing else occupying the room. It was barren.

Merlin stood at the edge of the rug, unblinking and silent. Gwen trotted up to the bed before hopping onto it without hesitation. "Well, the mattress has hardened since we were here last." she declared. The cat looked up to Merlin, her green eyes widening. "Are you going to sit?"

Merlin opened her mouth, but sound didn't come out. The last of her restraint was snapping at the memory of her home, smoking in front of her eyes. Memories destroyed, belongings gone... Her home, her life, her world. Everything was burnt, and she had just *watched* it happen. What could she say to her parents? Her brother? Hot tears were brimming at the base of her eyes as she thought of her parents. Hours spent watching her father carve the most beautiful pictures were all now transformed into shapeless kindling. Herbs her mother cultivated flew as embers in the wind, smoking until their spark had diminished. Her brothers belongings: both sets were gone. All evidence of her family's presence had dissolved.

"Merlin," Gwen's voice was grave and commanding. "Sit down." Without a thought, her feet followed the cat's instructions. Down she sank onto the stiff mattress, her boots leaving flecks of dirt and ash on the floor. "Listen to me," Gwen directed her. "I apologize for doing this again, but you need it."

A heavy force collided into Merlin's cheek, connecting with her jaw and pushing her face away. "Ow! Gwen, what are you doing?" Merlin exclaimed, her hand flying to the soreness on her cheek. Twice in two days she had been slapped by that cat, in the *same* spot no less.

"I'm trying to make you speak!" Gwen cried, jumping up and down on the bed. "Now is not the time to crawl inside yourself, we have things to do!"

Merlin gaped at the animal. "Crawl into myself? Don't you understand? Everything is gone! The house, the garden, Aspen's grave! It's all sitting in a pile of ash!"

The cat screeched, "Of course I understand! That was my home too! But is sitting here going to bring it back?"

"What do you expect me to do?" Merlin clenched her fists. "Pretend it didn't happen? My life was in there!"

"No, your life is in here!" Gwen pointed a claw at Merlin. "Inside you! There will be nothing but pain for you if you stay like this!"

Her fingers uncurled only long enough to grab wads of the bed's blanket, and squeeze until her knuckles were white. Every fiber of Merlin's being wanted to leave the house, find her home, and claw through the rubble until she found the sheriff's corpse. Even then, she wanted more. Merlin could never harm Rainault again, but she could find something close to his heart—a family, a business, something he put his passion into. As difficult as it would be, she knew she could find *something*.

"Lyn," Gwen said gently. "Can't you see that this hurts you worse than it can ever hurt him? The more you look back on things that are gone, the more they take what you have now."

Merlin looked away. "Don't quote my father to me."

The cat sighed, and made a quick leap to the ground. "I won't. But you have to make a choice right now, and I can't do it for you. You told the knight you would go north, and you promised Daleon you would see him at the front. Are you going to let a house hold you back?" The cat stood for only a second, before turning away and walking towards the door.

With red eyes, Merlin watched her go, conflict twisting her heart into knots. Her voice came out broken. "I was ready to leave, but I wasn't ready to have nothing I could return to."

Gwen looked back, and for the first time Merlin could see pain's imprint on the cat. "Neither was I."

G

The stairs creaked as she leapt down each one, putting distance between herself and Merlin. She was already shoving down the pain she had allowed to rise for just a moment, but the task was proving more difficult than she expected. Something she locked up this securely was not easily shoved aside. *If only... no.* Even in her thoughts there was no use complaining. Gwen would have to ignore it and hope that Merlin would come to the right conclusion.

On the main level, she found neither Jack nor Lancelot, so she headed straight to a brown door by the stairs. It led to a kitchen and dining room that had been added onto the boot after Jack's father, Tergus, had taken it as compensation from a giant named Paul. One of the last of his kind, Paul was a lumberjack in Sher who cut down Tergus' beanstalk. It still hadn't grown back, but Jack was hopeful it would eventually. Gwen suspected the stalk wouldn't grow ever again, but she wasn't going to tell Jack.

Stretching first, Gwen leapt into the air, wrapping both paws around a slim handle on the door. Her weight and downward momentum brought the door swinging open with a click. The cat gave a small cry as she swung outward and lost her grip on the metal. Everything spun as she spiraled through the air. "Aaah!"

"Careful!" The air was knocked out of her as someone, Lancelot by the sound of it, caught her.

Gwen's sight wobbled dizzily, a table and chairs spinning upside-down before finally settling back into their proper positions. "Thank you," she said as the knight set her down.

"Of course." He sounded a bit distracted.

Gwen looked up at him, noting the sword that hung at his side, and the concerned look he wore. "What is it? Did Jack threaten you or something?"

"Of course I did." Jack appeared from behind Lancelot, setting three bowls of steaming food on the dining table. He had expertly carried them from the old, half-dead stove he owned. "You think I'm letting a knight waltz into my house with you two in tow, *without* taking precautions? Now that I think about it, I should throw you both out right now before my hair turns gray."

Gwen rolled her eyes. "Oh please, our presence can't be that stressful."

He snorted. "I can feel years of my life fading away every time I see either of you."

Next to her, Lancelot sighed before moving to the table. "This doesn't have any carrots in it, does it?" he asked halfheartedly. "Because I nearly died the last time I ate one."

Jack glanced at the bowl of food. "Give me a moment and I'll get you some."

"Really?" Gwen drawled. She hopped onto the table, peeking at the bowls. Two of them were filled with rice and what looked like spinach. It smelled salty, with hints of basil and thyme. The third had milk inside it.

"Oh, calm down." Jack stopped his course into the kitchen and instead sat down at the table. The knight also took a seat, inspecting his bowl for any flecks of orange. "How about you explain, rather than complaining?"

"Didn't Lancelot tell you?" Gwen asked, biting the side of her bowl to pull it closer. She lapped the milk and purred.

"He wasn't satisfied with my explanation." Lancelot informed her. "Frankly, I'm not either. I hardly know what happened, and I was the one who had to fight those monsters."

"That's a little rude, don't you think?"

"No." Lancelot pointed his wooden spoon at her. "Those birds were terrifying."

Jack coughed. "Don't tell me you missed the Cockatrice?"

Gwen flattened her ears into a horizontal line. "No…"

"Guinevere," the leprechaun warned.

"Fine!" The cat glared. "Yes. There was a sheriff who wanted healing from Merlin, but when she refused, he came back with five Cockatrice." Jack's face grew several shades darker in annoyance. A deep sigh welled up inside Gwen and came out in a rush. There was no getting out of explaining it, so that is what she would do. Gwen took one more sip of milk before launching into the events of the last two days, starting with the military's denial, Merlin's plan, Lancelot's offer, and ending with their escape from the house. She wasn't sure how Merlin would feel about Lancelot knowing of her plight, but at the very least he should understand a piece of why Merlin was so desperate.

Getting to Daleon had been on her friend's mind for the past two years, driving her to pick up a sword and delve deeper into the regions of her power left uncontrolled. Though Merlin had always enjoyed her mother's trade, the new stress had choked all the joy from her studies. Watching the change in Merlin over the last ten years had almost been frightening, and now was no different. Of course, she wasn't the only one who had changed.

"That's it," she said as she finished. Jack sat back in his chair, one hand stroking his beard. A hazy fog glazed over his eyes while he took in her story. Lancelot also sat quietly, his face pensive. Gwen plopped her head down on the table, flicking her eyes between the two, trying to determine their thoughts. It was difficult with both adept in masking their opinions.

She had just considered leaving when Jack finally said, "How will the Lynwood's know where you are?"

Gwen frowned. "I'm not sure..."

"I'll have to send a letter, then." Jack nodded to himself. "That should explain it all. Did you say the sheriff had Talin's disease?"

"Yes," Gwen affirmed. "I can't believe he actually expected her to heal that."

"Could she?" Jack asked. Gwen opened her mouth, but closed it just as quickly. Merlin acted like she could, but would the Rideon really let her?

"Excuse me," Lancelot sounded apologetic. "You keep mentioning it, but what is Talin's disease?"

The cat tilted her head in his direction, feeling the grains of the wood through her fur. "You don't know?"

Lancelot shook his head.

"He wouldn't." Jack took a bite of his rice. "Not after the Massacre."

A flicker of irritation shot across Lancelot's face. "Would you possibly enlighten me?"

CHAPTER 7

Gwen snorted. "It's the Limit, for ivirian's anyway."

The knight stared blankly at her.

"He's going to need more than that." Jack told her. He turned to face Lancelot, who straightened ever so slightly. "You know that elves can't break their promises, else some horrible accident befall them. That is their Limit. Every kind of myth has one. Ivirians, they grow ill. It was named after a terrible ivirian by the name of Talin, oh, three hundred years ago?" Jack tapped the table. "He was awful, abusing his Rideon gift on so many innocent myths and humans. Eventually his bones began to leak, and no physician or healer could make it stop."

Gwen perked up. "It's difficult to put an exact cause on the sickness, but most people believe it comes from using their power for evil."

"Yes." The leprechaun looked a little annoyed at being interrupted. "After he contracted it, several more ivirians complained of the same disease, until it became shameful to have it."

Lancelot cupped his chin. "So all myths have this limit? Do elestiels have one too?"

Gwen let Jack answer those questions. "Yes we all have one, and no, elestiels don't." He glared. "There is only one kind of elestiel that I know of that has a limit, but that is a side matter. Mostly you have the freedom to do anything, without any repercussions."

"I see..." The knight nodded, setting his utensil down. "How is it that our records do not speak of this?"

"It's hard to record things when you're dead." Gwen told him. "Jack, is there any meat for me?"

Jack jerked his thumb towards the door. "Got a mouse somewhere in there. You can have him."

Gwen rolled her eyes. "Oh joy, I get to chase my meal."

"What do you mean, dead?" Lancelot asked, his eyebrows drawing together.

"Slaughtered?" Gwen tried again. "Murdered? Massacred? Which word would you prefer?"

"I—" the knight floundered.

"A hundred and sixty years ago, it became an unspoken law that no one should share information with humans." Jack said. "And then, even if we had wanted to share, we couldn't, because we were being hunted down and killed. The elestiels of that time were ruthless and unforgiving, not bound by any agreements that our leaders, the elves, had crafted."

The knight ran a hand through his hair and down his face, like he was ashamed of his ancestors. "That... makes sense. I should have guessed your meaning."

"Well, don't beat yourself up over it." Gwen hopped off her chair. "It was a long time ago, and none of the humans from that time are still alive."

"Humans," Jack grumbled. "They die so quickly, it's no wonder they make the mistakes they do. They forget to learn from their errors, and ignore their history. Sure, they can build anything, but what good is that when they destroy what one generation makes for another?"

An offended look came into Lancelot's eyes, but he quickly smoothed it away. "You said every myth has a Limit, do you?"

"Obviously." Jack crossed his arms. "Leprechauns turn into Gremlins should greed overtake them. As you can see, *I* am an honorable businessman."

"Yes, yes," Gwen tossed her tail back and forth. "And trolls turn into stone when they lose their aspiration. Gnomes are reduced to paranoid puddles if they abandon peace for industry. *Everyone* has a limit, it's just that most groups prefer to keep them secret."

Jack stood up from his chair. "That's enough storytelling, I've gotten my answers, and so have you." He nodded to Lancelot, moving towards the stove. Jack pulled out another bowl and scooped rice from an iron pot. "Now take this to Merlin, and don't come back down here. I'm tired of talking to you." Jack turned and glared at Lancelot, who obediently took the bowl from the leprechaun, albeit rather gingerly.

Gwen stifled a laugh and trotted towards the still open door. "She may not take it," she called back.

"I'll bring it anyway." Lancelot said, though uncertainty lay in his response.

CHAPTER 7

L

He carried the bowl up the creaking stairs, his head a whir with the information he received. The human belief that myths were untapped sources of power was wrong, very wrong. If anything it was the elestiels of the mainland that had true freedom. Individual gifts for every person, a signet for each, and the ability to do whatever they wished with it. No wonder Merlin had been so adamant about keeping her promise. An elf was *literally* bound to their words.

A rock hit the bottom of his stomach as Lancelot stopped just before an open door. He needed Merlin to come with him, desperately. There had to be some way around her promise, some alternate course that would allow her to help him. He sighed quietly before marching up to the doorway. The room inside was practically empty, except for a bed, a rug, and Merlin. She sat on the bed, staring blankly at the rug while her fingers played absently with her bracelet's sword charm. The one that, for some inexplicable reason, turned into a full-length sword. How she ended up with an imbued weapon was beyond him.

Pressing his mouth into a tight line, Lancelot knocked on the door. Merlin looked up to him, wordless questions in her eyes. "Um," he hesitated. "Jack said to bring you some food." He held up the bowl.

"Ah," she nodded slowly. "I'm... not really hungry."

A pinch of sympathy spurred him to step into the room and put the bowl of food by her. She looked at him with a raised eyebrow. "You walked all day, and hardly ate breakfast. You should eat." He put one hand on his sword's hilt, rubbing the metal uncomfortably.

"Are you threatening me if I don't eat?" Merlin pointed a finger at the sword.

His mouth shot open, ready to deny it, then paused. If he showed too much pity she might just get mad at him. "Yes, I am," he said. "We have a long walk ahead of us, and if you don't eat we won't even get halfway."

Just for a moment, a small spark of amusement lit her face. She tied the bracelet around her wrist, and said, "Do you always threaten people you've just met?"

He shrugged. "I'm a knight, threatening people is my job."

"I meant regular people," she said, the edges of her mouth pulling up into a tiny smile. "Not criminals."

"True, but you didn't specify before." He took a step back, raising both hands placatingly. "I'm afraid you can't take it back now." The knight watched as she shook her head, and took the food by her side. Satisfied now that she was eating, Lancelot turned around and headed for the exit.

He made it two steps before she said, "Thank you."

Lancelot paused, then, swiveling on his heels, he said, "You're welcome."

Merlin pushed back a few strands of her hair. "I'm not talking about the food."

The knight raised an eyebrow, questioning her with his expression.

She frowned. "Rainault would have killed me if you hadn't been there. So thank you." Her spoon made a little thwack as she poked the bowl. "You didn't have to, but you did."

"On the contrary," He raised his pointer finger. "I would have died as well, had I not intervened. But regardless, I did promise to protect you. You can count on me for that as we travel, without having to thank me." A knight's oath was not something to be taken lightly, for it held his honor and title until the promise was fulfilled. Perhaps it wasn't as binding as an elf's word, but he hoped she would understand the significance.

"Well, whatever the case, thank you." Merlin dipped her head down so she could eat the meal.

"You're welcome." He pursed his lips. "And I'm sorry about your house."

"Me too." She spoke so quietly he almost didn't hear her response. Feeling his discomfort return, Lancelot hurried out of the room.

M

Not long after the knight left, Gwen returned. She didn't speak to Merlin, just curled up on the rug. The silence was worse than arguing, because at least during the heat of a fight, Merlin could pretend she was right. Without that, all she was left with were Gwen's reasonable arguments and her own disjointed anger. The cat was right, but every time she thought of silencing her emotions, her gut tightened, and she would remember the house again; broken, and in flames.

Gently, she set the now empty bowl on the ground, letting her head rest against a pillow. It was soft compared to the mattress below her, and prompted Merlin to burrow further into the warmth of her blanket. Maybe sleep could draw her in and wash away the strains of the day. Merlin shut her eyes, wondering if it was even possible to calm down after everything that happened. Her worries were needless, however, because a minute later she felt the first pulls of sleep, and let them carry her far away.

Heat sweltered against her cheeks, stinging her skin and searing her hair. She was in her house, and orange flames bent and twisted around her in a curtain of blinding light. Gripped in her hands was her brother's sword, frozen in a downward swing. A loud crackle erupted from somewhere in the house, and suddenly Rainault was there, kneeling before her, his hands pressing against her blade. Dark blood dripped from his palms where the blade cut into his flesh, sliding down his wrists, and curling around his arms.

Merlin's gut wrenched as he let out an ear-piercing laugh, a mangled mix of agony and hysteric joy. She felt her body fight harder, forcing the sword closer to his neck and further into his palms. His laugh turned into a sneer, which morphed into a wide, malicious grin. Tensing, Merlin felt blinding fury swell inside her.

She was going to kill him.

More than knowing that she could, the resolution to act on her pain was coursing through her like adrenaline. It was a strong resolve, the kind that would not waver. Her mind scrambled to sort through the new thoughts and emotions, sudden doubt causing her to hesitate. Was she really going to kill him? Her stomach was repulsed, but her heart was torn in two. His life over a building that could be replaced? Could she really do that?

Again Rainault laughed, and she felt her blade shudder upwards. If she didn't decide right then, he would get away. Her eyes swept from the sword to his taunting face. The blood rushed to her head, and blinding emotion overcame her conscience. Merlin threw every bit of force she had into cutting down Rainault. She wanted to wipe that arrogant look off his face.

Down the sword went, nothing stopping it now. At the last second, before it met Rainault's throat, Merlin closed her eyes. Her instincts screamed their unwillingness to see the act, proving too strong to be ignored. Yet, even without her sight, she could feel it through the sword, and hear it in the air. The metal made a clear squelching noise in front of her, then warm liquid splash against her skin. It dripped down her cheek and across her shaking hands. Shivers crawled up her back and a dark feeling pressed down on her shoulders.

She tried to squeeze her eyes closed tighter, already regretting her decision. Instead, Merlin felt her eyelids begin moving upward on their own. She gasped as her eyes opened wide. Every nerve went numb in absolute horror at the wreckage before her. She was standing in the outskirts of a town, black plumes of smoke billowing from ashen homes. The walls were pure black, yet glowing bright orange. Her legs took a trembling step forward, and then another. Above, the sky was stained a vibrant crimson, and speckled with pitch clouds that stuck in globs of messy black.

No longer could she control her shaking limbs, her wobbling vocal cords. Not even her head would tilt back to let her see how she arrived. There was only the sky and the vague awareness that she was walking.

A scream wound tightly in her throat, too stuck to release, even when Merlin finally stopped moving. Her neck ached as her head finally lowered. Control snapped back into her body, her trapped shriek escaping into the smoldering town. The scent of iron filled the hot wind as it blew across the desolation, drops of red spreading over the drenched ground. Humans lay before her in steaming heaps, the slices on their bodies dyeing the grass beneath. Merlin's arm quivered as she held up her hand, realizing for the first time that her fingers grasped a sword. Its handle was made of two twisting silver dragons with hateful ruby eyes.

Blood dripped from the serpents open mouths and down along the gleaming blade. It coated her hands, dried on her neck and cheek, covered her boots. She gagged, dropping the sword as her feet stumbled backwards. What had she done? She covered her mouth, fighting against the metallic smell which filled her nostrils. It had been her. Merlin knew it in her heart—she had killed these people. Why? How could she cause such destruction with a single sword? What made her

CHAPTER 7

steal their lives? Her eyes fell to her empty hand, her thumb rubbing over her red fingertips.

Their final screams were splattered across her, and for a moment, she thought she could hear them, their wails of agony. But that was not so. There was nothing but the silent brush of wind blowing through the carnage, spreading the stench of death in every direction. What had she done?

8

A Pointed Conversation

L

Sunshine was breaching the trees overhead, warming the ground where Lancelot sat. Several ivirians had either flown or walked by Jack's shop, but none could see past the illusion of trees that hid him. Even a group of soldiers marched by, all the while unaware of the knight. Only the animals could see him, and they appeared unbothered by his presence. Although, at one point a squirrel hopped over Lancelot's outstretched leg, clicking furiously at the audacity of him being in the way.

"You're not the only one," he muttered to the animal. Jack didn't trust him any further than he could throw him, and he was right to do so. Lancelot tucked his knee and sighed. There were truths he simply could not unveil, despite the leprechaun's insistence on hearing them. Besides, he would be leaving with Merlin the following morning, so there was no point in trying to win Jack over. Lancelot absently ran his hand through the grass, skimming over pebbles and dirt until he found a stick. The bark crumbled as he picked it up, so he began peeling off the rest of the dark clumps without much thought. After a while he had skinned it entirely, leaving only bare wood.

"*Lancelot.*"

He flinched and looked up, scanning the empty forest. It sounded like someone called him, but had he heard wrong? Straining his ears, Lancelot rose quietly. One hand slipped to Solaris, filling him with both the comfort and loathing of having a weapon at his side. His eyes narrowed. Was there a flicker of someone's presence in the forest? How far away were they to be so faint?

"What are you doing?" The knight jumped, spinning to face Jack. His arms were crossed and he appeared unamused.

CHAPTER 8

Lancelot cleared his throat. "I thought someone was there."

"And you were going to throw a stick at them?" He gestured at the twig in Lancelot's hand.

The knight gave a disgusted huff and tossed the branch away. "I'm starting to understand why Merlin's personality is what it is. Tell me, is her family like you as well?"

Jack laughed curtly. "Oh no, they're much kinder than I am."

"Hm," Lancelot frowned. "Do you require something of me?"

He opened his mouth, then closed it. The knight could tell he was holding back a snarky comment. "Lunch, I've made it. Come inside." Jack shoved his hands in his coat pockets, heading back into the boot. Lancelot covered his face with a hand.

The *boot house*.

He would never be able to swallow that.

"Hurry up, boy!" Jack called.

With one last wary glance at the house, Lancelot headed back inside. He didn't bother to stop in the living area, heading straight into the kitchen. A loud noise was coming from behind the door, like a scuffle or scream. The knight threw open the door, his eyes falling first on the table where Jack sat grinning, then to Merlin, who looked exasperated. Lancelot was surprised to see her out of the bedroom, especially looking... normal. But Gwen took the title of most surprising.

The cat was bunched into a tight springing position, hissing loudly with her head close to the ground. Five feet from her sat another cat in a mirrored position. It was large, fluffy, and pure white. Lancelot inched to the side so he could see the cat's face. Its eyes were a bright sky blue.

"We meet again, cockroach!" Gwen sneered.

"What on earth?" Lancelot exclaimed.

The white cat yowled.

"Oh-ho," Gwen almost laughed. "You take that back!" In the blink of an eye both cats smacked into each other mid leap, falling to the ground in a tangled pile of claws and fur.

"Gwen!" Lancelot and Merlin cried out in unison.

They gawked and floundered at each other for a moment, as Jack said in a less concerned voice, "Nimbo, don't get blood on my floor."

Merlin whipped her head towards the leprechaun. "Jack!"

He shrugged and took a sip from a cup in front of him. "Stop Nimbo." Jack's cat ignored him and proceeded to claw at Gwen's face. The leprechaun looked back at Merlin. "I tried."

The cats made a remarkable roll across the kitchen floor. "Eat dust, you oversized pillow!" Gwen shouted, pushing Nimbo's face flat into a wooden plank.

"That's enough!" Merlin darted to the scuffle, dodging claws and grabbing the black fur.

"Let me go!" Gwen screeched, swiping her paws out wildly. "I'm going to make that ostracizing oaf into a white rug!" Nimbo plopped down on the ground, flattening himself to the floor. He stuck his pink tongue out at Guinevere.

Lancelot squeezed his mouth together, withholding a laugh. "I believe I'm missing something," he said when he finally had the snicker under control.

"On that note," Jack coughed. "Let's eat."

M

Cold slices of pork were the main course, with thin slices of bread served on a plate, and a bowl of carrots in the center of the table. Merlin took her portion quickly, trying to act natural. She noticed the knight give the bowl of orange vegetables a dark look, but he said nothing. Instead the room was filled with scraping sounds. Gwen was raking her claws into Jack's table, and glaring straight into the wall.

"Gwen," Merlin sighed. "Jack took Nimbo away, can you please stop?"

"I am going to skin him and turn him into a shaggy rug to be tread upon." Gwen growled through her teeth.

Lancelot set his sandwich down. "Why do you hate him so much?"

Waving away his question, Merlin tried again. "Enough with the violence, please. We're leaving tomorrow, so there's no need for this."

CHAPTER 8

Gwen snorted. "I'm very glad you're doing better, Merlin, believe me. But that flapjack has crossed the line too many times. Calling me unlucky, hmph! I'll show him what unlucky really means." The cat pulled back her paw, dragging it down the wood once more.

"Perhaps murder is not the best option?" Lancelot suggested.

"Stuff it, Lance." Gwen hissed. "It's the *only* option."

The knight flinched. "I told you not to call me that."

"All right, that's enough." Merlin clenched her fist. "Gwen, cut that out before I lock you in the guest room. You're being rude. And Lance," he scowled at her, "Your name is too long, so choose between Lance and Lot."

"Fine." Gwen snapped. She pulled back her claws and plopped her head down against the table with a thump.

"Must you shorten my name?" Lancelot asked. "It's fine the way it is."

"Ha!" Gwen tilted her head in his direction. "Guinevere is a fine name, but look at me now. I didn't get a choice, so you don't either."

Merlin nodded. "Yes. So which will it be?"

The knight sighed, setting his bread back on the plate. "Lance will do, if you insist on this."

"I do."

"That's settled then." Jack announced, returning to his seat in the room. The leprechaun raised an eyebrow at the claw marks in his table. "Really? Act your age, cat. I will charge you for that."

"Oh please," Gwen flicked her tail. "I added character."

"It doesn't need character." Jack leaned forward. "It *needs* to last until I die, which won't happen if you scratch holes in it." Gwen rolled her eyes, but refrained from arguing further. Jack looked over at Merlin, "And you, did you leave a note with Myrtle to explain what happened to your parents?"

Lance gave a startled cough and Merlin winced. "I wrote one, but it... burnt up."

Jack sighed and, for a moment, he looked just as sad as she had been. The emotion vanished as quickly as it came, replaced by his usual hard stare. "Fine then, I'll see him myself. Meanwhile, you can head to Rob. You'll need his help."

"Rob?" Merlin repeated, freezing in her reach for a carrot. "Why him?"

Jack raised his eyebrows sternly. "You are trying to find one soldier in the midst of an army. You'll need a crook to find out exactly where Daleon is, *and* you'll need a way of sneaking into their ranks. Preferably a method that will keep you from getting arrested in two bats of an eye."

"You're not even going to try and stop her?" Gwen marveled. "Forget blinking, one step in and they'll give us the rope. I don't fancy being hung."

Lance tilted his head in curiosity. "You hang people?"

Gwen rolled her eyes. "No, we drown them. *Of course* we hang criminals. It's an experience I would appreciate not having."

Jack huffed. "Guinevere, they don't hang cats."

"And besides," Merlin scowled. "He can't stop me anymore than you can. I am going to my brother." She turned to Jack. "Daleon is at Port Sal Azure, he told me so in a letter I received."

"But you don't know which ship he's on." Jack argued.

"I'll find out when I'm there."

Gwen laughed. "That's a bad idea."

Merlin squeezed her fists. "It's not an option. I have nowhere to go if not to him. My parents are somewhere in Logres right now, so there is no chance of joining them."

Jack rubbed his forehead. "You act as though you can't stay here."

"I can't." Her heart squeezed as the words came out without thought. Merlin closed her mouth to stop more from being said, caught by her own apathy toward Jack's offer. But what she said was not false, she *had* to leave.

Merlin dared to look up at Jack. He was looking at her with more exasperation than anger. "Fine. If you want to get arrested, that's your choice. I'm not going to stop you. But I'm only sending you with enough food to reach Robin. If you're going to get arrested, you'll need someone experienced with you. It's only smart."

Merlin sat back in her chair and huffed. "I don't have a problem meeting Robin, I just don't want to waste any more time."

"If you head to Loxley, it won't be out of your way." Jack told her.

Gwen looked up. "Will he even be there?"

"He always is this time of year, for a short time anyway." Merlin pulled one leg onto her chair, and wrapped an arm around her knee. "It's been a while though."

"Ahem," Lancelot cleared his throat. "Who is Robin?" He had been very quiet for the past few minutes, so much so that Merlin had forgotten him entirely. A pinch of guilt prompted her to pay more attention to his question.

"He's—"

"A crook." Jack interrupted. "A good one too. One of the best in Sher."

"He's a thief, yes." Merlin glared at Jack. "I don't know why you insist on calling him a crook. It sounds awful."

"I call him a crook because that's what he is." Jack insisted.

Merlin rolled her eyes. "Either way, you'll probably hate him, Lance."

The knight ran a hand through the longest strands of his silver hair. "Wonderful. Will he at least be able to get us to the border?"

Merlin glanced at Jack, then shrugged. "Probably?" He made a good point, but there was no way of knowing until they found Robin. "We'll have to ask."

The knight laced his fingers together and smirked. "It's nice to know our plan is well thought through. I'd be worried if we were only vaguely certain of what we're doing."

Jack grinned. "Well, now that you're all on the same page, we should gather your supplies."

They spent the remaining daylight finding backpacks, food, and various other important items. Merlin made sure to supply herself with many leather pouches for collecting herbs, and cloaks were given to both elestiels. Really, Merlin didn't need a cloak, but it would be nice to have a second, longer one over her purple half-cape. Finding the items took longer than she expected because Jack's house was cluttered beyond reason, and the items they needed were always in the hardest places to access. By the time they finished, it was late in the evening, bringing Merlin back to the bare guest bedroom, staring at the ceiling.

Here she was, determined to leave but mourning it all at the same time. Many years ago, when she was still learning to control her gift, her parents brought her and Daleon to Jack. He was able to help her in ways her parents were incapable of, as they were both ivirian. Jack's particular gift for illusions helped create scenarios that would have been impossible to experience elsewhere. The leprechaun was more like a grandfather than a teacher. Yet, in the aftermath of her home's destruction, she was leaving his house, the only other place that felt safe.

"You could stay." Gwen said from the corner of the room, as if Merlin had voiced her thoughts.

She rolled on her side, closing her eyes firmly. "No, I can't."

Suppression?

L

Dim light filtered into the room as Lance stirred awake. Outside the sun was just beginning to climb the sky, and inside wood groaned beneath the press of weight placed on each step of the staircase. Lancelot struggled to sleep through the previous night in the uncomfortable bed, and when he finally did, he fought to keep hold of the light, feverish sleep descending over him. However, now he was awake, and it was not the stairs that pulled him from his anxious dreams.

"Lancelot?"

Head pounding from the aches of restless sleep, Lance rolled out of bed, landing quietly on the floor. He reached for the sheathed sword sitting against the wall by his bed.

"Lance."

It was the same eerie voice he heard outside, but it was so much clearer than before. Lance scanned the room, knowing there was nowhere for someone to hide. It was as empty of living beings as it was furnishings. A bead of sweat slipped down Lance's forehead, his eyes darting to the door. Could a voice penetrate the wood so clearly? The knight squeezed Solaris's grip, silently drawing the blade as he crept forward. Carefully, he pressed his ear against the door. There was only the smallest sound coming from somewhere on the first level.

Gently, Lancelot turned the door's handle, wincing at the soft click it made. His heart raced as he descended the stairs, raising his sword upon entering the dim main room. A black rug of shadows covered the floor and spread out over the piles, brightening from red to orange near the fireplace. Tiny flames flickered in the dying embers, illuminating the silhouette sitting in Jack's chair, their body turned away from him.

Lancelot tilted the blade towards them. "Name yourself," he declared.

The person twisted around, a white cat on his lap. "You're up early." Jack chuckled quietly. He stroked Nimbo's back.

"It's just you..." Lance lowered the sword's tip, pinching his nose bridge with his empty hand. He let out a relieved sigh.

A small smile spread across Jack's dimly lit face. "Apologies for Nimbo. He doesn't care enough about waking those who sleep."

"It wasn't the cat," he told him. "I thought I heard someone call my name." He glanced sideways at Jack. "It wasn't you, was it?"

The leprechaun patted Nimbo's head thoughtfully. Beside him the fire crackled, its flames curling around the blackened wood. A shiver ran up Lance's spine as the orange tinge of the room flickered to a dark red. It was far too quiet.

Sitting straight, Jack tilted his head and answered. "It was not."

"A dream then." Lance muttered, more to comfort himself than anything else. Despite his declaration, he knew the voice had not been a part of his dream in any form.

They were silent for a moment, until Jack asked, "Do you believe in ghosts, Sir Lancelot?"

"Ghosts?" Lance repeated. He sat in the empty chair he had used the day before.

"Spirits," Jack corrected. "Tormented souls that have been tied by curse or bond to this world."

The knight let his blade rest on the tops of his knees, wishing he had brought the sheath down with him. "I do not." He raised an eyebrow at Jack, a voiceless request for explanation.

"Neither do I." Jack leaned forward. "But you do remember what I told you yesterday?"

For a moment the elestiel stared in confusion, before Jack's meaning dawned upon him. "You said it holds the victims' final cries inside it." Lance peered down at the black steel. "But it didn't cry, I heard my name."

"Yes..." Jack rubbed his cheek. "But the previous owner warned me of the voice. I haven't heard it myself, but he said it was the only reason he was willing to part with the sword. It scared him, I think."

"This is some sword you've sold me." Lance grumbled. The weapon did not appear haunted, but then again, how was he supposed to know what a haunted sword looked like? He frowned. "And while we are speaking, how long did you discuss this with the last owner?"

"We had a cup of tea." Jack admitted. "And I may remind *you* that it was *your* decision to buy the only sword I have that craves blood. It's some sword you purchased."

Lance suppressed an eyeroll. "Very well, fine, but I—" he paused. "Did you say craves blood?"

Jack picked Nimbo up from his lap and set the cat on the floor, earning him a hiss from the creature. The leprechaun stood, picking up his cane to lean on. "I told you that it should be stained red. Most of its previous owners were assassins that passed the blade between each other. Solaris, The Point Between Sun and Moon. That's what they called it. Between morality is what it means, I *suppose*."

"I have problems with everything you just said." Lance began.

Bang! Bang! Bang!

The front door shuddered from the force of the knocks, and a loud feminine voice called out, "Jackel Hymes, we are a suppression squad. We know you are housing three suspects in the burning of a citizen's home. Surrender them now, or we will come in and take them."

Lance was on his feet by the second word, but Jack was faster. The leprechaun grabbed their leather knapsacks and shoved them into Lance's arms, pushing him to the stairs. Jack's face had lost all humor and was gravely serious. His words came out in a rushed whisper. "You need to leave, go upstairs to Merlin. Gwen knows where the secret exit is hidden. Tell her to take you out that way."

"What?" Lance shoved his foot into the furthest corner of a step, stopping Jack's push. "We can't abandon you!"

"Don't be foolish." Jack stepped back. "I'll be fine if *you* aren't here."

The door shuttered again. "You have until the count of ten to come out and surrender them, or we will take them by force." The voice cried. "One!"

"I am no coward!" Lance snapped. "I will not run away and leave you to clean up our mess!"

"Two!"

Jack grabbed the knight's collar, pulling so hard Lance nearly toppled from the imbalance. "You listen here! If you stay everyone will have to fight, and I do not intend to let Merlin do that." He snarled in a hush. "You take both of them away from here *now*, and if *any* harm comes to them, from whatever source, know that nothing will stop me from killing you."

"Three!"

Lancelot gritted his teeth, heart pumping fast. He wanted to help Jack, but the leprechaun was right. This was the only way to lessen the chance of fighting and avoid any violence. Lance had to do as he said.

"Four!"

"Fine, we'll leave. Let go of me!"

Jack dipped his head, sighing as if he really hated letting Lancelot go with Merlin. His distress was evident, but when he looked back up his eyes were determined. He let go of the knight's collar and growled, "Then get going."

Lance straightened, glancing at the door. He could sense at least seven creatures on the other side, each moving to a position at the front of the house. From upstairs a door opened, and then he heard Merlin's voice. The situation would become far worse if she came down. He refocused on Jack, who was striding to the front door. He looked back at Lancelot, glared, and pulled open the door.

He saw nothing after that, because the knight launched himself at full speed up the stairs, taking them two at a time. A loud creaking racket followed him to the upper levels of the boot. Merlin was standing at the top, hair a mess and a half-asleep Gwen draped over her shoulders. Lance had no time to register Gwen's half dazed questions, or Merlin's either for that matter. He took three steps to her and forced one of the bags into her arms, slinging the other over his shoulder. Gwen made a surprised meow and rolled off Merlin, smacking against the ground. Lance bit his lip as shouting came from below them.

"What's happening?" Merlin asked, transferring the bag to her own shoulder. "Where is Jack?"

"No time!" Lance ran down the very short hallway to his own room, shouting behind him. "Gwen, find the secret exit, now!" He snatched Solaris's sheath and his satchel, clipping on the belts as quickly as possible. The sound of metal on metal screeched from the left as the knight made his way to Jack's room. Gwen and Merlin were standing at the far end of the bedroom, a trap door now opened next to Jack's bed.

As soon as Lance entered, he shut the bedroom door behind him. Jack could probably stall for another three minutes before whoever was out there came in. Assuming it was a government-sanctioned group, they would systematically move through the house, which gave them another minute. He turned to look at Merlin and Gwen, both wearing matching expressions of confusion and annoyance. Lance sighed.

"A suppression squad is outside," he told them.

The effect on the two was instant, their eyes clearing of the confusion. Gwen hissed and jumped down the trap door while Merlin pulled out her charm bracelet. She pushed it onto her wrist and followed Gwen. As they disappeared, Lancelot couldn't help note that they didn't have a problem leaving him behind. Withholding a glare, he moved to Jack's bed and grabbed the frame with both hands. He pulled at the furniture, intending to use it as a buffer. Surely it would only hold the door for so long, but at the very least it would slow the squad down. He heaved again, and the heavy bed moved two inches forward.

"Hey!" Lance twisted around to see Merlin's head sticking out of the exit. "Are you coming?"

He yanked backwards. "One... Minute!" The wood groaned and suddenly released from its fastenings, moving freely from its spot on the ground. The bed made a heavy thump as he dropped it in front of the door.

"Lance!" Merlin hissed. A shout came from below, accompanied with pounding footsteps going up the stairs.

The knight spun around, dashing straight to the exit. He jumped inside, passing Merlin, who was on a ladder, on his way down. Their exit dropped into a circular room with one spiraling hallway, and the only light for the room was shining through the walls. The sticky, oozing green walls were dripping with juice and condensation. The entire room smelled of the sickly-sweet sap that ran through the beanstalk they were standing in. One big drop would have splashed into Lance if he hadn't moved.

Snap went the trap door as Merlin jumped from the ladder. She eyed Lance suspiciously. "Where's Jack?"

"Outside." Lancelot took a step towards the tunnel. "He told me he would be fine. So we should leave like he said."

Merlin gripped the bag on her back. "Are you crazy? It's a suppression squad! They won't bother talking to him, they'll just arrest him!"

His chest tightened as well as his fists. "Jack gave us an order. We should follow it."

"There's no use in that!" She put one hand on the ladder's rung. "No one comes back once they're arrested. They'll kill him!" Merlin pulled herself up the step.

"We don't know that. All we know is that he said to leave." Lance dodged another drop of sap. "He is wisely stopping us from fighting, so we must go."

"There's no avoiding a fight."

Lancelot stared speechlessly at Merlin as she started pulling herself up the ladder again. Did she think that she could stop whoever they were by herself? What was she going to do, heal them to death? Wasn't she the one who implied they were powerful?

Before Lancelot could bring up any of these excellent points, a loud crash came from above them. Both elestiels froze as creaks started spreading out in Jack's room.

Lancelot stared at the trap door, speaking quietly through clenched teeth. "Merlin, we need to go. *Now!*"

She was hesitating, but the steps were getting closer to the door. Merlin slowly, slowly brought herself down. As soon as her feet touched the ground they both took off down the tunnel. It wound down in a tight curve all the way to the bottom of the beanstalk. There was a closed brown door at the end, but Lance barged right into it, bursting out the back of the stalk. Open forest was spread out before them, Jack's house at their rear. Merlin skidded past Lance as he skirted by Guinevere, who was crouched by the shoe house. Her fur was standing on end as she gazed at the trees.

"Have they spotted us?" he asked.

"No—" Gwen's sentence was cut off with the whiz of a small throwing knife embedding itself in the boot, inches from her nose.

"Over here!" Someone shouted.

CHAPTER 9

The cat shrieked, taking off faster than a man on fire. "RUNNNN!" she shouted, the black feline dashing past an already running Merlin. Abandoned again, Lancelot had no time for exasperation as he began sprinting over tree roots and past rocks, creating a cacophony of snapping noises with every twig he stepped on.

ZZZIIINNGG! An arrow flew straight past his eye. The knight's head jerked to the side while his gaze followed the projectile as it stuck in a tree. As he passed it he saw that it wasn't a normal arrow, rather it was a twig, deformed and twisted into a sharp point. Lance ducked under a huge branch, trying to work out how any craftsmen could design such an arrow. Perhaps a human might be able, but surely myths would not have any man-made weaponry.

ZING! ZING! ZING, ZING! Four more arrows were swallowed by the forest, one grazing Merlin's coat. Lance could hardly process that the arrow bounced off of the purple garment, let alone the fact that she barely noticed it. He looked over his shoulder, trying to locate the archer or whoever was shooting at them. The hasty look sent newfound energy pumping through his legs, and pushed his pace up to Merlin.

Behind them flew an ivirian, his beating wings blurred from speed. His arms were extended and his red eyes were glowing like hot coals. He wore a dark outfit not unlike Rainault's uniform, his skin a rusty brown. Behind him the forest was bucking and writhing as branches grew into a tangled web. The dark oaks reached for them like claws. Even twigs from the ground responded, rising in the air and hurtling themselves at the escaping elestiels.

Lancelot yanked Solaris out of its sheath just in time to bat a sharp twig from his face, and a second a moment later from his stomach.

"Who is that?!" Lance screeched, vaulting over a sudden crack in the ground.

Out of the corner of his eye, he saw Merlin look back. "Sands!" she responded in a similar scream. "He's a Growth Ivirian!"

Ivirians of the Growth Order, capable of reviving the most desolate plant or burying an entire town under the soil it stood on. Avalon had only the most basic information on the four orders, each being; Growth, Purge, Tear, and Gale. Lance wished he knew more, but at least one property of their power was certain. Growth Ivirians *had* to touch the ground in order to work their gift. So how was this one using his power while flying?

A half-baked idea came into his mind, one that needed polishing but wouldn't receive any. It was insane, and might get him and Merlin killed, but it was better than being run down by the ivirian who could clearly fly faster than they could run. With one last leap over a root, Lance skidded to a stop and dug his feet into the dirt and leaves on the ground. He spun round with his sword, facing the dark swirling mass of angry nature. Good plan or not, he had to try something.

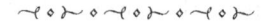

M

Gwen was left behind somewhere—the elestiels were simply too fast for a cat to keep up with. While Merlin was worried about Gwen, most of her mind was occupied by avoiding dangerous plants and anything that could look possibly like a myth's home. Dragon Blossoms were fairly common in the northern areas of Sher, so the chances of stepping on one were high.

To her side, the knight suddenly stopped fleeing, and she screeched to a halt five paces past him. He had his sword pointed to their attacker, but neither Merlin nor the Growth Ivirian believed that would change the situation. At least, that was the look on the soldier's face as he slowed several yards away, hovering in place.

"What are you doing?" Merlin barked. Lance ignored her, holding his sword tightly. The black blade seemed to blend with the shadows of the forest, growing darker despite the rising sun. Her chest tightened. Surely he was not going to fight a Growth Ivirian in the middle of the woods, where *everything* was a plant? She whipped her head back, noting the amused look on the soldier's face. Behind him the trees curled like snakes.

"Merlin Lynwood," The ivirian's voice sounded deep and earthy, despite his young appearance. "You are both under arrest for murder and treason. Do not fight, and you may yet be given a merciful death."

"Murder?" Merlin narrowed her eyes. "I didn't murder anyone, you've made a mistake." While she spoke, she took a step towards Lancelot, whispering under her breath, "Plan?" He didn't seem to hear her.

CHAPTER 9

"If there is a mistake, we will uncover it during your trial." The ivirian eyed them with a narrowed glare. "A clean arrest will look better."

"Oh joy." Merlin turned unceremoniously to Lancelot. "He isn't listening to me, like someone *else* standing here." she said angrily.

His face was completely blank, but when he faced her, she thought she could see calculation in his eyes. Gently, Lance tilted his head in her direction, and spoke one quiet word. "Decoy."

Merlin was confused for only a moment. It was so obvious she was embarrassed she hadn't noticed earlier. Merlin grinned crookedly and looked back at the ivirian. "Forget what I said, I surrender. I'm tired of running." She moved backwards, away from the knight. Behind her was a fairly large tree, and that was where she needed to stand, assuming Lancelot was right.

The ivirian looked suspicious. He turned his red eyed gaze at the knight. "If you *both* come with us quietly, there will be no need for violence. Then we may sift through your crimes, those alleged and witnessed."

Lancelot gripped his sword tighter. "I wish that were true, but I'm afraid that won't be possible."

The soldier sighed, and thrust out his wrist. The forest responded immediately, shooting out three branches towards Lance. Fast as he could be, he dodged the first two and leapt onto the third, running along the top. He was heading for the ivirian, who now brandished a long, curved sword. From the quick glance Merlin took, the blade appeared to be white like fresh snow; a cold substance she only saw once before. It melted immediately back then, right in front of her eyes.

Regardless, she could not see anything more because right then she took the last remaining steps to the great tree, and swung behind it. The sword charm activated as she spun. A small squeal escaped a short ivirian as she fell to the ground, bark flying off the tree as the blade stuck into the wood. Merlin had missed her by inches, and now the myth was staring up at her with wide eyes.

"Y-you..!" the ivira spluttered.

Oops. Merlin thought. *I didn't mean to hit that hard.*

The second Growth Ivirian scrambled away from Merlin, bright blue eyes locked on the sword. Merlin gritted her teeth and yanked out the blade, starting toward the soldier. She was obviously a rookie who relied too much on her power. She wasn't even carrying a weapon as a part of her uniform. All she had were the usual dark pants clasped around her ankles, and a halter shirt that showed off the military band around her arm. Her skin was the only unique thing about her. It was a pale and translucent white, which displayed blue and purple veins running across her body. Well, that and her long white hair was somehow straighter than even Merlin's own hair.

"Listen, I don't—" Merlin started to try reasoning with her, but instead of listening the soldier drew a half circle in the ground with her foot. Warning bells rang in Merlin's mind as the soldier stomped forward, roots springing up from the dirt. She gasped as the plants flew with deadly aim, leaving barely enough room for her to dodge. Each root crashed into the tree with a loud crack, meanwhile Merlin swung her sword straight at the ivira's neck. Too late did she remember the soldier was defenseless, but there was no stopping her sword now. The weapon was already in motion.

Before the edge of the blade could reach its mark, a wall of coarse dirt sprang into the air. It swallowed Merlin's sword nearly up to its hilt, pulling her into a rough stagger. A fist flew towards her, and her muscles clenched in response. She received the blow smack in the nose, knocking back her head, Merlin's body following suit. Through her clenched teeth came a breathy growl, which soothed the pain only briefly. Her hand tightened around the sword, and in seconds she had pulled herself back up.

Another punch swung her way, but this time she was ready to dodge it. Merlin released the sword and whirled around it, her hair fanning out wildly as she tackled the ivirian. Bright wings spread out underneath their owner as Merlin slammed her hard against the dirt. She screamed and clawed at Merlin's arms, but her nails couldn't pierce the purple cape.

"Please... give... up!" Merlin pleaded, one hand searching the ground for a rock. The ivirian continued struggling, pushing and twisting as best she could. A crazy look spread out on the ivira's face, and she desperately shoved all her weight to one side. Merlin yelped as they rolled through the dirt. Tiny stones jabbed into her back and arms, twigs snapping underneath the two of them. The ivirian reached up and grabbed a clump of Merlin's coppery hair.

"OWW!" Merlin howled as the ivirian twisted the clump. Merlin's left hand shot out and she grabbed the white hair of the ivirian. Tugging hard, she mimicked her attacker in everything but strength, because she could only tug so much while her other hand searched the ground. Thankfully their rolling stopped on a particularly rocky patch of earth. Merlin's hand slid over the rough ground, latching onto something cold and hard. The pain in her head intensified, throbbing from the ivira's grip. Merlin swung her clenched hand up, the rock tucked inside it colliding with the ivirian's forehead.

The ivira shrieked one last time, pulling Merlin's hair even harder before her eyes rolled back inside her head. There was instant relief for Merlin as the grip on her hair melted away, and the ivirian sprawled unconscious on the ground. Merlin rolled to the side, panting heavily. Her back was stinging as she shakily stood up, dirt on her face and in the ends of her hair. She pulled out a twig and frowned.

This is why I wear a ponytail.

From her left a loud cracking sound came from the hill Merlin had just rolled down. Her eyes widened as Lancelot hurtled over the crest, landing against the ground several feet away. His momentum carried him through three bouncing rolls, stopping only when he banged into a tree trunk.

"Lance!" Merlin hurried over to him, leaving the unconscious soldier where she lay. The knight quivered as he lifted himself onto his elbows, shaking his head. Merlin crouched by him, taking a quick moment to determine if he had any life-threatening injuries. "Did you beat him?" she asked after a second.

"I'm fine, thank you." Lance spat, trying to push himself up further. "Thanks for asking."

"Obviously you're fine." Merlin retorted. "But what about the soldier?"

Lance glared openly at her for possibly the first time, and pointed. "There." Following his gesture, she saw the bronze ivirian kneeling by Merlin's assailant, his sword lying on the ground next to him. Gently, he lifted her in his arms, brushing her hair away from the bleeding wound.

"What have you done?" He looked over to them, hate burning in his eyes. By his feet, small pebbles dislodged from the packed earth.

Merlin swallowed but found her throat dry. "Nothing that can't be undone," she told him. "I can heal the wound if you let us go." Her eyes stayed focused on stones. Now that this ivirian was touching the ground, he could use his gift to any extent against her. There was no chance of her beating him, and Lance had already lost. Although, with his fire ability he *should* have had an upper hand. Merlin would have to ask him about it later, if they escaped.

"Elestiels," the ivirian growled. "You golden eyed fiends would even bargain healing for your own gain."

Merlin snapped, "Anyone else would do the same, we're no anomaly. Besides, it's her own fault for being unprepared."

"Merlin," Lance's tone was warning. "You're making it worse." The knight pulled himself into a sitting position, and nearly tipped over. Merlin winced at his tight expression. She had overlooked his ribs, at least three of them were cracked. That settled it. Merlin put one steadying hand on the knight's shoulder, and turned her attention back to the ivirian. There was no chance of fighting their way out of there, not with Lancelot injured.

"Listen," she began. "Even if I don't heal her now, my friend and I can leave."

"Is that what we are?" Lance grumbled.

She ignored him. "You can't fight us without putting her in danger as well. We're no murderers, but you can't guarantee that our fight won't make her injuries worse."

The ivirian considered, then answered, "I can wait until my team has finished dealing with the leprechaun. They'll be here soon. You can't escape us all."

"I'm willing to bet we can, but either way, you have no idea what kind of injury she has. I might be the only one able to heal her, and I won't do it if we're arrested." Merlin waited, but instead of arguing, the iviro just sat there thinking. Her bluff didn't appear to be working, and his team would surely arrive soon. Merlin would never be able to get them away from so many soldiers. Her heart began beating faster as she tried to think of something that would help their situation.

"Healers don't fight." the ivirian said suddenly, looking down at the unconscious ivira again. The light in his eyes was dimming.

A tiny spark of hope ignited in Merlin, and she quickly said, "This one does."

He glared at her, looked at the unconscious soldier, then glared back up at Merlin again. She could tell she had won when his eyes completely lost their glow, fading back to a normal red. "Heal her, but know that we will follow you. And when we find you, I will bury you alive."

"Fair enough." She nodded to Lance. "But I'm healing him as well."

"Fine." The ivirian turned back to his fellow soldier, and Merlin helped Lancelot up, guiding his arm over her shoulders so he could lean on her.

"This is a bad idea," he whispered as they moved closer to the ivirians.

"Do you really want to run with those injuries?" Merlin asked.

Lance glanced down at her—albeit not that far down—and sighed. "I've done it before."

They stopped right above the unconscious soldier, giving Merlin enough time to shoot the knight an angry scowl. "Maybe mention that sooner next time."

He sat down. "Maybe I will."

"Your quarreling is pointless." The soldier carefully set the ivirian down. "Heal her before I change my mind."

"All right." Merlin began drawing her signet. "Just be quiet and let me work." To his credit, he did stop speaking after she asked him. It took only a few moments to connect with the Rideon, after which she began working on Lancelot. Mending his ribs was simple enough, but she had to take care not to burn through his energy in the process. When that was finished, she wove the skin back together on the ivirian's head, taking care of any damage inflicted underneath. With the soldier, Merlin spared no energy, as one of them being incapacitated was probably a good thing. Between the two of them, it only took her a few minutes to heal both injuries.

Just as she was about to disconnect from the Rideon, Merlin felt a twitch from the nearby trees. She turned and scanned the foliage, trying to locate what caused the disturbance. Beyond the hill, voices started filtering to her.

The suppression team had come.

Merlin hoped Jack had been left alone once they found his house empty, but she couldn't dwell on that. She disconnected herself from the power, and Lance sprung to his feet.

"Why isn't she waking up?" The soldier picked up his companion and shook her slightly. His voice held so much desperation that Merlin could not leave his question unanswered.

"She'll wake up within the hour." Merlin told him. "Her energy is simply depleted." The assurance did not seem to ease his concern, but there was no time left to speak any more words of comfort. Voices which had been quiet were now loud enough that it was amazing their owners were not upon her already.

Lancelot beckoned to Merlin, and she ran towards him. Together they left the soldiers sitting by the hill, waiting for the rest of the suppression squad to arrive.

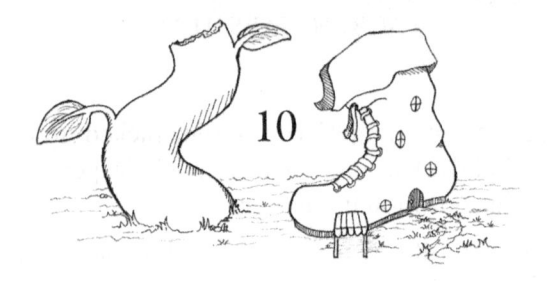

From Dust to Dust

Merlin leapt over a root, looking over her shoulder. So far their only pursuer was Guinevere, which would have been great if she wasn't so worried about Jack. If they were not being chased, the squad must have stayed with the leprechaun. He could take care of himself, but the soldiers were stronger. Far stronger than one leprechaun. Merlin glared at a patch of mourning lilies as she raced by them. Somehow she had to get back to him, just to make sure everything ended well.

"Guys!" Merlin stopped running at Gwen's shout, and to her right Lance also froze. Gwen had stopped a ways back, next to a large toppled tree trunk. The end of it was covered in tall yellow grass that stood like stalks, and small ivy with four blue-green leaves sticking out.

"Gwen, now is not the time to collect bluemint." Merlin hissed.

Even from a distance, Merlin could see the cat give her an unimpressed look. She pointed her tail at the wall of plants, and walked straight into them. The vegetation completely swallowed the cat. Merlin gave Lance an uneasy frown before backtracking to the trunk and crawling past the leaves. Inside, the trunk was covered in bright green moss that traveled the length of the fallen tree, and little pink flowers sat untouched in small rays of sunlight peeking through the trunk's bark. Merlin gave a momentary gasp before crawling further in, positioning herself in an upright sitting position.

"Moss-camelia?" Merlin gently touched the tiny petals. Its leaves made tea that soothed fear, and oil which prevented sickness.

"Yes." Gwen nodded. "This seems ideal to hide in, though it is a little cramped for you two." Though the trunk was tall enough for sitting, it was very thin, and the two elestiels had to tuck in their knees and rest their feet against the opposite wall. From the open end far to Merlin's right, a cool breeze blew through the tunnel.

Now that she had stopped running, Merlin could feel her skin growing hot under her clothes, and even more so, her nerves were sizzling. For a moment, she had forgotten her cares upon sight of the moss-camelia, but now her mind was grounded once more. Merlin flicked an ant off her shoulder and looked at her companions.

"We should start heading back soon, and quietly."

Gwen's eyes widened, and Lance sat forward. "Merlin, we can't go back," the knight said in surprise.

"He's right," Gwen agreed. "Jack told us to leave, and we really won't be any help."

Merlin took a deep breath, trying to grab hold of her temper before it erupted. "The suppression squad will take Jack in our place. He's outnumbered, and he isn't powerful enough to take them all. Not in an outright fight."

Lance maneuvered his sword as he spoke to her, resting it horizontally on his lap. "He gave us orders. As I said earlier, we should follow them. If we returned, it's likely we would be caught and make Jack's situation even worse. As of now they have no proof he hid us, just baseless accusations."

Merlin curled her fingers into a tight fist. "They *can* charge him for aiding us. We have to go back. I can't let him take the fall for my mistakes."

"What mistakes?" Gwen waved a paw. "The only crime we've committed is not killing Lance here. They want to know what started the fire, which will be somewhat easier to solve once they pull Rainault's burnt corpse out of the wreckage."

She started to lose hold of her anger, a single strand connecting her temper to her self-control. Merlin could feel the thread pulling taut even as she argued, "I can't just leave him!"

Lance shook his head. "You must. We have somewhere to go, and we will not arrive if we are taken prisoner by the soldiers."

Merlin's thread snapped.

"You only want to reach Norestere faster! You don't care about Jack, but I do! I can't leave him because some suicidal knight wants to

CHAPTER 10

play hero and save the world!" Lancelot stared at her, his mouth parting and his fingers tightening around his sword hilt.

Gwen glanced at the knight, then looked at Merlin with a face that almost appeared like *she* had been the one insulted. "That was uncalled for."

"I don't think so." Merlin let her words sharpen the attack. "He is only with us because he wants to find some non-existent prince. On its own, that's fine, but this involves us now. Jack's safety is more important than any fictional prince he believes in!"

Her words sat in the air between them, bringing tension that rivaled even the moment Merlin first met Lance. Inside she could feel her conscience poking into her, a voice telling her that she was acting beyond unreasonable. Unfortunately, the voice was small, and as Merlin leaned against the trunk, it was drowned out by her mind's insistence on the accuracy of her words. There was only one reason why Lance traveled with them, and that was to convince her to join him. Jack would hardly worry him, regardless of the possibility that the leprechaun could be imprisoned—or worse, hung.

Still, as she watched him hide his stunned pain beneath a cold mask, Merlin felt her fury crack, just a little bit. It was not enough to make her apologize, but it did suppress any further attacks. If more was to be said, he would be the one to speak.

Lance seemed to realize that after several silent moments. "Yes, I want to go north." he started, sounding unsure at first, and then bitter. "But let me remind you that I head north because I want to *save* lives. I don't needlessly turn my back on anyone in danger." His frigid gaze snared her own. "It is you who willingly sacrifices others."

Lancelot may as well have slapped her.

Merlin's gut clenched and her blood boiled. "How dare you. I have never done so!"

Gwen yowled in surprise, but Lance held his ground. "My quest is to end the continuous death that has plagued us for two and a half years." His volume rose. "By refusing to help me, you are purposely turning a blind eye to the many casualties of the war!"

"Guys..."

"It's my fault for getting Jack involved," Merlin shouted back at him. "But it is not my job to save them! You cannot expect me to carry the weight of *your* war on my shoulders when I have nothing to do with it!"

Lancelot finally matched her glower. "Does the myth forest not touch the lands of men? Is it some special forest that lies on an island? You *are* part of this, whether you acknowledge it or not!"

Merlin raised herself onto her knees and leaned forward. "I would not count myself a part of your squabble if I had been accepted into the military at my first request. I am no human, and I am not a part of this war!"

Lance rose to meet her. "You're wrong! And one day you will see that!"

"Guys!"

"What?!" both elestiels screamed as they turned to look at Gwen.

The cat's tail swished back and forth, her eyes narrowed. "This is a hiding place! I did not bring you here to let every bird and beast know exactly where we are! If you want to continue arguing, leave this place now! But if you plan to stay here, you *will* be silent!"

Merlin slammed her mouth shut, stopping any further protest from coming out. Her heart was pumping hot anger through her blood, and her jaw ached from clenching it. Yet despite her dark emotions, she knew Gwen was right. They needed to stay hidden, and yelling was not going to help that. Even so, as Merlin sat back she sent an icy glare at Lance, who received it with restrained ire.

"Very good." Gwen nodded, patting the moss beneath her. "Now, we will not be going back."

"Gwen!"

"No, Merlin!" The cat turned her unfeeling eyes on her. "You and I have known him long enough to know that he can take care of himself. You're not thinking clearly or you would agree with me." Merlin looked down, biting her tongue. Even if Gwen was right, she was asking her to abandon someone she had known her *entire* life. The cat patted Merlin's leg. "He'll be fine. Besides, if we go back after he told us not to, we will be the ones in danger."

Merlin inhaled deeply and blew out as much anger as she could. Gwen's reasoning could hardly be argued with, no matter how badly she wanted to ignore it. Sighing, she gave up. "You're right."

"I know." Gwen's tail flicked, and then a claw appeared on both of her front paws. Merlin blinked in time for the cat to stick the point into her leg, and the other into Lance's knee. Both of them yelled in pain before remembering the *be silent* rule.

"Guinevere!" Merlin hissed, grabbing her thigh. "What is wrong with you?!"

"Yes, what was that for?!" Lance winced.

Their third companion simply turned up her nose at them. "That was for arguing. Even if we are all strangers to each other, we're a team now. Or at least a group. So none of this, the 'war is your fault' stuff. Both of you. There are three people responsible for this war, and that would be the King Regent, the King of Avalon, and the assassin that killed King Tharin."

"Thanks for the lecture." Merlin grumbled. She glanced a little shamefully at the knight, who looked rather the same. "Sorry Lance."

He rubbed the hilt of his sword. "My apologies as well," he hesitated, "I was too harsh..."

"No." She shivered. "Don't deny what you said, I know you still believe it." The knight frowned, eyes falling to the ground. How low must he think of her to believe she didn't care at all about innocent people. Merlin tried to straighten her back against the wood. His opinion shouldn't matter, but somehow she wanted to show him that she wasn't as heartless as he thought. She wanted to prove that she did in fact care, but that it also wasn't her responsibility to take care of them. Merlin closed her eyes, resting her head against the tree. Knights and their silly values.

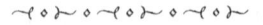

G

As a child, Merlin was chatty and friendly. Gwen only knew her for a year or two before that part of her disappeared like the morning fog. It was gone in a swift recession that swept away any traces of lingering charity. Guinevere watched it happen to Merlin and—though she still appreciated the person that Merlin had become—she sometimes wished that she could turn the lively side of her friend back on. Now was one of those times.

After leaving the hidden trunk, they made their way northwest. Traveling through the spider's web of mangled roots was difficult, as it criss-crossed over tangled grass. Not only that, but their way was made much worse by fissures that split the earth into clefts of rock and clay. Gwen knew they should be trying to find the Mason Line, but Merlin was the one leading, and making any sort of protest seemed out of the question. Neither she nor Lance had spoken, aside from what was immediately needed, and frankly, it was rather childish.

Their argument had clearly bothered both of them more than Gwen first thought, so there they were, hiking around enormous cuts in Sher. The black cat ducked under a root that was particularly close to the ground and came face to face with a rabbit.

"Hello." Gwen muttered. The cottontail blinked its black eyes at her, and shot off. Gwen watched it spring between tufts of grass and moss with a sigh.

That was it.

Three hours of walking in near silence was enough for her. Pulling herself out fully from the root, Gwen hopped up onto a dark branch that rose in the air high enough to bring her at eye level with the petty elestiels. "Ehem." Gwen cleared her throat. "Lancelot, would you like to hear about these fissures we've been traveling around?"

The knight pulled himself out between two wedged roots and stared at her. "I didn't think they were anything remarkable."

"Of course not." Merlin scoffed from ahead. She twisted around to look at the two of them from her spot near the edge of the deep divot. "Why would you?"

Gwen resumed her bouncy march along the root, feeling somewhat pleased that they had both spoken. "Now, now, it's not his fault. We're in something of a special circumstance. We both have access to the records in the Bristlecone Library, as well as having very old acquaintances."

"You've been to the *Tem'Casivir*?" Lancelot sounded awed.

Gwen raised an eyebrow. "Is that what you call it?"

Lance hopped over a bush. "It means ancient library in Allmen's tongue, although there's more meaning behind those simple words."

"I see," Gwen made a great leap from one root to another. "Well yes, we went with Merlin's brother, Daleon. Spent considerable time reading, which brings me to these fissures! There are hundreds of these all throughout Sher, they're historical marks that no ivirian would dare close up."

Lance gave her a curious look. "Why is that?"

Gwen grinned wide enough to show her fangs. "Because they're axe clefts, from the Giant's Siege."

"Really?"

"It's obvious." Merlin called back again, still scornful. "The giants came down from the north with swords and axes large enough to fell whole cities! It's amazing there isn't more damage."

"I'm aware of a giant's size." Lance shot a dark, unseen look at her. "But that was a thousand years ago. I would have thought all the marks left had been covered over."

"It's somewhat out of respect for the fallen." Gwen told him, rubbing her paw. "So much happened then... Many myths and humans died in that siege, as well as you golden eyes. Humans first created Irode Powder from Irodnite then, and our capital, Nottingham, was founded. Erasing the scars would be the same as wiping away their sacrifice, and everything else that occurred."

"I see..." Lancelot said as they came around the end of the fissure. Gwen hopped off her root and trotted alongside the knight.

Both of them seemed in better spirits, so Gwen posed the question that most plagued her mind. "Merlin, perhaps we should find the Mason Line?"

Merlin was ten paces away from them, so Gwen had to repeat herself in order for Merlin to hear her. The elestiel scowled when her question became clear. "I'm trying Gwen, but there is an unusual amount of swiftfoot on the ground, so I can't quite make out the trail."

Gwen looked down at the plant to which Merlin was referring. It was small, with thin, pointy leaves that were light green around the edges, and a deep red that bordered on pink down the middle. Swiftfoot—while incredibly difficult to kill—was invasive and easy to plant.

"Should we really be aiming for the most used path?" Lance asked cautiously. "And what does this plant have to do with our traveling?"

Gwen sighed. "Poor, ignorant Lancelot. We're not explaining enough to you, are we?"

The knight looked unamused. "With the exception of your obvious patronizing, you are correct."

Merlin waved her hands in exasperation. "Fine, *I'll* explain it for you. Act seventeen, Protection of Property. Anyone caught trespassing on land not owned by themselves or without permission, is subject to the retaliation of said landowner, in whatever way they deem appropriate. Meaning, if we get caught on someone's front lawn, they have the right to kill us."

"That sounds like a terrible law." The earlier annoyance which had laced their previous conversation was starting to rise again between them. Lance pushed past Merlin and started following the swiftfoot. "And these plants?"

Gwen watched Merlin turn two different shades of indignant red, then answered the knight. "Swiftfoot is specifically planted in order to guide travelers to the Mason Line. Merlin knows where plants are supposed to grow, so that's how she and her brother travel. No one likes it on their property, but they hate trespassers more."

"There, now you know." Merlin snapped, and in turn stomped forward, past the knight and between two large bushes.

Blinking at her, Lance looked to Gwen. "It seems I've upset her." he said, though the words were tight.

"No kidding." Gwen soured. "That's what happens when you tell someone they're responsible for the war, or rather, the deaths in the war."

Lance stepped to the bushes and pulled them apart for her, snapping twigs as he went along. "I did not say that."

She looked up at him as she passed. "Didn't you?" An unsettled expression came over Lance's face.

From a distance Merlin's voice shouted, "Are you coming?"

Gwen brushed a blade of grass off her fur and stepped over a spiky rock, heading towards her friend's voice. Past the bushes lay a grassy clearing which sat on the edge of an enormous fissure spanning twenty feet in width. Long grass hung over its edge and patches of tiny, white daisies mingled with swiftfoot. The only way to cross the cleft was a stone bridge with two rails on either side. Towards the middle Gwen could see a bent part of the fence curving inwards, as if something heavy had bent it.

The cat marched right up to Merlin and sat on her back feet. "Are you insane? A stone bridge? Really?"

"You wanted the Mason Line, well there it is. On the other side." Merlin waved at the bridge. It only took one look from the cat to make Merlin facepalm in regret. "I'm sorry, Gwen, but this is the best I can do. Unless he can fly..." They both turned and looked at the knight.

Lance raised both of his hands apologetically. "Not at the moment."

"But you can fly?" Gwen repeated, looking dubiously at him.

He ran a hand through his hair. "No...?"

"What exactly can you do, then?" Merlin asked. "Because I saw you manipulate fire exactly like a Purge Ivirian, and flying isn't something they can do without wings."

Gwen cocked her head to the side. "Exactly like the Purge Order?" Ivirian gifts, while not very unique between persons, were very different from elestiel gifts. Their power worked on an elemental basis, and varied in strength, not expression. Of course, there were some ivirians who had additional skills, but even those gifts were finite.

"My power is not flame manipulation," Lancelot insisted.

"Then what is it?" Merlin pressed.

Gwen noted Lance's quick grip on Solaris. "It's complicated, and not something I like to talk about."

"If you can fly us over the fissure," Gwen told him, "it's worth sharing."

"No, I cannot." He frowned. "My feet are as stuck to the ground as yours."

"That doesn't explain what your power is," Merlin pointed out. "Or how you use it without a signet." Gwen looked curiously at Lance. A being that could use the Rideon *without* a signet was unheard of.

"I have one!" Lance started tromping to the bridge. "I just don't want to tell you."

"Why?" Merlin hefted the bag up on her back. "What are you hiding?"

He stopped short at the beginning of the bridge. When he turned, his face had a mischievous look spread across it. Gwen blinked in some surprise at the change of demeanor the smirk gave him. "Anything important about me that would interest you," he called. Merlin's cheeks flushed a red so deep that Gwen could not help but guffaw. It was easy to laugh at both his distrust and Merlin's indignance.

"Fine, then *Mr.* Knight," Merlin stressed the improper title and moved forward. She stopped in front of Lancelot, her posture itching with a challenge. "You can be the first to cross the bridge, or are you too scared?"

Gwen's light mood fell. "Merlin…"

"I am not one to accept false challenges." Lancelot told Merlin, holding her gaze. He leaned a little closer, and Guinevere could see the tension between the two rising. "But I can make an exception for this." The knight turned swiftly around, striding through the remaining distance between him and the bridge.

The cat felt her stomach flop and twist, but Merlin simply grinned. "This is a bad idea." Gwen fretted, already sprinting after the knight. "Lance, wait!" She made it just past the beginning of the bridge when Lancelot reached the middle. Something loud and hard banged beneath their feet, a heavy thump that pressed against Gwen's ears and made them squeeze with pressure. Another thump sounded, this time shaking the bridge so hard that all three of them stumbled and swayed.

Up rose a hand carved from gray rock, its fingers clasping around the bent part of the bridge. A second hand sprang into view and wrapped around the railing, cracking the rock between its fingers. The creature pulled itself up and over, its legs curling in against its thin body. The stone troll was covered in rocks like scales, sharp and jagged. It towered over them with its disfigured face, staring blankly at them. Gwen gaped as it let go of the rail, letting dust and pebbles fall from the bridge.

The troll lowered its face, pointing its large nose down at them and staring with empty eye sockets. "Who are you?" rumbled its deep, hollow voice. "Who crosses my bridge?"

For a moment, there was no sound except the scraping of Lancelot's sword being drawn. Gwen shook her head and stepped forward. The knight seemed wary of attacking, but just in case he tried something, Gwen needed to attempt talking first. "Sir! We are travelers, simply making our way to the pass!"

Maybe, just maybe she would be able to stop the troll from throwing them over the side. If she could avoid a lengthy conversation they might have a chance. Gwen backed away from the troll, only to run into Lance's boot.

Above he whispered, "What is that?"

Merlin scooted closer to them. "It's a troll."

"You sent me across a bridge with a troll under it?" Gwen kicked Lancelot's leg as he hissed at Merlin.

The troll groaned again, leaning even further down. It spoke slowly. "Travelers? Why do travelers whisper deceitfully amongst themselves?" The cat started sweating, feeling even smaller than normal. The troll continued to speak in its earthy voice. "Spies whisper. So tell me, why do the giants send weak twigs like you to trample on my dignity?"

"Giants?" Lance repeated. "We were not sent by them, or anyone. We came of our own volition."

The troll sat up straighter. "I... do not believe you."

Gwen flexed her paw. "Sir, we are not from the giants, which should be apparent by my companions. Giants hate humans, I believe everyone knows that." On the word 'giants' her voice wobbled and squeaked. It was true indeed that trolls of any faction hated humans and their golden eyed counterparts, but trolls especially hated giants.

"There are no humans in your trio," the troll breathed, faster than his other words. "Nor does your breath hold life. I see only the shells of tragedies long looked over, the consequences of evil being ignored. Why do the giants insist on sending such shadows to test us?"

A gust of wind blew smoothly over the bridge. Gwen shivered, and two hands wrapped around her. She gave Merlin a questioning glance as the girl picked her up. "Sir, I don't quite understand your meaning."

The cat sighed internally. *What is she up to now?*

"Of course not. This forest is so blind, only those without eyes can see. What you do not know, lifeless girl, is that we are all on the brink of death, one step away from returning to the dirt we are made of." The troll's hands gripped the sides of the bridge as he spoke. The rumbling of his voice gained more emotion as he went on. "Your employers disagree and argue with meaningless dribble as their ally. They know not that they waste what little time we have in this land. Thus they send you to test our resolve. *My* resolve."

"Excuse me," Lance lowered his sword. "How could this be described as a test? We simply want to pass your bridge, nothing else."

Something that sounded like rocks clashing together came from within the troll. "Fool. We are the only ones aware of the impending doom that lies before this world. Yet, your employers insist on mocking our beliefs, sending you small flies in the path of life to scurry over the top of our homes. They know we detest the sight of such flippant creatures, who have no regard for the time they have been given. As is the case, I must relieve the forest of such useless beings, by sending you down the crevice from which I came." The troll started to rise, using its arms to push itself up onto its scrawny legs.

"Wait!"

Gwen yelped as her whole world blurred from the speed at which Merlin shoved her into Lancelot's arms. The cat wobbled in his loose grasp, hissing at the girl. Merlin was ignoring her though, stepping closer to the troll. It stopped moving, and had its full attention on Merlin. "If I understood you correctly, you said that we waste time, and that is why you hate us?"

"Yes." There was irritation in its rumbling.

"Well then, I respectfully disagree."

Gwen stopped hissing. "Uh, Merlin..."

"No." The cat looked up at Lance. His eyes were determined as he said, "She is correct."

The troll eased cautiously back to its seat. "How can you say so?"

"I can say it easily enough." Merlin crossed her arms. "If you believe that the world is ending, again, that is if I heard you right, then we are being very productive. I am traveling to see my brother, which seems like more than a good enough reason to be alive. Your belief that the world is going to end just makes it more important for me to see him."

"I do not see how this is productive." The troll cupped what looked like its chin. "You waste time traveling, spending energy so unnecessarily. Better to stay in one place, and gather dust from the ground, unbothered by anyone or anything."

"It may be that way for your people," Lance began. "But for us it is important to work for something, even if it is to see a relative. Spending time to search for something does not seem futile, rather it feels like progress. Should we not spend our time building, instead of doing nothing whilst things get worse?"

"And if we did stay still like you said," Merlin continued. "Wouldn't we all be in danger of dying uselessly? Wouldn't that be a true waste of time?"

They stared at the troll, who was so still it could have been a statue. Gwen glanced behind Lance's arm. Would they be able to run fast enough should the troll decide to attack? And what if the suppression squad was back there, hunting them even now? Gwen frowned for a moment as she was struck with a sudden thought. How did the soldiers know to look for them?

The troll suddenly moved, lowering its hand to the bridge. "Nothing you do will matter in the end. So there is no reason to feel accomplished in life."

Merlin's shoulders drooped. "Then you will still throw us off?"

Gwen felt Lance's arms tense at Merlin's question. The troll was staring at them again, hopefully contemplating the decision. "No," it said, sounding half unsure. "But if you ever step on my bridge again, I will."

Merlin bowed slightly, grinning at the troll. "Thank you."

Lance set Gwen down, but looked nervous. "Sir, why are you letting us pass?"

The troll stood, little bits of stone rolling off his shoulders. "There is something within your party, a presence I have yet to feel in any group of travelers that's passed me. I see your past tragedies, but there is something..." It stopped, looking down at the crevice below. "Something." It nodded and jumped off the bridge, disappearing from their sight.

Gwen peered over the side, murmuring to herself, "Something."

The Coward's Company

B

Lillacae hung limp in Bristol's arms as he flew up and around the trees which covered a large hill. Her glittering wings swayed in the wind, and her skin was icy beneath his hands. Bristol held her tighter as he flew towards the sounds of his squad. They were much farther away than he'd realized. The squad *should* have been right behind him when he went after the elestiels. If they had, he and Lillacae would not have been so easily defeated.

They had promised him a simple training mission, something harmless. The Phantom Trial was the last thing between Lilla, and her entrance into the suppression squad. It was a test to make sure her power was ready for fighting. Bristol glared at the path before him. Lilla should never have been in any real danger.

"Stop!"

Bristol swung his legs forward, pressing the tips of his feet against the tree in front of him. He bent against it and pushed off, turning in the air. Bristol flapped his wings to steady himself, and to keep from flying straight into his captain, Koa.

As she stopped, her arms and legs flew out in similar fashion, blowing her long, brown braid out before her. "Bristol, what is the meaning of this?" The rest of the squad appeared behind her, each performing the same halting technique as Bristol had on separate trees.

"Where is Brull?" Bristol demanded, his words slipping into a yell. Koa's red eyes flashed, but she motioned to the soldiers nonetheless. The entire company descended to the ground, and he felt just the smallest bit better with the feeling of dirt between his toes. At least, not as powerless.

CHAPTER 11

Not far from him, long evergreen hair swished outwards from the rear of the group, and an iviro the shade of pale ivy hurried forward. Bristol grinned with relief as he recognized the shine from Brull's draels. The reflective stores of water were scattered all across his face and arms, laying like drops of morning dew. It gave him a strong resemblance to a leaf after summer rain.

Brull pushed his leather bag aside and said, "Give her to me." He took Lillacae from Bristol, who was promptly grabbed by Koa. She pulled him several paces away, her eyes darting to the unconscious ivira.

"Tell me what happened. Where are the suspects? How was Lilla injured?" Captain Koa's usually reserved face darkened as her eyes narrowed.

Bristol took a step back and bowed his head. "I am sorry Captain. They escaped. Lillacae was injured by the elestiel, though the one claiming to be Merlin said she healed her."

He dared to look up at the captain, and received a livid expression of frustration. Though she was shorter than him, he felt small under the weight of her stare and guilty under the glare of her silver captain's token. "If they were healing Lillacae, how did they have time to escape?"

Bristol tensed. "She was injured..."

"So you let them go?" Koa's voice was strained.

"I'm sorry, Captain."

"Sorry does not save your job." He flinched, Koa continued. "You are a part of a suppression squad, Bristol. You can't be soft! Do I need to remind you that today was Lilla's final exam?"

"No, Captain."

"Hm." She sounded dubious. "Then do I need to remind you of the consequences of letting them go?"

Bristol put one hand on his left arm, feeling the cool token that marked him as a soldier. "Can you ignore it just this once?"

"No, *she* cannot." Another, darker voice spoke. Koa closed her eyes and straightened, smoothing the wrinkles out of her billowing pants. Behind her stood their commanding officer, the sight of which always made Bristol's stomach turn.

Brown strips of cloth were wrapped around his head and arms, covering every patch of open skin apart from his eyes. He wore a black tunic with slender sleeves—of which the cuffs were stuffed inside his dark gloves—and a robe with wide sleeves that ended above his elbows. A hunting knife rested at his side, and a hood was pulled over his bandaged head. Every action seemed to hurt him, though the pain did not stop him from heading where he wished. The dull outfit was not what disgusted Bristol, however. That was reserved for the officer's wings.

They were robbed of the one beauty ivirians truly cherish: Color. Gray and murky were the sharp, bat-like limbs which hung from the ivirian's back, the ends a tattered and burnt mess. Holes were speckled throughout them, like the officer let someone stick a hot poker through their membrane. What fire could rob the wings of their natural shade, Bristol did not know.

"Sir," Koa turned and saluted. "I don't believe it was intentional—"

He cut her off. "I find that very unlikely, since we both just heard his confession."

Bristol's nerves fired, and he dropped to one knee, clasping his fist over his heart. "Sir, I simply did what I thought was right. My companion was injured, and I needed a physician's aid."

"Stand up," the older ivirian commanded. "As of now I have neither the time nor the inclination to punish soldiers who commit treason under their moral banner. Should we catch these criminals, you can consider it forgotten. If not, then I hardly see reason for the rest of your squad to take the blame when it was your mistake. Understand?"

"Yes, Sir." Bristol stood as instructed, meanwhile Brull marched up to their group.

The healer had a strange look on his face. "Captain, Sir... Bristol." he added Bristol's name after a moment of thought. "Lillacae is fine. She shows no sign of any injury. In fact, she's pristine. I've never seen anyone so perfectly healthy before, albeit she does seem very tired..." Quietly, Bristol let out a sigh of relief. He looked over at the still unconscious Lilla, and smiled just barely.

"That's settled then." Bristol turned to Koa. His captain had evidently overlooked his trespass, and returned to her normal reserved self. She spoke with firm resolution and authority. "Brull, take Phoral, Leif, and Claeo, and go after the suspects. Do not engage, but make sure we can find you."

CHAPTER 11

Brull pressed both of his arms against his side and bowed, accepting the mission from her. When he rose, Brull glanced at the old ivirian. "Sheriff Rainault, are you still against being healed? I know I can offer some relief to your burns before I go."

Rainault shook his head decidedly at the healer, and brought out his sheriff's token from his bag. As he twirled it with his fingers, he said gruffly, "These burns are a reminder of my subordinates' destruction, and my failure to stop those mongrels. I will have no healing until Merlin Lynwood has been caught."

His words sobered them all.

When the squad first found the sheriff, he had been sitting by the smoking carcass of a house. Many questions had been asked, but few were answered. In what little information he did give, was the revelation that his *entire* squad of soldiers had been killed by the two elestiels hiding inside the house. One looked Avalonian, and the other, which had fairer skin, appeared Gressan. It wasn't until the day after they found him that he gave them more specifics, such as the name of the female elestiel. Apparently, this Merlin Lynwood, had been hiding in Sher for many years, undetected by the government.

His story had thrown the whole squad into a violent fury, propelling them to chase after the criminals. However, even upon Rainault insisting the woman was responsible, there was a small seed of doubt inside Bristol. Could an elestiel have effectively hidden for years in the forest without being caught? Was that plausible? If it was, why would she kill so many soldiers, knowing full well it would make her a target of highest priority?

Bristol frowned, squeezing his sword's curved hilt. The woman seemed genuinely confused when he leveled the charges at her before. With such thoughts playing in his mind, he said, tentatively, "Sir, is it *absolutely* certain that those elestiels caused the fire? Perhaps it was an accident?"

As soon as the words left his mouth, he tensed. All the other ivirians visibly froze. The sheriff's demeanor changed like the flip of a leaf in fall. A small opening in his mask revealed Rainault's black eyes, glittering brighter than any winter moon. It held the determination of a wolf who had spotted its defenseless prey. The old ivirian was radiating hate.

"They are responsible for the loss of my wings, my health, and my squad. I can still taste the ash like vinegar burning in my throat." Rainault shook as he spoke, his voice dripping with infernal rage. "I can still feel the splinters embedding themselves in my skin even as it seared off. The screams of my dying comrades remain in my ears even now. No, those golden eyes are not innocent. Do not let them fool you."

In comparison with such anger, Bristol felt hollow. It was as if his own emotions were drawn from within him until nothing was left inside. Any response which may have come from him was swept away before he could speak.

Brull cleared his throat as he left them, and Bristol envied his escape. At the same time, another iviran came flying over the hill, a rope in his hands. It hung from him to the ground, where a short leprechaun walked with his hands bound. His sweater had mud caked on its hem, and his clothes were all wrinkled from his journey hither. Something silver hung from his neck, and his face was set in a scowl. Jackel Hymes, although his house had been difficult to find, was captured in the end.

"This is why we split up?" Bristol muttered.

"We have questions, and he has the answers." Koa responded. "Though he may not give them willingly."

Bristol flinched as the sheriff started toward Jackel, growling darkly, "Then we will pull it from him one tooth at a time."

Koa sent Bristol a hard look, and unwillingly he went after the sheriff. Rainault stopped by the prisoner, who had been escorted by the ivirian called Grazer. Grazer was of the same Order as Bristol, but they were very different in appearance. For instance, Grazer's skin tone was deep orange, like clay, and he was bulky in stature and build. Usually ivirians were strong but thin, allowing their hollow bones to make up for the extra weight of their muscles. Grazer detested frailty, and so sacrificed his speed for strength. It made him the slowest of their group, but also the one best equipped for hauling prisoners around.

He was snapping at the prisoner when Bristol arrived. "Be quiet, you jackrabbit!"

Jackel pulled at the rope around his wrists. "I will not! You're all fools if you believe for a *single* moment that this chump deserves respect! You should be arresting him!"

CHAPTER 11

"That's enough!" Rainault brought his knee up into Jackel's stomach, faster than Bristol would have thought possible given his injuries. He flinched as the leprechaun fell to his knees, coughing and gasping. The sheriff grabbed a fist full of Jackel's orange hair and yanked his head upward. "I have three questions, and you will answer each one. Where are they going, who is the boy, and what is their purpose?"

Jackel stared defiantly at the sheriff, keeping his mouth shut. Bristol's nerves buzzed. Killing prisoners was not legal, and yet he could sense the urge building inside the sheriff.

"Sir..." he began to voice his worry, seeing some semblance of his own concern in Grazer's posture.

Rainault released Jackel's hair only to seize his collar. Up the leprechaun went, his feet dangling above the ground. "I asked you kindly." Rainault sneered. "Do you wish for more pain? Answer, and I will let you go!"

Jackel shuddered, but he held his head high. "Make me, you overgrown moth!"

Bristol tensed as Rainault shook in anger, then froze. The sheriff's cold eyes appeared to be fixated on the prisoner. No, no that was wrong, Rainault was looking at something specific. Something silver around the leprechaun's neck. The sheriff's bandaged head tilted to the side as he stared silently at the pendant.

Swallowing, Bristol glanced at Grazer. The other soldier gave him a look that plainly showed his discomfort and confusion. Once again, this time with a questioning tone, Bristol said, "Sir...?"

"So, that's it..." Rainault murmured, almost like he hadn't meant to speak aloud.

Jack's face contorted in confusion, and Grazer put an uneasy hand on his sword hilt. "What is it, Sir?"

Jack gave a short cry as Rainault let go of his collar, and in one fluid motion, grabbed the silver chain. It snapped as the links broke apart, slipping from the leprechaun's neck in seconds. Rainault quickly held it up, examining the engraved pendant. From the ground, their prisoner lost all the color in his face, and the smug attitude he had been courting disappeared. Whatever that pendant was, it scared Jackel.

"Sheriff," Bristol glanced at the prisoner before continuing. "What is that? Does it tell us where the fugitives are?"

"No..." Rainault looked up at him, and Bristol could see a hungry light in the sheriff's eyes. "But it might tell us something else." He wrapped the chain around his hand and curled his fingers around the pendant. Then he spoke again, and his voice hissed in such a perfect impression of a snake, that Bristol recoiled in surprise. "I wondered why a leprechaun would give charity for anyone, but that was not why you did it, was it? It was your greed that made you assist them, wasn't it? Well, in your lust you gave away not their path, but something far better." Jack flinched as Rainault finished. "I appreciate your service."

With that the sheriff whirled away, marching straight to Captain Koa. Bristol stared in surprise for a moment, then hurried after him, leaving Grazer with the now subdued prisoner.

He reached the two in time to see Rainault hold up his clenched fist. "I must go to the Mayor, immediately."

Koa's eyes narrowed slightly. "We are in mid pursuit, Sir."

"I'm aware of that, but this cannot wait." he snapped.

The captain kept her face blank as she asked, "Would you care to explain *why* you must go? The Mayor is busy and far away. It will be weeks before you could reasonably return."

"This is more important!" Rainault pulled his fist back to his side. "Just follow the culprits until I return. Do not apprehend them without me."

Koa frowned, then bowed her head slightly. "Yes, Sir."

Bristol squeezed his mouth shut before he could object. The sheriff's order was outrageous! Its tactic and its practical use were a huge waste of time. They *should* arrest the elestiels as soon as they found them, but if their captain agreed to it, there was no use in complaining. They would follow the elestiels, and they would wait.

Ah, Sweet Ivory Bishop,

    Of course I do not truly distrust you. There are many people against me in this world, but you are not one of them. I simply worried that you were growing complacent in such a secluded forest, but I see from your observations that you are keeping up with the important matters near you. Forgive me for assuming ill of you. It is true that Ivory Rook keeps me informed, but it is not the same as being there with you. I am surrounded by walls of stone and ancient men. You are free in the open forest. It is not that I dislike this place, but I find the lack of true conversation tasking. Though I will soon be free of them, I hope to remove them should the occasion arise earlier than expected.

    I digress, this is not what I have written to you about. After receiving your letter, I have begun to make the necessary arrangements to aid in your journey. While I can do nothing about your circumstance, I can assist in expediting it, as long as you ensure that they don't discover you whilst travel is underway.

    On the subject of my uncovering the culprit, you asked who was nagging me. Unfortunately, it will be difficult to rid me of the Minister of Defense, but I await your solution, knowing it will be quite amusing to watch. He still nags me even now, but has moved on to another subject, as I appeased his original concern.

Now, you said you have a guess about this powerful weapon; I would like to hear your thoughts on it. My spies have still not determined its location, though it is likely that my lovely neighbor, his highness the Onyx King, has it locked tightly up in his castle. If you know more than those actually on the board, pray write and tell me so I may begin to prepare for it. Perhaps you can also retrieve more information from the Marble Rook, though you can't ask directly. Loose lips sink ships, as I've been told.

I have some new information for you, and hopefully it will be of use. A report came in that troops have been amassing in the port of Sal Tri, and despite their assurance otherwise, it is probable that they intend to begin fighting. The infilling of troops likely implies that their forces are depleted inside the forest. This may assist you in hiding, though it won't help me. It's quite gratifying to think the Jade King has finally decided to join our squabbles.

Farewell, and try to avoid being caught.

Ivory Knight

12

The Child

M

"You sent me over a troll bridge!"

Merlin threw a couple twigs into the fire, watching sparks fly into the air. After walking most of the day in mutual silence, they ended up in a cave below ground. The opening was partially covered by grass, and after being thoroughly searched inside, it was deemed safe. Now Lance and Merlin were sitting by a makeshift fire while Guinevere slept in the corner.

The knight unclasped his sword belt, dropping the weapon down beside him. He ran a hand through his hair as he continued speaking. "I know you don't like me, but really, sending me needlessly into danger is too much! I could have *died*."

Merlin sighed, pulling her legs up so she could hug her knees. "Look, I'm sorry. I shouldn't have done that." As an afterthought she added, "Though, you were being annoying."

He glared at her—now the second time he had done so—and shook his head. "Not enough to be thrown off a cliff."

"Not all bridges have trolls under them." Merlin pointed out. "And really, this one was probably the most reasonable in Sher."

"That's not comforting." Lance leaned on his elbow, holding up his head with a fist. "Should I be worried that you will send me into sinking sand next?"

Her heart squeezed in annoyance, though Merlin knew he had a right to be frustrated. "No, you don't. There's nothing more I can do but apologize, which I've already done. Take it or carry on being angry."

The knight gave a short, exasperated laugh. "That's not how it works, Merlin. I get to be angry, because you clearly tried to kill me."

"As you wish." Merlin conceded. She turned away from the knight and opened her pack, pulling out some of the provisions Jack had given her. She took a bite of the bread, chewing it bitterly.

Lance spoke again, and when he did it was in a calmer voice. "That troll mentioned something about giants, does Sher house them still?"

She glanced at the knight and set down her bread. "Yes, but only southern giants. They're smaller, less indestructible, and they don't want to invade the mainland, as far as I know. The few giants I've met seemed peaceful enough."

"Except in regards to trolls apparently." He sounded a little dubious.

Merlin frowned. "Apparently that's the case. There are many divisions between the myths here. Trolls hate the giants, and everyone else hates the elves. I'm not surprised at all."

"Maybe your laws have encouraged this feud," Lancelot mused. "Isolation breeds dissension."

Merlin flinched and turned to him. The subject easily irritated her, but for once she had to restrain her temper. "Perhaps, but we appreciate our privacy too much to do anything about that. When the elves still ruled Sher, the myths and humans lived close together, which allowed them to be taken advantage of. We may not be united now, but a kingdom that hates each other is harder to control."

Lancelot frowned. "That would make living peacefully very difficult."

"Yes, but I would much rather live here than in a human kingdom." Merlin wanted to say more, but she hurriedly took another bite of her food to keep herself from speaking further.

"My kingdom is not perfect," Lance told her, averting his eyes. "There are laws I would change, but that is the case with every kingdom."

A breeze blew into their cave, blowing the fire back towards the wall. Merlin put away her food and began searching inside her bag for her purple cloak. The knight made a good point, and if Merlin considered it, he was likely right. But the working of Sher's government was of no concern to her, and likewise, Avalon was not either.

The thought brought back Lance's words from earlier. *Does the Myth Forest not touch the lands of men? Is it some special forest that*

CHAPTER 12

lies on an island? You are part of this, whether you acknowledge it or not! Merlin frowned at the dark fabric she found in her pack, rubbing her thumbs across the threads.

What had her brother said all those years ago, when they found out he had been drafted? *Well, I guess it's not surprising. We're neighbors to both kingdoms anyway, there was no way to stay out of it. Not completely.*

As she pulled the cloak tighter around her shoulders, Merlin couldn't help but wonder about her own words. To both Lance and Daleon, she firmly argued against participating in the war, but was that right? Merlin closed her eyes, picturing another ivirian, his eyes a light brown, skin a pale blue, a smile that was too bright for anyone to own. Aspen, the one reason, the one drive she had to remember. She mentally shoved all her doubts away, turning her head from the cracks growing throughout her resolve.

"Merlin?" She jumped, startled by the knight's sudden appearance next to her. He looked concerned, brows knit together. "Are you all right?"

"Ah yes." Merlin blinked. "Why—?"

Lance moved back to his original spot, and shook his head. "I was talking to you and you didn't hear me. What were you thinking about?"

Still a little put off by her scare, Merlin shrugged somewhat awkwardly. "Nothing important. What were you asking?"

He gazed at her with suspicion, catching the firelight in his golden eyes. "*Empa'ru E reolu?*"

Merlin glared. "That's it, you have to stop doing that. You *know* I don't understand you."

He nodded. "That's the point." Merlin scrunched up her face, already preparing to argue when he held up a hand. "What I was asking before was how long you have known Jack. I am still curious."

She raised an eyebrow cautiously. "Why do you want to know?"

"He seems... knowledgeable." Lance's face darkened. "I didn't think he was very old, but you've just mentioned him in connection to the elves. Is he old enough to have known them?"

For a moment she debated within herself, then answered. "I've known Jack my whole life. He helped me learn how to control my gift."

Merlin looked down at her clenched fist, thinking of the hours he had spent teaching not only her, but her brother as well. Her mind hopped to the present, and her heart squeezed. Had the soldiers left Jack alone? Was he safe? If only there was a way to know for sure.

Pursing her lips, Merlin carried on, trying to comfort herself. "And yes, he is old enough to have met my ancestors. Sher's tyrant king and queen. He's seen many things, a lot of them I don't know. I don't think Jack told my brother or my parents either."

"Would your brother have spoken with Jack?" Lance asked.

"Of course." Merlin turned up her nose. "Daleon trained with Jack the same as I did. He would have been more interested in Jack's political knowledge than I would."

"I see." Lance tilted his head. "Then you must have trained to use your sword with your brother?"

Her heart sped up for a moment, beating quickly. "No, I only started two years ago." Merlin wasn't the most proficient at sword fighting, but she only began learning in order to enter the military. Thinking about it made her heart ache, and she suddenly had the desire to change the subject. Merlin looked over at Lance and asked quickly, "Do you have any siblings?"

A reflection of the same anxiety she felt rippled across his face before disappearing quickly. "An older brother, actually."

The similarities were not lost on Merlin, but something about the way he spoke made her wonder. "Is he a knight too?"

The cat in the corner started snoring intensely. Lancelot sighed. "Yes. It's required for every male in my family to become a knight."

"That's..." Merlin bit her lip. What should she say now? It wasn't like she knew anything about nobility or their families. All she knew was that she didn't want to go back to talking about her own. "Do you get along?"

His face became tight and stolid as he said, "No." The bitterness that filled the single word was so intense Merlin dared not continue questioning.

I wonder what happened to make him dislike his brother so much, she thought. It would take a great force to disrupt her relationship with Daleon, but she had to acknowledge that not everyone was the same. Still, Merlin was curious as to why he sounded so hurt.

Instead of questioning him further, she said, "We should get some rest. We have at least a week and a half of travel left before we reach Robin, and I doubt we'll find such a nice cave again." She received a nod as her answer, while the knight removed a blanket from his pack. Her bag contained a blanket, a coil of rope, a few water skins, and a very small amount of food. She frowned. There were a few other items, but nothing edible.

"Lance, do you have any food in your bag?"

Merlin looked back to where he was unfolding the cloth. "Yes, it's in my satchel. Do you need more?"

She peered at the small bag he had been carrying. "Um, now that you mention it, how does that thing hold a book and all our food?"

"It's imbued," he told her flatly. "You can put anything nonliving inside, and you are the only one who can take it out. I thought it would be helpful."

"That *is* nice." Merlin agreed. "How much can it hold?"

"I'm not sure, but I know I'll sense when it's becoming too full."

"I see..." Merlin uncurled her cotton blanket, stretching it out over her legs. "That will definitely be useful."

"I figured as much."

Gently she rested her head against her arm, staring at the now horizontal fire. It was slowly getting smaller and smaller, shrinking down to the embers that would keep the cave warm throughout the night. For some time Merlin lay there with her eyes on the shifting reds, until finally sleep took over all thoughts.

The next day Merlin was able to find the Mason Line, the stone path sitting proudly amidst the untamed forest. It really was a welcome sight to all of them, as now they could walk without fear of stumbling across uneven ground. Progress became much easier, and thus faster, while they remained on the walkway. With that being the case, it didn't take long for a week to pass as they headed farther and farther north. Merlin's initial worry was that someone would recognize Lance, and then attack them. But even though they did pass a few merchants, the hoods of their cloaks kept them from any extra attention. Every time they passed a traveling myth, she found herself silently thanking Jack for providing the cloak to Lance.

It wasn't until noon on the eighth day that they were stopped on the road. Lancelot froze by the edge of the path, pulling back his hood. He looked confused as he stared into the forest.

"What's wrong?" Merlin asked, pulling back her own hood. She couldn't see anything besides the normal trees and plants, unless he was concerned about the squirrel that had just hopped between trees.

"Don't you hear it?" he asked. Merlin frowned, walking closer to him. For a moment she heard nothing, and then...

Her frown deepened. Someone, or something, was screaming at the top of their lungs. Even with the long distance, she could hear anguish and pain in the screams. Lance stepped forward, but Merlin grabbed his arm.

"What are you doing?" He started to pull against her grip.

"It could be a trap!" Merlin hissed. "There might be pixies out there, and they always cause trouble."

"I agree." The cat sauntered over to them, looking unperturbed. Gwen narrowed her eyes as she stared at the knight. "We need to move on."

Merlin kept her eyes trained directly on his face. If she let go of his arm he would probably bolt. "Lance!"

"No!" Now Lance made eye contact, and the elestiels began battling through the connection. His mouth curled down into a frown. "They're calling for help! Trap or not, I can't stand by while they might be in danger."

"And what if they're not in trouble? We should walk away!" Merlin gritted her teeth for two seconds, feeling a momentary pang of guilt at the hurt expression on his face. "Listen, not everyone in this forest is friendly. Most of them want to cause as much mischief as possible!"

"I refuse to turn a blind eye on a cry for help." He yanked his arm from her grasp, unsheathing his sword in the same motion. "You might be willing to ignore the need of another, but *I* am not!"

Merlin's eyes widened as he dashed away from her. "Lancelot!" she called, anger boiling in her stomach. The knight ignored her call, heading at top speed in the direction of the voice. She and Gwen stood there, watching him disappear into the forest.

What is wrong with him?! Merlin looked between the forest and the road, trying to decide what to do. This knight was far too righteous for their circumstances, and even worse at following common safety principles! However, if there really was someone out there who needed rescuing...

"We could keep going..." Gwen suggested.

Merlin had only one moment of temptation before sighing deeply and flicking out her sword. "No, let's go."

She launched herself off the ground, sprinting in the direction Lance was heading. Gwen yowled in pursuit as Merlin began weaving through the web of trees. She scrambled under and above large roots, leaving the cat behind in her rush. The feline was simply unable to keep up with Merlin's increasing speed. The farther she went, the more pained the wails became, until they suddenly stopped. A wave of silence swished back into the forest, sucking out any remaining sound. Merlin's heart pounded as she kept barreling towards the direction she last heard the scream. Why was the cry gone? Was Lancelot all right?

Her worry grew increasingly larger as she searched for the knight. He couldn't have gone far, could he? Merlin hopped over a large rock, nearly running right into Lance. Her balance tilted as she skidded to a stop several paces away from him. Whirling around, she came back, already trying to sense any injuries that could have been inflicted. It was a futile attempt.

Lance was kneeling on the ground, unharmed physically but shaking all over. In his arms lay a young ivirian, his wings drooping and gray. The child's skin had a pale greenish tint to it, and there were thin red lines looping his neck, far smaller than ordinary rope. Merlin covered her mouth to keep a horrified gasp from spilling out. A tremor ran through her as for a moment, she was not seeing the child, but someone else entirely. Blue hair instead of black, and brown eyes instead of yellow. Hurriedly she blinked away the image, sinking to the grass in front of the knight.

"Can you save him?" the knight asked, not lifting his head.

Merlin cringed. His whole body was etched with the desperation she had heard and seen so many times throughout her life. "Lance..."

"Can you save him?" he yelled.

"No!" Her heart twisted. "I can't bring back the dead."

Lance's trembling grew worse. "He was alive, Merlin."

There it was, that shooting pang of guilt.

He looked up at her, eyes glistening with tears. "The boy was alive when I got here. He was trying to tell me what happened!" Lance spoke through his teeth. His eyes were red. Merlin could barely swallow as his expression went from pain to anger. "He was *alive*, Merlin!"

"Stop!" she ordered, voice breaking. Tears were forming beneath her own eyes now. She knew exactly what he was implying. "How could I have known? I'm not so powerful as to sense when someone needs me! This could have been a trap!"

"But it wasn't!" Lance squeezed the child, wiping the tears away with one hand. "And you could have saved him if you were here."

Merlin stood, scrubbing the tears from her cheeks. She couldn't look at the child, not now. But she wouldn't let Lancelot continue insulting her either. "It's not my job to go running every time someone gets hurt! I have the power to heal, but I never chose this! I was born without any option of a different path! You can't blame me for every bad thing that happens!"

"Not everything," His voice lowered and cracked. "But this..."

Merlin remained there staring at the knight, trying not to cry again. Why did Lancelot always blame her for everything? Anytime something bad happened, it was automatically her fault. If she had known before, of course she would have acted immediately. She would never want this.

While they sat there quietly, Guinevere came trotting forward, taking in the scene. She sighed. "I heard your argument. Why is it always blame with you two?" Gwen's ears dropped. "It's neither Merlin's fault nor yours, Lance. All the blame is placed on whomever did this."

Merlin looked down at her boots. She wanted to believe Gwen was right. The person who did this was the one on whom all the anger she and Lance felt should be placed.

Gwen looked at both of them very seriously. "We can sit here and cry, or we can go do something about this. Which will it be?"

CHAPTER 12

Merlin glanced at the knight, eyes meeting. Neither spoke, but an understanding passed between them. Her fingers curled into a tight ball. "We'll go. But first," she looked down at the child. "I think we should find his family."

It didn't take them long to find the house where the iviro lived. He was too young to have been far from home, and he didn't have any supplies indicating travel. For safety, Merlin and Gwen were the ones who went up personally, but their worries were useless. Once the family saw their child, they didn't have any attention for even the elf before them. Merlin nearly started crying again as she walked away from the house, the sobs of the parents still carrying through the walls. Her heart felt like it was being ripped into a thousand tiny pieces, even more so than when her house had burnt. That at least could be rebuilt. The child on the other hand could not.

There were no footprints on the ground when they returned to the place of the attack. Merlin crouched beside the imprints of Lance and the iviro. She wasn't a tracker, but surely there should be a footprint or something that marked the opposing force.

"Do you see anything, Gwen?" she asked, turning to look at the cat.

Gwen was poking her head out of a patch of tall grass, flicking a beetle off her claw. "No I don't."

"I do."

Merlin jumped up, rushing to where Lancelot was crouched. Sitting on top of his glove was a shiny silver thread, bright enough to be noticeable, but thin enough that Merlin was amazed Lance had seen it. The thread led into the forest and around a tree. Maybe it was just Merlin, but the forest seemed to grow darker the farther her eyes followed the thread.

"Is this metal?" she wondered, picking up the thread from Lance's palm. He nodded, drawing his sword as he began following the string. Silver thread was expensive, anyone who just left it on the ground was either extremely wasteful, or setting a trap. Her misgivings deepened as the three of them followed the thread, with Merlin coiling it around her hand as they went. Every ten feet or so, the thread they were following would end and another would start up a small distance ahead. The strings changed color every time one strand ended, ranging from the brightest blues to the shiniest pinks. There was not a single color that could not be easily spotted if you were looking for it.

Merlin frowned as she picked up the end of the last string. The purple thread led straight to a wall of tall hedges with a single door fitted between them. Trees surrounded the wall on all sides, and even when Merlin poked her head out she couldn't see the end of the hedges. To add to her concern, there were no birds chirping or squirrels scampering around the trees. It was utterly devoid of any forest chatter that was so common in every other part of Sher. Basically, the door screamed *"trap"* in every possible way.

"Maybe we should climb a tree first?" Merlin suggested, eyeing the door dubiously. "Or at least enter strategically?" They all knew this was a bad idea, so caution should be the natural decision, right?

Lancelot swung his sword in a full circle, like his wrist was itching to use the weapon. "Not this time," he determined, marching forward to the door. It made a loud splintering sound as he kicked it in with the heel of his boot. The knight didn't wait to enter.

Merlin sighed, rubbing the side of her head. Her nerves were already strained from earlier, but the knight was pulling them past their limit. "He's going to get us killed, isn't he?"

"Probably." Gwen admitted, following Lance into the hedged area. Merlin gave one last glance at the forest around her before following her companions inside. As soon as she took three steps past the door, she heard a loud crash, and swung around. The door closed itself, slamming so hard in its frame that it was visibly stuck.

"Oh look," Merlin drawled. "It was a trap."

Gwen appeared by her feet, looking up at the girl. "Indeed, but look where it led."

Confused, she twisted around. There were no trees poking up anywhere inside the hedged area, instead there were several poles stuck into the ground. Each pair had a white rope tied at the top and strung to the pole nearest, forming what looked like a clothesline. Sitting on top of the ropes were tapestries. The closest pair of poles had one giant tapestry draped on its rope, and to the left sat another pair with three smaller weaves on it. Merlin could see several more sets overlapping like scales, such that there was no way to see from one end of the hedge to the other.

Gwen sidled up to the large tapestry before them, swatting a tassel hanging from the edge of the fabric. Merlin had to admit that the workmanship was excellent. She had never seen the ocean before, but from what she heard, Merlin would expect it to look like that—with giant curls of vibrant blues and rolling spans of beige ground skirting around the ends of the image.

The cat rose up, sitting on her hind legs for support. She flicked out one claw and poked it into the tapestry. Merlin was about to scold the cat, but was stopped by a shrill whistling sound. It blew out from the tapestry in a steady stream of high-pitched whining until the cat removed her claw. Merlin lowered her hands from their place over her ears.

"Strange." She reached forward with hand, ready to touch the threads.

"Please don't do that."

Merlin spun around, her eyes latching onto the speaker. The woman before her looked surprisingly human, with long, curly brown hair and a pleasant face. Merlin could see that she had pointed ears, and her skin had a light pink tint to it. The woman was also wearing an impractical white dress that hung in folds at her feet.

She was beautiful, which made Merlin all the more wary. Her sword had reverted back to its charm, but now she summoned it again into her hand. In Sher, there was one general rule that every child was taught; if it's pretty, it's dangerous. That applied to everything, even objects like flowers. Anything pleasant had the ability to harm if used incorrectly.

Merlin also had not forgotten why they were there. If this woman wasn't the iviro's killer, then at least she might know what had happened. "Who are you?" Merlin asked, trying not to sound like a threat. She was aware that summoning a sword didn't help her case, but whatever the scenario was, she wanted a weapon with her.

"My name is Ardene." the woman said, taking a step forward. "Now that I've answered, please keep a handle on your pet. My works take forever to finish and I don't want them to be torn apart by that animal. It hurts me."

"My pet?" Merlin looked down at Gwen.

The cat winced. "Meow...?"

Ardene took another step, but Merlin held up her sword, keeping the tip level. "Stop." Ardene froze. Merlin moved herself back a step. "An iviro was killed not far from here. I followed a trail of thread from him to this place. Was it you?"

Ardene smoothed down her skirt, expression unconcerned. "Yes."

Merlin squeezed the sword, her knuckles turning white. "How could you? He did nothing wrong."

Her head tilted to the side, Ardene speaking calmly. "He didn't want his tapestry. That was insulting and infuriating enough to kill him. All that time I put into making it, and he simply turned away."

"That doesn't give you the right to kill him!" Merlin gritted her teeth, trying to control the anger inside her. Out of the corner of her eye, she saw Gwen shoot off between the tapestries. Hopefully she was getting Lance.

Ardene took a step forward. "I do have the right. Just like I'll have the right if you don't accept your tapestry."

"What?" Merlin stared at her. "My tapestry?"

"Yes." She inclined her head to the left, directing Merlin's gaze deeper into the maze of threads. "I wouldn't have let you find me if I didn't have one for you. Every picture I make is for someone specific, completely personal to them. Yours is this way." She started to move, walking between the fabrics.

Merlin's mouth fell open some, her disbelief heightening with every second. Should she risk killing Ardene now, or wait for Lance? Merlin could use her sword, but she had never killed anyone with it. Ardene stopped and looked back, obviously waiting for Merlin to follow. What was she going to do? What could she do? The elestiel straightened her back and made up her mind, lowering her sword.

Ardene nodded, smiling sweetly as she resumed her course. She led Merlin slowly through the scattered tapestries, brushing her hand along each one as she passed. If it wasn't so unnerving, Merlin might have enjoyed the walk. Some of the works were so beautiful they surpassed the ocean she had seen. There were mountains, full skies, castles, and even a picture of the silver sands in the north. The amount and the quality made her more nervous. How could one person make all these in a single lifetime?

After five minutes of walking, Ardene finally stopped. She turned and moved to the side, sweeping out her arm dramatically. "Your tapestry, Merlin."

13

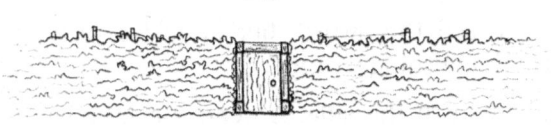

THE WEAVER

M

Merlin stared at the tapestry, struggling to take it all in. It was large enough to be a blanket, and it immediately stole her complete attention. Shivers ran up and down her back as she looked at it, feeling nauseous after one glance. Every thread was either black or red, twisting throughout the sky and ground. Burnt buildings sat scattered across the picture, and crows flew in the sky. Merlin covered her mouth, feeling repulsion cling at her throat. She could see bodies laying on the ground, Ardene had even taken the time to weave terrified expressions over their faces.

"W-what is that?" Merlin stepped back. It was disgusting, but she had seen it before. The black and red painted town, how had she seen it? It felt familiar, like a distant memory overshadowed by fog.

"You don't remember?" Ardene sighed, twirling her finger in her hair. "How disappointing. This happens too often to be amusing anymore. I guess I'll just have to remind you."

Merlin lurched forward to stop her, but Ardene's fingers were already brushing across the face of the tapestry. Each of the threads blazed like the sun, stinging Merlin's eyes. She tried to raise both hands to shield herself but was unable to move.

What is this?! Her vision began to dissolve at the corners as her breathing became faster. "Ardene!" she panted, ears pounding with a dizzying ring. The darkness crawled to the edges of the glowing tapestry and framed it in shadows, pulling her forward, sucking her into the dismal scene.

The ground came straight at her face, or rather, she was falling straight into it. Merlin threw out her arms to stop the fall, catching her weight on her palms. For a second she froze there, holding herself up in surprise. Where was she? Merlin looked up from the ground, taking in the unfamiliar sights. She was laying at the entrance to a village, a settlement surrounded by the most barren landscape she had ever seen. All around her, there were blank, grassy hills rolling on and on without a single tree popping up from the ground. There were mountains in the distance, but they did little to help with the monotonous landscape.

When she tried to look back, her head refused to move. Her mind was a spectator in her own body, able only to make the smallest of actions. Irritation flared as she tried again to force her head to turn. The effort was useless. Merlin glared as instead her legs responded, pushing herself upwards to stand. She wanted to turn, but aversion swelled inside her. Merlin had to go into the town. She had to. Her direction reversed, thrusting her forward into the village.

Little children stopped playing to watch her walk by, hushed by some unknown conviction. Their eyes bored into Merlin as she stopped in the center of the village. There, at least a dozen villagers went about their various tasks. None of the adults seemed interested in her presence.

What now? Merlin thought, as her arms began to move on their own. For some reason her body knew what it was supposed to do even though her mind didn't. Merlin stared as her fingers grasped the hilt of a sword she thought was unfamiliar, but also recognized somehow. Its grip was made of smooth black leather, with a silver knob at the end. Several tiny red jewels made a ring around the knob, matching the cross shaped hilt. The silver of the hilt had been shaped into two entwined serpents. Both creatures were poking their heads out hungrily, teeth pointed to strike. It took a moment, but she recognized them for what they were—dragons. Merlin's skin began to crawl as she brandished the sword, shifting her hand to a maneuverable position.

One of the village women looked up and set down her basket, coming forward to Merlin. She looked kind, with crinkles around her eyes. "Hello, is there something I can help you with?" Her voice was gentle and friendly.

Only when she finished speaking, did Merlin feel the intent of her actions surface. Panic sizzled in her gut. Deep inside her, two warring emotions vied for dominance. One ordered Merlin forward, crying that her inaction would enact dire consequences of which she could not handle. The other was a cry to not give in, to stop and turn away. Merlin's eyes flicked from the woman to her own left wrist, latching on to the item there. She wouldn't normally wear anything on that arm, but to her surprise there was a chain wrapped over it multiple times. Hanging from the chain was a silver pendant she didn't recognize. It appeared to have a flower engraved across it.

For some reason, when she looked at it she felt desperate, and cornered. There was something important about it, that much was obvious. Merlin looked back up at the woman. The second emotion inside her spiked and fizzled out as her heart dropped. Whatever that pendant was, it knocked the fight from her. The first emotion snapped its cold jaws around her heart, snuffing out resistance and replacing it with binding commands. The woman in front of her stepped back, her eyes trained to Merlin's face. Some of her intent must have been evident in her eyes. Either way, it was too late.

The villager screamed as the sword in Merlin's hand flashed across her. Something in her gut pulled taut, and Merlin wanted to scream, to cringe, to stop. But she wasn't in control of this body. Someone shouted from behind her, and she heard heavy footsteps.

"What have you done?!" shouted a man as Merlin whirled around. He was charging at her with a broom. Two other men and a woman followed behind him with similar cleaning instruments. Anger was scrawled over their faces and threaded through their bodies.

Dirt clung to Merlin's boot as she slid her foot into a proper stance. Her muscles tightened and she drew back her arm, both hands clasping the sword. When the first man reached her, she sidestepped and swung her blade in a large half-circle, sweeping the point up the man's chest. He screamed but she paid him no mind, twirling around a second pursuer and slicing down the woman's front. Blood sprayed into the air as she turned back around, whipping her sword up to meet the man's rake. He was pressing so hard and so close against her sword that she could see the veins popping out along his throat.

It was only because she was an elestiel that her arms didn't give out. The man roared and doubled his force. Merlin gritted her teeth and smacked her head into the man's face. For a split second, he gasped in pain and his attack lightened. She didn't let him have the chance to stay his mistake. A simple dodge and the ragged sound of metal ripping through flesh filled her ears.

Merlin let her sword dip slightly as she turned around. More villagers had appeared in time to witness her attacks, and the expressions on their faces told her they would never let her leave without answering for them. She let her sword touch the tip of the grass, blood slipping from one blade to another. They were wrong. She would not be the one left forever in the village, unable to leave again. If only there was something she could do to stop it, but there was not. There was nothing she could do to stop herself.

Merlin gasped as she was suddenly pulled out of the village, the wind knocked clean out of her lungs. Her vision spun wildly until her knees trembled and gave out. For the second time, she thrust out her hands to stop herself from receiving an uncomfortable embrace from the ground. Merlin coughed and tried to fight back the bile that was worming its way up her throat. The utterly too tangible vision had left her veins pumping with a flood of unnamed emotions—or maybe not so nameless. It was desperation, like she was a mouse trapped in a corner, with nowhere to go.

"There, there." Someone patted Merlin's shoulder, and she quickly rolled away, twisting to face Ardene. The woman looked completely unrumpled, even pleased. She smiled at Merlin. "Now do you understand?"

"No!" Merlin tried to fight off the lingering fear. "What *was* that?!"

Ardene wilted. "I was just showing you my inspiration. It's so irregular for someone's pain and destiny to be so entwined. I quite enjoyed making this." Ardene brushed the tapestry again, and for a scary moment, Merlin thought it would take her back into the village.

When it didn't, Merlin scrambled back to her feet. "I don't know what pain and destiny have to do with this. Tell me what you just did!"

"I showed you both of those things." She shrugged. "My weavings let me access pieces of your past and future. You have seen this village before, therefore I have seen it."

"But I've never been there in my life." Merlin squeezed her fists. "I don't know what you're talking about."

"You have seen it." Ardene insisted. She blew some hair out of her face, seeming annoyed. "You had a dream last week, or maybe it was a little longer than that. The dream was of this village. I wouldn't have been able to connect with you if you hadn't."

"I don't..." Merlin frowned, eyes darting back and forth. A memory was trying to tug its way forward in her mind. When she had been with Jack, yes, it was then. It hadn't been a dream. It was a nightmare. The red village, was that what she did? How could Merlin inflict that much destruction with her powers and a sword?

"See, you do remember!" Ardene clapped. "Now you can take your tapestry, and I can take your life."

"What?" Merlin stepped back. "Take my life?"

"Yes." She grinned. "I have lived for two thousand years by giving up my time in order to provide people like you with insights into their futures. I'm only able to do that because of the time I receive from people like you. In other words, I give up my time, you give up your life. Simple, right?"

"Uh, no?"

A shadow came over Ardene's face, or maybe it was always there. Merlin swallowed, attempting to take yet another step backward, only to find she was unable. She looked down at her feet. Why couldn't she move? Merlin pulled, but her foot only managed a few inches before being yanked back down. She looked back up at the now sneering woman.

"You don't have a choice," Ardene spat.

Merlin's eyes widened, she had to get away, *now*. But she couldn't move her arms either. They were stuck, just like her feet. She gasped as her wrists were suddenly pulled upward. Thin, almost invisible strings were wrapped around her hands and snaking down along her arms. Merlin looked back at Ardene. A smug look replaced the sneer on her face.

"Don't do this!" Merlin tried to sound as reasonable as possible. "I'm really not worth the effort!"

"I think not," Ardene started walking towards her. "You have—"

Slice! The clear sound of a sword pierced the air in front of Merlin. Her mouth fell open as Ardene's head toppled right off her shoulders. The body crumpled to the ground, revealing Lancelot, his sword still tipped downward from his slash. The knight's eyes were filled with worry as he stared at her.

"Are you hurt?"

Merlin gaped at him, speechless. An intense wave of relief welled up inside her, so quickly she was startled by its vehemence.

From behind his leg, Guinevere peeked out, her ears and fur standing on end. The cat blinked at her, then looked up. "Lancelot! What did you just do?"

He looked down at the feline. "What do you mean? You said to save Merlin!"

"I didn't say to chop off the person's head!" Gwen jumped in outrage. "You can't just kill random people unless they're on your own property!"

"She was clearly going to attack Merlin!"

"But she hadn't yet!" Gwen snapped. "She could have been making tea for her, you don't know!"

At that point in the conversation Merlin regained her voice. "Hey!" They turned to look at Merlin, to which she shook both wrists. Her arms were starting to hurt from the tiny threads digging into her skin.

"Right, sorry." Lance hurried over to her, avoiding Ardene's body. With two swipes of his sword, he cut down the threads holding her arms. Merlin handled the strings holding her feet.

"Thank you," she told them both, leaning her palms on her knees to calm her hammering nerves.

"What happened?" Lance asked. "Gwen just told me that you found the killer. She didn't say you were trapped or anything."

"That's because I wasn't when she left." Merlin grumbled. Quickly, she recounted the conversation she had with Ardene. When she got to the part about her vision, she wavered slightly. Just thinking about the village made her stomach flip. Even so, she described as much as she could. "It was unsettling to say the least."

Lance looked troubled. "You said it was a human village?"

"Yes."

"And you had a bracelet too?"

She nodded. "It had a pendant on it that I'd never seen before, silver with a flower imprint. I didn't look close enough to see what kind of flower it was, though." Her words just seemed to make him more worried. Merlin opened her mouth to ask why, but the cat spoke before she could.

"Uh, the body..." Gwen's green eyes were getting bigger and bigger by the second. She pointed her paw shakily.

Merlin spun around, eyes latching onto Ardene. Her body was breaking down into tiny bits of ash and dust, swirling around in a circle that climbed high into the air. As they all watched, the dust started clumping together to form blackened legs, arms, and a head. The nearest tapestry, a separate work from that of Merlin's, began unraveling at the same speed as the limbs were being formed, slithering up to the body. Each string grabbed hold of the charcoal limbs, spiraling themselves upward in tight coils that left the body completely covered. The last thread wound itself around the head of the figure, leaving a colorful human-shaped form slumped in a standing position.

For a very long minute they stood there, unsure what to do or say, frozen in place. Then the figure shuddered, rising in perfect imitation of a puppet on strings. Two pointed white eyes opened in the middle of the head, large and tilted, like that of a snake. It raised one arm, stretching out three long fingers, causing the sound of snapping bones to come from them.

A violent shiver ran across Merlin's spine as the head turned to her. "How dare you." Ardene's silky voice crept out of the creature. It took a step forward, but so did Merlin, repeating the action that the knight had taken previously. Her sword tore through the thread-covered neck far too easily. Ardene stumbled back from the force, catching her head in her hands as she tried to regain her footing.

"What are you?" Merlin gasped, watching Ardene put the head back on the neck.

"I am a weaver, you foolish child!" she screeched. Threads from other tapestries lashed out and wrapped around the arms and legs of Ardene, creating a spider web around her. "You couldn't kill me if you wanted to! I have lived longer than society, longer than the borders this kingdom resides in! I am the being closest to immortality that you will ever see!"

Any attempt at innocence in Ardene's voice was gone, revealing the violent shrieks that made up her real voice. Merlin almost wanted to put her hands over her ears to avoid the screech. Unfortunately, she wasn't given that choice, as the weaver was done with theatrics. Ardene grabbed the wooden pole that had been holding a tapestry, pushing off the rope that was tied to it. The bottom of the pole had been carved to a straight point that was now aimed at them.

Merlin gulped, stepping backwards towards Lance. "Run," she mumbled, before twisting around and fleeing past the cat. It was not the bravest thing Merlin had ever done, but Ardene just had her head lopped off twice and was *still* alive to tell the tale. Her sword disappeared as she wove through the sets of poles, throwing herself sideways behind a particularly large tapestry. Three heartbeats later, Gwen shot straight into Merlin, the cat's claws digging up the ground in a large puff. The girl caught Gwen at the same time Lancelot barreled behind the tapestry opposite their own. He skidded to a stop behind the fabric and dropped to the ground.

The three of them sat there, panting and staring at each other, waiting. Two heartbeats later, Lancelot whispered, "How do we kill her?"

Merlin glanced anxiously around the corner of her hiding spot. Nothing there yet. "I don't know," she hissed back. "Nothing can really be immortal, right?"

"Of course not!" Gwen wriggled out of Merlin's grasp, glaring at her. "Didn't you listen to her? She said she was *close* to being immortal. Close to not dying means you're still very much able to be killed!"

Merlin nodded, trying to remember their conversation. Was there a way to kill her?

Somewhere not far from them, she heard the weaver scream, "Come out now, you miserable brats! You have to pay for damaging my work! Do you know how long I spent on that?"

The tapestries! Merlin grabbed the bottom of the work in front of her, rubbing the frigid ends. What was it that Ardene had said to Merlin...? *It hurts me.* From the side, Merlin caught Lance's eye. The knight looked like he was about to charge into danger, *again*.

"Wait!" He froze in place, looking at her. Merlin wasn't entirely sure if she was right, but maybe, just maybe, it was the threads that were keeping Ardene alive. The way the tapestry had unraveled to revive her kept repeating in Merlin's mind, and the more she saw it, the more she was convinced.

"Show yourself, or I will be forced to kill all three of you!" demanded the weaver's approaching voice. Merlin swallowed. There was no choice, even if she was wrong, it would be better than running. She turned, ready to yell to Lance. "Th—"

"Got you!" Ardene's arm thrust out from behind the tapestry, grabbing Merlin's throat and lifting her above the ground, feet dangling.

Merlin gasped and grabbed the weaver's arm, grimacing at the feeling of thousands of threads beneath her fingers. It was as if a slick, bumpy sleeve had replaced all the skin on Ardene's arm. She heard the distant sound of a sword, but everything was slowly being drowned out by the ringing in her ears. She could hardly see, her eyes blurring as her lungs began to burn. Was this it? Was she going to die? Merlin tried in vain to suck in another breath. If she was going to die, then she needed to warn Lance and Gwen. She had to tell them, now!

"Hurt... tapestries!" she cried, the last of her breath forced out in those two words.

"No!" Ardene screamed.

The pressure around Merlin's neck released abruptly as an ear-splitting whistle broke through the fog in her mind. Merlin fell, hitting the ground with a heavy thump. Around her the world spiraled in dizzying circles as air flowed back into her lungs. Merlin coughed out saliva, pushing her hands against the ground to lift herself up. She needed to help Lance, but her mind was working at the speed of a slug.

The tapestry they had hidden behind was now cut straight down the middle, slowly unraveling from the cut. Lance's sword was on the ground beside it, and the knight himself was wrestling with the weaver. Merlin watched as he pushed harder against Ardene, who was struggling to deal with both him and Gwen. The cat shot back and forth between Ardene's legs, sinking her fangs into the creature's ankles and clawing at the strings around her calves.

Now was the time for Merlin to help. She had to do something about the tapestries before it was too late. Gritting her teeth, she thrust herself to a standing position, summoning her sword as she guided her hand towards yet another tapestry. The blade appeared in time to slice through the woven fabric, releasing a sharp whistle once again. Merlin cringed with the loud snap each thread made as the work began falling apart. From behind her she heard Ardene wail, shrieking at her to stop. Merlin paid her no mind as she cut more and more of the works. Every time she moved to a different tapestry, she threw as much power as she could muster into the sword. Soon the air around her was filled with loud, pained whistles from each slice.

Merlin lost count of the weaves she tore, hacking at any form of fabric in her vision. When she thought her ears couldn't handle any more of the shrieking, Merlin turned back in the direction she'd come from. Surely she had sliced enough to make a dent in Ardene's power? Merlin skidded to a halt in front of the scene. The weaver was still very much alive and angry, fighting pole on sword against Lance. Guinevere was busy using her claws to destroy other low hanging fabrics, but it wasn't helping much. Ardene had too many tapestries, and they were all fueling her.

Hope drained out of her. There was no way Merlin could cut down enough to kill her. One person couldn't accomplish this by themselves, not without finding a way to destroy multiple at once. But how could Merlin do that?

She squeezed her empty fist tightly. With two arms and one sword, how could she make any difference? A terrifying moment passed in which Merlin grasped for an idea. One came as she stared at Lance, her feet responding before her mind registered her plan. She dashed forward, slicing down Ardene's back.

"What?" A surprised scream came strangling out of the weaver as Merlin thrust her blade into Ardene's chest. The sword went straight through her body as if there were no bones to get in the way. Unfortunately, the wound wasn't damaging enough, because almost instantly Ardene began putting herself back together.

"Lance," Merlin looked up at the surprised knight, speaking quickly. "You have to use the pole to make fire. Burn all the tapestries!"

His eyes widened, looking from her to the pole. "I can't!"

"What?! But you did before!"

"Not anymore!" Their argument froze as a guttural howl from the ground rang out.

L

Before Lancelot could do anything, both he and Merlin were pulled in opposite directions with such force that his feet pulled up the grass and dirt. Strong threads wrapped around his waist and wrist tight enough that he almost dropped Solaris from the shot of pain. *Not good,* he thought, straining against the bindings as best he could.

"That is *it*!" The creature—what had Merlin said its name was, right, Ardene—stood up and pulled out Merlin's sword from its chest. Lance watched as she threw it to the side, expecting it to go back to its owner. Instead of doing anything helpful, the sword simply stayed flat against the grass.

"I will not have you boorish brutes tearing apart my artwork and refusing my generous gift!" Ardene sounded strung out and whiny. Lance glared as she stepped closer to Merlin, who was now ten feet away and sneering.

"Some gift, it has no function worth the price! How can I enjoy the tapestry if I'm dead?" Merlin spat on the ground, which wasn't very ladylike, but definitely appropriate.

"You're not supposed to enjoy it. I am!" Ardene stomped. "And now you've gone and wrecked so many of my beautiful pieces! I ought to etch their likeness into your body before I strangle you with the threads of your future!"

"Now hold on—"

"Never!" Ardene screeched, the threads around Lance tightening in response. Something at the base of his wrists snapped, and he gasped out in pain, slumping slightly on the ropes that held him up. Throbbing pain quickly overtook all his nerves as the weaver continued. "Before this day is over, I will be roasting your empty bones until even the ground hates your remembrance. But first!" The stringy creature spun around so that she was facing Lance. "I'm going to kill your friend!"

She stomped over, picking up her pole on the way. Lancelot forced a grin, smiling in the midst of pure anger. "I'm afraid I'm not the one to kill if you're trying to bother her. That would be the cat."

"What?" Ardene's blank white eyes somehow conveyed all the irritation that came through her voice.

"Hey!" Gwen yelled.

"Really?" Ardene moved back to look at Merlin, giving Lance a good view of the now infuriated girl. "You couldn't make fire, so you're trying to get Gwen killed first? What kind of knight are you?"

Indignation began to combat the pain stemming from his wrists as Lance tried hard not to glare at Merlin. It was not his fault that he couldn't control fire anymore, but at the very least he should have mentioned it to her. Lance gritted his teeth, scanning the surroundings as quickly as possible for something that could work. Merlin was unfortunately a healer, so her power would be useless, and Gwen was just a cat. He could try Ardene's gift, but he knew so little about it that he might hurt himself rather than help.

The weaver made a spitting sound, returning to face Lance. "I don't care if you are her mortal enemy, I will kill both you and the animal." He glared at her directly, an expression he normally refrained from. Of all the times not to be surrounded by people, this was the worst.

"*Try me.*"

Lance flinched, recognizing the male voice as the one he heard at Jack's home. He looked back at Solaris, which was hanging so loosely from his grasp that he might as well have dropped it. Was it really the sword? It had the ribbon dangling from its handle, but was that enough?

"*Try me!*" the voice repeated, this time more urgently. Lance stared, unsure what to do or say.

"Ignorant, distracted child!" Ardene barked, directing the pole so that its point was aimed straight at Lance's heart. "Take one last look at my face before I kill you, and think forever upon it, whether it be above or below this pitiful forest!"

"*Lancelot!*" screamed the voice.

Fine! he yelled back through his mind, forcing two fingers to extend to their full length. The shiny white ribbon responded immediately, the loop swinging up into his hand on its own. Lance transferred his grip to the ribbon so that Solaris hung only from his clenched fingers.

Exclamations of alarm escaped his attacker's mouth, but the knight ignored her, instead focusing on the rope. Power rushed through Lance, flooding his senses so that they buzzed with even the slightest movement. The sensation was like the hum of a great swarm of bees.

The comfort didn't last, as one second it was a pleasant heat that dulled the injuries in his hands, and the next, it shifted into a blazing fire, boiling him from the inside out. Everything in his line of sight, the tips of Ardene's feet, the grass, the tiny rocks that lay embedded in the dirt, were bathed in a purple hue that was slowly shifting towards the deepest blue. The pain was so intense that Lancelot could hardly hear, let alone understand what was happening around him. He was being swallowed by the fire, its blazing pull drawing him far away from his mind.

"*Don't fight it.*" The words of the voice cut through the heat like butter, becoming clearer the more it spoke. "*Nothing will happen to you for now, so let it roll over you. Don't build a wall.*"

It wanted him defenseless, but if Lance ignored the voice, would it really help? The knight squeezed both eyes shut, relaxing his mind and muscles so that the heat could flow over his skin. Whatever was happening, he was the one in control, it was his power now. He could always stop and release it if needed.

"*Good, that's right!*" The male voice was now so clear that he might have been standing next to Lance. "*You handled that well.*" With his last word, all the heat left Lance's body as if it had been sucked away.

Slowly, feelings other than temperature came back to the knight, one at a time. Coarse little bumps were poking into his legs, and wind was blowing over his face. Someone was yelling something, but he wasn't quite sure what it was, and even though his eyes should have been working, he couldn't force himself to open their lids.

What... was that? His thoughts tumbled around in his mind.

"*That was a small taste of my power, Lancelot. You're welcome.*"

But, who are you?

"*I am Solaris, and I would prefer to have this conversation when you're thinking a little more clearly.*"

Lance mulled that over for a heartbeat. "*I believe you caused this.*"

"*Fair enough. But look what happened, I'd say that was worth it.*"

What did he mean?

Again Lance tried to open his eyes, pulling them open by sheer determination. Black smoke was the first thing he saw, blowing in clusters as it danced around the air above the burnt ground. Charred bits of woven fabric lay tossed on the blackened grass, and the few wooden poles that remained standing were burning like torches.

The knight pried open his mouth, staring in shock at the wreckage. "Did I do this?"

"*We did it. You're welcome.*"

He looked down at the steaming black sword. "You already said that."

"*You're still welcome.*"

"Lancelot!" His attention shifted quickly to the elestiel who was running towards him, cat on her shoulder. Merlin looked torn between worry and anger.

"*Well, well. You've been traveling in fine company, haven't you?*"

"Be quiet." Lance growled under his breath as Merlin slid into a kneel beside him.

"Are you hurt? Did you burn yourself?" she asked.

"No, I'm fine." he reassured, but the words didn't seem to do anything except annoy her further.

"Right, you're fine." Merlin repeated, brushing some dirt off her palm. Before he could try to reassure her, she placed her hand on his forehead, sending shivers running down his face and neck.

"*Wow, now I'm jealous.*" Lance swallowed a retort to the increasingly irritating voice, not wanting Merlin to think he was crazy again.

Merlin pulled her hand back, swinging it up and down like it hurt. "Well, your skin is burning, but I guess that's what happens when you set yourself on fire."

"What did you just say?" he exclaimed, turning his head so fast that it sent the world spinning.

"Careful!" Merlin grabbed both of his shoulders to steady him, which was good, because if she hadn't, he probably would have fallen over.

"Lance, if you don't calm down, Merlin is going to make me fall while she fusses." Gwen scolded, adjusting her place on top of Merlin.

Merlin frowned at the cat. "Stop moving or you will! I didn't promise to carry you."

"But the ground is dusty…"

"Please," Lance said slowly. "Just explain to me what happened."

14

The Voice Inside the Blade

L

Merlin insisted on healing him before any explanations were given, saying that his energy was low enough that it made *her* tired. Lance didn't complain, being the subject of said exhaustion. Surprisingly enough, she didn't need to heal his wrists. It seemed as though the power had rid him of any damage to his body, along with roasting the surrounding vegetation. All Merlin really did was replenish his energy levels, which he still appreciated as she then insisted they had to leave before someone saw the smoke.

As it was, Lancelot didn't hear what happened until they found a hollowed-out tree to hide in, and by then he had grown fairly annoyed. Not only did he have to travel in ignorance, he also had to endure Solaris' constant chatter. Talk, talk, talk; that's all he did, rarely even needing an answer. But even *that* would have been bearable if he had talked about important things, not about the squirrels he was seeing, or the giant trees, or the excessively interesting tortoise that passed by a rabbit.

Would you mind giving me a chance to think properly? he asked, as he plopped down inside the tree. Merlin and Gwen came in after, all three shifting to be as compact as possible.

"Goodness me, your highness, so sorry for disturbing you. Guess I'll just be quiet now, even though I haven't been able to see for the past, what, twenty-three years?"

But you don't have to narrate everything to me, right?

The sword made a sound that was probably supposed to be a snort.

"So, you wanted to know what happened," Merlin started. She was fiddling with the charm on her sword, which meant she must have retrieved it before they left. "Well, Ardene was about to skewer you with her spear, and I have to say, pointing her to Gwen wasn't very brave."

"I was trying to stall her," he defended. "She wanted to kill us, as you *just* pointed out."

"So you thought sending her to attack me was the best option?" Gwen rolled her eyes. "And I thought we were friends."

He sighed. "I won't do it again." Lance looked at Merlin. "You said Ardene was trying to kill me?"

"Yes." She nodded. "But you suddenly burst into flames, there wasn't a part of you that wasn't covered."

"How did I not burn?" He stared at his hands, as if further inspection of the skin would reveal new injuries.

Solaris made another scoffing sound. "*Obviously that was me. I did say that you wouldn't get hurt.*"

Merlin frowned. "I don't know. But what I do know is that as soon as you lit up, a bunch of sparks went flying off of you, which created more fire wherever they landed. I mean, you were spreading the fire, I think."

"It happened so fast that Ardene couldn't hurt any of us." Gwen added. She scratched her ear. "I was surprised she died that quickly. I mean, she bragged a lot about being unkillable."

"That's what happens when you tie your life to something flammable." Merlin observed, sliding her bag into the only open space left. "Anyway, after she turned into a pile of dust, Gwen and I found cover until you stopped shooting blue flames everywhere. That's what happened."

"That's it?" Lance ran a hand through his hair. "Why couldn't you have told me this earlier?"

"Because I didn't understand what was going on, but I know you do." Merlin said flatly, pointing an accusatory finger at him. "You said you couldn't make fire, and then you did exactly that. So now I want you to explain. You owe both of us that much." Gwen nodded in agreement, and they both stared.

"I... can't." Lance rubbed the side of his arm, glancing between them. "I shouldn't."

"Your gift is making fire." Merlin exclaimed. "I just want the details."

"My gift is not creating fire!" He squeezed Solaris's sheath. "But I'm not supposed to tell just anyone."

"If you want to keep traveling with us, we need to know. I'm not going to tell anyone, if that's what you're afraid of." Merlin leaned her head against the tree.

"Neither will I." Gwen agreed, sticking two claws into the wood. She started dragging them down the wall. "You can trust us."

He raised an eyebrow speculatively. "I don't mean to be offensive, but the two of you have demonstrated your willingness to leave me behind several times over. As well as your disregard for my own personal safety."

Merlin's eyebrows rose. "That's not true. Sure we might leave you behind, but when you wanted to run off, I told you it was too dangerous, out of concern for *your* safety. I even went after you to make sure you were not being attacked."

"She's got a point."

Be quiet. I know that.

Lance sighed, rubbing the sides of his forehead while he considered. The three of them had been through a lot, but was it enough to trust them with this? Originally, he had been willing to tell them, but that was under the assumption that Merlin would come with him to Norestere. What would he do if they reached the pass, and she refused? Someone would be wandering around with the knowledge of his power, in an enemy kingdom, no less. Still, she was telling the truth about following him. Maybe not as quickly as he or the young boy would have liked, but she still came. Despite her prickly words, she did care.

"Lance," Merlin spoke gently, prompting him to look up at her. Her expression was softer than any look he had seen on her face, a stark contrast to the glare she normally wore. "I promise not to tell your power to anyone whom you haven't given me permission to tell it to."

His eyes widened and his mouth cracked open. Even Gwen looked surprised, an ear even flattened horizontally. Elves can never break their promises; that was what she said before. Yet here she was, making a promise to him anyway. Merlin continued to silently stare at him, her golden eyes saying more of her determination than her words communicated.

Here was a promise he could trust. All those reminders never to believe someone hadn't included an elvish promise. Merlin might be the one person whose words he could actually have faith in. He knew she would not have promised if she hadn't meant it. After taking a deep breath, Lancelot released the air slowly.

His shoulders dropped as he made up his mind, silently apologizing to his father and brother. Hopefully they would understand. If not, well, it would be too late by then. "I'll tell you, but Gwen, I need you to promise me the same."

The cat stopped clawing at the hollow, her demeanor shifting into seriousness. "My promise won't be as convincing as Merlin's, but you can rest easy knowing that I will keep this from spreading to unwanted ears."

He nodded, accepting the cat's words. "All right. Then first you should know that the fire wasn't mine. It came from Solaris."

"The sword?" Merlin peered at the sheathed weapon.

"Hey! That's my secret!"

"Yes." Lance patted the handle. "I'm not sure why, but as soon as Jack sold it to me, I started to hear its voice in my head. I was ignoring it before, but when Ardene tried to kill us, it got louder."

"It has a voice?"

"Yes," he nodded. "I promise I'm not crazy. When I was using the fire, it guided me as to how to use the power. It helped me."

"Lance, I would have preferred you ask me before telling her."

"Sorry, one moment Merlin." Lance sighed, glaring down at the sword. If he couldn't stay focused she would think he was crazy. "Telling them about my power means explaining about you."

"Still, I should have a say in what gets said about me. You may be the one swinging this blade, but we're partners now."

"I was partners with Merlin first," He stopped, flicking his eyes towards Merlin. Her face was looking more shocked by the second. "Gah!" He waved a hand. "It's the sword Merlin. I can't prove it to you, but I promise it speaks."

"I believe you." Gwen offered, poking her head towards Solaris with more interest. "It looks strange enough to talk."

CHAPTER 14

Merlin shook her head, blinking. "I believe you too. It took me a moment, that's all. Keep going."

A relieved smile pulled across his face, but before he continued, he asked Solaris, *Can I continue?*

"Yes, but I have more to tell you later."

Thank you.

Out loud he said, "Even though the flames came from the sword, I was the one controlling them. Which brings me to my own power. I..." He hesitated, then tried again. "I can copy any power or skill I come across."

The two of them gave him surprised looks, but Merlin was the one who spoke. "So, like a mirror?"

"Sort of." He nodded. "But seeing them doesn't mean I can use their gift. You asked what my signet is, well, it's not normal. I was born with a mark on my back that allows me to access my power at all times. All I have to do is touch your ribbon, and I can use your gift."

Gwen tilted her head. "Ribbon?"

"Everyone has a shiny ribbon that hangs from between your shoulders on your back." Lance told them. "Normally I try to forget their presence, but I always see them. They come to me when I reach for them." It was actually the reason he bought Solaris in the first place, as the sword had one of the pearlescent ribbons attached to it.

"So you can copy *any* Rideon gift?" Merlin sounded awed, which was exactly what he did not want.

"Yes. I haven't found one I was unable to mimic, but as I said before, I'm not limited to a Rideon gift. I can copy skills as well." Lance ran a hand through his hair, which proved difficult in the tight space. "If I was fighting someone more skilled with a sword than I, simply touching their ribbon would let me gain their skill for myself."

"How long does it last?" she inquired.

"About a day, unless I decide to willingly release it."

"Isn't there danger in taking a power you don't understand?" The cat looked genuinely concerned.

"No." He flicked a bug off his shoulder. "I understand everything about the power when I use it. It only becomes dangerous should I be overwhelmed by it, which is what happened with Solaris."

"*Wrong.*" Lance jumped. The sword had been so quiet, he had forgotten it was there.

What do you mean?

"*Yes, you were overwhelmed, but I did that on purpose. It was the only way to acclimate your body to the intense heat of my power. If I hadn't, you would still have been able to use me, but it wouldn't have been very safe for your friends.*"

Oh, well, thank you.

"*You're welcome.*"

Lancelot looked back at Merlin and Gwen, who were both sitting quietly. He couldn't bring himself to break their silence, but he also wanted to hear their thoughts. His power made him one of the strongest elestiels in all the land. It was a miracle that he had been able to escape Avalon with the number of eyes watching him. Would this revelation make them wary of his presence in the forest, or would they expect him to fight single handedly for them? He dreaded that over all other options.

"What's wrong?" The knight flinched as Merlin spoke. She was looking at him like there was something on his face.

"Nothing, why?"

Merlin tilted her head. "You know we won't say anything."

"Yes, I know." Lance averted his eyes once more. "I was merely wondering what your reactions would be."

Gwen snorted from her spot on the ground. The cat *had* paused in her scraping of the tree, but now she returned her claws to the wood. "You have a powerful gift. Elohim was generous with you." With the noise from her claws she sounded somewhat harsher, emphasizing some of her words by splitting the trunk's walls into tiny cracks.

"It's true." Merlin leaned back against the wall and set her gaze upon him. "There have been people in history like me, none so gifted, but close enough. With you, there hasn't been anyone equal."

He let that sink in as far as it would. Though she meant it as a simple compliment, he knew just how true her statement actually was. Her point was more of a fact than a benefit. Facts were not inherently bad, but the impact this fact had on his life was more than a detriment.

If anything, it was an aggressive and active roadblock delighting in the suffering it caused him.

Merlin shifted in front of him, making the space they sat in feel even more cramped. "I do have a question," she asked as he and Gwen readjusted according to her position. "Why is your power a secret?"

Why, she asks?

His power was secret because his family had insisted that it was safer. His power was secret because he was far *too* powerful. His power was secret because he didn't want people to look at him like he was some kind of tool... some kind of weapon.

"I keep it a secret for my family." Lance told her. "My kingdom holds power above anything else, and if a knight was blatantly more powerful than our current king..." He shook his head.

"I see."

Lancelot rested his head against the tree. He couldn't say it out loud, but he could think it at least. *You don't see, not really, but thank you for trying.*

⚜ ⚜ ⚜

The next day they woke up early, cramped, but ready to carry on heading up the Mason Line. Mist covered the inside of the forest as they traveled, holding onto the murky weather for the days that followed. The farther they walked, the colder the mornings became. Chills had even begun slipping into the latter parts of the days, which affected the forest visibly, thinning its trunks. Lancelot's thoughts were on this as he pulled his cloak tighter around him. Despite it being the late morning, there was a chill blowing between the trees, and a heavy smell of moisture clung to the air. Above the treetops the sky was probably covered in clouds preparing for rain, which made the inside of the forest darker, and the moss over the trees brighter.

The dreary atmosphere made Lance miss Avalon, its green valleys and hills, the tall mountains with snow tipped peaks. He also missed the river Kogen, which ran across the northeast corner of his home. There were parts of the river deep enough for trade ships to sail in, but the area that ran by his home was known for the colored stones that lined the banks. The king even proclaimed it as a national reserve to discourage the theft of the shining rocks.

"You're a lot more sentimental than I first realized, Lance."

The knight sighed, raising his hood so he could see forward. *Do you read all my thoughts? Because I will sell you without a moment's consideration if my privacy is gone.*

"Calm down." Solaris soothed. *"I can read both your thoughts and memories, yes, but if you get annoyed I can always return to the sword for moments when you need to be alone."*

Perfect, then in that case...

"Hang on, I need to talk to you. I told you before that I would need to explain."

Lance glanced over his shoulder at Merlin and Gwen. They were quietly having a conversation, so it would be fine for him to have his own. *Very well, explain what you would like.*

"Thank you. You're so considerate." The sword cleared its voice loudly before continuing. *"Now, I know you think I'm an imbued item, but I am not. I'm much more interesting than that book in your bag."*

If craving blood is interesting, I guess you're right.

"I don't crave blood. That's a superstition that my owner before the last owner before the last owner came up with so that my owner before last would buy me."

Lance's stride halted for a moment as he tried to wrap his mind around the sentence. *You might have to repeat that to me.*

"Forget it. Just know it's a superstition. I've seen my fair share of death. I'm in a sword for goodness sake! But honestly, to insinuate that I crave blood... goodness. A sword is an object, the person swinging it is the one who wants to kill everyone."

Are you done? Because if you're just ranting, I'd like my mind back.

"Fine, the point is, I'm not a haunted sword. In fact, I'm not really a sword at all. The weapon is more like a room I've been stuck in. Does that make sense?"

I'm not uneducated, Solaris.

"No, but you are about to hit that tree."

Lance yelped as he swung himself around the tree trunk just in time. The knight glared at the sword hilt. *Thanks for the warning,* he thought sarcastically.

CHAPTER 14

"*You're welcome.*" The sword hummed for a moment as the knight adjusted his direction. Merlin gave him a strange look as she passed by, but Lance tried to ignore it. She didn't have a voice talking in her head at all times.

So if you're not a talking sword, what are you?

"*I am a phoenix.*"

Lance gaped at the weapon. *But those don't exist.*

"*Of course we do.*" Solaris snapped. "*There were many of us, all living on an island far from the mainland. If we had been left alone, that's where I would be now. Spending time with my wife, instead of being stuck inside this sword.*"

Lance frowned. *Explain.*

"*Twenty-three years ago, a group of elestiels found our island and hunted down all of my kin. We should have been able to stop them, but they came at night when our powers are weakest. I was attacking the first owner of this sword when he cut me down. I thought I was dead until I woke up inside it, with him dead and me stuck.*"

Lance clenched his fists tightly. Everyone knew that the last major massacre had been a hundred and sixty years ago, when the elestiels of that time rose up with the humans to kill the myths living among them. They feared the combined power of the creatures and sought to stop a possible uprising. It was a black spot on the history of their world. To think that another slaughter happened after that... Lance gritted his teeth.

Do you know which kingdom the humans were from? Are you sure they were elestiels?

"*All humans look the same to me, but I do know there were many elestiels. I saw one stab a sword straight through my wife's heart, and another took a life from each of my sons.*"

Lancelot stopped in his tracks. He could feel a steely anger emanating from the sword, but for his own part, he felt dismay. *I'm sorry.*

"*I am as well. A phoenix can only die three times before we are gone completely, and even then, when we die, our lives start over. I will never get to see my family again, not as they were.*"

The air around the knight grew colder for a moment, the trees rustling from a brush of wind. Lance winced. A dark suspicion crept into his gut, spurring him to ask, *You really don't know who was responsible?*

"I saw him, but I don't know who he was. Though I could recognize him, I'm sure he's changed much in the time I've been trapped. His sword would be easier to remember. It reeked of the Abba, though its power was twisted."

Lance started forward again, moving away from the trees and back towards Merlin and Gwen. The two had left him behind, but they weren't so far that he lost them completely. He could tell that Merlin was looking back at him, though his mind—while slightly pleased—only just noted it. A new string of questions sprung up from what Solaris said, and Lance intended to ask them all. *What is the Abba, Solaris? I haven't heard of it before.*

"Really Lancelot, with all the training you went through, how is it that you know so little of the myths and our culture?"

If you went through my memories then you would know that the Avalonian records have very little information on Sher. They were burnt up twenty years ago, and as far as anyone else knows, phoenixes don't exist!

"Fine, fine. You call Elohim's power the Rideon, we know it as the Abba. I assume that makes sense to you?"

Lance rolled his eyes. *Yes, Solaris. It makes sense.*

"Don't be mad at me. You're the one asking silly questions."

Well I have another, so try not to be too annoyed. I want to know why they were attacking you. Do you know?

"If I knew that, I would have told you already. One day I will find the man responsible, I'll force him to explain his actions, and then I will claw his eyes out myself. Only then will I be satisfied to search for my people."

There's that bloodlust...

The sword hummed with annoyance. "It's my duty to avenge them. You would do the same if your friends and family were killed in front of your eyes."

CHAPTER 14

Maybe, but can I tell Merlin and Gwen about this? We might be able to find some way to get you out of the sword. The book I have could give us an answer.

"If you would like, but I don't really trust them. The cat has a shifty look about her. I almost expect her to claw you in your sleep."

Lancelot started laughing at this and quickened his walking so as to catch up with the others. *While I appreciate the concern, Gwen couldn't do anything to me if she tried. Which she won't.*

"Then tell them if you want."

He did want to, and did so when he caught up with the two. They had walked much farther ahead of him than he had realized before, but it didn't stop him from relating most of what Solaris said. As he explained, their expressions turned darker, matching the shades of the forest.

Guinevere hissed when he finished. "Sounds like it was a small faction of elestiels, not another group from the kingdoms."

"That's what I was thinking." Lance nodded, gently stepping over what looked like a red daisy. Despite the path being made up of stones, flowers were haphazardly growing along the sides and between the cracks. "I think the book might be able to help get Solaris out of the sword, but I'm not sure where to begin looking for the people responsible."

"If a group of elestiels did this, they were probably doing it under someone's orders. Someone *powerful*." Merlin observed, also stepping over the flower. "It could be really dangerous to try and avenge his family, not to mention getting anyone who's helping him killed. I don't know about you, but I have somewhere I'm supposed to be. Not that I don't want to help him."

"*Hmph. I'm sure she's just saying that.*"

Lance ignored the angry comment from the sword. "I feel the same. The next time we stop I'll ask the book. Maybe there's someone better suited to help." The knight looked down at the sword fondly. It hadn't been with him for very long, but it was a fine weapon. The blade was carefully crafted, well balanced, and granted him access to a gift at all times. Trying to find a different weapon that compared to Solaris would be difficult.

"Uh, excuse me, I don't want to be sold. I'm pretty sure your power is what lets me see out of the sword, and I don't want to lose that."

Lance sighed. *But I can't stop my mission to help you.*

"For now, that's fine."

The knight sighed and looked up to his companions. "It seems that he would prefer to stay with me."

Merlin raised an eyebrow. "Really?"

"It may surprise you," Lance said in some annoyance. "But I'm actually an agreeable person."

"Hmm," She glanced up and down at him. "It does surprise me."

He shook his head. "I don't know why I bother talking to you."

"I don't either." She grinned.

"Ha!" Solaris crooned. *"This is great. You definitely can't sell me, I'd miss this entertainment."*

Oh, be quiet.

"If you two are done, can we get moving?" Gwen hopped from her perch on a thick tree root. "We've finally made it to the Hall of Untamed Moss."

Lance blinked. "What?"

Merlin patted the root Gwen had been sitting on. "It's a very old stretch of trees that has been standing since before Sher was formed. It's just around this bend." She pointed back to the path, which remained straight for six feet and then turned abruptly to the right. The trees around the bend were the same width as the rest, but Lance could tell that it was denser than the forest behind them. He tilted his head to the left, and glanced at Merlin.

"Will there be more people in the hall?" he asked.

"I don't think so." She held out her palm, possibly feeling the weight of condensation in the air. "It's too cold, and I believe it will rain later. It's not good weather for traveling."

"Then we best get moving." Gwen called, already at the bend of the path. "You two are going to want to see this."

The two elestiels gave each other a look before heading after the cat. When they turned the bend, Lancelot understood why the cat seemed

CHAPTER 14

so impatient. It was like taking a step into a whole new forest of bright greens and yellows. Every tree was covered in a thick layer of moss that extended from the ground to the top of the dark trees. Above, the branches reached out over the path to create a ceiling of leaves and hanging ferns. On the ground mixed in with the grass and moss were many red and pink flowers that sprouted in untainted growth with full petals and color. Even with the sky preparing for a storm, the hall was coated in yellow shades of sunlight, only minutely darkened by the brewing rain.

"That's quite a sight." Solaris observed.

"Yes it is." Lance muttered.

Merlin stepped past him and bent down by a patch of flowers. "Moss-rose; its leaves are good for burns and other skin related injuries. I wish I could pick some. I'd like to take some of the moss as well. I've heard it heals in a similar manner to my gift..." She looked up wistfully at the trees.

Gwen sauntered past Merlin, bouncing as she walked. "We're already criminals, what's another felony? No one's going to know."

Merlin glared at the cat. "I'll know."

Lancelot heaved his pack up farther on his shoulders, marching into the hallway. "Amazing, you have honor towards plants."

"Don't judge." Lance looked back to Merlin in time to see her stand and scowl. "You're the knight who broke his own kingdom's laws in order to find me. Who has more honor for their kingdom? Me, or you?"

Lance narrowed his eyes. "My honor is not endangered by entering Sher. I have a duty to protect my kingdom, and I will do whatever I must to accomplish that."

"That's one way of looking at it."

Guinevere popped up by Lance's leg and tilted her head to the left. "Breaking the law doesn't seem very honorable in any situation, no matter the reason behind it."

"Well—" His words were left unfinished as the sound of loud footsteps began marching through the woods.

15

Robin

M

"It's a patrol!" Gwen growled, darting off the path and into the forest. Merlin withheld a sigh and grabbed Lance's arm, dragging him to the nearest tree. The knight offered no resistance, following her hastily to the hiding spot. They could all view the path from there, but those on it could not say the same. A squirrel skittered across the road as the origin of the noise came into sight. Right away, Merlin saw that it was not a patrol. Six ivirians marched alongside a horse, swords hanging from the sides of their long tunics, wings bouncing gently. Merlin spat on the ground when she saw the rider's outfit.

White wool robes were draped across his shoulders and down his back, concealing any wings of his in folds falling past his feet. His other clothes were the same milky color, except for the dark gloves protecting his fingers from any blistering caused by the reins. A hood with a specially designed front covered the rider's head, forming a point past his nose which allowed only his mouth to be seen. If there was any doubt as to his identity, a gold chain hung around his neck, displaying a circular medallion with leaves engraved at its center. He didn't have his wagon with him, which meant he had already collected the day's taxes, and had his cut stuffed within the folds of his robes.

"Who is that?" Lance whispered.

"A tax collector," Merlin grimaced. "The one official everybody hates. They wear that hood to hide themselves because it makes it harder for landowners to identify the one responsible for over-taxing them." Lance frowned, keeping quiet while they watched the party progress. Merlin shivered as the collector tilted his head, looking to the left. Her father once told her that their presence was the price of freedom, but surely there was a better system to fund the government.

One that didn't include a specific person taking more than they ought whenever the guards with them weren't looking.

As they watched, a bird began hooting in the distance, a sound kind of like a twisted cuckoo. Merlin narrowed her eyes. She knew that sound; she was sure of it. Her attention shifted to the trees as a whizzing sound broke the forest's silence. One of the ivirians gasped in pain as the arrow collided with his chest, knocking him to the ground. Shouts began flowing from the group of ivirians, the horse rearing up from shock.

Two more arrows shot through the air in glorious arches, one landing in a guard and the other embedding itself in the farthest ivirian. The arrows were spot on, their precision killing both in one salvo. The collector's horse reared upward again, this time throwing its rider off the saddle before bolting away. The rest of the guards surrounded the fallen figure as another two arrows flew at them from the forest. One hit its mark, driving its point into the heart of the ivirian, while the other rammed into a solid wall of dirt that lifted up from the ground.

Lancelot started forward, but Merlin put a restraining hand on his arm. It was becoming a common occurrence between them. "We can't get involved. They'll arrest us without a second thought." He looked like he wanted to fight, glancing at the ambush again. For a scary moment she thought she would have to hold him back, but instead he nodded, returning to his spot beside her.

"If you say so."

Merlin blinked. He actually listened to her?

Another shout drew her back to the fight. The archer must have found a way to move through the trees, because now the arrows were coming from all directions, shot precisely through open cracks in their defense. Soon, all the guards were down, leaving the tax collector by himself, hands raised and trembling.

"P-please! Just take my money!" he yelled, cringing with every creak that came from the forest. Merlin watched the collector grow steadily more terrified as no answer came from the woods. Where was the archer?

A slight snap came from the forest, and then, "If you insist!" called the archer.

Merlin's eyes widened as the familiar, cocky male voice came from above. Her head snapped up to see him as the unmistakable sound of taut string was released. The tax collector whimpered loudly as an arrow sank into his chest.

Steps sounded from the tree to their right as she stood up, catching a glimpse of someone jumping off the branch. Her eyes followed the motion to the path, where the archer landed in a squat. From where she stood, she could see part of his face, more specifically, the wide smirk.

The rest of his face was covered by a hood that matched the collector's in every aspect besides color, his being a deep green. His sleeveless tunic stretched to his knees, and tall leather boots were laced up his calves. The vambraces on his arms were also leather, but ran long to protect the undershirt's sleeve from the bow string. A full quiver hung at his hip, and his bow swung crookedly from its sling across his shoulders. The weapon was made of a sandy wood, with little notches carved in lines originating from the grip.

It was definitely him.

Merlin turned to look at the knight, who was inspecting the person with a look of mild disdain. "That's Robin."

His face crinkled in disbelief. "Him?" The knight leaned out to look at Robin again. The thief had moved to the tax collector and was fiddling around with the robes.

"Yes, him." Merlin answered, rolling her eyes. "Jack already said he was a thief."

"A crook, if we're being exact." Lance squared his shoulders, stepping out from behind the tree. "But if you say he's a friend..."

"Wait!" Merlin was almost too late as she pulled Lance back. Any later and the arrow would have gone straight into *him* instead of the forest behind them.

"Thanks," he said, moving back behind their tree.

From the path Robin's jeering voice called out, "Well, well, what do we have here? Who hides behind a tree like a coward?"

Merlin sighed, taking a small step out from the tree. Lancelot reached out to stop her, but she waved him off. "Robin, it's Merlin, the coward behind the tree." The sarcasm was only intensified by the extra volume she used to get the words over to him. Inhaling, she took another slow step, that one movement taking her into the open. Robin was still by the tax collector, but he had one knee down with his bow drawn back to its full extent.

If he shoots me, Daleon is going to kill him.

"Don't shoot, it's me."

For a moment he knelt there, arrow pointed at her heart. Then he lowered the bow. A grin spread from one side of his face to the other. Robin stood. "Merlin! What are you doing here?"

Instead of answering, Merlin hurried forward, spanning the distance in a few moments. "Hugging!" she announced, pulling the archer into a large embrace. How many months had it been since she'd seen him—seven, eight? Regardless, she squeezed him tightly. In the wake of her home's destruction, her old friend felt safe and familiar. The emotions welled up inside her, stronger than she realized they could be.

Oblivious to her thoughts, Robin laughed. Wrapping his arms around her, he said, "Well then, maybe I should stay away more, if this is the reception I get!"

Merlin pulled back, scoffing slightly. "Don't be cocky, this is a one-time thing."

He grinned. "We'll see. Now, who is that?" Robin pointed, Merlin's eyes following his direction. Lancelot came out of the forest, Guinevere by his feet. The knight was looking skeptically at them, or more specifically, at Robin.

"That's Lance, my traveling partner. He's a knight from Avalon." Merlin told him. "Gwen's here, too."

"Hello." the knight said, walking tentatively over to them.

"Traveling partner?" Robin frowned. "Don't tell me I've been replaced?"

Merlin withheld rolling her eyes, but the cat simply snickered for her. "Nothing for you to be replaced in, Rob." Guinevere marched up to him, tilting her whole body at an angle to peer up at him. "Where's my dinner? Did he fly away?"

"*Pico* did not fly away." The thief frowned. "He'll be back in a moment, and no, you still can't eat him!"

"Hmph!" Gwen turned up her nose and strolled off.

"Anyway," Merlin took a step back. "We were on our way to find you in Loxley, but I guess we would have missed you."

"No, I'm on my way there now." Robin told her, bending down to the tax collector's body. He felt along his arm until he found the man's face, and carefully closed his eyes. Then he gingerly reached into the man's robes. "I stopped for this." Robin pulled a large leather bag from the body and shook it. The contents made clinking sounds, identifying themselves as coins.

"You're robbing him after you killed him?" Lancelot sounded disapproving, maybe even disgusted.

Merlin turned and glared, but Robin responded in a jovial manner. "You're right, I should leave it here for the body, because he needs it *much* more than I do."

The knight's mouth curled into a frown like he'd tasted something sour. "Your name is Robin, you wouldn't happen to be Robin Hood, would you?"

Robin bowed, raising the bag of money with his hands. "My reputation precedes me even in Avalon. That's wonderful."

Merlin shook her head as Lance continued to frown. "I thought as much. Our kingdom has to constantly deny affiliation with you. Now I see why Sher hates you so much."

"Well I wouldn't be doing my job properly if they liked me."

"Perhaps you should look for another occupation."

Robin flashed a grin. "I think I'm suited for this one, thank you."

Lance grimaced, but here Merlin stepped in. "That's enough from both of you." She frowned at the knight, who returned her expression with indignation. "We're in need of your help, Robin."

"I assumed as much," he turned in response to her voice. "Though, in general I am great company. As for why you need me, I have yet to guess."

"I'll explain," Merlin glanced down at the fallen tax collector. "But this isn't the place."

"Hm," He fingered the bag of money. "In that case, we'll head to my camp and talk there. But Pico's the one who knows the way, so we'll have to wait for him."

Merlin winced. "Pico...?"

CHAPTER 15

"Mhm." Above them, a loud bang sounded from the sky, blowing a chilly wind from the east. Merlin shivered as a single large drop of rain splashed against her forehead.

"Great." she muttered, pulling her hood farther on her head. Lance did the same with his hood, casting worried looks up at the roof of trees. Bits of deep blue clouds were all that could be seen of the sky above the leaves.

"I suppose that means it's going to storm," Robin mused. "It has smelled like rain all day."

Merlin nodded, then face palmed. *Nod to the one guy who can't see it, wonderful.* She fixed her mistake quickly, voicing her agreement as a flapping sound came from the sky. The noise snapped Merlin's attention up to the trees as another loud crack of thunder erupted from the sky. Leaves fluttered down from the branches at the same time as a deranged, screaming bird crashed through the canopy.

"Ack!" Merlin gasped as it collided into her, sending her stumbling backwards. The force was enough to knock her into Lance, who in turn stumbled back into Guinevere, who was standing conveniently behind him. They all fell into a tangled mess of wings, legs, and arms on the path, just missing the thief, who had an amused smirk on his face.

"I feel as though I just missed something hilarious," he observed.

"Sands, Pico!" Merlin growled, pushing the owl off her.

The bird chirped and fluttered away, careening from left to right until he hit the ground. "Robin, Robin! I saw those guys!" Pico's voice was just as crazy sounding as the last time Merlin heard him. The bird's complete unconcern for the two people he had just knocked over was evident as he flapped up to Robin, who stretched out his arm for the owl.

"Uh, Merlin, would you mind getting off me?" asked the knight, whose leg was trapped beneath her.

"Oh," She scrambled up and away from the knight, brushing off the dirt that had collected on the knees of her pants before offering a hand to the knight. He took it, and she pulled him up. Meanwhile, Pico started dancing from leg to leg on Robin's arm, breathlessly speaking at top speed.

"I saw the guys, Robin! Just as you said, just as you said!"

"Looks like he's also the same." Merlin had to agree with the cat, who thankfully managed to avoid the crash. Gwen gazed up from her spot on the ground, watching the owl with hungry eyes.

"That's enough of that!" Robin pulled his arm back while Pico was still jumping, letting the small bird fall straight to the ground. "Calm down."

The brown owl straightened on the stones, twisting its head to peer at the thief. "Sorry."

"That's better." Robin crossed his arms, tilting towards the bird. "Now, you saw the patrol I asked you to find?"

"Well, I don't know about that." Pico poked his beak between two feathers. "But I saw a bunch of the birds with those pointy sticks you showed me. They fly so strangely, but they should be here soon."

Merlin covered her face with a hand. "Ivirians, Pico. Ivirians! They're not birds!"

"All right." Robin nodded to them both. "Pico, please take us back to the camp. That patrol will be on us in no time."

"You're letting him lead?" Lance questioned, looking half panicked at the thought.

"Of course. He might not act like it, but Pico has an excellent sense of direction." The discourse might have continued longer if another crack of thunder hadn't interrupted the two men. Large drops of rain were falling sporadically through the trees, but now the numbers were increasing in speed and amount. All the rain was making the surrounding forest extra cold, and the darkness of the storm didn't add any warmth. Poor Guinevere even had to hide under the bottom of Lance's cloak to avoid the downpour.

The one good thing the water did was startle the bird into following the thief's instructions. He led them off the path into the forest with a loud squawk, weaving between the trees just fast enough to stay in the front, but slow enough not to lose them. They walked for some time. Without the path of stones to follow, they had to trudge through the plants and the mud that coated the ground beneath the moss, and all in the dark. The further they went, the more Merlin was glad that Pico could lead them, as navigating the criss-crossed web of forest would have been extremely difficult. There was one point where they came to a deep dip in the ground with a single root spanning the distance, high enough to cause serious damage should one fall.

It took Merlin a whole minute before her slick boots hit a wet patch of bark and slipped.

Oh, great. Her arms wrapped around the side of the root, water pouring down her sleeves and across her face. She could hear Robin calling out in front of her, but the noise of the rain made it difficult.

"Pico says that we're almost there!" he shouted.

Had Merlin not been hanging onto the branch with all her might, she might have been happy at the news. Alas, with her feet dangling and the bark growing steadily wetter, her view on everything was slowly becoming more desperate.

She began to slip from the tree, prompting her to shout, "A little help?" Merlin tried to push her nails between the cracks in the bark, but all that amounted to was her slipping even farther down the branch. Her breaths came out in quick shallow pants as the bark suddenly gave way, her hands flinging wildly for something to grab. At the last second, she felt something grab her wrist so tightly she nearly cried out from the pain. It felt like her arm was pulling out of her shoulder from the strain of hanging by one limb. Just before it became unbearable, she was hoisted up and onto the root, now thoroughly drenched.

Merlin spat out the rainwater, balancing carefully on the log. Warily, she tested out rotating her shoulder. When it worked, she let out a sigh of relief. "Thank you!" she said loudly, looking gratefully at the crouched knight.

He grinned from under his hood, replying in similar volume. "I'm starting to get tired of saving you!"

An exaggerated eye roll was all the response she gave him, as they were beckoned by the thief to hurry. The rest of the way across was traveled without another slip. Once everyone made it over the root, Pico continued, taking them to the base of a large, mountain-shaped hill. It was too small to be deemed an actual mountain, but it was large enough to have a set of caves sitting at the bottom. The owl took them straight through the middle opening and into a maze of corridors encompassing the inside of the hill.

When they first entered, Merlin thought that they would *literally* be following blind, as caves have little to no light. Thankfully, her worries were groundless. Inside, the rock walls were covered with glittering golden light that swayed with the draft from the cave's mouth. Each gust changed the color from gold to green and green to gold, providing a light only bright enough to walk in.

A closer look provided the origin of the glow. "Dragon's Gold." Merlin muttered, thinking over her mother's lectures concerning the different mosses in Sher. "It should be harmless, as long as we don't eat it."

"Why would we eat it?" Lance asked, pulling up his dripping hood to get a better look.

Guinevere poked her head out from under the cloak, sniffing at the moss closest to her. Merlin pointedly glared at the feline. "I meant her, specifically."

"How dare you." Gwen sprung out from her hiding spot, pouncing on a clump of moss. "I don't eat *plants*."

"Stranger things have been eaten." Merlin retorted, pulling down her own hood. With a scowl she wringed the ends of her hair, watching the water splash against the ground.

"As much as I'd love to hear this continue, we should really keep going." Robin called from a short distance away. Even with the light of the moss, shadows seemed to cling to his arms and legs, outlining the shape of a clenched fist. "These caves aren't empty, and I can't promise that the fungans will appreciate us being here."

Merlin frowned. "There's a colony here?"

"Yes."

"What's a fungan?" Lance asked.

As they started walking again, Merlin explained. "Fungans are tiny creatures that look like mushrooms, except they have legs, arms, and most importantly, a brain. They regularly live in large groups in caves and ravines, sometimes hollowed tree trunks. Usually they're peaceful, but when it comes to larger people invading their homes, they are *extremely* territorial. It would be best to avoid them."

"Which we will." Robin carefully stepped around a jagged rock that had several tiny beetles crawling along the top. "I made sure to set up on the farthest end from their homes, because I'm brilliant. No need to thank me."

Gwen expertly jumped over a pile of rocks, landing with a snort. "No one was planning to."

From the front of the group, Pico hooted excitedly. "Home!" The bird did a quick horizontal loop through the air as they walked into a circular room. A small fire ring was laid out in the middle, with a larger pack thrown to the side and a blanket rolled tightly on top. The wood inside the ring was not lit, but at least it wasn't soaking like the rest of the forest.

Robin walked into the campsite and waved a hand. "Welcome to my current home. Please, make yourselves comfortable, but watch out for the spiders."

Merlin rolled her eyes, pulling out her backpack to fish for her blanket. While she did, Lance came into the room, looking around at it. "How long have you lived here?"

"Two weeks? Maybe three?" Robin set his bow and quiver against the wall, grabbing two small rocks sitting by the bag. "I tend to lose track of time easily."

"This is definitely a step up from your last hole in the ground," Gwen observed. "This place isn't ankle deep in mud, and it has a roof."

"The government doesn't allow non-natives to buy land, my dear Guinevere." Robin placed a flat hand on the ground, feeling the space slowly until he hit one of the ring's stones. Then the thief scooched himself closer, holding up the two rocks and striking them hard. After a few attempts, a spark shot off the rocks and into the wood, a small fire bursting to life. Merlin made sure to lay her blanket close to the flame so she could dry off.

Lancelot set up his own spot opposite from the thief, pulling off his boots and setting them closer to the heat. He sat back on his palms, staring at Robin. "You're blind, aren't you Robin?" The question did not seem to hold any offense, so Merlin kept her mouth shut.

"Mhm." Robin grinned. "And before you ask, no, I wasn't born like this. It happened when I was six? Eight?"

"Seven." Merlin corrected. "How do you always forget that?"

He shrugged. "I don't need to remember, because there's normally *someone* by me who already does. Like you. And who tells a beautiful woman to stop remembering details about you? That's asking for trouble." Merlin glared, while Lance started coughing. Robin picked up a stick and began poking the fire. "I feel like you're glaring at me, but it's hard to tell."

Gwen sprawled on the moss. "She is."

"Well, that's normal." Robin sat back. "Anyway, now that we're safely out of the way of any prying eyes, tell me why you're here."

"All right." Merlin peeled off her cape, laying it on the ground. "I guess this starts when Lance arrived."

"No, just before that." Gwen corrected. "When you got the letter."

Lancelot cleared his throat, setting Solaris at his side. The knight rested a hand on the sword, a concerned look crossing his face. "Are you going to tell him everything?"

Merlin frowned. "If I can't be honest with him, then why should I expect him to be honest with me? Besides, I've known him for a long time. He's trustworthy."

Robin chuckled from his spot. "In the name of honesty, that's really only reserved for my friends. I'm afraid that doesn't include your knight here."

"As long as you know the feeling is mutual, that's good enough." Lance said, shooting a distrustful look at the thief.

After sighing both internally and externally, Merlin began explaining to the thief exactly what happened, starting from the military's refusal, Lance's presence, and ending with finding Robin. She made sure to be as thorough as possible, with the minor exception of things she'd sworn never to speak of. Lancelot looked partially panicked when Merlin was telling the thief of their escape from the weaver, but the worry was wiped away when she said nothing of his power. It would take a lot more than simply explaining things to Robin for her to break her promise, a fact which Merlin hoped the knight would understand.

She did, however, tell Robin of Solaris after receiving permission from the sword. It was difficult to tell the thief's reaction with his hood pulled down, but he was likely surprised. Regardless, Robin asked not a single question throughout her entire explanation, instead listening attentively. The only stop came from Pico, who woke up from his sleeping and cuckooed loudly, asking Merlin what a Jack was before falling back to sleep. Eventually she finished her story, which took long enough that the group was able to make themselves dinner while she spoke.

Merlin set down a slice of apple, watching Robin carefully.

"So that means you're another elestiel." he said, pointing a finger in Lance's direction.

"That is correct," Lance nodded. "I didn't realize there were more of us here beyond Merlin."

"Oh, I'm not one of you guys." Robin grinned. "I'm just a regular human." The thief flipped back his hood so that his face was on full display. His hair, a dark brown, had lengthened since the last time Merlin saw him. The strands were pulled into a short ponytail at the back of his head, tied tightly with a leather string. His skin had taken on a darker tan as well, though it was still a little lighter than Lancelot's. Most importantly, his hazel eyes were staring blankly at the knight.

Robin's grin grew and he winked. "I know, I know, I'm extremely handsome. That's why I wear a hood all the time."

While Merlin didn't completely disagree, she retorted anyways, "How do you know? It's been a while since you've seen yourself."

"That was extremely rude," Robin said in a pained voice. "But I can hardly deny it. I know, because every time I take off my hood, I instantly get twice as much attention, and my companions get none. Several of them have complained that I should be uglier so as to avoid being caught."

"I think they may have exaggerated." Merlin crossed her arms. "Moving on, I was hoping you could get us to the border. Secretly, if possible. Lance and I will go our separate ways after that."

"Not necessarily," Lance interjected. "Remember our agreement."

"Yes, I remember." Merlin pursed her lips, a pang of guilt shooting through her. The agreement had simply been that she would keep an open mind about continuing with him. Surely he had already realized that her opinions were unchanged? Even if she was inclined to stay on friendly terms with him, that didn't mean she was going to give up joining her brother just to travel around with the knight. Still, she did agree to his demands when he made them, so starting an argument to get out of it would help nothing.

"Listen, Merlin, now is not a good time to be near the border." Contrary to his usual attitude, Robin gave her a somber frown. "I was sent word from Yon that the Avalonians are mounting another strike against Logres. It's supposed to happen tomorrow. Who knows how long it will last, and when it does finish, the surrounding area is going to be in disarray. All the ivirians in the vicinity will likely be called to Akiva."

Of all the times for an attack, why did Avalon have to choose right then? Merlin squeezed her fist tightly, directing her anger toward the fire. It was not as if she wanted to stay at the border for very long. All she needed was to get across it and the pass to reach the other side.

"How did you find this out?" Lance's eyes widened, catching the firelight in his golden irises.

"I have contacts." Robin crossed his arms, directing his face in Merlin's direction. "I'm sorry about your house, but I think you should go back to your parents. It's safer and won't end with you in a dungeon."

"I came to you so I wouldn't get caught." Merlin's heart started to beat faster with every word. "There's no going back for me. I have to join the military. I'm dead if I don't."

"No, you're arrested for sneaking into a military post and impersonating a soldier!" Robin snapped sharply. "I can't escort you into danger like that. I won't. Your brother would never forgive me."

"I'll go with or without your help," Merlin insisted. "There isn't anything you can do to stop me, so please make this easier and get me past the border."

"I refuse."

Merlin gritted her teeth, breathing deeply. Getting to her brother would instantly become ten times harder without Robin's assistance. She needed him on her side if she was going to get to Daleon. Not only that, how could he think she would get caught so easily? There was more to her than just being a guide or a healer.

"I'm not weak anymore." she asserted, trying so hard not to be harsh that her voice wobbled from the effort. "You don't have to protect me like you used to, neither does Daleon. This is what I want to do. Can't you support me in this?" She stared at him intensely, knowing that his eyes couldn't see anything more than the faintest smudge of her figure.

"She won't be alone." From the side, Gwen popped up from her lounged position. The cat inspected Robin with her wide green eyes. "I'll be with her, and when we find Dal, he'll be with her."

Robin shook his head. "No, no I still won't."

CHAPTER 15

"Perhaps you could ask the book?" Merlin broke off her silent pleading to look at the knight. He seemed pensive, holding up the book with a frown. "If it says you shouldn't help us, then don't."

"This is the question book, right? How exactly am I supposed to trust *your* book's answer?" Robin asked. "It could just say what you want it to."

Lance smirked crookedly, brushing aside his hair while he sat the book down in front of Robin, avoiding the fire. "Frankly, I hope you don't join us. So even if it is rigged, you would get the answer you want. It's a win for both of us, don't you think?"

Merlin glared daggers at Lance. She knew that he had no control over the book, but what if it gave Robin the excuse he needed to not help her? Begging wasn't her most favorable option, but it at least was sure to only work in her favor, unlike the book. Was Lance doing this to get rid of Robin?

"How does it work?"

"You don't have to do this." Merlin told him. "Can't you just help us without it?"

"Ask the book your question once you've opened it. Then it will respond." Gwen explained. "It's in front of you."

Robin nodded, patting the ground until he came upon the book. Merlin felt her throat dry as he gently flipped open the cover. They all silenced as Robin sat in front of the blank pages. The only sound came from the sleeping owl and the crackling fire. Merlin's breath caught in her throat.

"Well," Robin started. "Should I help Merlin get into the pass?" The page blurred, scrawled words forming on the cream-colored pages.

Merlin moved closer to Robin, squinting at the dimly lit pages. *Not only should you help her, you should go with them too. It will be very good for you, trust me.*

"Ha!" A smile broke out on Merlin's lips. She read aloud the words for both Robin and Lance. The two men each wore similar expressions of annoyance as she finished.

"It never gives me extra information." Lance grumbled. "Why would it give him more?"

"At least that settles it." Gwen nodded.

"And why should I go with them? Tell me that, book." Robin's voice was steady, but Merlin could hear an underlying current of suspicion. Her eyes set back on the changing book, waiting for its answer. When it finally came, she stared at it in surprise, eyebrows raising.

On the page it said; *Because finding something is easier when one has a guide that knows the way. Go with them, it will be worth it.*

16

A Rhythm Lost

J

Thick shackles of iron were the only tether keeping the leprechaun upright as he leaned against a tree. The chains were unnaturally sunken into the bark-covered wood, high enough that his arms had no choice but to hang from his hands. The skin beneath the iron was ripped and raw with pain, but thankfully the rest of his body was mostly unharmed. The ivirians seemed unwilling to injure him, so instead they were lugging Jack across the forest as they tracked the runaways. Despite the absence of torture, he grew more distressed with each passing day. The missing weight around his neck was far heavier than the pendant itself had ever been. If he had only put it back in its box all those days ago, none of this would have happened. Jack shivered despite himself, causing his wrists to scream in pain again.

The entire suppression squad was huddled beneath a grouping of trees that the ivirian, Bristol, and Graser, the big one, had manipulated into a domed roof. Outside the ring of trees, rain poured without pause, beating against the ground in loud rhythmic taps. Even without standing in the midst of the water, it was freezing beneath the trees.

One of the soldiers, an iviro with long pale blonde hair and lavender skin, stomped his foot against the ground. His two wings, each shaped similarly to a dragonfly, fluttered in response to his annoyance.

"This is ridiculous." he spoke angrily. "We've had them in our sights for so long, and yet we have done nothing. Now the rain has drowned the sound of their footsteps. We've lost them!"

The captain of the squad sat silently by the base of the trees, sharpening a dagger with a small rock. Bristol stood next to her, and beside him was an ivirian whose skin was paler than a summer cloud. She took a step forward, waving her hands in a placating gesture. "Claeo, the Sheriff said to wait. We'll find them again once the rain stops."

"That could take weeks!" Claeo turned around briskly, the long drapes of his kirsco fanning out as he stomped over to Brull. "If you would do something about this deluge—"

"I hardly think that's necessary." Brull glared at Claeo.

"Yes, Brull is right." Another ivirian agreed. She was sitting closer to Jack than the rest of them, and her voice was soft and dainty. "We are not supposed to catch them yet, and besides, the rain is not for us to control."

"Am I the only one who finds this suspicious?" Claeo shook his head. "If Rainault wanted them captured, he would let us grab them now. We could easily overtake them. There would be no escape!"

At that, Jack let out a laugh which caught their attention. Several of them leered in his direction, but he ignored them entirely. "Oh don't mind me, I agree. He's playing you fools like a fiddle."

Claeo shook his head. "See, even the prisoner knows this is wrong!"

Bristol crossed his arms. "He'll agree with anything in his favor."

Jack rolled his eyes, wincing as his wrists rubbed against metal. "Or maybe I'm just smarter than all of you." Then again, maybe he wasn't.

The lavender ivirian plopped down by the opening of their refuge. "Regardless, I see no reason to carry on this foolishness."

A loud scrape came from the captain's knife, drawing the soldiers' attention to her. Koa lowered her knife, swinging its handle into her palm by the hilt. "That is not for you to decide, Claeo." Her voice was stern and cold as she spoke. "Whether it be foolish to your eyes or sense to the others, it does not matter. We *will* obey our orders."

Jack silently inspected the ivirians as she spoke, watching the ease it gave some, but also the jaws that clenched. He could see in Bristol a small spark of the unease which had consumed Claeo. Or rather, he saw the good sense that had donned upon the soldier. If only they could see that Rainault was lying, then maybe Merlin would be safe. She and the ignorant knight were probably unaware they were being followed, and even if Gwen noticed, he doubted it would be in time to save them.

The angry soldier hit his fist against the ground suddenly. "I will obey what is right! How can you ask us to swallow this when we all know this is wrong?" Cleao prodded each of the soldiers with a hard stare. Many averted their eyes. The healer, however, did not look down. Brull stood straight and marched over to Cleao. The younger ivirian gave him an indignant expression, which was wiped away the moment Brull drew his sword. The curved blade found itself under Cleao's neck in a flash of speed Jack had not seen Brull use before. The rest of the soldiers all sprang to their feet—except Koa—several reaching for their own swords.

"You speak mutiny, Cleao." Brull growled darkly. Jack could see the younger ivirian sneering at Brull, but he didn't attempt to move or even use his gift. It could have been the weapon against him, but Jack could see that several of the other ivirians were hesitant to make a move as well. Detached but observant, he noted with some interest that the ivirians with only two wings—like Cleao—were holding back from drawing their swords.

So they were very aware of the power difference, then. Four dragonfly wings could beat two, but bat-like wings could defeat them all. Yes, that was it. Jack saw Cleao's eye go from the weapon to Brull's four shimmering wings of olive green.

"My words have enraged even you?" Cleao growled. "Does that not show us all that there is something wrong?"

"That's enough!" Brull turned his head, letting Jack see the tight anger in his eyes. "Captain, what is your opinion?"

The scrapes of Koa's second knife against the rock stopped. Between the soldiers a heavy sense of precarious silence hovered. They seemed to be tilting towards a fight, but her presence was holding them back. The captain stood, sheathing the knife with a small thump. "My opinion is in accordance with the law, and you all are currently not. Lower your swords before I arrest every one of you."

The sound of four swords being sheathed fought against the pattering rain. Brull pulled his sword away from Cleao with the air of someone itching to use it, sheathing the weapon with a loud snap. "As you wish." Brull stalked back to his prior position.

"That was interesting." Jack muttered.

"Hardly."

He jumped, which made the shackle cut through his left wrist. Blood trickled down his arm slowly, while the captain gave him a look of pure ice. She had no sympathy for the pain her voice had caused him.

"Captain!" Cleao scrambled to his feet. "Surely you hear the sense of my words!"

"I hear complaining." Koa crossed her arms. "And I hear treason. It is not our job to question our orders, Cleao. I obey the law, and *you* obey me. I will not have anyone else in this squad break our code. Do you understand?" For a moment Jack thought she was looking at Bristol, but before he could decide, her eyes were back to Cleao.

The soldier clenched his fists, and begrudgingly bowed his head. "Yes, Captain."

"Good." Koa directed her hard gaze to Jack. "Now, old leprechaun, I do not wish to hurt you, but if you continue to speak, I cannot promise your safety. I will not let dissension be encouraged."

Jack grinned. "A parting word then? Before I'm banished to silence?"

She pressed her mouth into a tight line, tensing every muscle as she gave a small nod.

"Thank you, you're very generous." He kept the sarcasm at bay for her sake. "That sheriff will do something illegal in the future. I know it, and you do too. When he does, I hope you will treat him the same as you have treated these soldiers."

"That is all?" Koa asked suspiciously.

"It is."

Her head tilted in contemplation. "Then we shall see, leprechaun."

Lovely Ivory Knight,

Many things have transpired since last you requested information. The Marble Rook has flown past my expectations and intrigues me to no end. To think such a power existed... but I get ahead of myself. A secret was shared recently in such an innocent and naive manner, I nearly gave myself away by laughing. Truly, the Marble Rook should have taken better care that their words would not be carried in the empty forest for all to hear. Promises were made, but none that affect me.

Now, let me just say, I was right. Your predictions were correct, and so were mine. I do believe that makes our score equal. In any case, the Marble Rook has a remarkable gift that I shall outline for you in the second page of this letter. Here, though, I do believe I should note that my own senses tell me there's more inside the Marble Rook that has yet to be shared. Perhaps a skill, or a new level of power? I have yet to decipher it. When I do, I shall share the answer with you.

However, that does bring me to a pressing question: Should I kill our Marble Rook? Such power is difficult to handle, and may do more harm than good. Write to me with your answer quickly, as the further they progress the harder it will be to remove the Marble Rook easily. Even now it would be difficult, but at the very least possible.

Anyways, thank you for the information. I have already experienced the lack of soldiers and made good use of it. As of yet, I have not heard any rumors of the Jade King joining this fight. No whispers, not even a rebellious idea spoken out in restlessness. If the Jade King truly plans to enter this war... we will have to be wary of which side he chooses. Assuming he chooses one at all. It is difficult, when one is surrounded by fighting, to abstain from it for long. You know that, though.

Now, the next subject is the detailed account of the Marble Rook's gift...

Ivory Bishop

17

Merry Woodsmen

L

The rain finished its tormenting downpour by the next morning, leaving behind mist, mud, and clouds that kept the bright light of the sun captive behind them. Everything within the forest had the fresh, clean smell that only rain can produce. A smell that was somehow heavy. It weighed against Lance's skin as they trudged their way through the forest. Despite the mud and the cold temperature, the greenery was a rather pleasant sight. Alongside cleaning the air, the rain had given new life to the hue of the vegetation, breathing vibrance into the plants.

Still, traveling with a thief meant they had to avoid the *oh so important* Mason Line that Merlin found. Lance almost felt sorry for his boots as he and Merlin made their way over the forest floor. Whenever he took a step, the ground seemed to swallow his foot, and it would make a horrible noise when he tried to remove it. His only relief came from a clear creek that crossed their path, as it had stones running along the width of it.

Regardless of the water, Lance was still envious of Robin and Gwen. Those two were moving from branch to branch, high in the trees and out of clear sight from the ground. When Lance could see Robin, he had to marvel at the way he moved through the trees, never missing a step or trusting a weak branch. Such ease of movement had to have been sharpened through years of practice.

"*I agree.*" Solaris's dry voice said. "*Is it certain that his sight is gone? He moves like any other person. Better in some cases, and worse in others.*"

Lance yanked one foot out of the mud, placing it flatly against the first rock in the river. *They wouldn't lie about his blindness, but I agree that his movements are too accurate.*

"Exactly. I don't trust him or his bird, and I know you don't either. He gave no reason for why he is suddenly helping us, and his aim is too accurate to be unassisted. Perhaps you can convince Merlin to abandon him?"

I doubt it. Lance glanced sideways at Merlin, who was attempting to remove her own shoes from the ground. *But maybe she can give us some insight or information that would alleviate our distrust.*

Solaris made a sound that Lance had long since determined to be a snort. "By all means, ask her. If she gives unsatisfactory answers, I hope you will use me to get rid of the problem."

You really do have no scruple with violence, don't you?

"Words fix problems temporarily. Only something that cannot be undone is a true solution."

Lance frowned, hopping from one stone to the next. "But is it the right solution?" The sword said nothing in return to this question.

"If you're not careful people will say you've lost your wits." Merlin's words contained a layer of amusement that Lance did not fail to pick up.

"Maybe I have," he admitted lightly, offering his hand to assist her. "Having a sword speak to you will make anyone question their sanity."

With her hair pulled back, there was nothing to stop Lance from seeing the indignance on her face. For maybe the twentieth time, he marveled at how easy it was for her golden eyes to convey anger. Irritation seemed to be her first reaction to anything. Regardless, Merlin did take his hand, pulling herself up onto a bumpy rock. She let go promptly, wobbling as her footing stabilized.

Lance pulled his hand back, flexing it out fully. Surprising warmth was beginning to spread through his fingertips, crawling down his palm. A shadow feeling of her hand still rested on top of his. Quickly, he moved from his stone to the next, shaking his head to clear his thoughts. Now was not the time for that; now he needed answers.

"Speaking of questions, I have a few." His voice stumbled awkwardly along with his movements across the rocks. "How is it that Robin can shoot if he is unable to see?"

"I wondered when you were going to ask me." The noise of the creek almost drowned out her remark. Fighting the urge to look back, Lance made another careful leap to the next slippery stone. After a moment, Merlin continued speaking, raising her voice to be heard. "Robin can't see, but the animals and bugs in the forest can. He simply listens to their instructions. That's how he shoots."

Tilting with eyes fixed on his next step, Lance called, "Are you telling me every single animal can speak?"

"Yes! Or rather, they have the ability to let certain people understand them."

Solaris scoffed, *"That's very far-fetched."*

Says the talking sword.

"So, all the animals in this forest just talk to him? That hardly makes sense." Lance said aloud.

"I don't quite understand it myself, but he said not every animal will talk to him, and there are some that can't. The ones that can recognize him help by shouting out the directions he needs, or by letting him feel their surroundings. He told me he's never gone astray listening to them."

The bugs direct his aim? A small wave crashed over Lance's rock, drenching his leather boots as he hopped to one of the last stones. Shooting by direction could be done, but it was very difficult, and even then, the chance of hitting the target was slim to none. Obviously there was more to the thief than what could be seen outwardly. Lance made the last few jumps back onto stable ground, as stable as mud can be, anyway. Merlin joined him with two, he had to admit, graceful leaps over the remaining stones, sending splashes of mud out from around her feet.

A pleased expression donned her face. "Is that all you wanted to know?"

"No." He faced the path. "I would like to know why Robin changed his mind about helping us. The book's answer makes no sense to me."

"You mean the answer it gave when you were trying to get rid of him?" Her voice was light with mockery.

His cheeks flushed. "You're the one who said I wouldn't like him."

"Fine, that's true." Merlin went past him, stepping from the ground to a large tree root that had pulled itself up from beneath the ground. Dirt and tiny patches of moss covered the top of its deep brown bark. "I'll give you the answer, but we have to keep up with Robin and Gwen. We're almost at his home, but if we're not with him we could get into some serious trouble."

"Very well..." Lance followed behind her, making sure he wouldn't fall off the root.

"Good." Merlin adjusted the backpack on her shoulders. "In that case, I'll tell you. Robin is looking for something, and the book said it would help him find it."

"What is he searching for?"

She glanced over her shoulder, and when she spoke, her voice was solemn. "Something worth seeing."

Lance took a moment to ponder that. It seemed to be an honorable search from a thief without reputable character. Then again, maybe everyone had that same goal, to find something worth seeing. Wasn't that what he was doing?

Solaris made a coughing sound, which startled Lance out of movement. Some distance away, Merlin also froze. She was looking skeptically at him. Her eyes seemed as though they were trying to judge his reaction, whatever it may be. Lance was unsure why, but her expression prodded a thought. Robin said he was not born blind, rather it had happened in his childhood. Was his blindness an injury, then? If it was, then why hadn't he gone to Merlin?

Lance pursed his lips. Tentatively, he asked, "Could you heal his eyes?" The pleasant atmosphere of their conversation dwindled, but the question didn't seem to have surprised her.

Merlin's shoulders drooped. "I could," her normally solid voice dipped into defeat, "but he won't let me."

The knight looked down at his carefully balanced feet. He wanted to know why, but how could he ask? There were some things that no one wanted to talk about. Was it really his business to know? With a sigh, Lance looked back up, still not sure what to say. He was met with empty forest, Merlin nowhere in sight.

For one heartbeat Lance stood there, staring blankly, eyes glued to the space she had occupied. Then a dose of alarm, not just his own but of Solaris' as well, sent every nerve in his body flying. His balance was gone, he was wobbling on the root, whipping his head left and right.

"Merlin?" he called. There was no sight of her, not a heavy footstep in the mud nor a group of fleeing assailants in the distance. She was just... gone.

"Lancelot, something is out there, can you feel it?"

At the same time as Solaris spoke, Lance felt them; people in the forest around him. Muscles tensing, he reached for his sword, grasping the handle—and Solaris' ribbon—tightly. Before he could unsheathe it something grabbed his cloak, pulling the hood up and over his head.

"Wha—" Lance jerked backwards, his face covered by the fabric. Ripping off the hood, he went for the sword once more, twisting around at the same time. Again, whoever was there pulled the hood up over his face from behind him. The second Lance pulled it off himself, a hand pushed at his shoulder, laughter breaking out from the trees above him. The shove was just enough to send Lancelot careening off the side of the root, which had climbed at least ten feet above the ground.

The knight and the sword let out simultaneous yells as Lance fell upside-down towards the ground. One second he was falling, the next, his body was jerked up harshly, one foot holding him midair. He swung in a spiral, eyes swimming, arms flinging out to stabilize himself. More laughter echoed through the trees around Lance. Whoever was out there was laughing at *him*.

"*Pulkata, tokata, es dar'ka! Ceva evera chuva!**" the knight swore.

"*Lancelot, calm down,*" warned Solaris in the knight's mind. "*You're not dead, that's most important.*"

I'm alive all right, for now! Lance puffed. The blood rushing to his head was starting to hurt. He glared at the trees as the spinning slowed to a gentle rocking.

Lance yelled, "Who's out there?"

In response there was more laughing, and something hard thwacked Lance's free foot, sending him spinning in circles again. The knight gritted his teeth, his stomach revolting from the movement. Hot, boiling anger had been brewing inside him, and now it was bursting. How dare they attack him without showing their face. Were they cowards?

---

* *Translated to, "Boorish, cruel, and foolish. The impertinent scoundrel!"*

He was no one's sport, tool, or toy, and he *never* would be. He would turn towards death before he allowed himself to be used that way.

"Come out and fight me, cowards!" he shouted, shaking a fist out at the trees. When nothing came back to him, Lance tried reaching the rope that held his foot in the air.

"That's not going to work."

Not helping! Lance groaned as his fingers just brushed the threads of the binding. The tips slipped and Lance flung back down, limbs swinging limply. He growled, clenching both his fists. Whoever had trapped him was still there, Lance could feel their presence, which meant that Merlin had to be with them. That meant he needed to escape and find her.

Solaris coughed. *"Easier said than done, my friend."*

"Oh, be quiet!" Lance huffed. He looked back up at the upside-down trees. "If you harm one hair on her head, I will make sure every one of you spends the rest of your life rotting in a dungeon!"

Someone chortled. "And who are you to be making such threats?" The voice sounded young and smooth. Lance twisted his head to try and see the location of the voice. Still there was no one visible in the trees.

"That is none of your business." He gritted his teeth. "Stop hiding and face me like men!"

In the tree above, there was a rustle of leaves and a thumping of something landing hard. Whatever the rope holding Lance was attached to, bent up and down as someone hopped on and then off it, landing in a crouch in front of his eyes. Frizzy red hair spilled out of the hood that covered the boy's face, an impish light gleaming in the two eyes that looked down at Lancelot. A foxtail was hanging from the boy's belt, along with a long hunting knife and a bow on his back. Everything about him exuded the kind of arrogance that only a youth could summon. The color of his skin, a pale yellow, and the color of his eyes, a light green, were no exception to this.

"Course it's my business. It's all of our business." The boy leaned down closer to Lance, who instinctively jerked his head back. "So you're going to tell us about it."

"I refuse." Lance spat, missing the boy entirely.

"You're not going to get anything out of him, he looks too stubborn." The second voice was more raspy, a bit like Solaris, except far younger. Behind the boy, another person appeared on the branch of a tree, hanging upside-down with his legs locked around the limb. Lancelot couldn't see him well, what with being tied to the rope and all, but the hood of the second person was hanging down so that Lance could see some of his face. He looked exactly like the boy in front of him. Were they twins?

"You might be right," agreed the crouching boy.

"I have no coins on me," Lance lied. "Just let my friend and I go."

That piqued the boy's interest. "Is that what you are? A friend? I've never seen you before though. What about you, Featherhead?" Lance blinked at him, his anger dipping into confusion. It felt as though he was missing vital information that was needed to understand a word they were saying.

"Why are you asking me?" the second person called. "If you haven't seen him, then I haven't. Must be new."

Lance opened his mouth, but a third loud thump stopped him from speaking. Another voice, this one slightly deeper, said, "You think he stole the Boss's spot?"

"Oh, hadn't thought of that." Tilting his head, the boy in front of Lance blinked at him. "Did you steal his place? He's going to be annoyed if you did."

"I don't know what you're talking about." Lance snapped. "Now get me down from here!"

In Lance's mind, Solaris decided to speak up. *"I don't think that is going to work, Lance. Instead of talking to crazy bandits, maybe just use my gift to burn them all?"*

The suggestion wasn't horrible, but Lance didn't get much time to consider it, because just then, a series of loud, ground shaking footsteps came slowly over to him. His head itched to move in the direction of the stepper. The only thing stopping him being a cool blade that had just been pressed against his throat.

A fourth, gravelly voice, this one much more serious than the others, spoke. Each word demanded Lance's attention with intense authority. "You have one minute to explain who you are, and what you are doing here, or I will send you to beg to Elohim in the Rideon."

Once again, Solaris remarked sardonically in Lance's mind, *"Now will you use my power?"*

Lance narrowed his eyes. *If I try to make any fire they'll kill me now.*

"Come on," urged the crouching boy. "If you don't tell him, he will kill you. None of us are going to stop him."

The blade pressed further against Lance's throat. He glared at the boy intensely. "I will not."

"Very well." The fourth voice responded.

"*Lance!*"

Lancelot grabbed at his power, connecting to the Rideon as the sword prepared to swing down at his neck.

"Stop!"

The crouching boy, the deep voice, and Lance all froze. Merlin's shout was familiar enough that the knight instantly recognized her, and subsequently followed her instruction. He was puzzled though, as the bandits also obeyed, freezing for several seconds. The sound of loud buzzing grew during those seconds, which caused the boy who was crouched to hop up and away, opening Lance's view. What he saw would have made his mouth drop open if he had been right side up.

A gray skinned ivirian was descending to the ground, his blonde hair flipping in the wind his wings created. He looked fairly advanced in age, with a hood and several belts with pouches hanging off them. None of that surprised Lance though. No, the shocking part of the appearance was the fact that Merlin was being carried down by the ivirian, looking completely unperturbed by her circumstance. Rather, she actually looked irritated at all of them, Lance included. As soon as the two had their feet on the ground, she was let go and on her way over, glaring daggers at the group.

"Miss Merlin!" the first bandit, the one closest to Lance, exclaimed. He sounded astonished and horrified as she marched forward, stopping a foot away from the knight. "You were supposed to go with Callin!"

Callin, the blonde headed ivirian, sidled up to them, a displeased look on his face. Now that he was closer, Lance could see a black eye-patch covering his right eye. "She was refusing to go with me, whining so much I had to come back."

Again, Lance felt that he was missing something important, but no one was taking the time to fill him in.

CHAPTER 17

Merlin pointed angrily at Callin, arguing, "I was not whining. I was trying to stop you all from making a mistake." She then turned her attention to the younger bandit. "Really! Does he look like a threat to you?" After her last few words she pointed at Lance.

"Hang on!" Lance cried out indignantly.

"And you!" Merlin squatted so she was around eye level with the knight. "What kind of knight allows himself to be trapped so easily? I have half a mind to let them continue without stopping them."

"Oh seriously, it's my fault all this happened?" Lance rolled his eyes. "I'm just an innocent bystander, being caught up in all your mess. Because apparently it *is* your mess, since you know these bandits."

"*Woodsmen,* mate. We prefer that." Both elestiels glared at the boy, who in turn gave them each an undaunted stare.

Merlin sighed, turning to look at someone Lance couldn't see. "Please cut him down. He's no threat to you."

A small worry popped up inside Lance as no one spoke. Would they leave him here against Merlin's wishes? If they didn't take the sword, he could get himself down, but as for finding Merlin afterward, that would be nearly impossible.

His concerns were needless, since then the fourth voice said, "As you wish." A piercing sound followed the speech, alerting Lance a half second before he fell that the rope was cut. Pain throbbed in his head and feet as his blood rushed back into his limbs where it belonged.

"Ow." he grunted, pushing himself up by his palms.

"*Think of it this way, at least you landed in the moss and not in the mud.*" Solaris was only a little comforting, but it would take more than his sword's words to settle his swirling emotions. Lance stood, brushing off clumps of dirt from his pants and shirt. Next to him, Merlin took a step forward, her eyes set on something behind him.

"Thank you for getting him down, Yon."

Lance turned around carefully, taking in the appearance of the fourth and deepest speaker. Never before had he seen a giant, but Lance had expected them to be, well, taller. Yon fell around nine feet tall, if Lance's estimate was correct, with a hulking body made up of muscles. The presence of such excessive strength and tight posture seemed to try and make up for the dearth of height the giant possessed, and from Lance's tiny, miniscule perspective, it did.

He felt even smaller as Yon bent forward, dark brown eyes inspecting Lancelot. "Miss Merlin, you're going to have to explain what a knight is doing here. Although, we might as well wait for the boss first. He's supposed to be back soon."

"No need for that!" Lancelot jumped back as Robin landed on the ground, Guinevere perched on his shoulder. The thief stood quickly, putting both hands on his hips. "Lance here is traveling with us, so it would be fortunate for you not to kill him."

"Boss!" the bandits all chorused the title, some with more exuberance than others. Even the giant seemed happy to see Robin.

"Yes, yes," Robin waved. "I have returned, and it's nice to see me isn't it? Well, even if you're not glad, it's good to hear your voices again. Except you, Callin." The ivirian promptly rolled his one eye, his four dragonfly-like wings twitching.

Gwen hopped from Robin to Merlin, peering up at Yon. "Have you gotten shorter?" she asked impertinently, the way only a cat could have done.

"You've just gotten taller." The giant nodded to the cat's position on Merlin.

Gwen nodded. "Ah, I see."

Here Lancelot sighed, covering his face with one hand, the other poised on top of Solaris. He was trained to be dignified in any circumstance thrown at him, but ever since coming to Sher, he was beginning to wonder if he had actually learned anything. He was always getting into situations he didn't understand, like now, with a group of thieves that Merlin apparently was intimately acquainted with. Just when he thought he understood what was happening, something new would come along and muddle it all up.

"Robin, would you make some introductions?" Lance looked up, Merlin was giving him a slightly less irritated look that he might have mistaken for pity had he not known her.

"Oh, right." Robin raised a hand to his forehead. "I forgot, Lance is here." The thief then began to point at each person as he listed off their names. The sight was quite silly, because the group had to rearrange itself in order for each name Robin said to fit with the person he was pointing at.

"That's Foxtail." Robin pointed to the first woodsman Lance had seen, unsurprisingly the one with a foxtail on his belt. The boy pulled off his hood to reveal two thin, pointed ears sticking out of shaggy hair. His ears were shorter than Merlin's, and he wore a superior smirk along with them.

"That's Featherhead." A second wingless boy did a flip off a tree and landed next to Foxtail, also pulling off his hood. He had to be a twin, because his face was practically the same as the first boy: a sharp chin, almond shaped eyes, and a devious smirk. The exception to their similarity was him being two inches shorter and having hair that stuck up like a rooster.

"That's Dirian." An ivirian that Lance hadn't seen before fluttered forward, gripping a bow. His skin was midnight blue, like his hair, which was pulled into a ponytail. It made his sky-blue eyes all the brighter. He wore similar clothing to the rest of the woodsmen: a hood, tunic, mask, leather vambraces and such. Dirian's countenance was a more mature version of the twins.

"And of course, Callin and Yon." Each respectively nodded, but the older two looked displeased as they did so. Robin grinned. "My woodsmen, some of them at least. Apologies for whatever they did, but it can hardly be helped. It's their job to keep people away from our base."

"And that includes killing anyone who wanders by?" Lance asked, raising both eyebrows.

Foxtail let out a loud snort. "Anyone foolish enough to walk around this place is neither friendly nor welcome. Sides, you have 'soldier' written all over your face. Don't he, Featherhead?"

"That he does," the second twin agreed. "If he weren't human, I'd have shot him where he stood."

"I am not human." Lance glared at both of them. "And shooting me would have been a mistake. Be glad you didn't."

The blue ivirian moved over to the twins, a haughty gleam contorting his features. "It's difficult to believe that after catching you so easily. Tell me, how exactly were you planning to stop us while hanging from your boot?"

Merlin spoke before Lance could say any of the choice words he had for the Woodsman. "We should probably keep moving. Loxley is close, if my memory is correct."

"Very close, Miss Merlin." Yon answered, nodding his head to the right. "We'll take you all there."

"Good!" Robin stepped over to the giant, looking up. His voice stayed at the same cheery tone, but his words were that of a more serious note. "Then you can explain why *all* of you are here, instead of leaving some at the base." The giant looked unswayed, but Lance caught the uncomfortable expressions on the twins' and Dirian's faces.

"Yes, Boss."

"Excellent!" Robin turned around and started walking away. His action was all it took to get his woodsmen moving, either dashing through the trees or by flying in the air. The knight had to keep up a steady jog to match their fast pace. A regular human might have had a difficult time if they weren't accustomed to the forest terrain.

While they ran, Lance took the opportunity to calm down, letting his anger dissolve with each footstep. His brother taught him this technique, or rather a version of it to help him control his feelings. Somehow it never worked as well for Lance as it did for his brother, at least, as far as he knew. How many years had it been since they were able to speak on civil terms?

Regardless, running cleared his mind enough to help him process the current situation. Obviously the woodsmen were also thieves, and probably helped Robin with all his schemes and thefts. That must be how they knew Merlin. Now more than ever Lance felt curious as to the nature of Merlin's relationship with Robin. To have known him since childhood, and to be acquainted with his troop meant that they must be very close.

What are your thoughts on it, Solaris? he asked.

The constant presence in his mind that was the sword stirred. *"Such relationships in my home meant that the two in question were, in human terms, betrothed. It is possible that's the case here, but I couldn't be sure."*

Lance cringed. *That's not what I was asking you about! How much of my thoughts can you hear?*

"All of them." Solaris said innocently. *"Were you referring then to the job of these wood dwellers? If that's it, then I agree with you. Honestly, they are so rude I wouldn't mind—"*

CHAPTER 17

I'm going to stop you there. I am not using you to kill anyone. If you truly can hear all my thoughts, then you should know how I feel about needless violence.

Solaris scoffed. "*You were perfectly willing to fight these thieves earlier. I don't think you really considered how much fighting you would have to do when setting out to stop a war, did you?*"

Lance stared gloomily ahead, silently taking his hand off the sword. The weapon felt so heavy, like a ball chained to his leg for him to drag or carry, never to be removed. Many times, he had relied on a sword to solve his problems, or remove them altogether. Some said that killing was the best solution to a problem—assumedly like the thieves he was with—but he didn't believe that. At least, that was what he thought. Ever since he entered Sher, he had been forced into situations that could be solved either by fighting or by talking. Every time he had chosen to fight. Was that all he could do now? Had he become the weapon they wanted him to be?

Solaris, tell me, you've seen my thoughts and memories. Have I followed the path he paved for me?

He felt the shift in the sword's mood, changing to something like unease. "*How dark your thoughts are getting, Lancelot.*"

As the group stopped, Lance shook his head, clenching his fists tightly. *They've always been dark.*

18

House of Suspicion

L

"Welcome to Loxley." Robin declared, as he hopped down from the trees. He grinned at Lancelot, waving along the bumpy, root covered ground which formed the path before them. Lance's eyes followed the roots to a line of trees that were sitting on the edge of a cliff. The only noteworthy aspects regarding the plants were their size, but every tree in Sher was twice the regular width of a normal tree. After all the startling things he had seen, Lance found himself overwhelmed by the monotony of it all.

Merlin let out an exasperated sigh next to Yon, stepping around the bored giant to reach Lance. Without a word, she grabbed the knight's hand and dragged him—with little resistance from Lance himself—right up to the edge of the cliff. "*This* is Loxley."

"*Now that's impressive...*"

Solaris was right. The cliff they stood on was the edge of an enormous circular crater carved out of the ground. Tree roots cascaded down the sides of the cliffs in thick strands that pooled at the bottom, spiraling upwards to form a trunk at its center. Sitting atop the roots sat a large house with three great bow roofs coming to a point at the top of an arch. Its walls were just as gnarled as the roots which held up the structure, and an air of pompous self-congratulation hung about it.

Lancelot took a moment to reflect on why the building struck him that way, and was hit suddenly with the realization. The house reminded him of the Avalonian palace, a building also covered in curved roofs and carved walls. That only left him with the question of how the house was placed on the roots in the first place. Unfortunately there was no immediate explanation. Instead there were three hanging bridges to entertain Lance's attention. Each connected to a wing of the house, two of which were some distance away, and the third which sat closer to their current standing.

"How is this possible?" he asked.

From the side he saw Merlin nod, as if he said exactly what she thought he would. "It's an old elf mansion. The perfect hiding place, really."

Lance glanced at her, expecting more explanation.

Merlin sighed. "Myths hate elves, so they don't like going near their abandoned houses. Thus a great hiding spot."

"Exactly!" Robin was standing on the nearest suspended bridge ten feet away, leaning on the ropes that held it up. "Spacious and discrete. Now, are you coming or not? Don't tell me the knight is scared of heights?" Lance narrowed his eyes in inspection of the closest bridge, noting that the ropes were made of what looked like braided straw.

He *was*, in fact, wary of the long distance between the bridge and the ground, but now he refused to mention it. There would be no indulging in the thief's criticism, especially after being so easily captured by the woodsmen. Within his mind, Lance felt Solaris agree, but he paid minimal attention to it. Stretching to his full height and squaring his shoulders, Lance made to move past Merlin, forgetting that she still grasped his hand. He was reminded when his movement abruptly stopped, jerking him in the opposite direction. Irritated, Lance turned and looked dubiously at Merlin.

"Sprites first." Merlin stood defiantly with her eyes on the swaying walkway. A reflection of his own concern was mirrored in her face, although she directed it towards the bridge. "They're lighter, so they can test it out."

So the twins were sprites: Relatives to an ivirian but lacking the wings and secondary Rideon gifts that ivirians occasionally had. The twins looked exasperated at her request, but Robin simply waved them forward. "As you wish, I wouldn't dream of letting you down. Foxtail, you go before Featherhead. Merlin is concerned about it's stability."

"Not again." Foxtail groaned loud enough for Lance to hear.

His brother shuffled forward. "She always does this. Let's get it over with." The two marched past Robin and across the bridge, carefully holding the guide ropes whenever the bridge swayed too much. While they did, Yon appeared with the two ivirians beside him. It struck Lance that the giant, while being on the small side, was probably far heavier than the bridge could take. His supposition proved correct by what the giant did next.

"We'll be off now." Yon said, just barely acknowledging Robin's nod before he and Dirian moved to a root. The ivirian crouched down, dragging his hands through the dirt in the shape of a triangle. Scorch marks appeared beneath his fingertips as he finished his signet. Immediately the plant shuddered, its bark reaching up over the two passengers' feet, and wrapping securely around their boots. Dirian's wings fluttered as the root shot forward, shooting down the cliff with its passengers in tow.

The second ivirian, Callin, sighed loudly and made a running leap off the cliff, his wings already in motion. It was now only the original party that stood together on the cliff side, as the twins had made a good deal of progress in crossing the bridge.

Guinevere, who had been silent for the past while, hopped off Robin's shoulder and announced, "That's enough dilly-dallying and hand holding. Let's go before the bridge really does snap." She started marching down the wobbly wooden planks, tail held high.

Robin tilted his head to the sky, where his owl was flapping in a circle. Briefly Lance wondered if it was safe for the thief to cross, but since the owl was present, it was probably fine. As he followed the cat, Robin declared solidly, "As you say, Gwen. But I should like to hear about this hand holding business."

It was then Lance realized that Merlin was in fact holding his hand, and she must have remembered it too, because she immediately let go. Not daring to look at her, Lance set out towards the bridge, moving as hurriedly as he could across it. Every time the bridge swung to the left or right, Lance would grip the ropes until his knuckles turned white. Only once did he make the mistake of looking down and, as suspected, he regretted it. To fall from their current height meant certain death.

"*Calm yourself, Lancelot.*" Solaris spoke gently while the knight placed a careful foot on the next board. "*You can fly with my power, so there's no need to worry about falling.*"

Lance laughed slightly. *I already knew that. Why are you bringing it up now?*

"*It can comfort you while walking. Even with all your practice it is much more difficult to fly with my gift, but I believe you would manage* in a dangerous situation. Learning to fly is usually easier to learn when thrown off the side of something."

Maybe for birds! Lance shook his head. *I have no intention of jumping when the bridge will take me where I need to be.*

"Fine, but we will need to try soon. If the ivirians persist in following you, then you will need to be able to join them in the air. My wings cannot break like theirs can. It may also speed up your travel."

I doubt it. If it was just Merlin and Gwen, maybe I could carry them, but Robin's coming with us too. That's far too much weight, and I refuse to even consider carrying him.

"Well, you still need to try, but we can finish discussing this later. It appears you've arrived."

Lance looked up at the arched opening, which was much bigger now that he stood closer. There were rectangular cutouts in the arch's wooden trim that led to an open slant in the wall. Above the large doors but below the cutouts were carved words in Allmens tongue, a northern dialect by the spelling. The words said, *Wash me clean, and wave my faults aside.*

"Merlin, what does this mean?" He stopped her with his question.

Merlin peered up to the arch and frowned. "I'm not sure of the words, but I know the openings once let water through. I've been told this used to be a lake."

Lance glanced once more at the words, thinking now of the empty chasm that the house sat in. Somehow imagining the house in the middle of water seemed to enhance its outrageous elegance.

~•~•~•~•~•~

Yon and Dirian were waiting for them inside the building, with a new ivirian beside them. Four bat-shaped wings rested at the ivirian's back, each membrane holding a dark yellow color that looked remarkably like gold. His skin was a dark purple, and his wispy, gray hair had little, spindly braids sticking out of it. Eye magnifiers and bottles hung all over his vest, there was even a row of stuffed pockets all around the bottom.

Each woodsman had the brooding expression of someone being forced to greet unwelcome guests. Lance surmised that it was him and his profession that made them suspicious. It could hardly be about Merlin or Robin. What could he expect from a group of thieves? Of course they would hate a knight. It wasn't like he had any pleasant feelings in return.

Yon cleared his throat, speaking heavily. "Robin, Dirian will take care of Miss Merlin and the knight—"

"Lancelot." Lance interjected.

The giant's face crinkled. "And Lancelot."

Merlin coughed. "We call him Lance."

Yon's eye twitched at the interruptions, but he held himself together well. "Please come with Luzel and I. There is much we need to discuss." The purple ivirian nodded. He must be Luzel.

Robin sighed. "Oh, fine. You're right about that." He turned to Merlin, taking her hand and patting it. Lance's mouth turned sour and he averted his eyes as Robin spoke gently. "I'll come find you later. Please keep the knight from killing anyone."

He looked indignantly back in time for Merlin to roll her eyes. "He's not likely to do that, but very well."

Robin nodded, visibly squeezed her hand, and turned away. The three headed down a wooden hallway to the left, its walls looked like trees reaching over the floor. Lance looked down at the smooth, probably marble, ground, trying to withhold any repulsion from his face.

"Miss Merlin," Dirian started. "Yon said to make sure you both get new clothing and a hot meal. May I take you to your quarters?" A quick glance down showed all the mud that had accumulated on Lance's outfit. Merlin was in the same predicament.

She tilted her head, glancing at Gwen. "You can go if you want."

The cat flicked her tail. "Yes, I believe I will. If you need me, I will be in the kitchen."

"Swiggle won't give you anything," Dirian smirked. "Not unless you're stealing it."

"We'll see." The black cat sauntered away from them, walking behind one of the tall columns that lined the hall. No sound came from her footsteps as she disappeared from sight.

While they walked, Merlin asked, "Where's Jax?"

CHAPTER 18

After a moment's thought, Lance decided that it was better to keep his mouth shut and listen, instead of interrupting. Solaris agreed so heartily that it was almost insulting.

"He's leading a group to one of the border villages, *the* border village, actually." Dirian glanced back as they started ascending an exposed staircase. "We were able to... obtain many pounds of flour and other provisions recently. They are to take and distribute it there."

"I see. Is that why Yon is in such a low mood?"

"Uh, no." The stairs ended after three flights, opening into a hallway lined with closed doors on the right, and three windows on the left. "I don't know all the details, but I believe it has something to do with the state of the pass. I heard from Scout that there is a lengthy battle going on right now."

"If that's right, then Yon is probably concerned for the surrounding homes and villages." Merlin guessed, giving Lancelot a strange look.

He just stared at her blankly, though inside his thoughts were a whirl with the news. Who started the fighting? Avalon or Logres? Were the soldiers faring well or would reinforcements be called in? If only he could stop this needless war sooner.

At that thought his brother's voice rang in his head, as clear as the day he had spoken to Lance. *There is a way to end the war, and it isn't in the folktales you've heard. It's in decisive action. But you're too much of a coward to go willingly. Must you persist in this until it becomes a matter of the crown's interest?*

Lance gasped, not loud enough for the others to hear, but enough to release some of the surprise. Tentatively, he rubbed his shoulder, trying to force the sealed memories back into the chest he previously stuffed them in. His brother wasn't there, and he couldn't dictate what Lance did. At least right then, while he was in a different kingdom.

Continuing in his avoidance, Lance returned his attention to Merlin's conversation. He might have put more interest into inspecting the passages they walked down, but there were too many exquisite carvings and patterns to take them all in. The house was far too fancy, to the point of being imperious. How ironic that it was now inhabited by a bunch of scrappy thieves.

"Several of the border villages have been struggling with food shortages, so we've been busy bringing food to them." Dirian turned right. "Jax has been busy dealing with that while Robin was away. He was gone for several months, you see."

"Really? What was he doing?" Merlin asked curiously. Lance leaned forward slightly, curious despite himself.

Dirian stopped at a round top door, turning around to peer at them curiously. "He didn't tell you?"

Lance shook his head, and Merlin responded. "No, he didn't mention it."

A distressed look fell on Dirian, a torn stance donning his posture. "I don't think I can say, then. Sorry, Miss Merlin, but I'm sure if you ask, Robin will tell you."

Merlin straightened. "All right. I'll ask him myself."

Dirian looked relieved, then directed his head to the door. "This room should have clothing for you, Sage is in there to help."

She moved forward, then halted in front of the door. "Will you help Lance?"

The knight withheld a smile, surprised by her consideration. It was rather touching, to be honest. The ivirian bowed his head in answer, which seemed to convince her. The door creaked when she opened it, her eyes flicking to Lance for half a second as she disappeared behind it.

Both of them stood there in awkward silence. Lancelot could feel the displeasure radiating off Dirian. The ivirian crossed his arms, scowling. "This way." He jerked his head to the left and walked briskly away without waiting.

Lance rolled his eyes. He could be diplomatic, but Dirian seemed like someone who would be offended with anything less than bluntness. "If you have a problem with me, I would have you air it. Or is it simply that I am a knight?"

"You're an *Avalonian* knight." Dirian called over his shoulder. Lance sighed and hurried after him. They stopped relatively soon in front of another door. Dirian leaned against the wall, glaring. "We all have good reasons to dislike you. Robin more so, even if he decided otherwise. There's nothing you can do to change my opinion."

Lance stood there, waited, then opened the door. "If nothing will change it, then I'll have to accept it. But tell me," he looked back at him, "why do you call her Miss Merlin? I hardly think she's the type to demand formalities."

"Ha." Dirian shook his head. "You haven't met her brother yet, if that's what you think. Robin's the only one who gets away with using just her first name, except maybe Luzel."

Lancelot scoffed mentally, saying, "Is he that frightening?"

"It has nothing to do with fear," Dirian sneered. "It's about respect... and power. Shouldn't an Avalonian understand that?"

Lance squeezed the slim handle of the door tightly. He did understand, completely. The king of Avalon could only rule if he was strong enough to hold the throne, and knights had to prove their ability in order to join one of the armies of the six governor generals. The king's personal guard was even more exclusive. Beyond even that, his own experience agreed with the unfriendly ivirian. Without power you were nothing more than a worm crawling in the soil. That was the way of Avalon.

His silence seemed to satisfy Dirian, his attitude reeking of victory. It caused an instant revolt inside Lancelot, but the knight refused to give Dirian the pleasure of arguing further. Instead, he summoned all the self-respect he had, and closed the door in a dignified manner.

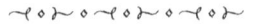

RH

Robin's office was on the highest floor of the house, separated from the hustle and bustle of the lower levels. He liked it because out of all the rooms, it had a very simple layout, with a desk and chair to the left of the rectangle and a bookshelf on the right. A doorway sat open on the far side of the room, granting access to the balcony. The balcony was his favorite place to sit since its guardrails were wide enough to slip his legs in between, and low enough that he could rest on the top of it. The other charm of the room lay in that all the insects avoided it. Excluding a single old female spider who was so grumpy at Robin's presence, that she refused to speak unless it was for complaining or a serious matter. Any bugs that did have the misfortune of entering the room were caught immediately by Madame Muffet's web.

"Afternoon, Madame. How's the fly trap?" Robin called out as he entered the room, feeling the wall for his straight walking stick that he had placed there months before. The smooth pole was right where he left it, propped by the door.

"*Get out of my house!*" Madame Muffet screeched from her spot above the balcony. "*Why must you always come back, and with extra people, too?*"

"It's a pleasure to see you as well." Robin walked forward, not needing the stick to help him find the desk. When he had seated himself, he produced the bag of gold he nabbed from the tax collector. He flinched as it made a loud clanking sound, followed by Pico's squawking entrance through the balcony's opening. The bird's claws made scraping noises, probably from clasping the guardrail.

Someone cleared their throat, Yon from the sound of it. He and Luzel were standing not far from the desk. "Robin, did you find him?"

Robin pulled back his hood, feeling the desk until he came to a top drawer. He pulled it open, and slid the heavy bag inside it. As he did this, he answered, "I did not. The records in Nottingham for such things are kept locked up, and even when I broke in, I found nothing. Someone must have destroyed them already."

Yon sighed, but it was Luzel's nasally voice that spoke. "They could have kept them somewhere else. Maybe they were not completely destroyed."

"That's possible." Robin admitted. "But if that's true, I won't be able to find them. There were no leads to such a change of location."

"If it is gone, then there's hardly anything we can do about it." Yon observed. "But there might be a way to ask the villagers there if they saw anything." He proposed it carefully for Robin's sake, saying it gently. An amazing feat for one with such a deep and serious voice.

What did Yon look like while saying it, Robin wondered. He shoved the thought aside, saying, "I assume you've already asked Jax to do that, seeing as he isn't *here*, and you sent him *there*."

"I told him I would send a raven should you return in time to give your approval."

Robin tapped his fingers on the desk. "You may send it, but he won't find anything. Most of the people who saw anything were killed.

I doubt any that lived would stay in the same village and be so exposed. Really, our only hope was in the capital."

"There is also your own testimony that could help." Luzel pointed out. "Should we go over it again?"

"We've already been over it too many times." Yon snapped. "Must we make him go through it again?"

"We might have missed something important!"

Robin straightened, clasping both hands resolutely. He *was* tired of repeating it. In fact, he was exhausted with the whole thing. But Robin had a duty nonetheless, and what's more, he couldn't be weak. He coughed lightly to get the two's attention. Doubtless they were staring, but that didn't affect him like it did others.

"I appreciate your concern, Yon, and your suggestion is not out of the question, Luzel. But at the moment I don't see how going over it again will help. It's out of respect for my parents that I do this, so I don't see the need to rush into more searching. Waiting longer won't hurt them any." He broke off there, halting as his stomach clenched. Robin waited until his gut untwisted before continuing. "It isn't that I don't want to continue; I will see this through. However, for now I am content to move on to other concerns. You both know harping over it will only make things more muddled than they already are."

Both murmured their agreement, but Luzel sounded less than happy. Robin tilted his head. "Luzel, don't worry. I will do what has to be done."

"I understand that, Boss." Luzel huffed. "I just wish you would take care of him hastily. The scoundrel deserves an arrow in both eyes."

Yon grunted. "I'm sure you *would* like that. If your sense of justice keeps growing the way it is, you'll end up like Callin."

Robin cracked a small smile. "I'm sure there can only be one Callin, but a similar replica might be manageable."

"You jest." Footsteps started marching back and forth, a sign that Luzel was pacing.

"I do." Robin nodded. "But while we are on the subject of filling someone up with arrows, I heard some strange rumors of a man able to live after being stuck with five of them."

"That's preposterous." Yon stated over Luzel's snort. "I thought you went for information, not groundless gossip."

"I did, yes. But the rumor was spread not just in the city, but through the travelers on the path as well. I heard them talking about it myself." Robin insisted. "Apparently, some guards found him past the western part of Akiva, a figure clad all in black. No one's seen his face, and when the guards attempted to check, he killed them. They say that an ivirian shot him several times before being incapacitated, and even now the figure has been roaming around the forest."

"That is foolish, completely foolish." Yon declared.

"I'm afraid I agree." Luzel said, his footsteps halting. "Seems like the government is trying to keep us on our toes, the citizens I mean. No one can survive five direct arrows."

Robin frowned. "I know that, but I believe that there is someone wandering about in black. Just before I met Merlin, Pico said he saw a person matching that description from above."

"Pico?" They said it at the same time, doubling the amount of unbelief in the word. With his name being said so loudly, the owl couldn't help but make a happy hoot.

"I'm here!" Pico fluttered his wings joyfully. "I'm here!"

"Yes, yes." Robin stood up, carefully navigating himself to the bird. He sat next to the animal, patting the top of Pico's head. The thief gently smoothed three feathers that tended to stick up on his head. "We know you're here. Why don't you try finding Swiggle and see if he'll give you some seeds?" That excited the bird so much that he flapped away without bothering to respond.

Behind him Yon stepped forward, his heavy footsteps making thumps as he walked. "The man in black is a matter for later. What I would like to know is why Merlin is here, and with a knight no less."

That was easy enough to explain, so that's what Robin did. He told the two everything he knew, from the burning of Merlin's house, to the knight's ludicrous plan. Though he tried to speak with less distrust when it came to Lancelot's idea, the thief wasn't completely able to accomplish that. The knight seemed like a well-meaning guy, and he *had* helped Merlin many times, but trying to stop a war with just a handful of people? That was suicide.

CHAPTER 18

Yon said as much when Robin finished. "You can't be helping them, can you?" he asked incredulously.

Robin spread out his arms helplessly. "Merlin says she isn't going with the knight, and the knight swears that he will be leaving the forest promptly. Besides, the book said I'll find what I'm looking for if I help them. I've got no other option."

"It's a book!" Robin sighed as Luzel's voice increased in volume. "How can you trust it?!"

"I just do." Robin said firmly. "There is no changing my mind, so don't bother. We'll set out for Aroth tomorrow." Silence fell upon his companions. Robin felt his skin crawl as he waited, a breeze blowing the ends of his hair. Surreptitiously he closed his eyes, the black smog he saw growing darker. The motion didn't help him calm down, so he just reopened them immediately.

Madame Muffet's creaky voice called out from her corner. *"Would you get those two out of here? They're scaring away the gnats! And what for? Nothing!"*

Robin looked up, directing his face towards the noise. "Sorry, but I doubt they'll go so soon. They have yet to tell me how the pass is."

"Hmph!" Madame's voice pitched two octaves higher in tone. *"Anyone can tell you how it's going! My seventy-eighth daughter, Shela, said that the Avalonians have launched a surprise attack on them Logres people! They've been fighting for three days now."*

"Is that so?" Robin asked.

Muffet gave a self important click. *"Of course it is! The last ant I ate was delivering her message to me. Now get them out!"*

Robin laughed, letting his head fall back down. Here was a perfect example of why he could still eat meat. Regardless, her news about the pass was concerning. Robin was now even less sure that he could get Merlin past the border without getting them all killed in the process.

"Uh, Boss?" A third voice was accompanied by the opening of his door. Robin recognized it as Dirian and waved at him. The iviro stepped forward, somewhere in the middle of the room. "Sorry to bother you, but Miss Merlin was asking about why you were gone. I didn't tell her, but she might come asking you."

Robin cupped his chin. "Right, I probably should have mentioned that. She's probably worried now. Thank you for letting me know."

"Oh, and Swiggle said dinner is warm, and that we had better come down before it's gone. Everything is pretty chaotic down there now. He was threatening Foxtail with a ladle earlier, and Gwen was chasing Pico when I left. I think I heard her yelling something about salt being great on boiled wings."

"All right, we'll be done in a moment." Robin grinned, picturing as best he could the things which Dirian described. Having not been born blind, he could still recollect the appearance of a few animals. It was no doubt a hilarious scene.

"Uh, Boss..." Dirian started again, sounding extremely uncomfortable.

"What else do you need to say?" Robin asked, rising from his position on the balcony ground. He held out a single hand to keep from hitting either a wall or a person. A sense of solidarity accompanied his arrival at his desk, which Robin sat behind while Dirian spoke.

"Is it really smart to have a knight here? He looks like a polecat with a mouse, and *we're* the mouse. Can't we turn him out?"

Neither Yon nor Luzel contested the young ivirian, a sure sign that they agreed. Robin pressed his mouth into a straight line, at the same time searching with his hands for a thin arrow from his side quiver. Slowly he rubbed the shaft between his fingers, carefully weighing his options. Sir Lancelot, a knight crazy enough to enter Sher, and apparently powerful enough to do so without getting caught. He hadn't come to assassinate the mayor, and he claimed to have been avoiding the troops, so he couldn't be after patrol routes. Additionally, everything that Merlin described went along with what the knight proclaimed himself.

"For now, I trust him." Robin decided. "If he does something wrong, then I'll take Luzel's preferred action and shoot him between the eyes. Does that satisfy the three of you?" The trio gave their begrudging agreement, which satisfied Robin for the moment.

19

Making Friends

L

There were no holes in the backs of the shirt and tunic they gave Lancelot, which was a relief since he didn't feel like sewing them closed. Unlike the ivirian clothing Merlin had supplied, these were for a man. One downside was that the new, brown clothing was of much lower quality than what he normally wore. Another was that the hood given to him made Lance feel too much like one of the thieves. Even so, he was not going to complain about the free outfit or the cold bath. After traveling for so long, it felt wonderful to be clean without washing in a river.

When he finished donning the clothes, he clasped his two belts around his waist, Solaris once again hanging at his side. The phoenix had retreated into the sword so Lance could think in peace, but as soon as the belt was clasped, he returned.

"*You take forever. I thought you'd be faster with the water being cold.*"

Oh, be quiet. Lance rolled his eyes, grabbing a stray cloth and drying the dripping ends of his hair. It was growing surprisingly quick without consistent trimming. If he didn't cut it soon he might have to put it in a ponytail. *You didn't have to endure that water. I'm fairly certain there was ice in there.*

Solaris's dry voice took on a mocking note. "*Aw, is his highness going to whine about the freezing water?*"

Lance glared at the empty room. "Obviously not. Why do you call me that? I asked you not to."

"*It's just fun, no need to be so uptight.*"

Lance sighed. *Please don't do it again. You're going to get me arrested for treason.*

"No one can hear me except you." An excellent point, but it didn't make Lance feel any better. He set the cloth back down to where he'd retrieved it and exited the room, pulling the door closed with a loud click. Dirian was waiting outside, sharpening a short knife against a flat oval-shaped stone. The blade screeched as he swiped it against the rock. His eyes lifted threateningly up at the knight.

"Took you long enough." The ivirian stood up straighter, putting the stone away in a pouch.

"So I've been told." Lance muttered.

Dirian raised an eyebrow, but said nothing. Instead he whisked himself back down the hallway they came from. The knight spent one heartbeat staring up at the ceiling in exasperation, then hurried after the ivirian.

They set off down the hallway, which was cold both in temperature and company. Lance's guide was clearly eager to get rid of him, or at the very least to minimize their time together. The ivirian's contempt emanated off of him with such force that he made it quite impossible for Lance to ask where Merlin was, or where they were going. That forced him to follow blindly, which was not something he enjoyed. At least he had the comfort of knowing that, should he find himself lost or abandoned, his power could lead him to someone. Though he usually ignored it, Lance could always feel the presence of anyone near him. Not strongly, it was more like a dull buzz. Currently there was a large group of people somewhere beneath him that he could sense the best. Unsurprisingly, the more stairs they descended, the more passages they walked through, the closer they came to that mass of people.

Though it took nearly ten minutes, they eventually made it to their destination. After navigating through so many passages and doors, Lance would never be able to find his way back. The woodsmen must have lived in the house for some time to know the hallways so well.

"This is the kitchen," Dirian told him. "We don't bother using the actual dining room for anything other than planning."

Here Lance had the pleasure of remaining indifferent to Dirian's insinuation. He couldn't care less where they ate, whether he was noble or not. Yes, he was used to nicer surroundings, but he never complained about their absence like other noble families he knew. Here was one area of his life they could not ridicule. He smirked as he moved forward, pushing the door open so that he could enter.

Chaos ensued in the kitchen as Lance opened the door. It was a warm, decently sized room with all the necessities of a regular kitchen: a fire pit lined with stones, shelves carved into the walls, an iron chandelier hanging from the ceiling, and a chimney lined with rock. Everything smelled of rosemary, salt, and other spices, all of which stemmed from the cauldron steaming and bubbling over the fireplace. Lastly, there was an extra room attached to the kitchen which held a table and chairs.

The kitchen would have been pleasant regularly, but with everything going on, all peace was broken. For one thing, a short, stubby troll with a bright red beard—which clashed horribly against his sickly green skin—stood holding a ladle like a club. He was threatening the sprite called Foxtail, who was trying to get around him to the cauldron. His brother hung upside-down from one of the beams, bowl in hand, cheering Foxtail on. Around them Pico circled wildly, screaming out howls and sentences of fright, while Guinevere leapt from object to object trying to catch him. There was another sprite Lance hadn't seen before standing in the center of the room, yelling at the animals to stop. The sprite waved her arms at Pico, the long white sleeves of her dress fluttering about.

Blinking twice, Lance looked back at Dirian, who appeared to be suppressing his laughter. He noticed Lance looking as Gwen darted by, yelling about salt. Instantly the smile dropped. Dirian said something about finding Robin and left. Lance opened his mouth, watching the door swing closed. What was he supposed to do now?

He was given an answer by the sprite trying to catch Pico. Her calculative eyes fell on him, and immediately she yelled sharply, "Grab the cat!"

Without much thought he obeyed, springing out in front of Gwen. The cat yowled and stuck out both front paws, screeching to a hasty halt. Lancelot wasted no time, grabbing Gwen up from the floor. She meowed angrily, swiping with her claws at his hands and face.

"Lancelot, put me down right now! I hate being held!" Gwen demanded, aiming a paw at his face again.

"I don't think so!" he said, holding her at arms' reach. "You need to leave Pico alone!"

Upon hearing his name, the bird halted momentarily in the air. "Got you!" the sprite shouted, making a high jump into the air to grab the bird. Pico cried out as he was dragged down, held firmly in the sprite's arms. Lancelot walked over, still holding Gwen far enough away that she wouldn't be able to hit him.

"Good job," the sprite told him. "My name's Sage."

"Ah." Dirian had mentioned her. "Lancelot. Nice to meet you."

Sage grinned, whipping her head back to move strands of hair from her face without releasing Pico. Lance smiled as well, it was refreshing to find someone friendly.

"So you're the knight that showed up with Merlin," she guessed, repositioning her arms. Lance noted that she had no honorifics with Merlin, so maybe it was just the men who spoke formally. That made it rather amusing.

"Yes, that would be me." he admitted, distracted from setting the now calmed down Gwen on the floor. "Now, don't eat the bird, Gwen. Honestly, I expected more from you."

Gwen rolled her bright eyes. "I won't eat him, but Lance, don't talk down to me just because I'm smaller. I'm actually older than you."

Lance raised his eyebrow. "How old do you think I am?"

"Ha." Gwen sat on her back legs, and spread out her front paws. "You're twenty-one, obviously. It's so easy to guess the ages of humans and elestiels. In your years I am twenty-eight." She looked smugly at him.

Sage broke into their conversation then. "Sorry, did she say she'll leave Pico alone? I'm tired of holding him."

"Let go please!" Pico said with a childlike plea.

"Yes, yes, I'll leave him be." Gwen acquiesced with a flip of her tail. The black cat didn't look pleased, but at least the craziness of the room was cut in half. The only loud noise left came from the twins tormenting the cook.

Sage let go of Pico, who hooted happily, flying around the room fully before landing on the back of a chair. Crisis now averted; Lance turned to Sage. "You mentioned Merlin. Do you know where she is?"

"Oh, she said she was going to come down here soon as she could." Sage brushed a few feathers off the sash tied around her waist. "How did you meet Merlin, by the way?" Lance explained that he had been looking for her assistance on a private matter and had been obliged to travel north with her. "Oh, I see. You have a sick family member?"

"Eh, no... but her healing might be of use later." Sage looked confused, but she didn't press the matter. To avoid a lull in the conversation, Lance asked, "You work with Robin, I assume. How did that come to be?"

She brushed a strand of dark hair behind her pointed ear. "The same way as everyone else, really. No parents, no home, most of the time no friends; all good reasons to follow him. Before, I at least had a job, a really nice one in the capital." Her face contorted into a scowl. "But one of the superiors stole some gold, and I was blamed for it. I would have been hanged with the rest of the criminals if I hadn't met Foxtail and Featherhead. They were getting the rope as well, so when Robin broke them out, he saved me, too."

The noise that had backdropped her story stopped with an abrupt, "Hey!" from a shrill voice.

Foxtail appeared by Sage, having abandoned his fight with the cook. The young sprite was grinning. "I heard my name."

Sage glared at him not unlike Merlin, except with more affection in her features. "Yes, but I hardly see how that means you get to interrupt."

He ignored her words entirely, looking at Lance. "What I wonder is why you're explaining your life story to him."

Lance agreed, but he was hardly going to say so. Sage was by far the friendliest person he had met in Sher, and he wasn't about to ruin that by questioning her openness. Again, a memory of his brother spoke in his mind. *If someone is willingly giving you information, don't stop them. Listen, discern, and remember. Hidden information isn't always the most important.* The memory was so faint in his mind that he almost didn't notice it. It was more of a subconscious instruction, a learned mindset.

Lance's train of thought stopped as Sage gave him a pitiful look. "There's no reason to keep the information secret, so why not? Besides, the rest of you are all acting like he has the plague. I'm extremely disappointed in you all."

"He's a knight, Sage." Foxtail pointed out, losing the humor in his voice. "I run from people like him every day. So do you."

"Is he chasing you now?" Sage faced Foxtail, crossing her arms. "You're being silly."

"That's unfair." Foxtail mimicked her arm position, stepping forward. "You can't expect me to accept this guy just because he hasn't attacked us yet. Not that I'm worried about him attacking us, he looks weaker than Swiggle."

"Now you're insulting him. Can't you just leave him alone? It's not like he's staying with us."

Lancelot listened quietly, surprised and touched. He wanted to say something in defense of himself, but Sage was doing an excellent job by herself, and he didn't think Foxtail would appreciate his interference. Although, her unwarranted kindness did strike him as suspicious.

"You're so paranoid, Lance. My wife used to worry as much as you do, it made her very unhappy."

The knight frowned. *Suspicion tends to save lives.*

"Yes, because Sage is definitely able to kill you."

The argument stopped as the door to the kitchen abruptly opened once more. Robin, Yon, Luzel, and Dirian all walked inside. The thief had produced a long walking stick which he used as a guide into the room, eyes fixed forward on the back wall. Both sprites, with the quick addition of Featherhead, stood straighter at the entrance of their leader. Pico, on the other hand, made a joyful hoot and hopped from his perch on the chair. The brown owl flew over to Robin, gently landing on his shoulder.

"Hopefully I'm not interrupting anything. I was told dinner is ready." Robin announced.

The troll left his guarding position in front of the soup to stand by Robin. He spoke with the same sharp voice Lance heard earlier. "Good thing you're here. These mongrels were practically attacking me! I told them they needed to wait for you, but that hardly made them blink!"

Robin patted the cook's shoulder, bending slightly due to being much taller. "Don't worry, Swiggle. I'll give the twins the privilege of cleaning our horses, since they have so much energy, but that's after we eat. I haven't had anything really good since I left Nottingham."

Prideful pity filled Swiggle's face. "Of course, no one cooks like I can. If you'll just sit at the table, Boss."

Robin nodded, heading past Lance and the sprites to the table in the side room. "Aren't you coming Lance? Or would you prefer a proper dining table?"

Lancelot sent a tiny glare at the thief. "Here is fine, thank you." He sat in the farthest chair from Robin, who had placed himself at the head of the table.

Robin spoke cheerfully, "Oh, good. We haven't got a dining table anyway." He twisted his head around the back of his chair. "Is it just the knight and I eating tonight? I hadn't planned on spending my evening alone with him, but if none of you are hungry..." Laced in his casual words was a threat that only increased in severity at the unfinished sentence.

Lancelot was not surprised to see the woodsmen hurriedly sit around the table. That left only one spot open, directly to Lance's right. No one wanted to sit near him, except the cat who was on his left. The seat was thereby reserved for Merlin.

But where was Merlin? Lance hadn't seen her for an hour now. It was making him anxious. After being with her non-stop for so long, it was difficult to ignore her absence. As Swiggle placed bowls of steaming soup in front of each person, Lance leaned over to Gwen.

"Do you know where Merlin is?" he whispered.

Gwen looked up and blinked. "Yes."

"Well, is she coming?"

A sly and mischievous light brightened the feline's eyes. "She's here." Gwen pointed her paw. Lance turned his head, and there Merlin was, standing by the fire ring next to Swiggle, who was holding two bowls as he spoke. His mouth parted in surprise as she turned with her own bowl to face the table.

She was wearing a dark green dress tied tightly around her waist with a cord. The outfit made her coppery hair brighter. Ending just above her elbow were houppelande sleeves that hung halfway down her sides, swaying slightly as she walked. Merlin also had one of her rare pleasant looks on her face, something between happy and uncomfortable. Her appearance was, as a whole, far different than the one Lance had grown accustomed to while traveling with her. Regularly she looked tense and on the verge of anger. Something about her new, relaxed manner made her look... breathtaking.

Solaris whistled, "*I agree. Not as pretty as my wife, but still pretty.*"

Lancelot coughed, looking back down to the grains of the wooden table. *Shut up.* Heat warmed his cheeks, no doubt an embarrassed blush. Thankfully his skin was just dark enough to lessen the visibility. Unfortunately, that didn't account for the cat who was studying him for just such a reaction.

"Mhm, she does look nice when she tries. Bet you never noticed till now. Did you?" Gwen observed both bluntly and unabashedly. His throat dried some as the cat watched him, slowly licking up milk from her bowl.

"That is... none of your business." His voice was dry as Lance pulled awkwardly at his collar, trying to loosen it. The garment was fastened with a hook and eye, so his efforts were futile.

"You're right." Gwen agreed, sounding like he had trusted her with a secret. The tone made him more anxious than when he had been tied upside-down. "It's not my business."

"Yes..." He dragged the word out, now unsure of what he was agreeing to. "That is correct, Guinevere." With one last nervous glance at the cat, Lance turned his attention to the people around him. Merlin had just made it to the table, and Dirian was looking over at her.

"Well, Miss Merlin, I didn't think it was possible, but you look nice."

"Better than you at least." she retorted, continuing to her seat.

As she passed, Robin said loudly, "Yes, you look great, Merlin. A sight for sore eyes, really. I don't know what Dirian's implying."

Lance shook his head as a few of the other guys chuckled. Merlin just rolled her eyes. "That means a *lot*, thanks." Robin laughed as Merlin finally arrived at her spot next to Lancelot.

"I never lie!" Robin lied as she sat. "So there's no need to distrust me."

Sage spoke from the other side of the table. "Not that I'm trying to be rude, Boss, but it's hard to take you seriously."

Robin huffed. "I don't see why. You look lovely as well. My opinion counts just as much as anyone else."

"Sure it does." Merlin smirked, setting a bowl in front of her spot, and a second in front of Lance. She raised an eyebrow at him when he took the spoon she offered rather shakily, but he ignored it.

"There! Merlin agrees."

"I also agree." Foxtail pointed his utensil at Sage. "You do look nice." Sage's pale green cheeks turned to a light blue in response.

"I'm glad you didn't kill anyone."

Lance glanced at Merlin. She had spoken so softly he almost hadn't heard her. He frowned. "I'm not likely to do that." It was roughly the same thing she had said to Robin, and the eye roll meant she knew it.

"One can never be entirely sure," she muttered, taking a bite of food.

"Your faith in me is touching, *Miss* Merlin." He smirked, starting to eat his own meal. The tangy liquid had chunks of cabbage and potato—no carrots thankfully—in it, and was so good Lance was almost able to ignore the glare Merlin was giving him.

Only almost though, because then she leaned closer to Lance, and said in a quiet, mocking voice, "I'm glad you think so, *Mr.* Knight."

She was too close. He felt the light touch of air from her words against his skin. Lancelot choked on his potato.

Merlin smirked and sat back in her chair.

Not long after, most of the group finished their meal and were called to attention by Robin. Sharp tapping sounds came from the bottom of his spoon as he banged it on the wooden table. He was met with a few confused looks, but Yon and Luzel seemed unsurprised. Lance set his spoon down next to his empty bowl, listening attentively.

Robin cleared his throat before letting his own utensil slide back into his bowl. "If I could have your attention for a moment," he began. "I know I just arrived today, and I had every intention of staying, but tomorrow I will be leaving again." The confused faces turned disappointed. "I don't know how long I'll be gone, but as usual, Luzel and Yon are in charge. I'm sorry you won't have the pleasure of my company, but to make up for it, tonight we will celebrate my return and departure. Swiggle, get the ale."

"On it, Boss." The cook shuffled off.

Robin leaned back in his chair, smiling. "I want you all to pretend you're extremely happy tonight. Got it?"

"Who's pretending?" Callin asked gruffly.

Lance muffled a snort as Dirian leaned forward. "Are you bribing us with alcohol, Boss?"

Robin raised both hands. "Maybe?"

Foxtail grinned from down the table. "Good. Then in that case, I say farewell heartily!"

A round of laughter ran across them, Swiggle bringing out the mugs. Most of the night passed away in that manner, with jokes, laughter, and a steady supply of ale. It was happy enough, but there was an underlying weakness in it. Everyone was trying their hardest not to be in low spirits, and one wrong word might make it all fall apart. It was obvious to Lance, as he was folded into the fun largely because leaving him out would crack exactly what they were trying to keep whole. Still, despite the strain, Lance allowed himself to enjoy the night.

It was all going well until the subject of Sage's discussion with Lancelot was brought up. She declared rather bluntly that Robin had a habit of hiring orphans and criminals to be his friends. Maybe just that one sentence in the dim light of their table party wouldn't have mattered, but Callin responded in the precise moment there was a lull in conversation.

"Oh, Robin only looks for orphans because they've got nowhere to go. The best people to do your dirty work are the ones who can't leave you part way. It's a genius idea that only he can think of, being without parents himself." Before he had even finished the sentence, Callin's gray face turned pale. His embarrassment turned quickly to defiant uneasiness, but the initial emotion still saturated the room. Everyone was frozen. Dirian still had a smile plastered on his face, eyes filled with apprehension.

Robin's face remained blank, but he gently set his mug down, pushing back his chair. "I think that's enough for one night. Be ready for work in the morning." Those were his only words before he turned around and walked out of the room, tapping his walking stick as he went.

Lance sat quietly in his spot, unsure of what to do or say. There was obviously something he was missing. He turned to ask Merlin but couldn't, as she had just risen. Her eyes were pinpointed on Callin. Though the gold of her irises were always pale, they were now frighteningly cold. Utter displeasure and disappointment lay in them, a withering stare of anger that would wilt even the most seasoned nobleman. Lance shivered, glad that he was not the recipient of that glare. Callin, on the other hand, appeared torn between shame and prideful confidence.

CHAPTER 19

It felt like hours before she turned and followed Robin out of the room, leaving silence in her wake. Guinevere trailed behind Merlin, hissing before she was no longer in sight. The cat's snarl seemed to loosen the frozen woodsmen. Luzel, who was sitting by Callin, brought a hard fist down on his head. The older iviro gave a short howl of pain.

"Why'd you have to go and do that?" Callin asked, rubbing his head.

"You old jackrabbit!" Dirian glared, wobbling slightly in his seat. It was amazing that only the twins had passed out. The older ones could certainly hold their liquor just fine. "Why did *you* have to say *that*?"

"It just came out," answered Callin lamely.

"Well you ruined a perfectly good night." Luzel told him, running a hand through his hair. "It was awful timing for you to say that. You know he just got back from hunting."

Callin looked down, grumbling, "I know."

"Um" Lance started. They all looked at him, their stares intense enough to dry his throat. "What exactly are you talking about?"

"You don't know?" Swiggle asked him as he placed two lit candles on the table. Previously the room was illuminated by the fire ring, but it too sunk alongside the good mood.

Lance rubbed his sword's pommel. "I only met him a few days ago."

Dirian slammed a fist against the table that startled Featherhead, who was snoring next to him. "You're right, you only met him a few days ago, so there's no reason to tell you—"

"No." The ivirian was interrupted by Yon. The giant sat in his large, elaborate chair, looking somber. "I will tell him."

"But Yon!" Dirian cried.

"No!" The giant's rumbling voice was stern. "You heard what Robin said the same as I. There's no reason to keep this a secret when Robin himself doesn't." Yon held up a hand to silence Dirian from further protest. "I know what you're saying, but avoiding a subject is not the same as hiding it." Yon turned his head to face Lancelot, leaned his elbows on his knees, and clasped his hands. In the darkness, the giant looked bigger somehow, and *much* more dangerous. Maybe that was because of his serious expression or the many weapons that adorned him. Either way, Lancelot sat straighter, meeting Yon's steel with his own.

"I'm heading to bed then." Dirian announced, glaring at the table irritably before he left. Callin also departed, leaving Lance with Yon, Luzel, and the sleeping teenage sprites. Sage gave Lance a sad look before she too left.

Luzel moved his chair next to Yon so that now they were both facing Lance. "Do you have parents, Lancelot?" the ivirian asked, pulling out a ball of white thread from one of his pockets. He began rerolling it, winding the string tightly around his middle and pointer fingers.

His chest tightened, Lance answered cautiously, "Yes, I do."

"Most of us don't, not anymore." Yon said slowly. "Robin included. But unlike the rest of us, who were abandoned too early to remember, he has memories of his parents. He wasn't abandoned, not by the Hoods."

"Hoods?" Lance repeated. He thought that was just Robin's stage name, something to keep the authorities away.

"It's their surname. The one we made up, anyway." Luzel paused looping the string. "It's not his actual last name, but we all use it, so does he. Robin Hood, got a nice sound to it, especially since he wears them so much."

Yon nodded. "He hasn't told us his real name yet, but that's beside the point. His family used to live in a town exactly on the border of Sher and Avalon, half in one kingdom, half in the other."

The knight nodded. There were two or three towns with that description that he knew of. It had never been ideal for the kingdom, but in order not to cause further tensions, they had been left untouched.

"Kete, that's the name of the village." Yon continued. "The town is poor now. They're taxed by both the Avalonian and Sher Government. Robin's parents were tax collectors of a kind, and had a habit of passing by the poorer homes. As you can assume, they made enemies that way. It ended for them when they were killed in their own home. Robin was seven and saw the whole thing."

"That's horrible." Lance muttered. It was repulsive that anyone should be cruel enough to kill two people who were only being kind, and in front of their child no less. "Was it..." He hesitated. The answer might be exactly what he was dreading. "Was it an Avalonian?"

CHAPTER 19

"No." Luzel answered. "It was a Sher official. An ivirian is the reason our boss is blind." Luzel glowered at the candle as he spoke. "Gave him a smack across the back of his head so hard he lost his sight."

A somber cloud descended on Lance as he sat there, eyes glued to the table. Whoever had done the act must have been horrid in more ways than one. But even in his disgust, Lance was also a little relieved. If an Avalonian had been the one to do it, he might have felt guilty. Certainly he would have returned home and done his best to hunt down whoever it was, but after so long, it'd be nigh impossible to accomplish it.

"That stinking worm threw Robin straight into the forest." Yon growled, his voice shaking with anger.

Both woodsmen were shivering with rage at the thought, as if the very act had been done to them instead. Such vehement anger at a hurt done to one's leader, even so long ago, was in some ways commendable. The observation sparked a seed of respect in Lancelot for the woodsmen, and subsequently Robin as well. Not that he would ever tell them, but he had to admire their resolve.

Gently, Lance asked, "Why won't he let Merlin heal him?" He had a guess for the answer, but he wasn't sure yet. Maybe they would tell him.

The woodsmen looked up, startled. "How did you know that, if you didn't know his story?" Luzel asked.

"She told me, Merlin, I mean." He was somewhat regretting saying anything at all.

"That sounds like Miss Merlin." Swiggle appeared once again, but this time he was empty handed. The troll pulled out a chair and sat down heavily. "Not giving you all the information when you ask, and then rolling her eyes when you don't understand." He shook his head, though he spoke fondly. A smirk tugged at Lance's mouth at the cook's declaration. Apparently he wasn't the only one she kept information from. Then again, he was keeping things from her as well.

Yon pulled himself together, casting off his surprise. "Robin is waiting for something to see. Whatever that means." His face turned darker. "Apparently his comrades aren't good enough."

"So I was right," Lance murmured to himself. They didn't seem to hear him, and carried on amongst themselves.

"Oh, stop complaining." Swiggle wagged a finger at the giant. "You wouldn't want our dirty faces to be the first thing you see after fourteen years. No one would! At the very least, Miss Merlin can be offended, not us."

"He does make a good point." Luzel nodded. "I avoid the kitchen as much as I can to save my eyes from seeing Swiggle's face."

"You best beware it now!" The old troll wagged his finger at Luzel. "The kitchen is where the knives are!"

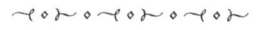

M

The steps leading up to Robin's office were dark and would have been extremely difficult to climb if not for the candle Merlin had procured. Even with the extra light she had to be careful, as the hem of her dress liked to slip in and out from beneath her shoes. She would have infinitely preferred her long riding pants, but Sage had none for her to borrow. The sprite offered trousers, but Merlin declined knowing that she would be wearing the pants for the foreseeable future once they left Loxley. Her olive riding pants were much more tattered than she realized, so she was forced to let them go.

Despite the fickle skirt, Merlin was able to make it to the top of the stairs, unharmed. There was only one room down this hallway, and she could see that its door was open. Merlin set the candle down in a small alcove in the wall, moving to the room's opening. Streams of moonlight poured in from the balcony at the far end, casting a silver glow over the few furnishings of the room. Pico was perched on the back of a wooden chair, quietly watching as she entered. The bird for once didn't make a noise, just stared sullenly. As she entered softly into the room, she made sure to gently stroke the top of the bird's head, which seemed to make him feel better.

It was on the balcony that she found the thief she was looking for. His arms were draped over the rims of the rail, feet dangling between the posts. The edge of the forest was far enough away that only the faintest whisper of the crickets reached the balcony. Robin tilted his head in her direction as she sat down, mirroring his position with the exception of his feet. Putting her legs through the rail would be too difficult with a dress.

Taking a slow breath, Merlin opened her mouth, ready to break the silence. "You were looking for him again?" she asked delicately.

Robin rested his head on an arm, eyes still trained out into the vast expanse of open air between them and the trees. "Do you know how exhausting this is?" he asked, more for himself than for her. "I've been looking for him since I was ten, and still I've found nothing. Just more anger."

Merlin bit her lip. She didn't want to say the wrong thing and make him feel worse, but gentleness wasn't exactly her strong suit. She tried anyway, saying, "Have you searched the capital? They might have records with his name."

Robin laughed wryly, which made Merlin cringe. "I just came back from there. They had nothing, not a single record from the time when it happened. Someone cleared them all out. It's like they knew I was coming."

"I'm sorry," Merlin rested her own head on her arms, staring out at the dark tangled mass of roots draped on the cliff's edge.

"I'm not."

Her lips parted, eyes flicking over to her friend. Robin could see nothing of the surprise on her face, but she could see him. He looked both determined and undecided at the same time. It was the exact opposite of his normal attitude.

Merlin laced her fingers together. "Why?"

"Because I'm not so sure this is the right thing to do." Robin admitted. "Holding on to this anger for so long is worse than being shot with an arrow or cut with a sword. I know from experience. And what does it add up to anyway? More rage and a chase that will seemingly never end. I don't suggest it."

"But," Merlin hesitated, "he killed your parents. He deserves the same treatment."

"Yes, he does." Robin frowned. "If he was to stand in front of me, I doubt I could just let him go. But what about after that?"

She sat up, drawing her eyebrows together. "After? What do you mean by that?"

He also sat straighter. "After he's dead. What am I supposed to do with fourteen years of bitterness inside me? Is getting rid of him going to also get rid of the anger? Or am I going to be stuck with that forever?" Robin shook his head. "It won't help."

"So," Merlin's stomach clenched, her emotions were telling her heart to speed up and clamp down on her sentiments. "You think that you should give up, even though he deserves to die?"

"No, I'm not giving up." The thief leaned back on his palms. His voice was calmer than hers. "I've come too far for that. But maybe... it's best I never find him."

Merlin shook her head, unable to grasp what he was saying. Let the ivirian go? After everything he did? "If someone killed my parents, I don't think I could just sit and do nothing."

"I know that." Robin sighed. "But I'm warning you not to go down this path. Don't be like me. Don't go down a road with no ending. Do you understand?"

Merlin crossed her arms, glaring at the sky, trying to calm her racing nerves. She knew exactly what and who he was speaking of, though he wouldn't say it out loud. His words of caution had already been said to her from her mother, and from her father. Each time her heart would clench so tightly she thought it would break.

Fearing the emotion, Merlin said, "You're very foreboding tonight. Is there something you aren't telling me?"

The thief pursed his lips, pulling his walking stick that was lying at his side up into his hand. It was his personal cue to the fact that he was about to stand, so when he did seconds later, Merlin was already on her feet. She eyed him narrowly, aware that her question was still unanswered.

"Robin?" she prodded, following him into the office. The thief ignored her as he walked farther into his room. He patted Pico's head as he passed, coming to a stop in front of his desk. Robin put both hands on the edge, leaning heavily. For three painstakingly silent moments Merlin waited for him to speak. When he did, she was listening intently.

"I'm not hiding anything, or... at least nothing like that. But I have a bad feeling about this, Merlin. Something isn't quite right, and it's not going to end well for us."

CHAPTER 19

She let that sink in, turning it over in her mind. "What caused this feeling? I can hardly see anything immediately worth worrying about."

Robin shook his head, speaking in a more disheveled way. "No, there isn't anything happening right now, though the fact that you don't worry about our plan is amazing. No, I'm talking about the sick feeling that has been sitting in my stomach since I came up here. I'm worried, Merlin. I'm worried."

20

THE START OF SOMETHING DARK

The next morning Merlin woke up feeling unsettled. She was in her room with Gwen, who lay curled up on a chair, the sky outside just starting to brighten. Somehow she had managed to wake up at dawn, so maybe her discomfort was due to drowsiness. Slipping her legs off the side of the bed, Merlin carefully moved to a side table. She lit the candle that was standing on the wood, and then pulled the pile of clothes she received from Sage out from inside the drawer. It creaked once as she pulled the drawer out, a loud cry that made Merlin wince. She glanced over at Guinevere, but the cat was only stirring, not awake.

Internally, Merlin sighed in relief, and proceeded to change into the trousers, shirt, and tunic that were in the pile. A green vest went over her brown tunic that laced all the way up the front. She was in the process of threading it when Gwen gave a yawn.

"Morning," Merlin called over her shoulder. Behind her she could hear Gwen stretching. When the cat said nothing, Merlin turned and raised an eyebrow at her. "You're awfully quiet." It was only when she said it out loud that she realized how true it was. The cat had been uncharacteristically quiet ever since they arrived in Loxley.

"I had an unsettling dream." Gwen said, sounding tired. She rubbed her face with one of her paws. "I must have been worrying too much, and it affected my sleep."

"You and Robin." Merlin grumbled, returning to her lacing. "I know why he's worried, so why are you? Do you also have some sort of bad feeling that you can't explain?"

"No Merlin, I can explain it well." Feeling the shift into a longer conversation, Merlin turned fully around so that she could keep working while facing Gwen. The cat was stretched out on the chair, flicking her tail back and forth.

"So, what is it then?"

CHAPTER 20

"Have you realized that in a few days, we will have made it to the border?"

Merlin pulled the leather string through one of the remaining holes in the fabric. "Yes, I'm excited to see Daleon again. I know we have more traveling afterward, but I'm so close now, I can feel it."

"Are you sure they will even let you stay?" Gwen asked, all traces of sleep gone from her. "What if we get there and they just send you back? You already got the letter saying you were declined."

"I'll just have to convince them." Merlin told her, tying the strings together at the top with unnecessary force.

"That won't work, and you know it."

"Why are you saying this?" Merlin asked sharply, spinning around to get her purple cloak. "You haven't mentioned this once. Not during any of the times we could have turned around."

"Really, and when could we turn around?" Gwen growled. "When we were almost arrested at Jack's place? Or maybe when you were almost killed by a thread-crazy weaver? And if we did go back, where could we go? Your house is unavailable, and your parents won't be back for another three months!"

Merlin's hands were starting to shake as she pulled her cape over her head. "Fine, if we don't have anywhere to go back to, and you just followed me because of that, why are you telling me now?"

"Because! Tomorrow we'll be at the front, and once we've crossed the pass we're likely to be arrested or sent back. I think that instead of going there, we should help Lancelot." The cat stood up, looking defiantly at Merlin.

The elestiel stared at her, open mouthed. Go with the knight? Gwen wanted her to follow a plan that was based on a *folktale*? "Ridiculous," she declared. "Utterly ridiculous. I am not going with Lance."

Gwen's eyes narrowed. "You haven't even considered it, have you? Actually going with him. Even though you promised to keep an open mind, you didn't think one moment about joining him! Unbelievable Merlin!"

"How is that unbelievable?" Merlin cried. "All along I've been saying that I am going to join Daleon. I have never said otherwise. What's surprising is that *you* actually considered it! You know his plan doesn't hold water."

The fur on Gwen's back was standing on end as she hissed at Merlin. "What you don't seem to be getting is that countless people could all be saved if you help him! I've been thinking about joining him since we left your house, simply based on that!"

"That's only if the plan works!" Merlin pointed out emphatically. "Chasing after a dead prince is not going to help. And it certainly won't fulfill my promise to Daleon!"

Gwen rolled her eyes, closing the lids as she sighed in aggravation. "Oh, that blasted promise. You keep using it as an excuse. You and I both know the exact words were, "I promise that I will follow you." That means you've already achieved your goal. The moment you started this journey, you followed him."

Merlin froze in front of Gwen, the cat panting from her anger. Why? Why was she challenging her on this? Yes, her promise had a hole that could be exploited, a way to get around its meaning. The idea had suggested itself to her through Gwen, who made a joking comment about it a year ago. But she never considered actually using it, especially not in this way. Not so she could go gallivanting off to Norestere with Lance. Even if she trusted him more, and would admit that he was an acceptable traveling companion, she did not want to go with him. Stopping this war was not her job.

Maybe Gwen saw a measure of her resolve, because her ears drooped, and she sat back down on the chair. "Merlin," she started gloomily, "I know you've never been outside this forest, but I have. I've seen the way humans live, how they're ruled. This war doesn't just take the lives of those fighting in it, it swallows those at home as well." With each word she sounded more pleading. "The people who rely on trade to have enough food and the ones whose sons are needed for work. It kills them in ways worse than those who die in battle; by crushing their hope, and starving them of food. Maybe not in every town and village, but in enough of them for it to matter. Can you not understand any of that?" Guinevere stared intensely at Merlin, eyes wide and reaching, trying to get her to agree.

A heavy lump formed in the back of Merlin's throat. The desperate emotion coming off of Gwen was almost tangible, but she couldn't bring herself to grasp it. The sympathy displayed was just out of reach, an emotion Merlin did not share. It wasn't that she felt no care for the victims of battle, because she did. But even so, it didn't change the fact that Daleon was simply more important.

Quietly, and with much reticence, Merlin said, "I don't know them, Gwen. I understand what you're saying, but I won't go with the knight. My brother always comes first. Always."

The light in Gwen's eyes died. The cat turned her head to the side, dropping her tail. "Dal isn't weak, Merlin. You make it sound like it's a miracle he's still alive."

Merlin pulled her bag from beside the bed. "He's not weak, but everyone is subject to injury. I'm the only one capable of stopping death."

"I know." Gwen muttered bitterly. "But you could be saving more than just his life."

Merlin was saved from further argument by a knock on the door. With a mutual glare between the two, Merlin hurried and opened the door. Lancelot was standing in front of her, Dirian at his right. The ivirian looked tired, but there was the faint trace of a smirk on his face, like he'd won a bet. Lancelot looked the opposite of Dirian, with a blank face that did nothing to hide the sad shadow covering his features. What upset him? Surely he hadn't been standing long enough to hear her argument with Gwen? Yet, even if he had, everything she argued was something she'd said before.

"Good morning." she said, testing out the greeting. It felt wrong on her tongue.

"I suppose, yes." He sounded as if his mind was not entirely there, which could mean Solaris was speaking to him, but Merlin had a sinking suspicion that was not the case. The possibility that he overheard her didn't sit well in her stomach, something like guilt was biting at her.

"Swiggle has some porridge for you before you leave," Dirian spoke up, his wings fluttering. "We came to get you."

"I see," Merlin replied mindlessly, turning her head to the side. A heavy weight pressed against her shoulders as Guinevere hopped off her chair, stalking past Merlin with an air of annoyance. The elestiel followed after the cat once she was sure she retrieved everything from the room.

Silence ensued for the first three minutes of their trek down to the kitchen. Awkward uneased hovered like a cloud, glaringly blatant until Dirian broke it. He rambled out a stream of idle complaints about waking up too early and the horrible headache he had from the ale of the previous night. The speech seemed to revive Lancelot a little, and he helped Dirian along with the conversation, saying he also had a headache, though it was manageable. Gwen still kept her mouth shut, and Merlin would have too, if not for being asked about the state of her head.

"My head is perfectly fine," she answered. "My gift is constantly healing me without my signet activated, that includes the effects of drinking."

"Have you never been sick, then?" Lance asked curiously.

"Not that I can remember." Merlin told him as they arrived at the kitchen. Swiggle was waiting for them inside with three bowls of scooped porridge. The hot breakfast passed by quickly with the conversation dissolved once again, and soon they were all headed back out. Yon, Luzel, and Robin were waiting for them in the grand hall connected to the exit, speaking in hushed tones. Robin had his bow slung behind him, and his side quiver was full again. A knife was strapped to the side of his leg, and there were small satchels attached to his belt. Pico was perched on Yon's shoulder, and Luzel had a tightly stuffed bag in his hand.

He handed it gingerly to Lancelot when they reached them. "There are plenty of supplies in there for you, but you shouldn't need it all. The border isn't far from here."

"Thank you." Lance slung the pack onto his back, glancing at Merlin before moving away. She sighed and faced her two friends.

"Thank you for your help." She shouldered her own bag. "It's been nice seeing you both."

"Yes, it has." Robin agreed. None of the worry from their conversation had transferred over to the morning, but Merlin figured he was simply hiding it. Yon might try to stop them if he knew about Robin's hesitance.

The giant crossed his arms. "You both stay safe. Patrols have gotten more frequent since the Avalonians attacked Logres. I think the Mayor is desperate to keep them out."

"You're probably right." Robin nodded. "That would start our own war with them."

Merlin frowned. "That might already be a problem." She looked over at the Avalonian knight.

"As long as they don't see him, it should be fine." Luzel sounded comforting as he came closer. He held up two pouches and put them gently in Merlin's hand. "These are crushed irises. They're decently powerful, so one sprinkle should work for a few days. There should be enough in there to last a week or two, if you're careful. It's not much, but it might keep you both from getting killed immediately."

"Thank you," she said again, closing her fingers around the bags. Imbued irises were particularly hard to cultivate, and even more rare to find in the forest. The power inside the petals made it both extremely useful and expensive. The amount he was giving Merlin was worth a lot of gold. Bestowing one of her equally rare smiles, Merlin hugged the old ivirian.

"All right, that's enough of that." Luzel patted her shoulder, moving away once more. "Gwen, you keep an eye on them all."

The cat was striding to the exit, but she looked back after being spoken to. "Don't I always?"

"She won't need to, because I will be doing all the watching myself." Robin exclaimed, crossing his arms in mock offense. "The amount of trust you have in me as a leader is beyond amazement. It's *so* nice to know that my men support and trust me."

Yon rolled his eyes, stretching to his full height. "Yes well, if you need your men, send a raven who's willing to make the trip. We'll be there as quickly as we can."

There was no effect on Robin other than a slight laugh as he turned away, waving his hand back and forth at them. "I'll see you both later. Don't burn the house down while I'm gone." Yon rolled his eyes once again as the small group exited the building.

As they started away from Loxley, Merlin felt a pang of homesickness. This was the third time she left a place that felt welcoming, like a bit of home had crept into her surroundings. Now that she was leaving what was likely the last familiar place she would enter, her heart longed for the house of her childhood. It had always been a place to ground herself and return to when she was unsure. Like she was now.

All her life, she had believed that keeping her family safe was the most important thing she could do. Being a healer meant that she was the best to do it, despite her brother's strong Rideon gift. He might be able to protect them in a fight, but she could keep them alive. Maybe, when she was younger, there had been a time when she didn't feel that way, when all she wanted to do was help those in need. But that wasn't her anymore. The world was more selfish than her six-year-old self could have comprehended. If she gave herself up to healing others, the world would snuff out those important to her.

Still, was Gwen to be ignored so easily? The cat was her best friend, and a highly intelligent cat at that. If she said that people were suffering and needed help, then that was true. Besides, didn't she owe Lancelot for all the times he saved her? At the beginning of their journey he promised to protect her, and even though she hadn't really believed him, he had done just that. The knight put his own life on the line to make sure she stayed safe. Not just anyone would do that.

Indecision hit Merlin's gut as she followed the group. Just like the last time they traveled together, Robin and Gwen took to the trees, moving speedily from branch to branch. That left Lancelot and Merlin to follow on the ground and over the thick tree roots. They traveled at a straining pace until the soles of Merlin's boots felt thin and weak. Every bit of upended bark stuck into the arch of her foot, pain magnified by the numbness that had taken over her toes. Stockings were of no use in the forest; the cold simply needled its way through the fabric.

Merlin pulled the sleeves of her shirt farther down her wrists, attempting to warm her arms. In the uneasy silence of the forest, she had noticed how different it was from the woods around her home. There the forest was lush and colorful, filled with life both in the trees and the animals that lived in them. Light seemed to find its way into that golden part of the forest, pooling through any crack it could find in the leafy roof. The flowers had been vast in number, and herbs lined small hills or grew by creeks. Her neighbors were pleasant too, if not bothered.

Here there were few people to be seen other than soldiers trekking through their patrol, as most myths had moved further into Sher. The trees were just as thick as the ones she knew, but their bark was a murky gray that cast dull shades over the surrounding plants. Even the dirt on the ground that had been muddy the day before was already returning to its normal, dry, crumbling state. There were barely any flowers, and the greens of the forest were all muted. Northern Sher was a cold, desolate forest that sunk its claws into travelers, forcing the gray gloom into their minds. How soldiers could bear to live in it, Merlin didn't know.

It wasn't, however, the forest's fault that it was like this. Merlin could sense even from where they were that power from the Rideon was being siphoned into the one thing keeping Sher safe from intruders: Akiva's Wall. Ivirians created it by growing tall thorny branches that hedged the entire kingdom. They filled the gaps between the thorns with gusts of wind strong enough to break bones, or geysers of fire so hot not even the Purge Ivirian controlling them could touch the flames. The most effective of the traps were those made from wind, but unfortunately most Gale Ivirians were terrifying hermits that not even the government could control. With so few of them in the military, hardly any of the wall was guarded by their overwhelming force. To compensate, Tear Ivirians would set up horrifying arrays of liquid traps to either drown, spear, or drain a creature's water from their body.

All the power it took to keep Akiva steady strained the forest, which was connected to the Rideon itself. A connection which had grown over the years because of the myths living within. Sadly, none of that knowledge made Merlin feel any better. She was still hampered by the dreariness of the forest, a reflection of her thoughts and emotions after both discussions with her friends. All they had accomplished was creating confusion by way of chiseling away at her resolve.

When they eventually settled into a cave just beneath a hollowed oak, Merlin was even grouchier than she had been in the morning. She tried releasing some of her pent up anger by starting a fire in the cave. Her ignition rocks practically quivered with the force she applied by scraping the two together. Sparks sprayed over the collection of dry, scrappy branches they had collected, but not a single twig caught fire. Merlin glared harder at it, trying again and again to light the wood.

She was close to throwing them when she was stopped by Lancelot. He put one hand on top of hers, smiling uncomfortably. "Uh, let me."

Merlin bit her lip as he held out his other hand, flexing his fingers towards the wood. Smoke slowly began rising from within the brush, and bright orange curls of light spiraled around the branches. Merlin glanced up at the knight, his eyebrows were drawn together from concentration. He had been covered in flames the last time he used Solaris' fire, so it was only now that Merlin noticed his eyes were glowing a vibrant red orange. She averted her gaze as he pulled his hand away from the heat, simultaneously removing his other hand from on top of hers.

"Thanks," she mumbled. He nodded and left her for his own part of the cave.

"Well, this is lovely," Robin announced. The thief was sitting against a crumbling part of the cave wall, a blanket rolled out beneath him. "We're all together in a cave again. Isn't this nice?"

Merlin shook her head, unrolling her own blanket.

When no one said anything, Robin spoke again. "All right, I don't know what happened in the very few hours I wasn't around you three, but we all have to be on the same page if we want to live through tomorrow. For the sake of keeping my wonderful self alive, can you all just forget whatever it is that's bothering you?"

Merlin frowned at her friend. "I don't think so, but I'm willing to pretend it didn't happen." Locking up her doubt might actually be a good idea.

"That's one person." Robin nodded. He turned his head back and forth around the cave, seemingly in the direction of Gwen and Lance.

"I'll endeavor to try my best, but unfortunately, I have serious problems that need to be thought over." Lance obliged.

Another pang of guilt sent Merlin frowning at the knight. Was her refusal one of the "*serious problems*" he was thinking over?

"I will also do my best, Robin." Gwen spoke up. "I'd rather live past tomorrow."

"Good." Robin nodded. "In that case, I will explain exactly what we're going to do tomorrow. We're about two hours away from the village of Aroth, which is a mile from Akiva. Once we get there, I will use a clever disguise to find where Daleon has been stationed. A post office should have the answer I need. While I do that, Gwen will lead you both to the town's exit, where you shall split ways. Lancelot for Akiva, and the rest of us for Daleon's post when I arrive. Understood?"

"Shouldn't *I* be the one looking for Daleon at the post office?" Merlin protested, placing a hand over her heart. "You're a wanted criminal. If anyone recognizes you we'll *all* have to escape."

"Ah, but you forget." Robin wagged his pointer finger at her. "You three are wanted as well, and when it comes to hiding in plain sight, I am the best. Alas, your gold eyes will draw too much attention."

"Not with Luzel's gift." Merlin pointed out.

"You asked me for help." Robin reminded her. She glared as he continued. "If this is supposed to work, then you will all do it my way.

CHAPTER 20

That village is full of soldiers who, given the chance, would love to arrest or kill us all. Except maybe Gwen." The cat purred contentedly. "So there won't be any arguments about who goes where. Not if you want to succeed."

"Excuse me, but I have a question." Lance sounded like he already knew the answer and hated to ask. "Merlin, you promised me that you would keep an open mind about coming with me. Have you still not changed your mind? I can't find Arthur without you."

All the guilty feelings came back to her as she looked sadly at Lancelot. He was annoying at times, but in general he was a good person and a good friend. Gwen was also staring at her, imploring Merlin through her eyes to say yes. For half a second Merlin considered going with him, she really did. But the force of her guilt fell short of the loyalty she had for her family.

"No, I haven't changed my mind. I'm sorry, Lance." Merlin sighed. Slowly, imperceptibly, she glanced at the knight. If she expected anger, there was none. Lance just nodded, accepting her response. "You're not mad?" The question was out before she could stop it. Of course he was mad, or at least frustrated. Who wouldn't be?

"Disappointed," he responded. Lance was straining, obviously he had more to say, but was holding back.

"The two of you make me speechless." Robin pointed a finger in their direction. "An important decision, and you're only discussing it now?"

"We've been a little busy." Lance offered.

"Oh?"

Merlin leaned against the rough wall. "Yes. It's difficult to talk while running away from soldiers."

The knight nodded, "Or avoiding trolls."

"Or trying not to kill each other."

Lance smirked, eyes twinkling for the first time in a long while. "I would never kill you, Merlin. I need you alive."

"I guess it was just me then, contemplating murder."

"No," Gwen swished her tail, "I wanted to kill you both."

"I'm starting to think I should have stayed with my woodsmen." Robin crossed his arms.

"There's no use in complaining now." Merlin stated. "You've already come with us."

"Yes, and you will do exactly as I said, *because* I came with you. Correct?"

Her heart squeezed, and she bit her lip. He had to bring that back up, didn't he? Still, he was right. She came to him for help because she knew he was good at these kinds of things.

"Fine," she muttered, grumbling it loud enough to make sure he heard.

"Excellent." Robin laid down. "Now all we have to do is not die, and the plan will be perfect."

"Right," Lance said seriously. "All we have to do is not die."

21

Batch of Shadows

The village of Aroth was built up in a line of tall trees that grew in a large marsh. The buildings were made on top of circular platforms with four ladders as the entrances, and thus the exits, which were separated to the four corners of the village. It was the closest village to Akiva besides a few military settlements made by humans before Sher became a kingdom for only myths.

Merlin paused midway up the ladder, gazing at the green marsh below. It was said that humans were some of the most creative beings in the world, and that they could make anything. Aroth was certainly a testament to that. Merlin's mother told her once that the trees in the village were false ash, a special tree in that its bark was used to calm injured patients so they could be treated. Unfortunately, though its medicinal value was high, the bark itself was very finicky. Whether cut or burnt, the bark would crumble into a cloud of highly potent mist, which made breathing difficult. In some cases the bark could actually render a creature unconscious. For those reasons, it made harvesting false ash extremely dangerous, and impossible to build atop. That is, until the humans came along.

They found a way to minimize their interference with the bark, saving the natural plant life in the marsh below. Had they made their home on the ground, many herbs would have been killed amidst the construction. As it was, Merlin was even able to collect some luel; a plant which appeared to be regular grass, except for its red tips. Luel was mainly used for pain relief and disinfection.

"Merlin, can we keep going please?" Gwen whined from her perch on Merlin's shoulder. Unable to climb the ladder herself, the cat had to hang on to Merlin's cloak with her claws. Her complaining successfully snapped Merlin out of her reverie.

"Yes." Merlin looked back up, renewing her climb upwards.

"You should listen to Gwen," called Lancelot from below her. "I don't want to have to catch you again."

She looked past her elbow and gave him a sour look. "I see your sense of humor has returned. But you know, one of these days *I'm* going to have to save you."

He gave her a small grin. "We'll see." Lance turned his head to gaze out at the trees around them, and the movement sent a pang of guilt through her stomach. It reminded her that they wouldn't be together long enough for that to happen. Merlin bit her bottom lip and climbed the rest of the way up in silence. Robin helped her up from the ladder onto the entry platform, and she in turn assisted Lancelot. Guinevere hopped from her shoulder as soon as Merlin was stable on the wooden platform, stretching out her legs with a pleased meow.

"*Sveit.*" Lancelot thanked her as he too found stable footing on the platform. At least Merlin assumed it was thanks. She nodded and moved away, pulling her hood back up.

"Don't bother." Gwen appeared in front of Merlin. "No one's here."

Merlin frowned, removing her hood so she could see clearly. Empty platforms peaked between tree trunks, and there were no guards to be seen. Aside from the present company, there really was not a single other living soul.

"Where are the soldiers?" Merlin wondered, feeling a shiver make its way down her spine.

Lance stepped farther onto the platform, scanning the empty forest. "I can't sense anyone. Didn't you say this place was overrun with soldiers?"

"A slight exaggeration," Robin admitted, sliding his pack off his shoulder. As he rummaged around his bag he said, "Two weeks ago the place held at least two companies of soldiers, according to my scouts. Aroth usually houses reserve troops in case of emergencies at the border. I don't like that they aren't here."

"It will make crossing the village easier." Gwen offered.

"Yes, but where did they go?" Merlin peered into the silent village. "Do you think they went... to fight?" she asked it tentatively, knowing full well the implications that arose with it.

"That can't be it." Lance responded emphatically. "Sher has been neutral for the entirety of this war. It would be disastrous for them to join now."

"No sense in worrying about that." Robin told them, standing up with something in his hand. He sounded somewhat pleased with himself. "Even if they did go off to fight, it's not likely to affect *us* right now. So we should just get a move on." He held up a segment of a smooth, beige pole, and flicked it sideways. There was a soft click, and the pole extended and snapped together. Robin gave a satisfied grin and set the bottom of his pole on the ground, resting the top on his shoulder.

Merlin shook her head. "One day you're going to have to show my father how you made that. He won't stop asking me about it."

Robin shrugged. "Sorry Merlin, but that secret stays with me. What will we humans do if our only defining skill is mimicked?"

Gwen snorted. "You'll find a new skill."

"Pardon the interruption," Lance broke in. "But I really think we should move." He gave the rope bridge to their right a worried glance. "There's something wrong with this place. It feels... stale."

Merlin raised an eyebrow at him curiously, but he didn't explain any further. Lance simply crossed his arms and glared at the trees, as if it was their fault the soldiers left.

"I agree. We should all split whilst we can." Robin started tapping his pole back and forth across the ground until he found one of the two bridges on the platform. He turned around and waved at the three of them jovially. "Farewell, Sir Lancelot. I hope we never meet again."

Lance grunted, "Likewise."

Nodding once more, Merlin watched Robin and Pico head away. For a moment her heart squeezed, her feet itching to follow after him. Unfortunately she couldn't, she needed to help Gwen get Lance out of the town. Even if she desperately wanted to know where her brother was, Merlin had to do this first. She was so close to achieving everything she set out for, she just needed to wait a little longer.

"All right, let's get going." Gwen trotted over to their bridge. "This will take long enough without wasting our time now."

Upon her words they set out deeper into Aroth, keeping as quiet as they possibly could be. While they walked, Merlin found that Lance was right; something was wrong with the village. Though not all decks had buildings upon them, the ones that did looked abandoned. Merlin approached a house to inspect the inside, but the windows were covered with dust inside and out. A couple decks had fire rings usually with marks nearby, where it looked like something had been fastened into the ground. Lance determined the rings had been unused for quite a few days, maybe even a week. He didn't say it out loud to her, but Merlin knew he was worried that it meant a hasty exit had taken place.

Perhaps more than the physical signs, the forest and village itself seemed stifled. The air hung frozen in place, and the trees barely ever rustled with wildlife. No wind, no sound, no animals. It was the kind of silence that sucked the air from your lungs, and the sound from your voice. Aroth was a shell of eerie and quiet threats, whispering danger at every turn.

"Lance—" Merlin started to ask him about the danger she felt, maybe a knight could tell her if it was needless. Instead of letting her finish, however, he raised a hand quickly, turning to face her on the swaying bridge they were crossing. Wooden planks creaked under their feet— Lance's eyes narrowed. For a long moment they stood quietly, allowing Gwen to arrive at the platform closest to them. Merlin watched Lance scan their surroundings, feeling with her own gift at the same time. What was he sensing that she couldn't?

Just as her power picked up a flicker of life beneath them, the closest tree reached forward and threw the bridge into the air. The support ropes snapped from all ends as Merlin's world spun upside-down. She let out a startled scream and flailed out her arms for something to grab onto.

"Merlin!" Lancelot's voice cut through the now raging wind, his hand appearing out of nowhere. Her world righted itself as he clasped her wrist, swinging Merlin toward a large tree branch. "I'm letting go!" shouted Lance, giving Merlin only a second before he released her wrist. Merlin yelped again, but this time it was from the sudden impact of landing precariously on the branch. She teetered back and forth on the wood, her balance sliding along with her body until she settled.

As carefully as she could, she turned around on the wood and gasped. Merlin could now sense several flickering presences in the marsh below, and she was sure they were each members of the Growth

CHAPTER 21

Order. They were attacking just like the suppression squad at Jack's house. That Growth Ivirian had turned the trees into a web of danger, and here it was happening again. She could see Gwen up on the platform, looking down with wide eyes. Lance was running along the top of one of the slithering branches, making his way towards her.

Merlin whipped her head back around, searching for a way up to the platform. She had never seriously wished for wings until *that* moment. A rumble brought her attention back to her branch, which was beginning to move like the others. Merlin couldn't stay still for much longer, so she quickly picked out the nearest branch and made a running leap. Merlin landed hard on the branch, and seconds later Lancelot did too. The wood bounced from the force of both landings.

Merlin spread her arms out to balance again, turning to see Lance doing much the same. "Is it the suppression squad? How did they find us?"

Lance stepped closer. "No time for that, I need you to trust me."

"Fine," she said hurriedly, looking backwards at the trees. Merlin could now see several ivirians flying towards them, swords drawn. "But—"

"No time!" Without warning Lance wrapped an arm around her waist and picked Merlin up.

"Not again!" she cried as the knight dashed off the branch. "Eeeh!"

Once again the world blurred as she and the knight soared through the air. Merlin grabbed Lancelot's sleeve and clenched it tightly, instinctively needing even the slightest proof of stability. Another screech threatened to burst out of her as they plummeted straight down, Lancelot's grip tightening around Merlin. She watched in terror as Lance swung out his feet, aiming and landing on the thinnest of branches. The limb responded furiously to the impact, bucking the two back up the way they came. Trees reached after them as they flew higher, shooting thin spikes at the pair. The knight expertly pulled himself and Merlin away, bending just out of reach of the projectiles. He repeated the motions a second time before his leap took them up to Gwen's platform.

The cat meowed in surprise and relief as Lancelot landed with Merlin on the deck. She felt her legs shake as he set her down, the knight gasping for breath.

"Thank you!" she said, taking several more deep breaths to calm her racing heart. "But what now?"

"Now," panted Lance. "We should run."

A shadow fell over them, and a rough voice said, "I agree," as the blade of a sword came crashing down.

RH

Robin paused, listening intently. He thought he had heard a scream somewhere in the distance, but he wasn't completely sure. Though Robin's hearing was superb, he could have imagined the sound, what with his nerves being so jumpy. He tilted his head towards where he knew a tree sat. The village was extremely quiet, except for the hushed voices of the insects and animals hiding away. It was only because they didn't want him to fall off the side of the bridges that they spoke at all.

Tapping gently along the deck, Robin asked quietly, "What happened here?"

"*We don't know.*" Came the sad and hushed answer. "*But we are scared.*" They clicked, letting him know that they were beetles. If only they were crickets, then Robin might be able to find out where all the troops had gone. He could try hunting for the bugs, but that would get in the way of finding the post office.

Conflicted, Robin inquired politely, "Excuse me, is there a post office here?"

An airy voice answered him. "*Yes, of course. Alias will show you the way, but please make sure the owl does not eat him. He has just exited his chrysalis, and would like to enjoy his new wings.*"

"Of course." Robin agreed. Once he got Pico to understand and adhere to their instructions, the butterfly made his appearance.

"*Follow me.*" Alias instructed, letting Robin borrow his senses. The feeling was always the same, a connection snapping into place like an arrow's notch to the bowstring. Robin flinched for a moment, and tilted his head towards Pico.

"Thank you, but I think Alias will be enough for me." he told the bird.

Pico hooted and removed his own link to Robin, relieving Pico's confused senses. The bird meant well, but it was difficult to sort out what the bird did and did not want him to do. Alias, on the other hand, knew exactly what he was doing, so connecting to the butterfly was much easier.

Standing straight, Robin began following the sound of the butterfly's wings, making sure to tap his pole back and forth as he went. When he came to another bridge, a wash of sensations rushed over him. The butterfly was giving him cautions and instructions all at once, which combined into a single warning feeling that guided him over the creaking bridge. Simply put, he knew what *not* to do, and thus, what *to* do at the same time.

In that manner he made his way through the village, trying and failing to ignore the unusual atmosphere around him. Every instinct—which usually saved Robin when he listened to them—wanted him to turn and leave Aroth immediately.

"Alias, are we close to the office?" he asked as he stepped off a bridge to a platform.

"We're here, sir." Alias answered. *"You may wish to alter your appearance some, as I see a picture of your hood hanging on the building."*

"Don't worry, I've already fixed that." Robin pulled his hood down, letting the butterfly see his clever disguise. It wasn't anything crazy, just a pair of sculpted clay tips that he could attach to his ears to make him look like a sprite. It was surprisingly convincing, and besides, no one had seen his face and known his identity at the same time.

"Well, I'll leave you then. The gnats will have to assist you." The gnats responded by connecting to Robin, just as Alias had said.

"Thank you." Robin said to all the bugs together. A hushed chorus of your welcomes came from the nervous insects. Smiling to himself, Robin stepped forward, holding out his pole to drag it along the side of the building as he walked. It made a loud thunk once he reached the doorframe, and the gnats began swarming by the door.

"All right." Robin muttered to himself, finding the doorknob and turning it. The knob clicked as the door swung open, the sounds of crinkling paper greeting him.

"Go away, I'm not open anymore." said an old and grumpy voice.

"Hmph!" Pico landed on Robin's shoulder and sneezed. "This place is a mess."

The crinkling paused. "Did that bird just talk?"

"Occupational necessity." Robin answered, making his way into the room. He had to be careful as he walked because of all the objects spread out on the ground. The gnats didn't seem to know what the objects were, just that he should avoid them. "Pardon the interruption, but I need a favor."

The postmaster grunted. "Whatever it is, I can't do it. I've had enough of this ghost town and I'm leaving. I should have gone with the rest of the militia, but my old bones don't move like they used to. Now I need to pack."

"Where *did* the soldiers go?" Robin asked in a hopefully nonchalant way. "I thought this was their camp."

"It was." More rustling came with the ancient voice. "But the mayor ordered everyone to move closer to Akiva about a fortnight ago."

Robin frowned and put a hand down on what felt like a table.

"You're by a counter, there are bookshelves to your left, and bags on the ground." Pico told him. *"The iviro has wings."*

The mailman, who couldn't understand Pico when he chirped, cleared his throat. "Your bird better not get into any trouble while it's in here."

"He won't." Robin assured him. He leaned forward, and directed his eyes to the area with the most sound. "Why would Mayor Faton move everyone? We're not joining the war now, are we?"

The old iviro lowered his voice conspiratorially. "I heard from the soldiers that one of our ships sailed out too far into Idella during an attack. The whole crew was lost in the crossfire of the human kingdoms, and Avalon lost a large part of its navy. More than that, there have been whispers of an Avalonian about the forest." The sound of packing came again. "If we're going to fight, now would be the time."

Robin pressed his mouth together tightly, pausing for a moment to consider the information. Avalon had lost part of its navy; that was a bad sign for his birthplace. If they lost any more of the islands between the north and south mainlands, Avalon would certainly lose the war.

CHAPTER 21

Additionally there was the matter of an Avalonian in the forest. It was too much of a coincidence for that intruder to be anyone other than Lancelot. No one knew that Robin was Avalonian.

"Sir," Robin began, feeling a new potent urgency. "I've come to find my friend's post. I know you're in a hurry, but could you please find him for me? His sister needs to see him."

There was a pause in the noise, and then the old postmaster said, "It's against regulation to have visitors. Why can't she wait till his term is over?"

"She hasn't seen him in two years." Robin squeezed his pole. "Who knows how long it will be until the war has finished. Please, she just wants to be with her brother again." He waited, hoping that his words would convince the mailman. There had to be pity somewhere in his heart.

The postmaster sighed heavily. "All right, but you better hope I find him quickly. I'm supposed to be out of here already."

"Thank you!" Robin grinned. "His name is Daleon Lynwood."

"Right, right." the iviro muttered. The sound of wooden drawers being pulled out began, papers riffling. For several minutes Robin stood quietly waiting for the old ivirian to find Daleon's name. He wished the iviro would hurry, but rushing him was hardly possible. While Robin was still, the desire to find Merlin continued to grow steadily worse. Something told him that he needed to find them before they tried to send the knight off, or trouble would come of it.

On that thought, Robin turned to his owl. "Pico, would you go find Merlin for me? Don't come back, just stay by them." Pico gave a crooked cuckoo and hopped off Robin's shoulder.

"Ehem." The postmaster cleared his throat. "Can you prove you know this iviro? Like I said, it's against regulation to give out this information."

Robin frowned. "His parent's names are Cavair and Philene, his sister's name is Merlin. The last time I spoke to him he was stationed at Port Sal Azure, I just need to know his ship's name, and if he's still there." It was now important to be quick, but the postmaster seemed determined to be slow. Robin waited impatiently as the ivirian hemmed and hawed about his decision.

Finally, the mailman said, "Well, I knew the name sounded familiar. I had hoped you were lying about knowing this person, I only recognized it because it came with the last batch of notices I got."

The thief tilted his head. "What do you mean?"

"I'm afraid your friend's name came in with the shadow batch. I'm sorry."

Robin's blood turned to ice as he understood the implications the man was giving him. A thick layer of weight covered his tongue as he tried to speak. He knew what it was, but he still had to ask, "What is the shadow batch?"

"You don't know?" The mailman sounded older as he continued, like a hundred years had been dropped on top of him. "Son, we call them shadows because the only way to see them is to look back, not in life, but in memory. Because they're deceased."

Deceased.

Robin breathed in slowly, letting the air fill his lungs steadily as the word stayed plastered in his mind. Daleon was dead. His friend, Merlin's brother, was dead. How was he going to tell her? This was going to break her heart. It would break her parents' hearts too.

Dipping his head low, Robin sighed. This was not the first time he had lost a friend; he knew there was no use in denial. There was only one question he needed answered, one answer to determine what he told Merlin.

"Who killed him?"

A hand patted his shoulder, gently. "He was on the boat I told you about, the one which sank in the battle before anyone could send aid."

So it was the war that killed him. It was not a death that had to be avenged. Robin's hand shook once. At least... at least he was saved from that anger.

"There is a letter for the parents, and one for the sister. I was going to mail them, but would you like them?" the postmaster asked gently.

Robin straightened, swiping the single tear that had slipped down his cheek. There would be time for mourning later, now he needed to find Merlin. Daleon would never forgive him if Merlin got hurt, and he certainly didn't plan to let that happen. He held out his hand towards the mailman.

CHAPTER 21

"I'd like the one for his sister, please. The second can be sent through the mail."

"All right." An envelope was set in Robin's hand, which he tucked inside his side satchel. "Will you give it to her?"

"Yes." Robin twisted around, walking straight out of the building without any problem. Outside he gave a shrill whistle, and a loud buzzing sound came to him. He crossed both arms as the gnats were replaced with a new swarm. They were dragonflies by the sound of their wings.

Perfect.

A single dragonfly buzzed closer. *"You called?"*

"That's right." Robin nodded. "I need your eyes."

Darling Ivory Bishop,

I have little time to attend to this, but your letter was insightful and begged a response. Now that I know of the Avalonian's secret, I am less concerned. The Marble Rook is intriguing, and I'm not in the habit of releasing pawns before they've run their course of use. Therefore do not remove the Marble Rook yet. If problems arise from this move, then you may do as you please to remedy the situation. Above anything else stay hidden, and keep yourself from any dangerous situations. Not that you can't handle yourself, but I worry what would happen to the others.

Aside from that, I have news of a different nature. You said you had not heard of the Jade King's movements, but he is indeed moving, and I bet the only people who don't realize that are the ones living in Sher. For a moment, I'll explain the facts. I have just received a notice that Sher ships have been loading irode powder on board for the past week. There's enough to level a fleet and then some. They must have been mining in the Talian Mountains for a long time to have so much refined powder.

We'll have to see which way the wind blows Sher, but I believe it will favor the right path. Even if that path is not what the Jade King has in mind. Still, his movements are making those around me nervous and unbearable. One of these days, my Ivory Rook might just lose all control and rid me of them. Regardless, as I've already said, there is little time for me to write this letter, so I will have to end here. It's short, but you understand my predicament. When I see you next, I will do my best to remedy this.

Ivory Knight

22

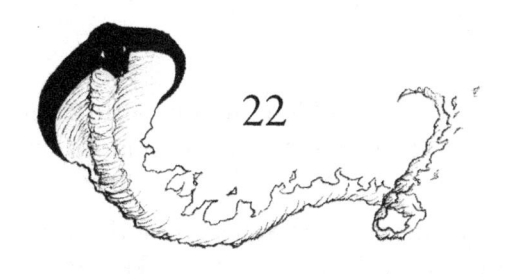

Lying Between the Lines

M

Merlin leapt away from the sword. It smashed into the ground, sending slivers of wood shooting in all directions. She skipped several steps back from the weapon, Lancelot and Gwen scattering to either side. The ivirian before them was dressed in a white tunic and kirsco, with thick ribbons criss-crossing his calves and a military token tied to his bare arm. Swallowing nervously, Merlin flicked her wrist to summon her sword, hearing Lance draw Solaris at the same time.

The purple skinned soldier brandished his curved blade, pointing the pearly steel at them with a sneer. "Halt, all of you. You're under arrest for treason."

Two blurs shot out from behind him, stopping in the air above the soldier. Merlin's eyes widened at the sight of two more ivirians. One had four green wings, long hair, and appeared to be a Tear Ivirian by the draels on his skin. The other had a long, brown braid and wore all red, aside from the military token on her left arm. She too had four dragonfly-shaped wings beating furiously to keep her in the air.

As Merlin took all the information in, the first soldier growled and lunged forward, blade aimed straight for Guinevere, who yowled in surprise.

Merlin gasped. Who would attack a *cat*? She tried to jump forward, but before she could one of the ivirians landed in front of her with a loud thump. Merlin skidded to a stop as the ivira drew a quick half-circle on the ground with her foot, followed by a second line straight through the middle. Bright red light blazed to life on the ground, a wall of flames springing up from the wooden platform. Fire spread across the deck, cutting off Merlin from Gwen, Gwen from Merlin, and Lancelot from either.

CHAPTER 22

"Ah!" Merlin cried out, holding up a hand to shield herself from the heat. She took several steps back, and bumped into the entrance of a bridge.

"What are you doing?!" she yelled over the fire. "You're going to bring down the village!" Even as she spoke, Merlin could see the ground shriveling into dark charcoal before it dissolved from the origin of the fire.

The ivira stood and raised her pale sword. "Merlin Lynwood, you are under arrest for treason!"

Merlin gaped at her. Was she actually arresting her amidst the fire? "Are you insane?"

The soldier simply tensed, preparing to attack. Out of the corner of her eye, Merlin saw Gwen leap past the fire onto the tree trunk holding their platform up.

The cat saw her and screamed, "Merlin, run!"

Merlin's breath caught in her throat, her feet moving before she could register what she was doing. In seconds she was halfway across the hanging bridge, her sword reverting to a charm. Another moment passed and she was over it entirely. She dashed across a platform and leapt onto another bridge. This one was much longer than the others she had crossed, at least fifty feet from end to end. Merlin gritted her teeth and leaned further into a sprint. She would be caught if the soldier got to the bridge while she was still on it. Then again, even if she reached the platform, she would have to keep crossing bridges and pray that Elohim would keep the ivira away.

Merlin withheld a despairing sound from escaping. The likelihood of a full escape was dwindling rapidly.

A gust of wind blew suddenly through the trees, sending the bridge into a violent swing. Loud snapping sounds erupted from behind Merlin, causing her to whip around. One of the ropes was cut, and the soldier was in the process of slicing through the second. Eyes wide, Merlin made a long jump from the bridge to the platform, landing in a roll that sent her straight into one of the false ash trees holding it up. Her back exploded in pain, throbbing where she collided with the trunk. She took several deep breaths while struggling to stand. The ivira in red landed knee to the ground in front of Merlin, splitting the wood beneath her weight.

Merlin glared as the soldier stood. "Leave me alone! I haven't committed treason, I was trying to make him leave the forest!" Merlin gripped the hilt of her sword, summoning it once more. Her lie was only *partially* untrue.

The soldier sheathed her sword, glared at Merlin, then said coldly, "You broke our law, it does not matter why."

What is she doing? Merlin thought, eyes on the sheathed sword.

"Fine." She raised her sword. "But I won't be captured without a fight."

"Please," The soldier sounded half amused. "You're an herbalist."

Anger flared inside Merlin, her lungs squeezing tightly. For half a moment, she considered simply charging straight at the extremely cold and somehow cocky soldier. Clenching her sword until her knuckles were white, Merlin dismissed the idea. Whether she liked it or not, the ivira was right. She was just an herbalist; her gift was useless.

As it became clear Merlin would not surrender, the soldier gave an irritated sigh, and repeated her signet. As she did so, a crazy idea entered Merlin's mind. She took a half step backwards and felt the tree, her hand hidden from sight. The bumps and edges of the bark were rough and crumbled when her fingers brushed them, but a large piece was still sturdy enough to withstand her grip. Merlin dug her fingers all the way underneath the bark as the soldier stomped her foot on the ground. Immediately, a spark of flame shot into the air, zipping straight towards her.

With a great heave and a loud crack, Merlin yanked the bark straight off the trunk. She let go of the chunk and covered her mouth and nose with her shirt, watching the bark sail straight into the approaching flames. Snapping and popping sounds exploded from the fire, along with a great, gray cloud of mist. The soldier gave a surprised cry as a fit of coughing overtook her. The fire swung crazily along the ground, as disoriented as its master. Merlin stumbled back as the flame crashed into the tree, igniting and encapsulating it. All at once the wood cracked and blew apart, spreading the mist out in a thick and heated fog.

The cloud washed over Merlin even as she ran for the secondary bridge. Inside she could hardly see a foot in front of her; the gray covered everything. It wasn't wet like morning fog, rather it was hot, dry, and felt like coarse dirt. One breath and it was like she swallowed a handful of sand, and seconds after that she felt dizzy. Merlin tried to hold her breath, pressing the fabric of her shirt harder against her face. Vaguely, she could see the outline of a bridge, and she leapt onto it. Three steps forward, and she broke out of the fog. Exiting the dust sent fresh air into her lungs, clearing the dizziness caused by the false ash. In the joy of the moment Merlin told herself that if she used herbs to fight again, she would need to make sure they couldn't harm her as well.

Springing forward on the swaying bridge, Merlin glanced back past the giant cloud to where she'd come from, though it was hardly visible. Lance and Gwen must have run in different directions, or they were still fighting those soldiers.

Her balance wobbled and she had to focus back on running. Hopefully they were doing all right, because she couldn't get back to them just yet. The boards beneath her creaked under the strain of her weight, crying out at the sudden use. Merlin gritted her teeth and made another long jump off the bridge, swinging out her feet to balance as she landed. Before she could make contact, two hands grabbed her arms, their grip tightening as the distance between Merlin and the platform increased drastically.

"Hey!" Merlin kicked frantically. "Put me down!" She looked up to her captor, and gasped in recognition of the iviro who had attacked them at Jack's house. His red eyes held their initial gleaming color, and his expression carried none of the indecision from before.

"I told you I would bury you alive if I saw you again." he reminded her. "If I put you down now, I will be forced to do just that." He glanced down at her and glared. "You're lucky she survived."

The soldier was speaking of the fair skinned ivira from before, Merlin was sure of it. "I told you my healing would work!" Merlin growled, attempting again to pull her arms free. "Put me down. You owe me!"

The soldier ignored her entirely, looking back up to the trees. They swerved around a trunk, and Merlin got a good look at the actual distance between her and the marsh below. Surely she would die if the soldier released her arms. Merlin swallowed nervously as she swayed in the direction of each turn, her arms aching from the soldier's tight grip.

He was flying at a quick pace, and his wings were buzzing loudly. This soldier certainly had a direction in mind, but what was it? "Where are you taking me?" she called up to him.

Again he ignored her. They were heading far away from her friends at high speed, and Merlin couldn't do anything about it. Had their plan been to separate them all along? Merlin spent a moment hoping that Gwen and Lance were safe, before the burning in her shoulders began to make thinking difficult.

She didn't know for how long they flew, maybe five, ten minutes? Eventually they came to a large tree that supported a wide platform with the help of two other great false ashes. Branches of varying widths spread out into the air above the platform, dark green leaves forming a thick roof. Though the foliage obscured her view, Merlin felt the barest trace of three creatures hiding amongst the branches. Of course, without her signet activated it was difficult to detect the lifeforce of a myth or other being. Regardless, Merlin could feel enough to recognize one of the wisps of energy. Even being twenty feet away was not enough to keep her from the wretched feeling of that carcass.

Merlin gasped as the feeling grew stronger. "No, no!" She felt her blood starting to boil as they entered the mess of leaves. The soldier set her down on a large branch, twisting her arms behind her back as he landed behind her.

"That was fast," said a voice as familiar as the smell of burning wood. "I only just sent you after them." Disbelief and anger coiled around Merlin's heart. She looked up to the top branch where an ivirian was sitting, one leg propped against the branch, the other dangling down. He was wrapped in dull, brown strips of cloth so that the only bit of him she could see were his eyes. The iviro also wore a long black tunic and shirt, and would have looked healthy if not for her power. Through her rising anger she sensed the burns running along his face and arms, the disease spreading throughout his core.

"Rainault!" Merlin snarled.

He was looking down at her, a smile within his words. "In the flesh."

A tremor slipped across her skin as she stared at him, the destroyer of her home, the iviro who destroyed Aspen's resting place. Rainault was disgusting, wretched, mutilated... and very much alive.

"Good job, Bristol." Rainault turned away from her, staring down past the branches of the tree. "Keep her there a moment, we'll leave once I've seen enough."

"Rainault, what are you doing?" Merlin shouted, struggling against Bristol's hold. "You should be dead!"

CHAPTER 22

The soldier tightened his grip on her arms. "You should stop talking." Bristol spoke with less venom than before, more like he was just giving her information. "Your friend will suffer if you don't."

Merlin pulled again once. "Lancelot is more than capable of defending himself, and so is Gwen!" Plus, she had yet to see either of them there.

"He's speaking of the leprechaun."

Merlin froze, her eyes wide.

Rainault sounded like he was gloating. "We brought him with us to ensure your cooperation. Trust me, I have *no* problem harming him to establish your silence."

The sheriff waved his hand, and Bristol put one hand on Merlin's head, forcing her to look up. There, chained between two soldiers, was Jack. He was sitting on the branch with both wrists shackled, keeping his mouth firmly shut. Merlin opened her own mouth but no words came out. If she spoke, would they really harm Jack? Was that legal, or did the soldiers just not care?

She jerked her head out of Bristol's grip, looking down in a small act of defiance. If only she had a power that could help them escape, not such a weak gift. As it was, there was nothing she could do. Nothing at all.

Silver sands! Merlin gritted her teeth, latching onto the one thought her desperation afforded. *Where are you Lance?*

"Here we go." Rainault said gleefully. "Everyone stay silent." Merlin saw him lean forward, and the other soldiers seemed to tense as well. They were each peering past the tree to the platform below. Merlin's nerves buzzed as she followed their gaze to find what was so fascinating. Her eyes widened at the recognition of the two figures standing below. Very soon their voices began filtering up into the false ash, and what they said felt like a slap across her face.

L

Lancelot smacked the butt of his sword against the back of the soldier's head, knocking him to the ground. He panted breathlessly, lowering the weapon now that the immediate threat was over. A ring of floating water dropped from its spot in the air, splashing into the wooden planks around Lance.

"They found us too easily," he said, out of breath but recovering quickly.

"*Yes, it's a wonder you didn't feel them following.*" Solaris observed as Lance wiped a trace of blood off his sword on the soldier's pant leg.

Lancelot sheathed Solaris and crouched by the ivirian. "I felt something, but it was faint and far away. I thought that maybe I was beginning to sense the forest's animals." He ripped off the bottom of his shirt and raised the ivirian's arm. Lance had given him a rather deep slash on his left bicep, a cut that may lead him to bleed to death. With a wince, the knight began quickly wrapping the wound, tying it tightly to stem the flow.

Solaris hummed thoughtfully. "*Well, since you cannot sense any animals, I guess that means they were staying far enough away to go unnoticed. It's not your fault.*"

Lance glared at the wrap as he tied a knot forcefully. "I still should have said something." he muttered, letting some of his bitterness show through his words. Now Merlin was off somewhere running from the soldiers, and Gwen was probably hiding in the trees. They were both in danger because of him. Not only because he wasn't there to help, but because he had entered the forest at all.

"*Enough of that.*" Solaris ordered. "*You don't regret it, so don't start blaming yourself now. First save Merlin, then find the cat, and then you get to feel terrible. Honestly Lance, when you make a decision, you've got to live with it. That's how life works.*"

Lance rolled his eyes, standing up in the process. "Thank you. That encourages me *greatly*." He began scanning the forest for any sign of life, something his gift would register or recognize if the presence was

CHAPTER 22

familiar. Specifically he was searching for Merlin. After a few weeks of traveling, the constant hum of her presence became far more normal than he would have thought possible. Without it he felt anxiety creep inside him, like a shiver slipping down his back. Lance felt it briefly when the woodsmen appeared, but he hadn't realized how bad the sensation was until right then, when she raced away and did not come back.

Of course, he had sped away from that platform just as fast as she had. The soldier didn't really give him a choice in the matter.

A flicker of movement caught his attention, and he saw a soldier flying through the air. The bright red of her clothes stood out against the gray trees like a beacon. Lance recognized her immediately as the one that chased after Merlin before.

"*Careful.*" Solaris warned as Lancelot dashed forward.

I know, he thought, following the flying ivira. She didn't seem to notice him following along on the bridges, but Lance didn't trust that. Even when he lost sight of her, he would pass a building and find her once again. What's more, the bridges he crossed were not quiet. The wooden planks squeaked—albeit not excessively—while he ran over them. With that in mind, it seemed like she was leading him, not flying unaware of his pursuit.

"*I feel a trap coming.*"

Lance agreed, though he wouldn't stop. If the soldier was leading him on purpose that meant he would likely find Merlin. Surely they would lure her to the same destination... right?

Solaris coughed in his mind. "*Or they just killed her.*"

Osor luchena!* snapped Lance. *Umha eu'pyl mae osetem.***

Solaris scoffed. "*I am helping you! You've got to be realistic about these things.*" Lance ignored him, doubling his speed. He clenched his fingers till they hurt from the pressure.

She wasn't dead. He would have felt it.

Ahead the soldier suddenly stopped in midair. Lance skidded to a silent stop behind her, every sense poised for action. The ivira hovered for one breath, two breaths, and then plunged towards the platform.

---

* Roughly: "Be quiet!" or "Be silent!"

** In Avalonian it is translated to, "Help me, or go away."

Lance surged forward as Solaris let out an exclamation of surprise. Before he could reach her, the soldier's wings snapped back into movement, all four extending at once. Lance froze on the platform, the soldier disappearing over the side of the deck.

Confusion rising higher every second, a flood of new sensations crashed into him. The knight tried to register the first soldier's exit, but at the same time he now felt at least *nine* flickers of power above him, and another on the platform behind the tree. Lance stared up at the foliage, but could only see empty branches and waxy leaves.

"What is this...?" he began, taking a step away from the tree.

"A meeting." The voice was deep and authoritative.

The knight whirled around, searching for the voice. The iviro was leaning against the second tree trunk, looking as if the position was equal to sitting on a throne. He wore a deep blue coat that looked remarkably like a human's dress coat, and remarkably unlike any ivirian garb he had seen before. There was a silver chain attached to his breast pocket that hung from a pair of spectacles. Behind the looking device sat pale red eyes set closely together, filled with intense cunning and self-importance. The iviro's red-brown hair was pulled back from his eyes but left hanging in the back.

Lancelot raised Solaris towards him. "Who are you?" he asked, trying to place the ivirian's face. He seemed familiar, but that was hardly possible.

"My apologies. I am Deputy Mayor Armble Reed." Reed stood straight, and tilted his head in Lance's direction. "And you are a prince of Avalon."

"*Uh oh.*" Solaris murmured.

Lance stood very, very still. He stared at the Deputy Mayor with such a blank face that he would have made his mother proud for concealing the utter surprise he felt. "I think you're mistaken," he said carefully.

"No, no." Reed shifted from the trunk and began to pace. "Bestial though you may be, I recognize you, like you recognize me. Denying it won't help you or your friend, so your charade can drop."

Lance had been glancing up into the tree once again, but now he faced Reed. He ignored the somewhat slanderous term for his kind, instead asking, "Where is she? She had better not have been harmed."

CHAPTER 22

"So, is she a spy then?" Reed mused, speaking in such a way that gave Lance the impression he was testing the idea out.

"She is not a spy." Lance raised his sword once again.

"*Maybe you shouldn't threaten the kingdom's second-in-command?*" Solaris piped up from the sword.

Lancelot ignored him promptly. "Where is she?" he repeated with more authority in his voice.

"How about this," Reed grinned towards him. "You tell me which prince you are, and I will tell you where she is."

Lance looked dubiously at him. This situation was beyond bad for him, but there was a piece of information he was missing, he could feel it. The soldiers in the tree made sense now that he knew Reed's identity, but the fact that he hadn't called them down was strange. Was Merlin there too? Could she hear them? What if the Deputy Mayor was bluffing?

"*Don't do it. It'll make things official.*" Solaris spoke with reason, his voice attempting to dissuade Lance.

I have to, he told the sword, already forming the words that he had hidden for so long. *I promised that I would protect her.* Lance met Reed's gaze and held it, standing straight, not backing down. This would change everything, but perhaps, just perhaps, it might turn out all right.

"Very well," he started, allowing notes of condescension to seep into his voice. "My full name is Prince Elyan Colm *Lancelot* Penthellion. I am the second prince of Avalon." He gripped Solaris's hilt tighter. "Now, where is my companion?"

In the branches above him, six of the presences abruptly left, flying away with increasing speed.

Reed didn't seem to notice, instead looking supremely pleased with himself. "I was right. Obviously, I knew already, but an admission from your own mouth makes paperwork so much easier, especially with witnesses."

"Enough chattering." Lance growled, his sword hand itching to attack. "*Where* is Merlin?"

Reed waved a hand in the direction of the fleeing energies. "Your friend has just been taken away, if you must know. Her and the other prisoner."

The knight twisted around, scanning the area with his gift. They were already growing faint. If he waited much longer, he might lose Merlin and Gwen—he assumed it was Gwen they spoke of—for good. That was only if he hadn't already lost them by hiding his identity. Merlin was probably furious.

Reed cleared his throat. "I am curious, your highness. What will you do?" His voice was silky. It laughed at the knight without ever uttering a single exclamation of joy.

Curling his fingers into a tight fist, he turned back around to face the ivirian. His temper was beginning to rise inside him, coiling like a spring about to burst. This ivirian had no idea whom he was taunting. He believed that his own power and that of his guards would be enough to stop Lancelot from going after Merlin. Well, he was wrong. Every weapon that the Deputy Mayor had available was doubled in the prince's own arsenal, and he knew how to use every one of them.

"*Elyan, calm down!*" Lance flinched and, for a moment, Solaris's words brought his anger to a crashing halt.

Reed took that moment to give a short laugh. "That was quite the look you gave me, your highness! Perhaps we'll make another deal. You can stay here and fight my guards and I, just like the bloodthirsty Avalonian you are, *or* you can simply talk this out with me. Frankly, I don't believe you'll be able to defeat us all, and even if you managed to, it would take a long time. By then your friend will be locked up tight, and I will be the only one who can release her. However, should you speak with me, I believe our respective countries can come to an understanding." He crossed his arms, smiling at Lance.

The look sparked his anger again, but this time he was back in control. Lancelot took a deep breath to steady himself, pushing his first, aggressive instinct back down into the chains he kept it in. He needed to be better than he used to be, and that started with diplomacy. Even if it was the exact opposite of what he wanted, which was to turn around and dash off after Merlin.

With great self-control, Lance sheathed Solaris.

"*Well done, Lance. Now stay calm.*"

I thought you preferred violence. Lance thought more to calm himself than argue, which Solaris knew.

Obligingly, Solaris responded. *"I prefer people to stick to their morals, and not change them in anger."*

After a second deep breath, Lance nodded to Reed. "Very well. We'll speak, but I expect my companions will be kept safe in the meantime."

"Yes, yes." Reed laced his fingers together and returned to his tree trunk, leaning against it rather informally. "Now, I assume you have yet to hear that Avalon has lost a large chunk of its navy?"

Lancelot bit his tongue hard to keep the shock from showing. The military lost part of the navy? But the fighting was on hold for the Avalonian ambassador to arrive in Logres!

"You know, he could just be lying."

Right. Lancelot swallowed a flinch. Aloud he said simply, "Information is hard to come by in this forest."

"That's true." Reed tilted his head. "Which raises the question, why are you here? Surely Avalon has not decided to provoke Sher *now*?"

Lance crossed his arms. Eyeing Reed with care, he considered his options. Of all the questions to ask, this was the hardest to answer, and the most expected inquiry. Weeks before, Guinevere asked him how he got into the forest, but she had failed to ask *why* he had been there. They accepted that he came solely for Merlin, that he journeyed to Sher with only that mission in mind. While that was partially true, it was not wholly accurate. Lancelot had been sent west by his kingdom with a secondary purpose, unattached to his own goal of locating Merlin.

Blood had been spilled, and thus was required. His father and brother needed recompense. They demanded the head of the one seated on the Logres throne, the king regent himself. Who better to claim such a hefty prize than the second son of the king, the one whose power could end the war? There was no one.

Through that desire Lance was granted the opportunity to leave the capital, and thus a chance of escaping the watchful eyes of those against his plan for peace. He had abandoned the party bent on assassination, and forced his way into the forest where he previously hoped to locate Merlin.

Unfortunately, he could not explain all this to Reed.

"*You could,*" suggested Solaris. "*It's not his ruler you wanted to kill.*"

Lance mulled the sword's words over in his mind, still silently analyzing Reed's expression. The latter seemed unbothered by Lancelot's hesitation. A calm smile rested upon the iviro's face as he waited patiently for the prince to make up his mind.

To tell the truth, or to lie; which was the right answer? Could he threaten Reed with the truth of his mission? Would the idea of assassination be enough to cause fear in the mind of the Deputy Mayor? Could Lancelot force him to kowtow beneath the strength of Avalon? On some basic level, Lance felt that he was unable. Not because he was weak, but because inciting such fear would go against everything he sought to become.

At last his mind decided and he said, "You think ill of us for this, but my presence here was not intentional. The southern border towns have had trouble with bandits running rampant in their towns. Whilst attempting to deal with them, I was... thrown into this forest."

Reed raised a single eyebrow. "Is that so?"

Lance nodded. "I have been attempting to remove myself from this kingdom ever since I arrived. Had I wished to see any of Sher, I would have joined the ambassador on his journey through."

"*Rubbish!*" Solaris observed. "*But well-spoken rubbish.*"

"I would be very interested in how these ruffians gained access to our wall." Reed cupped his chin. "I don't suppose you can shed light on their method?"

"I'm afraid I don't remember." Lance raised an innocent hand. "I was rendered unconscious during their attack."

His sword chortled.

Reed gazed at Lancelot, his expression indecipherable. "Then let us pass on from that matter." He waved his hand as if physically moving past the subject. "You mentioned an ambassador, I assume one headed to Logres. Does this mean Avalon really intends to surrender? I would have thought it impossible for your kingdom to do so."

"Negotiations are neither a sign of surrender or peace." Lancelot told him evenly. "Nor a sign of continued fighting. Their business is indeed with the Gressan regent, but only to speak."

Internally he wondered, *What is he fishing for?*

CHAPTER 22

"I have heard that the discussion would regard peace. That is what surprised me. I thought for sure the instigators of this war would not be the ones begging for its end." Reed's words belied the polite tones with which he spoke.

Coldly, Lancelot responded. "That was never proven."

"Regardless, your generals are quite split in their opinions on peace. I've heard that several of them are on the side of making amends with the young regent of Logres." The insinuation was clear, but the motive behind saying it was less so in Lance's mind. Reed had guts to speculate like that in front of him, though it was likely out of a mindset of superiority.

With no little tact, the prince spoke calmly. "You take a keen interest in our government, but as far as actually being there to see for yourself, I doubt you have had the chance. Perhaps you were.... *misinformed* by your ambassador." Lance emphasized his last words carefully, letting his tone dip just barely into a patronizing manner.

"I think not." Reed narrowed his eyes. "He informed me in a most serious manner. It was interesting, as he also said there were rumors that the second prince was planning a revolt!" His words were like a cat pouncing on a mouse, snatching up the tiny animal to play with and mock.

"That is ridiculous!" Lance snapped. "My loyalty is to my king, where it will always be!"

"*Careful, Lance!*" Solaris' ever warning voice chimed in immediately.

"Ha!" Reed looked like he'd won. "You deny it so heartily, I'm beginning to believe you are the rebel they say!"

"You insult my honor!" Lancelot vaguely felt one of the guards in the tree flinch, but he ignored it entirely. Start a revolt? What a horrible idea! The very suggestion was outlandish and wrong!

Reed openly glared at him. "I am simply settling my own mind."

Lancelot gave a short laugh. "I don't know what you're getting at, but making outrageous accusations like this gets us nowhere. Why should I bother speaking with you if you're simply going to spout nonsense?"

For a moment Reed said nothing, he simply stood and stared at Lancelot, thinking. What secrets lay behind the steel in Reed's beady red eyes? The contents of his thoughts were a mystery to the prince. Sher's Deputy Mayor was a master at concealing his mind, much like

Lancelot's brother. The comparison only served to resurrect Lancelot's prior anxiety. He could feel his muscles tensing once more in expectation of danger.

The silence was just crossing over to deafening when Reed finally spoke.

"Is it nonsense? Is it?" he wondered aloud. "A united front can do many things, but the divided will always fall. I am simply trying to prove that. To myself, and to the Mayor."

Lance frowned. "The Mayor has no need to wonder at another kingdom's unity, and assessing it through antagonizing me will not help you uncover it."

The Deputy Mayor turned on him harshly, his thoughtful expression sharpening into pointed clarity. "I have received what I want from you. As I said, I've settled my mind." Ice filled his voice as he kept speaking. "To continue now would only further prove that Avalon is headed for its own destruction, and no aid will avail it."

"You're wrong." Lance insisted, squeezing his fists as if the act could prove his point. It felt as if he'd just lost something important, but Lance wasn't sure what he was missing. If the myth kingdom was paying attention to politics in Avalon, that would suggest they planned to enter the conflict. But that idea was as outrageous as the notion that Lance would cause a revolt! Sher's neutrality was what kept it safe through all the human's conflict.

Gritting his teeth, Lance made a small prayer to Elohim, asking that the myths *not* join the war. As he did so, Reed gestured to the tree full of guards.

"I'm no longer arguing this point," he sighed. "Soldiers, take this prince and bury him somewhere he won't be found." Instantly all five remaining soldiers dropped from the branches above, surrounding Lancelot on all sides.

The prince gaped at Reed while his sword let out a string of curses directed at the ivirians. A glance told the prince that the soldiers were not a part of the suppression squad, instead, they looked like the Deputy Major's personal guards.

Lance went to draw Solaris, but one of the soldiers quickly put their own sword to his throat. "Don't move," ordered the ivira.

He glared at the Deputy Mayor, who was polishing his spectacles with the hem of his shirt. "You can't kill a prince without repercussions! Don't you know this will mean war between Sher and Avalon?" Lance shouted at the official.

"That's the idea." Reed said mindlessly, holding up his glasses to inspect them. A couple of the soldiers gave each other nervous glances.

"*He's lost his mind,*" marveled the sword.

Lance cried out loudly, "Are you mad? Do you know how many people are going to die if you do this? You're inflaming the war!"

Reed shoved his glasses back on his nose and pointed accusingly at him. "No, you are the aggressor here! Perhaps I might have been against fighting if I valued safety, but your presence has assured me of the right course of action. Avalon has been drained of its fortitude. You have no pride."

Lance sneered. "Remove your lackeys and we'll see who has no pride!"

Reed scoffed. "You are a bee with no sting. A fangless wolf. You bowed your head to me in a feeble attempt to overshadow your infirmity, as if submission could save your dwindling stature. Alas that nothing can hide the stink of failure."

Reed then let his facade fall, allowing Lancelot to finally see all that hid behind his practiced detachment. Utter contempt in its cruelest, purest form, blossomed and festered within the depths of the Deputy Mayor. It embodied his whole being, through his gaze and into his presence, all a corrupted atmosphere of disdain.

Captained by his vice, Reed proclaimed his malice with full solidarity. "You are the sum of your kingdom, Prince Elyan. *Weak* and *revolting.*"

In the presence of such hate, Lance felt frailty snatch him by the throat. His knees gave an involuntary shake. All along, Reed had been searching for strength, but what he found was what he had declared as truth: weakness in the heart of Avalon.

All because of Lancelot.

I've been chewed by a wolf this entire time without realizing it, and now he's spit me out, Lance thought, shocked. Too easily, Reed had wrapped Lance around his finger and pulled until a tangled knot had formed. Now, no amount of wrenching could get Lance out of the mess he stood within.

"Well?" Reed looked around at the hesitating soldiers, the shutters of his hate hidden once more. "I gave you all an order."

For a brief second, the soldier with the blade to Lance's throat hesitated. Then, something in her eyes shifted, and Reed must have seen it, because he nodded resolutely to the group, and turned around. His four wings began to beat in rapid bursts of speed, causing channels of wind to fling in every direction.

Lancelot felt his heartbeat increase as he saw that Reed was going to leave. *No, no he can't go!* his thoughts cried. *I can't let him go like this! Sher can't- I can't- if he leaves, if he leaves!*

Reed set off in a running leap, his wings carrying him higher into the air.

From the pit of his gut, a single, unyielding anger blazed to life as Lance roared, "*REED!*" The hysteric sound of his raging voice resounded through the forest, disappearing along with the Deputy Mayor.

Guilt and horror settled inside the prince's gut before igniting into a swirl of vengeful fury. Lancelot swatted away the sword at his neck. It cut into his hand as he did so, but the sensation was nothing new. With practiced speed, he drew Solaris, summoning fire from the sword onto the blade. The soldiers instinctively backed away, but their shimmering white ribbons were left sprawled over the ground. Lancelot held out his bloody hand, and the ribbons responded, flying straight into his sticky grasp. Power coursed through his body like lightning, buzzing atop his skin and along his bones.

A hot glow spread over Lance as fire poured down from his head to his feet, just like the first time he used Solaris. The sword was attempting to caution Lance, but he simply ignored the bird's squawking. His world narrowed to a single point of focus, the sound of the shallow breaths coming from the soldiers. The ivirians were trying to form their signets, but it was a useless endeavor. Still drowning within his complete focus, Lance bent into a fighter's stance, loosening his muscles which had tensed to the point of aching.

These fools had backed him into a corner, had wound Lance into a tight, angry coil. He couldn't stop the repetition of Reed's words in his mind, as constant as the ticking of a clock. *Avalon, weak, war, frailty,*

CHAPTER 22

mistake. All the dancing words only heightened his senses, to the point that every sound seemed to throb with pain.

Elyan twitched. A tremor ran slowly down his body. He released a breath, and then lashed out, flames responding to his wrath.

23

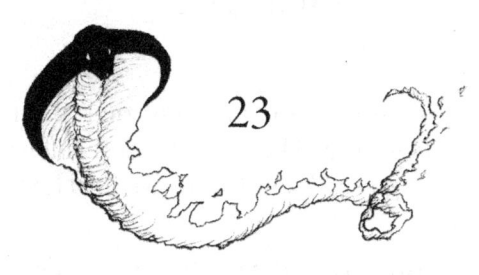

Farewell Future, See Me Now in the Shadow of Past

M

Their captors set Merlin down beside Jack once they were a far distance away from the Deputy Mayor's interrogation of Lancelot. Merlin flinched as she adjusted to a better sitting position. His name wasn't Lance, it was Elyan, and Elyan was not a knight; he was a prince. Part of Merlin was furiously angry with him for lying, and the other part of her was surprisingly sad. She was angry because he must have used her to get information about Sher, and sad because... because despite herself, Merlin realized she had actually grown to appreciate their friendship.

The thought put a sour taste in her mouth.

"Hey, Merlin?" Jack spoke quietly, keeping his eyes on the small group of soldiers who were listening to Rainault some ways a way.

Merlin started. "Ah, sorry. Are you all right?"

Jack scowled. "What- Yes *I'm* fine. What's wrong with *you*?"

"You're not surprised?" Merlin was sure he'd heard Lance's admission.

The old leprechaun shook his head. He sighed, "I already knew."

For a moment, she thought he had misspoken. "You *knew*?" She stared at him in disbelief, mouth partially open from surprise.

Jack began to respond, but before he could say anything of substance, the hushed voices of the soldiers silenced. Merlin turned only to find Rainault crouched a few feet from them. His eyes were easy to see now—clear, black, and dangerous. Just being near his sickness was enough to make her nauseous, and any close proximity to Rainault himself made her furious.

The sheriff's eyes were set on Jack, but they slid to Merlin slowly. She shivered inadvertently when they landed on her. "What do you want?" she asked, though she knew the answer. All he ever wanted was for her to heal him.

He tilted his head. "Would you like to know why you alone are ignorant?"

"What?" she exclaimed.

"Would you," he repeated slowly, "like to know why you alone are ignorant?" The quiet danger in his voice was unlike anything he had said before. It stood in stark contrast to his previous conversations with Merlin. After a moment, it became clear that he was waiting for her response.

It was awful how much curiosity appeared inside her when Merlin realized he was speaking of Lance's real identity. "I don't want anything from you." she said with considerable self-denial.

Rainault shrugged. "You're lying. I can see you *burning* to understand. I know something about burning... you made sure of that."

Merlin glared. "I didn't start that fire; you did. Blame yourself."

He shook his head, continuing as if she hadn't said anything. "I'll do you this favor now, because you may not be able to understand it later. I haven't decided if I'll cut out your tongue, or take both of your ears instead."

"You can't do that!" Merlin flicked her eyes to the soldiers, but none of them looked like they would help her. In fact, they each looked guilty.

Jack spat suddenly at Rainault's boot. "You're disgusting, and a mockery of justice."

Rainault shook his head. "That would be you."

He reached into his tunic and pulled out something shiny and silver. Holding up his fist, he let the chain slip through his fingers, a circular charm hanging from it. Merlin could see that it was a pendant with a flower—a bluebell, if she was a credible herbalist—indented in the center. A ribbon was wrapped around the stem, with two extra notches on either side of the flower.

Jack's face took on a pained expression, to which Rainault responded by turning his head to Merlin. "This is an Avalonian Royal Token. It is given as a promise that the royal who owns it will grant any request to the one presenting the token. I assume your friend was bribed with this for his silence."

"You assume too much." Jack growled. "I was not given that." Merlin looked between the two of them, her heart sinking. Who was she supposed to trust?

"Either way, you knew who he was, and that's treasonous enough." Rainault tossed the necklace at Jack, which bounced off him onto the ground. The sheriff stood, looking down at Merlin. "He told you he was a knight, didn't he? You obviously did not know that any heir in Avalon must become one of the king's knights. Then again, your knowledge of Avalon must be little indeed. Traveling with a savage prince, yet never realizing it. Avalonians are barbaric and crude."

Merlin stared at him with her mouth open, gaping in surprise. His insults hurt, but they were nothing compared to the betrayal and anger which was somehow growing worse inside her. She was used to being angry—it was a normal state for Merlin—but this was something new. It was a darker type of confused anger that she had yet to fully understand. At the very least, Merlin knew it came from the repeated slaps to the face she'd received from the events unfolding. All that aside, calling Lance barbaric seemed wrong. At the very least he was a liar, but barbaric?

"Yes, barbaric." Rainault said, as if hearing her thoughts. "That kingdom is known for the unchecked violence their people display. That's why they've been such a nuisance for everyone."

"I don't believe you."

Rainault shook his head. "Trust my hate. If truth can make you suffer, I have no qualms shoving it down your throat."

"Sir," the soldier who had been chasing Merlin interrupted Rainault. "We should begin taking these prisoners to Nottingham. The Mayor will likely want to deal with them himself."

"That won't be necessary, Captain." Rainault waved a hand at the soldier. "The Deputy Mayor has already given them to me in return for the prince, to do with as I please."

"He *gave* them to you?" she repeated, seeming surprised. From beside Merlin, Jack made a noise like a click, which the soldier caught. She looked at the prisoners, then back to Rainault. "Then... what would you have us do, sir?"

"Stay out of my way." Rainault instructed, pulling a hunting knife from his belt. "Don't interrupt me while I work. Then, when I am done, you can have what's left, Captain Koa."

Koa looked back at Merlin, and something about the soldier's face struck her as rebellious. It passed quickly, and the soldier bowed to Rainault. "Yes sir." Merlin watched her only chance of help stride briskly away, heading back to the captain's group of subordinates.

Rainault faced his prisoners, but Merlin spoke before him. Whatever she felt or thought of what had been said, there was a single truth that she would not ignore. "I won't help you!" she hissed. "Don't even bother asking me to heal you. I never will!"

The sheriff snorted, "Opinions can be changed." He stepped forward until he was able to crouch right in front of her. Merlin flinched backwards, but his hand shot out and grabbed her jaw before she could move away. Rainault squeezed tightly, sending throbbing pain through her head. With his other hand he raised his knife and pressed the cold steel against her cheek bone, the tip resting next to her eye. He slowly dug the blade into her skin. A gasp of pain escaped her lungs.

"Stop this!" That was Jack's voice.

"I think not!" Rainault was so close now that Merlin could see the enjoyment in his eyes as he forced the blade further into her skin. "You are going to heal me, even if it's the last thing you do!"

Again, Merlin gasped in pain. Her skin was stinging and screaming all at the same time. Her eyes watered from the constant push of his knife. Its edge stung more than any slash from a sword she'd received, and it just kept getting worse and worse. However, even with the steel pushing against her, Merlin still had the nerve to snarl, "I'll die before I help you!"

Rainault growled loudly, and abruptly pulled away from Merlin, yanking his knife out of her.

"Ah!" She brought her bound hands up quickly to her face, pressing them against the open wound. Blood was already trickling out from beneath her fingers, but the flow was stemmed for the moment. Head wounds always bled the worst.

"Are you all right?"

Merlin nodded to Jack, wincing from the movement. "For now." she answered. While her wounds always healed faster than most myths or elestiels, this cut would need her gift if it was going to stop bleeding anytime soon.

In front of them Rainault pointed his bloody knife towards Merlin. He was shaking terribly. "You! None of this would have happened if you had only healed me the first time I asked!"

"You don't deserve it!" Merlin snapped. Her words were slightly slurred from her injury and the way she was pressing against her cheek.

"You foolish rat!" Rainault shrieked. "You're a healer! If you aren't curing anyone, what is the use of your existence?"

"You burnt my house down!" Merlin screamed, pulling her wound open further. The pain made tears well in her eyes, but she kept yelling anyway. "You destroyed my brother's grave! You tried to kill me! You tried to kill my friends! I would sooner cut off my hands than let you live!" There she had to stop. The little healing her body was providing was just undone by her screams, and the loss of blood was making her head dizzy.

Despite her foggy mind, Merlin was still aware enough to see Rainault. He was growing more desperate by the second, but instead of falling apart, he was frozen. All his trembling came to a resolute stop.

That was when something strange happened.

It was like a shift in the wind that was one moment warm and the next frigid. Rainault's countenance flipped like a coin, and a sense of danger sent shivers down Merlin's spine. Beside her, Jack sat straighter, his eyes fixed on the sheriff, who seemed to be wavering on the precipice of some decision.

"That's enough of this." Jack spoke with bold authority. "You'd better leave us to the soldiers," he nodded to the group, "and be on your stinking way. Who knows what time you've got left to rot in this world."

"Jack!" Merlin gasped. Eyes wide, she tried to communicate to him that antagonizing Rainault was not going to help. The old leprechaun ignored her entirely, letting his gaze fall on something behind the sheriff.

Jack growled, and yelled again. "You've no legal way of forcing her to heal you, and no chance of convincing her either! You had better give up and crawl your way back to the hole you came from."

"Stop!" Merlin cried.

Rainault clenched his fist, and his wings fluttered just the slightest bit. "You're right, I have no *legal* way of getting cured."

Merlin felt the hairs on the back of her neck stand straight up. There was danger in the air—she could almost taste it. A foreboding shadow had fallen over them.

Heart pounding, Merlin began to speak, trying to get Rainault's attention away from Jack. Just as she started, Rainault moved forward. He covered the distance with such speed that Merlin momentarily missed his steps. Someone with his illness shouldn't have been able to move that quickly, but he defied her expectation completely. Before she knew it, the sheriff had crossed the distance separating the prisoners from him. Merlin let out a terrified cry as she saw him thrust his hunting knife straight into Jack's gut.

"Something *illegal* will have to do." Rainault snarled, wrenching the weapon out from within the leprechaun.

Merlin screamed, "No!" and launched herself towards Jack. Red tinged her vision. All she could see was the seeping pool of blood spilling out of him. Jack fell to the ground with a loud and horrible thud that resounded in her ears. Another wail of anguish ripped out of her, but the sound was useless in Merlin's attempt to reach him. For a terrible moment, she couldn't tell if she was moving forward or falling to the ground herself. Or maybe she was just crawling forward, pulling herself towards him despite the binds around her wrists.

Either way, her progress came to an abrupt stop as a blow to her head sent Merlin flying backwards. The world spun, and she bounced to a painful stop along the ground. Merlin could feel rather than see that she was right on the edge of the platform.

"Fool!" Rainault appeared before her and grabbed her neck with an iron grip. Merlin tried to scramble away, to break free from him, but he simply squeezed harder.

"Jack!" Merlin gasped. She could see him lying on the ground, his face paling by the second.

He needed her.

"Jack!" Merlin clawed at Rainault's hand, but his gloves made it impossible for her to inflict any damage. In vain, she struggled against the crushing force of Rainault's grip. "Let me go!" Her lungs screeched for air, so much so that she could hardly speak.

"I think not!" Rainault's voice was sharp and grating. "You refused my plea for health, so I deny his right to it. If you wish to heal him, you must save one person first, and that is me!"

Hot tears rolled down her cheeks in desperation. Merlin could *see* the life slipping out of Jack. He was dying, and she couldn't save him. Rainault would keep her there until she healed him or Jack died.

Hate filled her as she glared up at him. "I'll kill you." she promised, quiet at first then louder. "I'll kill you!"

"No!" Merlin flicked her eyes to Jack. He had one hand on his stomach, and was rolled onto his side. "Not you, Merlin. Not you!"

"I agree!" This time a female spoke. Something silver and shiny appeared under Rainault's neck. Merlin had to look out of the corner of her eye to see that the blur was actually a blade. "Sheriff Rainault, you are under arrest for attempted murder and assault. Surrender willingly, or suffer the full consequences of the law." Merlin strained to see the captain, was she actually helping them?

Rainault tilted his bandaged head up. "You would betray me? After I handed you a promotion on a platter? You caught a prince!"

"You broke the law. That is undeniable." the captain told him. "Release the prisoner."

Merlin coughed and pulled, but Rainault held fast. There was only a small motion, three taps of his pointer finger around her neck. Her heart stopped as she recognized the motion. "No!"

Her cry was not enough to warn them before his signet was completed, and chaos ensued. All at once there was a loud crackle, and a sudden blaze of fire roared up into the air. At the same time, the soldier jumped back, and a black blur fell from the trees above. Rainault gave a cry and let go of Merlin, who choked on the sudden return of air in her lungs. Her head was swimming, but now she could see that Rainault's fire was placed in a circle between them and the soldiers. She could also see that the black blotch was Guinevere! The cat must have jumped off one of the trees and landed right on the sheriff's head. He was trying to pull the feline off of him, but Gwen had her claws dug into the folds of cloth around his head.

Heat rose around them. Outside the fiery dome there were screams and something like the loud roar of a beast. Merlin looked from the cat to the wall of fire, trying to decide what to do. Jack was out there, needing her help, but now Gwen needed her as well!

The cat let out an angry yowl as Rainault finally yanked her away. "Curse you! I'll roast you alive!"

That clinched it. Merlin threw herself at Rainault, tackling the old ivirian to the ground. He dropped Guinevere with a yelp of surprise, the two of them rolling toward the fiery wall. In a mess of screams and punching, Merlin ended up with her back to the fire, swinging her fist at his head. The blow swung past him, missing his head by inches as he ducked. A gasp escaped her as he responded, a heavy fist smacking into her head.

"No!" Merlin felt the pain in her head swell to an unbearable amount, and darkness began clawing at her vision. "No, no, no!" Even as she hit the ground she tried to stay conscious, but her effort was futile. Despite her cries and pleading, Merlin's vision failed. *Jack, please, wait for me...* she pleaded, the darkness pulling her down.

⁃ ○ ⁀ ○ ⁃ ○ ⁀ ○ ⁃ ○ ⁀ ○ ⁃

L

The smell of ash sat on the wind. Lance hurried across a platform in the direction of the screaming, his sword gripped tightly in his hand. With every step forward, the sounds of battle grew louder, disrupting the once silent village. His head was still whirling with everything he had said, everything that he had *done*. It felt like a fever dream, rather than a memory. But no amount of delusion could convince him it hadn't happened. The smell of blood still lingered on his skin.

I snapped, he thought into the void of his own mind.

"*You sure did.*" Solaris spat. The sword was emanating irritation. "*I told you to stick to your principles, and you didn't listen to me. Now look what happened!*"

I'm sorry... I should have restrained myself. Lance felt like he was holding an ocean's worth of regret on his shoulders. Self-loathing did not even come close to describing the disappointment with which he regarded himself.

"*Exactly my point,*" Solaris agreed emphatically. "*While their deaths were warranted, killing them out of anger is worse than simply defending yourself.*"

I know that.

Solaris must have sensed Lance's guilt, as he let out a sad sigh. "*I know you do. I just don't want you to think I condone your motivations after I say that you should try to forget it. Now is not the time to wonder.*"

How can I? Lance asked as he crossed another bridge. *I killed all of them, Solaris.*

"*They were trying to kill you, too.*"

Yes, but don't you see? Lancelot squeezed his sword's handle tightly. *I could have simply left them unconscious. Instead, I... I was me again, for a moment, and I gave in.*

"*Listen, you made a choice, and you'll have to live with it.*" Solaris said with surprising gentleness. "*Though you may bear this for some time, you can dwell on it when Merlin is safe. For now it will only serve as a weakness. And if it needs to be said, you're you now, Lancelot.*"

The sword's words brought warmth to Lance's anguished heart, alleviating some of his inner turmoil. Solaris was not brushing aside his actions, nor encouraging them. Lance still felt all the guilt and anxiety that his memory inspired, but for now, he had more important things to worry about.

Thank you, Solaris.

"*You're welcome. But now I think you should focus on that hot mess in front of you.*"

"Hot mess—" he stopped, both in word and movement. He had finally come upon the platform making all the noise, and whatever he had expected, it was wrong. Five soldiers were spread out over the platform, one lying prone, another by her side, and the rest surrounding a giant snake. At least, he thought it was a snake.

The monster sat upon the platform, its base wrapped in a dome of flames, its pointed head reared high into the trees. The form of the creature was built from lashing and flailing flames of bright red and orange. It opened its jaws wide, and an ear-splitting roar burst out with a force that blasted wind straight into the ivirians. As Lance watched, several of the soldiers were blown clear off the platform. Many made

CHAPTER 23

hasty flying maneuvers to keep from plummeting, most of which sent them heading for Lancelot's platform.

One of the soldiers, an ivirian with pale green skin and wings, tumbled in a roll before he fell off the side, thrown closer to Lance than the rest. The prince sheathed Solaris in a breath, and in another, he leapt off his platform, one hand grabbing the edge. With his other hand, Lance grabbed the wrist of the falling soldier, biting back an exclamation of pain. His muscles screamed from the instant strain that pulled in opposite directions from either arm. Ringing began pounding in his ears as he gritted his teeth, trying desperately not to let go of the wooden planks. Splinters mercilessly stuck themselves into the tips of his fingers, and sweat began to slip through Lance's grasp on the ivirian's wrist. How long could he hold the ivirian before his hand slipped?

Shouts rang out above him, and another ear splitting roar shook the wood Lance was grasping. "Please... Fly!" he choked out through his closed teeth.

"I can't!" The voice was pained and uncontrolled. "My wing, it's bent!"

Please tell me he doesn't mean it! Lance thought as he felt the smallest slip of a finger.

"I'm afraid not." Solaris responded. *"He looks really bad... shall we try my wings, then?"*

No! More pain arched through his shoulders. Now was not the time to be trying to fly without practice, not when a single mistake would send them both into the marsh below. He could see the ground through a light fog: cattails and long lemongrass were growing upwards, and uneven rocks peeked through green water. If either the ivirian or himself fell, they would die on impact.

Another gust of loud, hot wind blew across Lancelot, sending the ivirian he supported screaming in terror. The soldier's fearful shuddering spurred momentum to build up and swing the two back and forth. The prince didn't know what was making the ivirian lose their sense, but if he didn't stop trembling, they would both fall.

"Uh, Lance!" Solaris's tone was warning and nervous, but Lance was having a hard time paying attention. Around him the temperature was rising, and red tendrils of light flickered in the corner of his sight. Sweat dripped down his face and coated his hands, stinging his eyes with each drop. His arm shook as the ivirian let out a second scream.

Tensing every muscle, Lance twisted his head around, gritting his teeth painfully. Nine feet away from him hovered the blazing head of the snake, the clear line of its jaw displaying an open mouth. Before either could brace themselves, the monster gave a shriek that was double the volume and heat of the previous, sending them swinging backwards.

"Solaris..." Lance exclaimed, his skin stinging as it burnt. His shoulder screamed from the strain. "Tell me you can control any fire!"

"*I'm afraid not, Lance,*" replied the sword solemnly.

As if it could hear Solaris' response, the snake drew back its head, preparing the fatal strike that would force the two into a freefall of flames. That left flying as Lancelot's best option. It was the only way for them to escape. He berated himself for not keeping that Tear Ivirian's power.

Taking a quick breath, Lance prepared to let go of the wood. The snake made a gasping, quenching noise that probably meant it was about to swallow them. Despite having no eyes, Lance was sure he could see a delighted expression come over the fiery monster. Steeling himself as best he could, Lancelot began to lift up his fingers.

Just as he was about to let go, a rushing sound rose around them. It snapped and sucked at the very air that floated carelessly above the ground, pulling it from every direction, even from inside the knight's lungs. Somehow the air was being drawn away, pulled so intensely that Lance nearly passed out from the suffocating loss of air.

Not only did he feel the pull, he could clearly see that the snake was not faring well either. The flames that made up its body and face curled backwards and shriveled into a thin, twisted caterpillar shape that wildly bucked this way and that. The giant monster writhed in uncontrolled agony as it shot higher into the air, screaming in protest. Two beats of a heart later, the entire snake was snuffed out. Uneasy silence descended upon them. It felt as though the monster would reappear, but the snake truly was gone. In its place remained only thick smoke and steaming black wood. The damage served as the only evidence of a fire occurring.

Stunned silence wished to grow, but Lancelot broke it. He yelled for help as loudly as he could, no easy feat for him as he had lost most of his breath. Holding the weight of two people was difficult enough with a firm grip, but now that he had released the slightest bit of his grasp, Lance knew he had only moments left before he fell. He began

CHAPTER 23

to call out again at the same time his right hand traitorously let go of the platform.

Wind rushed around the elestiel in a useless cushion as he fell, hurtling downwards with increasing speed. The rushing air covered his ears with airy hands, and despite the fact that he had fallen feet first, he'd somehow managed to maneuver himself so that his head would first receive the impact. All the blood inside Lancelot's head left him, and for a heart stopping moment he could see nothing.

Who knew how close he was to the ground when two things happened with swift abruptness. The first was him remembering that he should probably attempt to use Solaris's power, if, of course, he didn't want to die. The second, and more immediately helpful thing to Lance, was a quick jerk as someone or something grabbed Lance from behind, bringing him to a skirting halt. His eyes spun for a long moment, but the prince was vaguely aware that he was now being lifted up, and that a loud buzzing was coming from whoever was helping him.

"Oh, well done." Solaris drawled. "*I thought you were supposed to be strong and powerful, yet here you are, rescued by an ivirian when you have wings of your own to use! Shoddy knight skills, if you ask me.*"

I don't believe I did. Lance snapped, trying to settle his flipping stomach. Out loud he said, "Thank you."

From behind him a familiar voice grunted, "Same to you."

The knight raised a questioning eyebrow as the ivirian set him down on the smoking remains of the snake's platform. In the back of his mind, he noted that the ivirian who had saved him was the one who chased him before at Jack's house. Lance tucked that information away and refocused on scanning the area for Merlin. He couldn't see her anywhere on the smoking platform. Instead there was only one figure, laying flat and shaking terribly.

As soon as he saw Jack, Lance took off towards him, dodging gaping holes in the platform as he went. The leprechaun looked awfully pale, and blood pooled out of a wound in his stomach. *What happened?* Lancelot thought as he ripped off a piece of his ragged shirt to press against the wound. The old shop owner's eyes fluttered open, searching erratically until they found Lance.

"You!" he spluttered, sounding both weak and annoyed.

Lance tamped down on a rise of anxiety, forcing a similar annoyance into his voice. "Don't talk. You'll make this worse."

The prince looked back over his shoulder, but only three ivirians were on the platform with him, the rest were still on a neighboring deck. The soldier who had been prone previously was now half risen, her eyes and arms glowing red like her clothes. The soldier who saved him was by her side, along with another soldier. If he was correct, she must have been the one who destroyed the fiery abomination. The glowing soldier noticed him looking, and began to get up.

"If you have a healer, get them!" Lance didn't bother to wait for a response. His focus went back to the leprechaun, whose eyes were watering badly. "Their healer is coming." Lance *really* hoped that was true. "So just stay calm."

"No time!" Jack's hand shot out and grabbed Lance's collar tightly, pulling him closer. "Here!" Lifting his other trembling hand, he uncurled his stained fingers. In the palm of his hand was a silver chain with a circular pendant in the center.

"My token..." Lance exclaimed.

"I'm collecting the favor of this token." the leprechaun spoke quickly, quietly, and with great pain. "You must promise me to stop Merlin from doing what shouldn't be done. Kill the sheriff yourself if you have to. Protect her."

Merlin? Was she with Rainault? Did that mean he was still alive? Lancelot frowned, he was thoroughly confused. "Jack, I need to help you. I don't know where she is yet, but she's smart. She'll protect herself."

"No!" Jack gasped louder, trembling so hard that it shook Lancelot as well. "Promise me you'll stop her!"

"All right!" If Jack kept yelling he would lose even more energy. "I promise, I'll do it!"

Jack released his collar, falling back to the ground in a fit of coughing. When the spasms seemed to stop, he said in a calmer voice, "She can never kill someone, or her power... it will disappear. Understand?"

Lance's eyes widened. Jack didn't seem able to continue, but what did he mean, her power would disappear? That was impossible. "What are you saying? Nothing can take the Rideon away from an elestiel. You said so yourself!"

Jack's eyes were growing more distant and empty as he gazed at the treetops above. "Healers have a limit... Their good can turn to evil... don't let her..."

Lancelot drew his eyebrows together, more confused than before. "Jack, I don't understand. What do you mean?"

But Jack couldn't answer him. Small whispers of life had sustained him throughout his speech, now they were silenced. Only an empty shell remained: a cold, hollow body with no breath left to fill its lungs.

The light died in Jack's eyes... along with everything else.

Lancelot sat back on his heels, staring at the lifeless leprechaun. Shivers ran down his back and arms, numbing his heart. Jack was harsh and irritable, but somehow Lance learned to respect him. He knew that the leprechaun, with all his faults, was a good person who deserved to live his life till old age claimed his last moment. Except Jack would not get that. He wouldn't be able to live out his days to the fullest, and maybe it was Lancelot's fault. If he had just been faster in dealing with the soldiers left by the Deputy Mayor, maybe he could have saved Jack. Or before that, instead of speaking to Reed and ruining his country's chance for an alliance, he could have taken them all out. Anything would have worked, if it had preserved Jack's life. Instead all his actions, whether to prevent violence or participate in it, had aided in more bloodshed.

Tears welled up on his lashes, a drop rolling down the side of his cheek. Quivering, Lance reached out, and gently lifted the royal token out of Jack's palm, cupping it in his bloodied hands. Aching pain began to throb in his throat and squeeze his lungs.

The familiar presence of Solaris softly entered his mind. *"It's not your fault, Elyan."*

Lance closed his fingers over the token, bowing his head. Those words were the last he had heard from his mother, and now here he was, hearing them again. *Why do I keep hearing that if it's not because of me?*

"Because it's the truth."

The prince covered his face with one hand, bending forward. He stayed like that, even as footsteps pounded over to his side. A wail of anguish came from what sounded like Guinevere. At least she was all right.

More steps came forward, someone gasped. They were all seeing Jack now, his body splayed out on the wood. For a long time, nobody said anything, the minutes feeling like hours as they passed by. It was only when Lancelot felt someone place a hand on his shoulder that he raised his head.

The bronze skinned soldier with red eyes was kneeling next to him, his wings drooping against the ground. His face was ashen as he breathed, "I'm sorry," like the words were stuck in his throat.

"We all are." Now their leader was there, backed by the five other ivirians. They were kneeling in a group, each with a shame-filled expression. Their leader bowed her head. "We are *truly*... sorry." Her steady voice cracked. "He warned us. He told us that Rainault would do something like this, but I did not believe him."

Lancelot squeezed his mouth together, raising his head higher to stare at the crown of the trees above him. In the leader's voice he heard the same guilt that was sitting inside him, and he saw it in the reflection of the soldiers around him.

Jack realized this would happen... he thought. *But he died anyway.*

"*Maybe,*" Solaris answered. "*Perhaps he knew it was the only way for them to see the truth, so that they could help us.*"

Lancelot closed his eyes and took a single breath. In that breath he came to a silent resolution. With his last words, Jack made him promise to keep Merlin safe, to stop her from killing the ivirian responsible for the leprechaun's death. He didn't understand what the leprechaun meant about Merlin losing her power, but what the prince did know was that he would keep his promise.

Releasing his curled fingers, Lance let the token slide out from his palm. Carefully, he put the chain over his head, and rested the stained pendant on his shirt. Wiping the evidence of tears off his cheek, Lance turned to Gwen. The cat appeared battered, and one of her paws was bent at an unnatural angle. She wouldn't be going anywhere far until Merlin had returned. The pain must have been great, but that did nothing to disrupt her gaze. Her determined green eyes stared into his, conveying her permission.

Lancelot nodded just barely, and transferred his stare to the soldiers. "Will you help me find her?"

Chapter 23

They looked at each other, then at their leader. Straightening, she gave him a resolute nod. "We will."

24

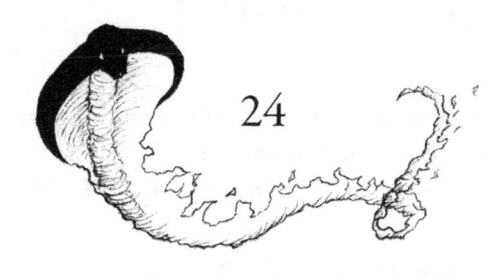

Twisted Justice

M

Pain throbbed behind Merlin's eyes and across the back of her head. As she opened her aching eyelids, she was met with a sideways view of rough wooden paneling. Laid on her side as she was, her bones hurt from the hard ground. She tried to move her hands, but her wrists were still bound tight. She felt the same sensation around her ankles, even through her boots. The one silver lining was that she could feel her head wound had stopped bleeding.

That thought cleared the fog in her mind as she remembered what had happened.

She'd tried to save Gwen, but Rainault knocked her out easily. He must have dragged her off somewhere like a coward. A wave of prickling needles crawled over Merlin's skin as her mind latched onto another memory. Eye's widening to an almost painful size, Merlin wriggled to her knees, using her hands to push herself up. Jack, she needed to get back to him. She had to heal him!

Her eyes searched the wide platform she was sitting on, looking for anything sharp. The platform holding her was bare except for a small hut with a thin garden encircling the house. Nothing pointy appeared, but her eyes did land on Rainault, sitting with his back against the hut's door. A hand rested over his face, his shoulders slumped.

She might have thought him to be asleep had he not looked up when she moved. "Don't bother struggling, there's nothing left for you back there."

Merlin swallowed and glared at him with all her hate. "What do you mean?" Her gut tightened. A dark feeling whispered that she knew what he was going to say, but maybe, just maybe, she was wrong.

CHAPTER 24

The sheriff dropped his hand so both arms were draped over his knees. "Obviously, that leprechaun is dead. I watched him breathe his last not fifteen minutes ago. You aren't *that* stupid, so you should have guessed."

Merlin collapsed to the ground with a hard thump she barely noticed. Tears welled in her eyes and trickled down her cheeks, sending shivers violently through her. When she lost her home, Merlin thought that a great hole had been cut out of her heart. Even before that, when Aspen died, she believed there was no way to recover the piece of her that was gone. Her soul had shriveled both times, and here it was happening again.

Jack, poor Jack.

Memories drifted in front of her eyes, bright and cheerful for a moment before fading away just as fast. Merlin tried to grab hold of the flickers of past times, of training with Jack, of watching him argue with Gwen. She could see the hours spent with her brother and the old leprechaun, learning to refine their connection with the Rideon. All her happy memories flickered and disappeared from her mind, leaving her with nothing but bitterness.

"Jack," the words tumbled out of her, "I'm sorry."

Her heart wrenched and twisted, her lungs squeezed the breath out of her. Merlin trembled, hunched over, and stifled her small cries with a hand. If only she had gotten back to him in time, but instead she was cursed to always fail. Why was she given such a pointless power? To be able to heal anything, and nothing at the same time... it was torture!

Why was she so *useless*?

Rainault appeared before Merlin. She hadn't seen him stand, but he was there now, crouched in front of her. A single wrap was undone from his head, revealing his forehead and eye, the skin around them burned to a glossy gray.

His voice was sharp as he asked, "How does it feel?"

"What?" Merlin blinked away more tears.

"How does it feel to know that you could have so easily healed him?" His eyes glistened. "I can't ask him what it was like to know you could have saved him, but that's fine. I already know."

Merlin seethed, feeling her face flush from the pure hate welling up inside her. "I am going to kill you. His life was worth a hundred of yours!"

Rainault shook his head slowly. "He was as insignificant as the ant under my boot."

Merlin growled, her stomach clenched in anger. She wished to say something in denial, but the words would not form.

Rainault tilted his head, he leaned closer to her. "The guilt is consuming you, isn't it? You know you could have saved him, had you left the cat to her fate. Now that he's dead, you have a thought inside of you that will spread its branches and grow until the only thing left is your utter shame, having failed to save what was *right* in front of you." His words were venomous claws that sunk their iron tips into her skin.

"No, no you're wrong!" Merlin shouted.

He hissed gleefully, "How long before you give up believing that this was not your fault, I wonder? How long until your desperation for atonement drags you down into the very pits of the disgust you direct at me?" It sounded as if he was smiling now, marveling joyously at his musings. "How long until you look like me, inside and out?"

Merlin couldn't breathe. Her lungs pumped up and down, but no air entered. "I know it's my fault! It's my fault he wasn't saved! But *you* are the one who killed him! It's your fault he's dead!"

Rainault stood abruptly. "Listen here, I would not have harmed a hair on his head had you simply cured me when I asked. It is *your* stubborn refusal that became the bane of Jackel Hymes."

The words echoed throughout her mind, tearing at the emotions raging within. If Merlin had healed Rainault, none of this would have happened. Jack would be alive, the knight—no, the prince—would have gone his way, and she would be that much closer to finding her brother.

But Rainault didn't deserve her help! She might have refused to help him, but his actions were his own. She didn't control him. He was the one who killed Jack. It was his volition. The fault of the wound lay on Rainault, but *she* was to blame for not saving Jack.

Merlin's breathing slowed, and the air once again began to flow into her lungs. The comforting sense of anger came back and wrapped around her like a hug, sharpening her thoughts. A dark idea danced into her mind and spread out in a banner of revenge. Perhaps the plan was too twisted, but her desire for revenge and her hate for Rainault were enough to convince her. After all, she had the upper hand. Rainault had yet to realize her sword charm was an actual weapon.

Merlin looked up at Rainault. "If I heal you," she sneered, "you have to promise to leave me alone, and never return."

His dark eyes inspected her, weighing her words. "That would be the deal."

Her heart squeezed tightly. "Then, I will heal you."

Rainault stared at her, his voice was icy with distrust. "I don't believe you."

"Fine." Merlin growled, turning her head away from him. "Then don't be healed. I'd say you have about," she focused on the rotting core at his center, "one week left before you die. My condolences to anyone foolish enough to care about you."

"All right!" he snapped. "Don't mock me, rat! You should be honored to heal me."

"Oh, really." Merlin scowled. "I'd be more honored to cure *dirt*, but by all means, keep insulting me. There really is no limit to your foolishness if you think calling me names will help you."

Rainault raised a hand to slap her, but stopped himself before he could. He moved backwards, sitting an arm's reach away from her. "Get on with it."

Merlin held up her hands, nodding to the rope. "You'll have to untie me first."

Waiting for him to decide was torture, excruciating torture. None of his face was visible apart from his eyes, making it impossible to determine what he was thinking. Merlin knew that anyone with a rational mind would laugh in her face and wait until she was actually telling the truth, but Rainault wasn't rational. He had been desperate enough to believe killing Jack would break her, thus it wasn't much of a leap to believe that she would heal him out of despair.

It seemed that her assumption was correct, because the sheriff leaned forward with his knife and cut the ropes around her wrists. As soon as the tension was released, Merlin raised both hands. In her right hand her sword grew, its blade resting on Rainault's shoulder, propped against his neck. With her left she grabbed his knife hand, twisting mercilessly. The weapon clattered to the ground, its owner crying out in pain.

"Don't move!" Merlin ordered, releasing his hand so that she could pick up the knife. Though her stomach flipped from touching it, she held on tightly, cutting the ropes on her feet before chucking the weapon over her shoulder and off the platform. "I'm glad you fell for that," Merlin muttered. She stood up slowly so that her sword stayed pressed against his throat.

Rainault glared at her. "I see your word means nothing to you as well as your gift. What kind of healer causes harm?"

"You'd be the first," she admitted. "That should make you feel good, right?"

"I'm dying anyway, so do you think this makes a difference to me?" He rose on his knees, forcing the sword to cut strips of his thin wrappings. "Kill me if it makes you feel like you've accomplished something, but it won't bring back your friend. You will be doing me a favor."

Merlin gritted her teeth. "I bet it *would* be nice, not struggling to breathe. Wouldn't it?"

"Exactly." He started laughing hysterically. "So good luck getting revenge on me!"

"Then I suppose I'll have to heal you," she mused.

Rainault's laughter stopped abruptly. "What?"

Merlin narrowed her eyes, and with one hand, she drew a large circle of glowing embers in the air. After drawing a second, smaller one inside the first, she forced the power into Rainault. In a regular healing she would be gentle, taking her time so that it wouldn't shock the patient's body and leave them crumpled in exhaustion. This time, she forced her power through his body without so much as blinking at the level of his energy she burnt up. Merlin clawed out every patch of invasive disease that was corroding Rainault's lungs and spreading through his respiratory system. She even fixed his wings, which had been the first to suffer mutilation by the hand of sickness.

The sheriff wobbled and toppled to the ground, lying on his side. Her healing robbed him of any newfound strength the cure afforded him. Merlin smiled to herself, stepping forward to reposition her sword.

"There, now you're completely healed." she announced, glowering down at him. "You could live for years... or a single minute. It depends

CHAPTER 24

on how long it takes you to bleed out." He gave a strangled gasp as she raised her sword, ready to stab him exactly where he stabbed Jack.

"Merlin, stop!"

She whirled around, leaving her sword pointed down at the sheriff. Lancelot was standing on one of the connecting bridges, a green ivirian behind him. He had Solaris drawn and was headed towards her. There was blood on his hands and his tunic was ripped, but he wasn't injured, she could tell. For half a second she was relieved, before she remembered that he lied to her.

"What are you doing here?!" she yelled, squeezing her sword tighter.

The prince stopped several feet from her, raising his empty right hand. "I'm here to stop you."

"Stop me?" Merlin puffed out an amazed breath. Who did he think he was? "You don't have the right to stop me!"

His face tightened, but that didn't stop him. "Merlin, you can't kill him! Jack told me—"

"Jack is the reason I'm doing this!" Merlin interrupted. "For him, for my house, Rainault deserves to die!"

"Yes, he does." Lance agreed. "But I will do it! You can't. I promised Jack that I wouldn't let you, and I mean to keep my word." Lance took a step forward, and Merlin raised her second hand, holding it palm out.

"Stop." She gritted her teeth, speaking through her locked jaw. "I don't know what possessed Jack to ask that, but I'm not letting you do this. He was my friend, and you barely knew him. It's my kill!"

Lancelot's face paled, which would have startled her had she been paying attention. His hand shook slightly as he raised it, now holding it out in a pleading gesture. Merlin raised her eyebrow, tilting her head as he took a step back.

"Listen to me," he started, forcing a calm tone. "What you're doing is not just avenging Jack. Torturing him isn't right; you have to see that! You're not meant for killing, Merlin."

"That's not up to you!" Her temper sizzled. "You don't get to tell me what I am!"

He took on a more desperate appearance. "That's not what I'm doing! Don't you see? You were given the power to heal. You're not supposed to be the one causing pain!"

From the ground Rainault gave a weak snicker. "That's what I said." Merlin looked down at him and growled.

"Be silent!" Lance barked, successfully retaking Merlin's attention. "Merlin, put the sword away. Let me take care of him!"

"No! I need to do this!" Her voice raised, and she looked back down at the sheriff, who was now gurgling fearfully with the sword pressed so close. "This is justice!"

"No it's not! This is revenge born of hate!" He paused, then continued. "If you kill him like this, it's the same as what he did to Jack!"

Her vision tinged red. "This isn't the same at all! He deserves this! Jack didn't!"

"The intent is the same! Don't you see that?" Lance pleaded. "Killing him out of anger will hurt you as much as it hurts him! Trust me on this; I've seen it happen before!"

"I wouldn't trust you with anything." snapped Merlin. "All I know is that he killed Jack, and I am going to be the one to take his life."

The prince gave a frustrated sigh. "You keep saying the same thing... you're not *listening* to me! I am going to kill him, but you can't do it!"

Merlin shook with the effort it took not to scream at him. He sounded just like Robin, suggesting that his parents should be left unavenged. At least Lance wasn't trying to keep Rainault alive, but handing him over? To someone so disconnected from Jack? No, she couldn't. Everything inside her revolted at the very suggestion of it. She had to do it. It had to be her.

"Merlin, Jack said that if you kill him, your power will disappear."

From the ground Rainault let out a tired laugh. "*That's* justice."

Silently, Merlin took her foot and stomped on his bent leg, twisting it so hard that the sheriff screeched in pain. From him she looked up to the prince, and shook her head. If Jack said she would lose her power, Merlin had no doubt she would. But what was so bad about losing it anyway? She was never able to use it on those who mattered to her, so why have it at all? At least this way she was avenging Jack...

Lancelot's posture tensed, his sword hand shook once, then it raised upwards. Realizing what he was planning, she let out an appalled breath.

"You think you can stop me before I kill him?" she asked incredulously.

"If I have to." He sounded miserable.

Merlin closed her mouth, steeling herself for a fight she sincerely wished not to participate in. She needed to be the one to kill Rainault, it was her job, her duty, her kill. Lance wouldn't be able to stop her fast enough.

Before either of them could move, a whizzing noise sliced through the air, an arrow flying an inch away from Merlin's cheek. The arrow stuck itself into the ground, its shaft vibrating from the force of the impact. Little flecks of feather drifted lightly down to the deck floor, responding to the vibration.

Eyes wide, Merlin twisted her head to the right, scanning for the archer. She didn't have to search long.

Robin's hood was pulled up and his form was rigid, his mouth pressed into a firm line. The thief stood on the platform with his bow raised and an arrow notched on the shelf. He was aiming the point directly at Merlin.

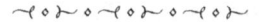

RH

Robin hurried across a bridge, making sure to maintain his hold of the ropes so as not to fall over the side. The dragonflies were doing their best, but they were terrible at judging space. Borrowing the senses of a flying insect meant Robin had to judge the distance between the ground and their eyes, and then convert that to his own height. It was hard at first, but now he was fairly used to it. Regardless, the insects insisted that they were leading him to Merlin, and for her sake he hoped they were right.

The smell of burning wood coated the wind, wafting in various strengths. Robin could smell it better the farther he went, and if he strained himself, he thought he could hear screaming. But even without that, his gut was basically shouting at him that there was danger.

"We're here!" one of the dragonflies squeaked. "*Just over that bridge is your friend, but she doesn't seem too happy.*"

"What do you mean?" Robin was already reaching for an arrow.

A second dragonfly spoke. *"There's an ivirian with her, his badge looks impressive. Your friend's got a bad look on her face. She seems to be holding him captive with her sword. I don't see anyone else."*

It was a soldier then, maybe even the sheriff Merlin told him about before. Growling quietly to himself, Robin stepped off the bridge and onto more stable ground. With help from the insects, he positioned himself behind the supporting tree trunk, ears straining to listen. He wanted to help her, but it was always better to get an idea of what was happening before charging into possible danger.

Merlin was speaking when Robin finished positioning himself correctly. "That should make you feel good, right?"

He raised an eyebrow beneath his hood. She sounded like she was taunting someone. *What is going on?* he thought.

"I'm dying anyway, so do you think this makes a difference to me?"

Robin gasped, stepping back into the tree so abruptly that the bark caught on his tunic. The air in his throat halted its course to his lungs, which hitched in tight anxiety. The dragonflies around him made a chorus of concerned noises, buzzing at his sides.

"Robin! Robin! What's wrong?"

The ivirian's voice, it was pulling dark memories up from the deeper parts of his mind. They pressed into him with overwhelming power and vice, pulling him away, out of Aroth, out of Sher. Back to Avalon, to the small town of Kete where he had been born. To his last memory with sight.

There was a wooden table sitting in the middle of a rectangular room, with bowls of steaming oats sitting on the table. Robin looked down at his own portion, wrinkling his face at the smell. His parents both had their own bowls, but neither seemed to notice the food's inherently disgusting taste. They were eating calmly, talking to themselves about... something. Robin's mother glanced at him, a concerned look in her green eyes. What were they saying?

A loud bang came from the door, and all three of them jumped. His father looked at the door, standing up only to be waved back by his mother. She stood and made her way to the entrance, pulling it open to reveal an ivirian. Robin stared at him, eyes wide. He had never seen an ivirian before. This one had dark gray skin, and dark blue wings that were shaped like the bat he had seen yesterday with his father.

"What do you want?" His mother sounded angry. Robin bit his lip, that was not good.

The ivirian pushed past her into the house, scanning with his black eyes until they landed on Robin. The young boy shivered as the ivirian grinned. "You two have been slacking," he said.

"What are you talking about?" Robin's father got up from his chair, moving to stand by his son. "We paid you last week."

"Not enough." The ivirian crossed his arms, and his wings fluttered. Robin watched them, fascinated by their glass-like appearance. They were just like the sky. "You're both in a heap of trouble."

"For what?" His mother shut the door and glared.

The ivirian tilted his head. "Hmm... tax evasion." he grinned. "Tax collectors who don't collect the tax. I've seen everything now."

"We collect what we can." Robin's father sounded angry now too. "This town can't afford to pay both Sher and Avalon. It's far too much."

"Father, who is that?" Robin asked quietly. He didn't like how the ivirian was talking.

"Hush." His father silenced him with a hand on his shoulder. Robin looked up, but his father's eyes were on the ivirian, whose smile had widened.

"I've been sent to collect your dues. Both of them." The hand on Robin's shoulder tightened, and he squirmed under its pressure.

"You can't have him." His mother moved to Robin's other side. "We won't let you."

"I'm afraid that's not how this works." The ivirian stepped back, unsheathing a sword from the belt at his side.

Robin's father grabbed both of his arms and heaved him up and out of the chair, thrusting the young boy into his mother's arms. "Here, hold him!"

"Father!" Robin started to wriggle, trying to break out of his mother's hold. He did not want to leave his dad. "Father!" Robin started to cry. He didn't understand what was happening, why couldn't he stay?

"Aulen," His mother moved backwards, her eyes on his father. Aulen grabbed a knife off the dining table. Robin stared, hoping he would look back at him, but his father's eyes stayed trained on the ivirian.

"I love you both. Now go!"

"No, Father!" Robin's mother covered his mouth to stop his screams. She started to back away, but he squirmed harder. He had to get back to his father and help! But his mother wasn't letting him go. The more Robin tried to break free, the tighter she held him, heading towards the back door. She didn't get far before the door opened, and another ivirian came into the house. A sword was in the iviro's hand as well, though he didn't attack. Robin's mother gasped and turned around, just as the first ivirian sliced across the front of Aulen's chest. Robin wailed underneath his mother's shaking hand, his father falling to the floor.

In two quick strides, the attacking ivirian was by his mother, yanking at the back of Robin's collar. The young boy screamed and flung out his arms as he was pulled away. Tears flooded Robin's eyes, making it impossible to determine exactly what he was seeing. Something dark flashed by him, and a heavy weight slammed into both him and the ivirian holding him up. The world went spinning while Robin himself flew backwards, the back of his head banging sharply into their table's corner.

His vision shook and blurred with the pain that was throbbing on all sides of his head. Robin cried and put a hand behind his head, feeling something wet on his fingers. He brought them back to look at, and screamed in fear at the red that coated them.

"Mother!" Robin looked around the room for her, terrified of the blood on his hands. He was having a hard time seeing with the room so dark and shaky. Still, he searched for her, his eyes landing on someone laying on the ground. Above stood the frightening ivirian, his sword coated in the same red as Robin's fingers. The young boy wailed and crawled to his mother, who had an arrow clutched in her hand. The tip was just as red as his mother's favorite dress. He cried, trying to wipe the blood off her.

"Take him," spoke the ivirian. Robin looked up at him, the ivirian was wrapping something around his hand.

"No! I want to stay!" the boy cried.

"Boss, the kid's damaged."

CHAPTER 24

"How bad is it?"

"I doubt he'll see again."

The ivirian looked up, then down at Robin. He crouched, forcefully grabbing Robin so that he could turn him around. The boy whimpered as he felt something touch his aching head. He heard the ivirian grumble something dark.

The other responded. "I don't think he'll want him broken like this. We could get into some big trouble."

The first ivirian growled, and picked up Robin, who kicked wildly. "Let me go!"

"We'll take him to the forest." said the ivirian. "The woods will make sure he does not survive."

Robin screamed and kicked and clawed at the ivirian to no avail. He was forced to watch with dimming vision as he was taken out of the house, both his parents still lying on the wooden boards of their dining room.

Covering his mouth, Robin felt his knees buckle. For fourteen years, he had rifled through that muddled memory, scouring it for any clue as to who had killed his parents. It had never been so clear in his mind, just a jumbled set of emotions and words. The memories existed as pictures of what happened without ever showing their meaning. Now he knew, whoever was with Merlin was the one who had been in his house. He recognized that calm, fowl voice that dripped with pretension.

Robin swallowed, trying to calm his nerves enough to stand properly. If he froze the ivirian might get away. At his side, the dragonflies sounded practically hysteric with worry.

"I—" he hesitated, "I'm fine. Please calm down." The dragonflies gave a combined heave of relief at his words.

"You're missing all of it, Robin!" one dragonfly called. "There's another person on the platform, and they seem to be arguing with the girl."

The thief jumped and returned to his spot, listening to the voices. "-will disappear." That was Lancelot, he must have joined them.

"That's justice."

Robin gripped his bow, recognizing that the ivirian had spoken. For a moment no one said anything, and then Merlin spoke, sounding half crazed. "You think you can stop me from killing him?"

Robin's eyebrows shot up, and he quickly pulled an arrow out of his quiver. She couldn't kill him, not now! "Friends, give me the layout please," he whispered. The insects quickly described what he needed, pointing out each person for him to consider. When they had finished, he pulled back the string, holding his form as they directed his aim.

"Two clicks to the left," one said.

"A notch down," another chimed in. *"And just a breath to the left."*

Robin let the bowstring slip out of his fingers, the arrow zinging from its shelf. He quickly drew another arrow and moved into the open, stepping onto a second wobbly bridge. His muscles tensed as he brought the string to the tip of his nose, aiming it to where he heard Merlin's voice. His body wanted to shake, but he refused to allow it. Any trembling would throw off his aim, and he would not let the ivirian see him that way.

"Merlin," the thief called, stepping onto the same ground as the elestiel. An army of ants started shouting a cacophony of positions and warnings to him as he spoke. "Don't do it."

25

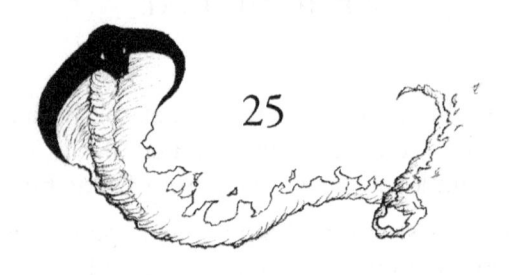

The Hated Man's End

M

"Robin?" Merlin stared at her friend, following the length of the bow up to his concealed face. "What are you doing?" How many people were going to try to stop her?

The thief began to walk towards her, motioning with his bow as he spoke through gritted teeth. "Step away from the ivirian, Merlin."

"I'm not moving," she told him.

He lifted his arrow a little higher, stopping five feet from her. The distance would ensure he didn't miss. "Go."

"You're not going to shoot me."

"I don't want to," Something in Robin's voice cracked, leaving an uncontrolled edge behind. "But I will, if you don't step away. I can only hold this arrow for so long."

Merlin squeezed her fist, clenching her jaw as hard as she could. Robin meant it. He was going to shoot her if she didn't move. But how could she, when the sheriff was right there, lying defenseless? The decision tore at Merlin from both sides of her mind, one pulling her away from the violence, the other screaming to end Rainault's life. Was she ready to possibly *die* just so she could kill him?

An angry growl burst from her as she pulled back her sword and stepped away, the weapon changing back into a charm. Killing the sheriff was already going against Jack's wishes, but trading her own life would be worse. He would never forgive her for dying because of him, and perhaps, if Merlin was honest, deep inside her there was a small voice telling her that Lance, for all his lies, was right. She still glared at them both, clenching her fists in a small act of defiance.

Rainault gave a loud sigh of relief, which stung worse than a hornet. Robin turned so that his bow was facing the sheriff, and let the arrow slide out of his hand. Merlin flinched as it collided in the wooden planks right next to Rainault's ear. A ripping sound followed it, and several more wraps around the sheriff's head fell off to reveal his shocked expression.

Merlin looked at Robin, brow furrowed in confusion. The thief didn't make a move for another arrow, instead he pushed back his bow and let it rest in its sling. He raised his hood from his head, setting it gently down on his shoulders. Just that simple act brought out the writhing anger which had hidden beneath the fabric. His sightless eyes filled with a wild and vengeful fury, threading its way through his face. There had never been such a force of emotion on Robin's face in all Merlin's time spent with him.

He retrieved his hanging weapon, pulling out an arrow to direct at Rainault. Rather than shoot, he spoke in a hiss that betrayed him to his own anger. "You recognize me, don't you?"

Rainault tried to push himself back, but his strength still had yet to return. Robin drew back the bowstring. "Don't you!" he repeated, growling louder.

Merlin begrudgingly glanced at Lancelot. Unfortunately, he seemed just as confused, though it showed with more subtlety than her own. Her heart squeezed and she looked back at Robin with her glare returned. The prince could hide anything that he felt was worth lying about.

"Yes." Rainault's wraps could no longer hide his fear. "You're Robin Hood. Everyone in my line of work knows you."

"Not that," Robin shook his head. "You knew me from before, in Avalon! You killed my parents. Don't deny it!"

Merlin smothered a gasp with her hand. How was this possible? Robin searched for fourteen years in hopes of finding the culprit, and after all that time, it had been Rainault? That was far too big of a coincidence to be true!

Rainault rose on the palms of his hands. "I've killed a lot of parents. How am I supposed to remember yours?"

CHAPTER 25

Merlin gritted her teeth and stomped forward again, ignoring the sudden exclamations from the prince. She needed to know if what Robin said was true.

"You'd remember this one," Merlin cried, "because you *blinded* the child. Tell us the truth. Did you do it?"

A sudden laugh came from Rainault as he looked between the two of them. "So the famous Robin Hood is blind? Who knew?"

Robin dipped the arrow's tip closer to the ivirian. "Answer her question."

With a gulp, Rainault closed his eyes, an expression of trepidation overcoming him. "Yes, I remember, but I certainly would have killed you if I realized you would be such a nuisance to the kingdom."

Merlin squeezed her mouth shut, attempting to silence the shock. Now she knew the truth; what Robin said was true. That iviro had slayed her friend's parents. Rainault had killed them, *in front* of Robin.

Robin's arms trembled. "Why? What did they ever do to you?"

The sheriff was starting to sweat, but still he rolled his eyes. "Nothing at first, but now I'm glad. I still have a scar on my hand from the arrow your crazy mother stabbed me with." he chortled. "It's her fault you're blind though. I would have kept you unharmed. If she hadn't made me drop you, you would still be able to see."

Merlin pushed her cape aside and grabbed the collar of his tunic tightly. "Stop stalling! Tell him why!"

"What do you want me to say?" Rainault wheezed. "That I did it because I hated them? Well, I didn't. It was a *paid* job! They're deaths were meaningless!" Merlin released his collar, sending him falling backwards.

Robin let his bow rest. "What do you mean, a paid job? Someone else wanted them dead?"

Rainault coughed and shuddered. "That's right. Keden wanted your mother's death, and you. Sadly, he never received his last purchase," he spat. "But who wants a broken boy, anyway?"

No one said anything while Rainault continued to pant from the exertion. There was a silent realization spreading through their tiny group, a whisper that reminded them of this one iviro's wrongdoings. At that moment, Merlin knew they each had the will to kill Rainault, and in some cases desired it. In truth, their silence was a simple, suffocating question that spun in their minds: Who was going to do it?

Before any of them made a move, a sound like the rustling of a small creak began to surround the platform. A whisper at first, it grew louder as it circled them, the noise becoming clearer the longer it continued. Something, or possibly many somethings, was hissing. The noise crawled along Merlin's arms and coiled around her neck, nipping at her nerves and making the hairs on her forearm stand up. Rainault whimpered. Her eyes slid down to him, but his gaze was locked elsewhere. Merlin followed his sightline to the patch of grass growing alongside the hut.

At first she saw nothing amiss, and then... Slowly, very, very slowly, she stood up. The grass was alive, growing longer, and swaying upwards in a curving pattern that identified them as one slithering animal only. Each green snake raised its pointed head, and several blew out little tongues of fire that glowed brighter than any other flame she had seen.

Again Rainault let out a terrified squeak, pushing himself back a few inches. Somewhere above the canopy a cloud must have covered the sun, because the world grew darker around them. Shadows along the sides of the house elongated, and a thick, wet fog of fear descended upon them all. The very air was rancid with an oily horror that coated Merlin's skin and restrained her voice. Her pulse quickened to a rhythm she could hear beating crazily within her chest.

Silently, from the pit of shade on the far side of the hut, someone stepped forward. Tongues of darkness slipped off what turned out to be a man, dressed in black pants and a tunic that split three ways over his legs. Gloves of the same shade covered his hands, and though he had no weapon, a bag hung from the belt at his hip. Where his head should have been, there was only a dark hood, filled with pure shadow, and vacant of any light that touched it. A single step from his approach sent the world into a terrifying spin before Merlin's eyes, her legs buckling.

As he walked towards them, she tried to move her feet, summon her sword, anything to feel less weak. Nothing budged. She was frozen in place, just like the others. The knight stood like a statue with his sword pointed towards the man, and even though Robin could not see the creature, Merlin knew he must feel the presence. Whatever it was, it felt unnatural, twisted. Its very existence was a writhing swell of unsettling energy that simply did not belong. She could feel it. His core was the same as Rainault, except where the ivirian's disease had been destructive, this was sustaining.

The hooded figure continued walking until his strides brought him before their small group. Merlin began to shiver as a voice slithered out around them, repeated hundreds of times over in unison. "Rainault." As it spoke his name, bark ripped off the tree holding up the platform, its collision with the ground hailed by a furious crack. The wood seized upon impact, molding itself into a writhing cobra. It reared its head, sap flinging from its fangs and dripping down the uneven grooves of its scales.

All pretense of confidence left Rainault's now visible face, leaving only his pure terror in place. "N-no, no ple—please!" His voice seemed to be working despite the horror, speaking out the sheriff's pleas in breathless fright.

The creature bent down just enough to grasp Rainault's throat and lifted him into the air. Merlin watched with round eyes, unable to stop him, unable to stop it.

"I made you a promise." A sea of malicious voices spoke. "And I intend to keep it." Rainault cried out, squirming in his hand to no avail. Merlin shook violently as the man pulled back his other hand and thrust it bare into Rainault's stomach. A squelching sound came out of the sheriff, blood spurting in all directions. Merlin gagged, and someone else gasped.

The creature jerked again, shoving his hand further into Rainault. Around them the hissing rose to an unbearable volume of rattling threats... and then, suddenly, it all went utterly silent. The snakes around them leaned towards their group, bringing back their lips to reveal fangs through their curved smiles. They were waiting for something, inclining their heads forward expectantly. Merlin slowly twisted her head back to the sheriff, forcing the movement through the shaking that encased her entire being.

Rainault's eyes fell down to hers, and then he screamed. The sound was ear splitting and sharp, like freshly cut glass being dragged against her skin. It only lasted for a second, but it rang in her ears, repeating over and over again. His shriek of agony burst forth alongside fire from within, consuming the whole of Rainault, even the air inside his lungs. Within a matter of seconds, the sheriff's skin became charcoal, blowing outwards in a cloud of ashy remains.

Quiet hissing returned as the creature lowered his hand, flexing his gloved fingers carefully. Merlin couldn't speak, horrified at what she had witnessed. He, it, whichever, had decimated Rainault, and she might have done the same. A vile taste filled her mouth, her stomach twisting into a coil of disgust.

It turned to face her, spanning the distance in two steps. Merlin stared into the pit of endless shadows under its hood, frozen. Out of the corner of her eye, she saw Lancelot move forward, but something brought the prince to a sudden halt. The creature paid no attention to him, raising his right hand. The glove was covered in ash and blood, the metallic smell enough to nauseate every one of Merlin's senses. He reached forward, she flinched, and he took hold of her cloak.

Confusion crept through her fear as he wiped his glove clean between the folds of her cape's fabric. Around her, the hive of snakes called out smoothly, "You're welcome." She trembled as he continued scrubbing his fingers. "He failed his mission, but I suppose I could collect them myself." Without explaining his words, the creature raised his hand to the side of Merlin's face, tapping the point of her ear. The sensation set Merlin free from her frozen stance, her feet pulling her backwards at last.

"W-who are you?" She hated that her voice wobbled.

The creature pulled his hand back, stepping away from the still frozen Robin. It tilted its hood. "I am your demise, and I am your savior," the snakes hummed. "I am Mordred."

Merlin glanced nervously at Lancelot, having not expected an answer. What should she do now? She was certainly no match for him, but maybe there was a way to stall him until Robin or Lance could attack?

She swallowed dryly. "What are you?"

"Fool." The long cobra of bark slithered forward, wrapping around one of Mordred's legs. It wound up his body and poised on his arm, opening its jaws to speak. "Now is not the time for you to ponder that which cannot be comprehended. Your mind is not capable of understanding my words." It was unnerving to watch a snake speak through so many voices at once. They each repeated the same words from all directions in a dizzying and sharp cacophony.

Merlin summoned her sword, gripping it anxiously. "You're right, I—I don't understand. But if you think you can attack us, you're wrong."

CHAPTER 25

"She's right." the prince agreed, finally speaking. "You're outnumbered."

"Am I?" The numberless voices swelled.

"You are." Robin held up his bow, releasing an arrow without warning at Mordred. Merlin held back a gasp as the creature grabbed the arrow from the air before it could hit its mark.

Mordred held the arrow up for inspection, before tossing it away, unbothered. Immediately, the snake dropped off the man's arm, his hood tilting towards them. "I will not kill you yet, but know your days are numbered fewer than you would previously have thought. We will meet again." While he spoke he backed away, the shadow beneath his feet growing larger. It reached up and covered his boots, enveloping more of him with every step until Mordred's entire body was submerged in it. Merlin gaped as he melted into a pool of shadow which stained the very wood underneath it.

They stared silently at the mark, silence filling their ears in uneasy peace. Merlin felt a tremor run through her legs, and this time she didn't stay upright. From behind her someone caught Merlin under the arms, sinking with her to the ground. She couldn't see him, but she knew it was Lancelot. Anger tried to return to her, but the emotion could grow no roots. Her mind was numb from the maelstrom of events in which she had just participated, overwhelmed by the absence of Mordred's presence. Not until he left did she realize how polluted the air had become, how with every breath, his corrupted core had seeped into the atmosphere around them.

Merlin leaned against Lance, trying to settle her writhing stomach. Though it didn't change the fact that he had lied, his core was untainted and calming, and being near him helped her nerves settle. Rainault was dead. He was killed not by Merlin, not by Robin, not even by Lancelot. Something evil had destroyed him, and for some reason, it was coming after her next.

Outside of Aroth, Merlin and the others stood quietly as they watched the soldier work. Graser gently placed Jack's body on the ground and performed his signet, a quick two step movement. When he finished, he placed both his hands on the ground, which responded immediately. The soil beneath the leprechaun began spinning and swirling like sand, pulling the body within. When Jack was fully covered, Captain Koa placed her hands by the pit, injecting her own power into it. Merlin swallowed uncomfortably as the earth turned to a dark red, then a brighter red, then orange. Steam rose from the ground, and even standing a few feet away, she could feel the heat rising off it.

It didn't take long for the two soldiers to finish the Elm's Ceremony. They put Jack's remains inside a dark brown urn made from bark off one of the nearby trees, and handed it to Merlin. The urn was the size and shape of a plate, with a small circle in the middle displaying the ashes inside.

Koa gave Merlin a pained look while she handed it over, lighting the small opening with the tip of her finger. Its spindly light swayed in the slight breeze blowing through the forest, but there was no danger of it dissipating. Once lit, the ashes would never go out, unless it was done by someone on purpose. Now she could only see Jack in the shadows it cast, the memories she had of him.

A hand rested on her shoulder; it was Robin. The touch seemed to bring back her emotions, ragged as they were. How many times had she cried that day? Enough to fill the rest of the year at least. But though her eyes felt like crying, she did not. Instead Merlin felt a burning and suffocating sensation in her throat. There was little she could do anymore. She could not get revenge for him, and she could not bring him back. Crying would do nothing for either of them now. That left only one question for her to ask.

Merlin swallowed hard and looked up to the captain, holding out the urn. "Would you take this to his shop? His cousin usually visits around this time, and his cat should have it." Poor Nimbo, he was going to be crushed.

Koa frowned, her hand gripping a knife holstered at her side. For a moment Merlin didn't understand, then it dawned on her.

"Oh, are you still going to arrest us?" she asked tentatively. Merlin felt Robin's hand tense.

"I... don't know." Koa admitted. "You broke the law, and we've been trying to catch you," she nodded to Robin, "for a very long time."

"Yes, and I usually take such good care to preserve my anonymity." Robin didn't say it outright, but Merlin knew his method for keeping his identity hidden involved deadly means. So many soldiers had now clearly seen his face, and any one of them could make a sketch. It would make his life a lot harder.

Koa shook her head. "You're all leaving Sher, right?"

Merlin winced. She glanced to the side where Lance was sitting, isolated and estranged from their group. Gwen looked like she wanted to approach him, but his dark expression seemed to be keeping her away.

"The prince will be leaving." Robin told Koa. "We haven't decided yet."

"I suggest you go with him." Koa turned her face away, her braid flipping. "If you don't, I can't promise not to arrest you now. The only reason I haven't is because I owe the leprechaun."

Merlin squeezed the urn in her arms. "Why?"

Koa's voice filled with guilt as she said, "He told us Rainault was lying, that he would do something like this. But orders are orders. We had no proof he was right."

It was Merlin's turn to avert her eyes. No wonder Jack had tried so hard to aggravate Rainault. He was trying to prove to the soldiers that Rainault was the enemy.

That selfless idiot, Merlin thought. A brief wave of bitterness rose up inside her at the idea of the soldiers failing to save Jack. She swatted it aside, though the pain began to swell again.

"Please," Merlin held out the urn, forcing herself to look Koa in the eyes. "Take this to his house. I won't stay in the forest."

The captain hesitated, then gingerly, she took the urn. She bowed her head, "We will return him to his home." Koa rose. Just for a moment, her stern face softened into a sad expression, and she said, "I'm sorry we didn't save him."

Merlin closed her eyes, inhaling deeply before opening them again. "I know."

The captain nodded and then was gone. When she flew away, the rest of the soldiers followed slowly behind. There was a minor delay, as they had to carry an injured ivirian up with them.

As he passed, Bristol stopped in front of Merlin. He presented none of the resentment from before, and when he spoke it wasn't with the growl he used to court. "Tell your prince, Lief thanks him."

"He's not—" Merlin stopped. "He'll get the message."

Bristol straightened. "Good." The iviro looked like he wanted to say more, but instead he just nodded.

Merlin watched him and the rest of the soldiers until they were out of sight, taking Jack along with them. She pulled her cape tight around her shoulders, until she remembered the blood smeared on it. Robin let go of her shoulder as she pulled it off and looked at the stain. Rainault's blood, his life that she had tried to take. If Jack were still with them, he would have been so disappointed in her. She could see that now. But her head knowing it, and her heart acknowledging that were two separate matters. Merlin couldn't be sure if she would ever be able to forgive herself for failing to save him.

"Merlin."

She faced Robin. He was only there because she begged him to come, and while he found out who killed his parents, he hadn't been able to avenge them. More guilt tugged at her conscience.

"I'm sorry," she started. "You didn't get to see Jack, and Rainault, I shouldn't have argued like I did. Maybe we would have had more time to question him..."

Robin gave a sad frown. Anger overtook him before, now he just seemed squashed. "I have more information now than when I started, even if I didn't get to stick an arrow through his eye socket." Robin fidgeted with the tip of his bow. "I'll have to live with that."

"I'm sorry. I guess I understand what you meant now," Merlin squeezed her bloodied cape until her knuckles were white. "When we talked before, you said the bitterness wouldn't go away. You were right."

"I did say that." Robin crossed his arms. "But you know I wasn't talking about this."

"How much do you know of what happened?" Merlin asked, avoiding his last sentence entirely.

Robin sighed. "I talked to Lance, or I guess Elyan. He and Gwen told me everything."

"You know he lied to us before." she muttered. Merlin couldn't help but glance at the prince. Gwen had finally decided to go over to him, and they were conversing quietly. He must have felt her looking, because he turned to meet her gaze. Something like an apology was sitting between them, as if Lance was attempting to communicate it with his eyes alone. Merlin quickly looked away.

"He did." Robin agreed, unaware of her discomfort. "But Jack knew about his identity before the rest of us. If he trusted him, there was a good reason behind it."

Merlin bounced her heel on a rock. "He could have told me. Jack lied."

Robin nodded. "Yes, he did."

Merlin crossed her arms, closing her eyes to stop another wave of pain coming from her restrained emotions. "How did you recognize Rainault?" She opened her eyes. "Robin?"

The thief flinched. "I remembered the voice. If I'm correct, Rainault should have gray skin and black eyes, bat-like wings and black hair?"

"That fits him." Merlin cleared her throat. "Fit."

Robin shook himself, and straightened, pulling something black out of his satchel. "Listen, I have to tell you something."

She cocked her head, noting the slight urgency now added to his voice. "What is it?"

Robin tapped the tip of his bow, fidgeting nervously. Merlin felt her concern rise steadily as he said nothing. There was something he needed to say, but he was obviously having a hard time with it. Waiting for him to resolve to speak might take a long time, and her nerves couldn't take that. Carefully, she sat on a large rock near his position, facing the thief.

"What *is* it?" she repeated, her voice serious.

Robin looked torn, his eyes fixed on some point behind her. Whatever he was holding he kept covered by his hands and out of her line of sight, which made her more curious as to what it was. Her curiosity made her feel worse inside, like she was somehow disrespecting Jack.

"Robin, can you just tell me?" Merlin wound a strand of her hair around her fingers. "Is something wrong?"

The thief sighed, running a hand through his loose hair. "I..." His shoulders slumped, and he held out the object. It turned out to be an envelope. The letter was smooth except for a small crease in the top corner, with Merlin's name written clearly on it in white letters. Directions to her home were written alongside her surname in handwriting that looked familiar, but the writer's name was nowhere on it.

'What is this?" she asked, taking it gently. A black envelope was reserved for government use only.

A shadow crossed his face, and Robin sank to a crouch, seemingly more from his own emotion than to be at the same level as she was. Robin cleared his throat, then cleared it again. "Merlin," He sounded heartbroken. "Your brother... he's dead."

26

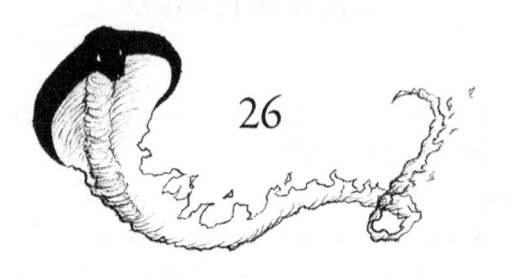

A Healer's Decision

M

Dead.

Dead.

Your brother is dead.

The phrase seemed to echo with less meaning each time it repeated in Merlin's mind. *Daleon is dead. Daleon is dead.* Her brain simply couldn't handle the information that it had just been given. Her ears felt like cloth was being held against them, keeping her from really hearing Robin. Her brother couldn't be dead; there was no way. Sher's military was not engaged in fighting with any kingdom, so how could Daleon be gone? Instinctively, her eyes flicked back to Robin. He was still speaking to her.

"I know this is hard. I'm sorry it came at such a bad time, but I couldn't hide it from you, not with any good conscience. The postman said that his boat was caught in a battle between Logres and Avalon a few weeks back. The ship sank, along with everyone on board."

Merlin's hearing stopped again. Her breathing slowed. She sat very, very still. Any awareness of her surroundings flickered and died with her sensations. There was nothing now, no air or sound or smell. Her hands may have been touching rock, but they were unaffected by the cold surface. Even the temperature, once a mild breeze, dwindled until it was utterly gone.

Light was meaningless, and darkness had no sting. Where her composure was trying to reform after Jack's ceremony, there was now simply... despair.

Not cold despair that sat within a person and held them down through heavy fits of pain. Not hot despair that clung to the skin in burning, stinging tongues of fury. No, her despair was consuming. It was utterly silent. It was a ball of impenetrable numbness that removed everything except the beat of her heart and the thoughts that slowly crawled before her eyes.

Dead. Her brother was dead.

She would never speak to or see him again. There would be no more traveling through the forest together, or collecting herbs for their parents. For two years she had worried that he would be injured, crippled or worse, and she wouldn't be there to help him. When she silenced those worries, the threat of death loomed in her mind, but always, *always*, she persuaded herself that he would be spared. Yet, here she was, alone, without any family. Aspen was gone, Jack was gone, Daleon was gone, and her parents wouldn't return for months. What would she do without him?

Would she just go home and return to the ruins of her house? She had no skills in construction, not practical ones at least. The truth was that she had nowhere to go. Yet, worse than that was the emptiness of the world without her brother. The war had taken her purpose, her direction. The past two years of her life were to prepare herself for joining the war to protect him, and through that, her parents. The three myths she wholly cared for, now brought down to two. What else was her healing for, if not to protect them?

Except here she was again, not having saved anyone.

It was useless.

She was useless.

Merlin's vision spun in a dizzying circle that caused nausea to swell in her gut. It only slowed when a flash of glossy black caught her eye. Merlin held up the letter, transfixed to its dark paper. It snared her frayed and quivering mind. Now it was clear that inside it held words written by her brother. His last words to her... ever. Were they apologies? Requests? Did it hold comfort? That seemed far from plausible. How could such a thin letter ever contain enough for that?

Her hand moved forward, trembling. Apprehension made her pause before slipping her fingertips under the seal. Weakly, Merlin released the flap so that sandy sheets of paper were uncovered. She took a breath, closing her eyes. Slowly, she pulled out the papers, unfolding them carefully. Courage, she needed courage to open her eyes. Whatever he had written, she needed to see it.

CHAPTER 26

Trembling ever so slightly, she cracked open her eyes and began to read.

Hello, Merlin...

How are you? I guess that's a foolish question if you're reading this, so maybe, how were you? I hope you were well. Our commanders requested that we write these letters at the behest of the Mayor, and, I mean, the paper and ink was free... But don't get me wrong, I'm writing this for you, and for Mother and Father. The Mayor simply gave me more paper than I had on my own, so I can afford a little more space to write.

However, now that I'm here, I wonder if it was such a good idea. Sitting in this room like I am, I don't think I've ever heard such a quiet group of soldiers. I can actually hear the scratching of their quills. One ivirian, Estol, his breathing is so loud that, if he did cry, it might be quieter than holding it in. Their emotions hang so heavy in the air that we can all feel them. I know, because they are my feelings as well. Asking us all to sit and write these goodbye letters was like putting a chain around our necks and hanging a stone from them.

It's not because we're afraid of dying, no, but because of the reminder. I've seen so much death here, Merlin. And I really do mean I've seen it. My job has always been to watch from the crow's nest, and to warn of any vessels entering our territory. Through my eyeglass, I can see the fighting ships on the lake, both of Logres and of Avalon. I have seen indomitable ships snap in half, and its crew jump overboard within seconds. There are times when the water is no longer blue, clouded over by blood and irode powder. And the noise... I have heard screaming, and shouting, and the iron clash of sword against sword.

Once there was a great shaking, like an earthquake, and one of the ships was engulfed in an enormous cloud of black smoke. Wooden boards splintered off the main vessel and flew so far in every direction that I worried they would hit our ship. The noise it made was just like the roaring of a griffon, except it was multiplied so many times over that the very waves around it shuddered and trembled. What manner of power it was, I do not know. But there was an elestiel in the midst of the waters, hanging off the bow of an attacking Avalonian ship. What happened to the men on the destroyed galleon... I don't believe I want to know.

From within Akiva's borders, I know the people believe that we are far from this fight, that simple neutrality makes us free from the violence. I'm sure Old Argathon would tell you that we have no part in it, and he would be partially right. The first thing you learn here is to avoid confrontation with any human ship unless absolutely necessary, so actual fighting does not really occur.

But what they don't understand, even what you couldn't possibly know, is the effect of two years' constant and prolonged anxiety. One step into the north, or on our main port might be enough for you to feel the tension that we all seem to live with. The weight of responsibility, the shivers of hearing atrocious battles, the constant threat of joining their war... We are the line between you all and the fighting that rages onward. One mistake by us and that could be it: Sher drawn into a war that the humans are unable to end.

A single step in our bay and you would feel the ever growing worry that plagues us. The fear, that plagues us. I still have yet to endure the horrors of actual combat, but I can't say my time here has been pleasant. It makes me appreciate what life still remains untouched in the forest, untainted from the strain of brewing provocation. It's because of that appreciation that I now arrive at what I'd like to say to you.

When we were younger, I did my best to help you see as much of the forest as possible. I knew our parents would not have let you out of the house otherwise. They're great, but we both know they are too protective, especially over you. I thought that if I took you to places where people needed help, it would help with your gift and with your future in the forest. For a while it seemed like it was doing good, you were making a name for yourself, however small, as a caring individual. People became welcoming to you, even though you had pointy ears and golden eyes.

But when Aspen died, you sank into yourself, and stopped helping as many people. You grew up to be such a distrustful person... I hate to be so blunt, but it's my last chance to tell you without hearing your antics on the matter. It is that thought that bolsters my honesty, so don't hate me later.

I wish for the younger sister that was so happy before, so filled with laughter and kindness. Your constant chatter used to easily irritate Gwen and I, but once it was gone, I wanted it returned. Seeing you ignore the needs of others on the slight chance they may betray or hurt you, was worse than being drafted. You were given a gift to heal those who had no other means of recovery, and because of one ivirian, you gave up following that calling.

I said nothing while this happened because I was unsure of how to approach you. My hesitance only exacerbated the issue, and I left without telling you what I thought. That may be one good thing this war has done. Now that I'm hundreds of miles away, and have seen this waste of life on the lake's surface, I can express to you my thoughts on it.

There is something precious about life, something delicate and frail. One wrong move, and it will break. Once it has, there is no going back. You have always had the ability to mend that breach before it snaps entirely, to protect the weak. Don't stop because of those who are ungrateful. Ignore them, and keep healing and saving lives. Your power is too special to withhold, and yes, I know you didn't choose this power, but no one ever gets to decide what gift they're getting. It is the sender's job to know what is best fitted for the receiver. Trust me, Elohim didn't make a mistake. Your role is simply to accept the gift, and use it. How, I don't know. I would have said that your job seems fairly obvious, but maybe there's more.

Either way, Merlin, I hope you will take what I said to heart. I guess I'm now somewhere farther than the port of Sal Azur, but one day I'll see you again. Please find and tell Robin that he'd better keep an eye on you. I'm entrusting your protection, whatever amount that you need, to him. Oh, and tell Jack that I appreciated all the training he gave me. And Gwen, tell her to stick with you since I no longer can.

I guess this is all. It's time to say goodbye, but Merlin, don't be too sad. I'll meet you in the Rideon, just like Grandfather described. All right? Farewell, and remember these words. I'll see you then.

Daleon

Gently, Merlin set his letter down. She drew in a deep, deep breath, and held it in with her tears. Though her body shook, and her eyes ached from the strain, she refused to let them fall. *Don't be too sad*, he told her. Merlin covered her mouth, pressing her hand hard against her skin.

For several moments, she sat there on the rock, crying without tears over the brother taken by war. It was not until the soreness of her throat grew too painful to handle that she was forced to take several calming breaths. Fresh air helped steady her mind, though it couldn't take away the pain of her brother's death. The truth was that she would never see Daleon again. Another round of weeping threatened to burst out of Merlin.

Don't be too sad.

Daleon's words came back to her again. It was such a rude thing to say to her, and yet it was definitely something her brother would tell her. He wanted her to be happy, to help people and heal injuries. Him, their parents, Gwen, even Jack wanted the same thing. What did Merlin want?

She looked down at her hands, which were trembling uncontrollably. *You're not meant for killing*, that's what Lancelot had said. If she wasn't meant to fight, then was she really stuck healing the wounded?

What's so bad about that? A memory of a past argument came to her suddenly. She could see her brother, arms crossed and shaking his head while he spoke. It was just before he left for the north. *I'd rather spend my time saving others than tearing them down. Imagine a life like that: one where you're only able to kill. That would be horrible, I think.*

All right. Merlin responded to her memory with an answer completely opposite to what she actually said to him. *I'll follow you one last time.*

Daleon wanted her to help people, so that's what she would do.

Merlin stood from her boulder, realizing for the first time that Robin had left her to be with the others. For some reason, she felt like a weight had been lifted from her at the same time as more pressure piled onto her shoulders. In her shadow, she would carry the memories of her brother and teacher, and instead of going back to her house, she would follow Daleon's instructions. Even if it meant dealing with a lying prince.

Folding the letter carefully, she tucked it back into its envelope. Once the letter was stashed in her satchel, Merlin walked briskly over to the trio. They stopped speaking when she halted in front of them.

CHAPTER 26

Gwen blinked up at her, tears in her eyes. "Merlin…" Her voice was filled with sadness.

Tears might overwhelm her if she spoke of Daleon again, so Merlin shook her head, turning to face Lance. He looked guilty, but shame had not robbed him of his resolve. While his expression told her that he felt bad for lying, it also said he would do it again in a heartbeat. Merlin was sure of that.

A nice comforting bubble of anger strengthened her, and she said, "I have made a decision."

Lance nodded.

Hesitating once, Merlin squeezed her fists tightly, and declared, "I will help you find Arthur, and end this war."

"Are you sure?" Lancelot asked, his tone serious.

"Yes." She turned away from the group, scowling at the grass beside her boot. "I'm sick of all this fighting. It's finally time someone put a stop to it."

My Ivory Knight,

    I see that your last letter was penned with a tense hand, so now, let me amuse you instead. I have witnessed something very funny, well, a sequence of funny events. I watched our marble pieces scramble about as each of them tried to escape from the forest. Overall, it was quite futile. I won't bore you with details of the chase, but I was able to overhear interesting news. You see, all this time, I was observing none other than the second prince of Avalon! There, that should cheer you up. Knowing where he is will help you, I'm sure. However, if it does not, I suggest you alleviate your irritation on one of the servants. No one will miss them.

    Passing on from that, however, our Ivory Pawn has decided to move. From now on, traveling will be harder for me, and I doubt I will be able to write to you for much longer. Such being the case, you had better make it up to me as you've promised, or I might just become angry. Alas, I have too much information to carry on that train of thought.

    Our Jade Pawn is dead now, and I'm quite glad for it. He ran his course of use, unlike the Marble Rook, whom I'm glad I did not kill. His mind is dwindling and taut in a most interesting way. You see, I watched an outburst that was truly terrifying from an onlooker's perspective. I believe his temperament could be useful, with time, though we will need to stay rather slow to utilize it well. Regardless, all our pieces have converged and are headed off to find our 'dear' acquaintance.

All trivial notes aside, we must discuss the Jade King's involvement. I can now say definitively that he is planning to join the war. I heard it from the Jade Bishop himself. They are wrong to believe joining the war will help them, but it should make things rather inconvenient on one side. I do find their supply of irode powder suspicious, and the fact that they transported it openly means they must have more. Perhaps they plan to blow both human kingdoms out of the water, and if that is the case it will be a massacre... again.

If you wish to delay their involvement, I suggest you send Ivory Rook. He would make short work of the matter, although I believe that would be too hasty. As it stands, we should benefit from their movement. Besides, even if we wanted them gone, there might be an even safer and more innocent way of ridding ourselves of the problem. Think on it, and I know you will be able to come up with something.

That's all for now, unfortunately I have no further information. As said previously, I will soon be so far offshore that I won't be able to assist you easily. I may even be unable to send you letters and reports, which will be a sad day for me. At least I know that I'll get to see you eventually, which makes this bearable... for now.

Ivory Bishop

Acknowledgements

All right, I have to thank the rain in the sky first, and coffee. Definitely coffee. Without either, I would not have this book. Period.

Moving on, many people helped me with this book, whether it was helping me with my ideas, giving their own suggestions, or putting up with my weird questions. So now I'd like to take the time to thank them. Mom, Dad, thank you for providing me with a home to spend the time needed for writing and publishing this, and understanding that writing was more than a hobby. Mom, you worked with me on so many ideas and for so many hours, I appreciated it all so much. Dad, thank you for reading and giving me your honest thoughts.

Isaac, thank you for listening to me ramble and ask questions, every suggestion has been incredibly helpful. There is also the small matter of you reading through my entire book to give me line edits. I appreciate that more than thanks can convey. Pearl, you were stuck hearing every random rant, ramble, idea, question, and fact from me, thank you for that. I dedicated my entire book to you, Ezekiel, so you aren't getting more. Aunt Jamie, thank you for reading my book over and over again. I couldn't have considered this as done without your editing. Thank you to the rest of my family, you all know what you did for helping me.

Ms. Wendy, thank you so much for everything. You are the best writing teacher I could ever have asked for, you're amazing. Not only did you teach me everything I know about writing, you read the entire first draft of my book as I wrote it. I can't say thank you enough. Sandra, thanks for listening to me work out my ideas, and for reading my story. Thank you, Calen, for beta reading my book. Your enthusiasm and comments made me laugh and find new joy in my story. Last but *certainly* not least, thank you, thank you, thank you, Megan. The process of publishing would have been all the more terrifying had you not been there with words of wisdom and guidance.

Thank you everyone who had a hand, small or large, in my book.

Pronunciations

NAMES

Alias: *Ah - lie - us*
Ardene: *Are - dean*
Argathon: *Are - ga - thon*
Armble: *Arm - ble*
Aulen: *Ole - an*
Bristol: *Briss - tole*
Brull: *Bruhll*
Calin: *Cal - in*
Cavair: *Ca - v - air*
Claeo: *Clay - oh*
Daleon: *Dal - ee - on*
Dirian: *Dear - ee - an*
Elohim: *El - oh - heem*
Elyan: *El - ian*
Estol: *Ess - tole*
Falen: *Fal - en*
Faton: *Fay - ton*
Graser: *Graze - er*
Guinevere: *Gwen - ev - ear*
Hymes: *Himes*
Jackel: *Jack - el*
Koa: *Ko - ah*
Leif: *Leaf*
Lillacae: *Lill - ih - kay*
Luzel: *Loo - zel*
Myrtle: *Murr - tole*
Penthellion: *Pen - thell - ian*
Pico: *Pea - co*
Philene: *Phi - leen*
Phoral: *For - ull*
Rainault: *Ray - nault*

Solaris: *Sole - air - iss*
Swiggle: *Swig - ull*
Talin: *Tal - in*
Tharin: *Th - air - in*
Yon: *Yawn*

LOCATIONS

Avalon: *Av - ah - lawn*
Akiva: *Ah - key - va*
Aroth: *Air - aw - th*
Ghara: *Garr - ah*
Idella: *Ih - dell - ah*
Kete: *Keet*
Logres: *Lo - gress*
Loxley: *Locks - lee*
Norestere: *Nor - eh - steer*
Nottingham: *Not - ing - ham*
Sher: *Sure*
Sal Azure: *Sal - ah - zoo - er*
Talian: *Tuh - lee - ann*

SPECIES

Elestiel: *El - est - chi - el*
Cockatrice: *Cock - uh - trice*
Fungan: *Fun - gan*
Ivirian: *Ih - vear - e - an*
Leprechaun: *Lep - ra - khan*

NATIONALITIES

Avalonian: *Av - il - own - ee - ans*
Gressan: *Gresh - ann*
Gharan: *Gar - an*

Plant Catalog and Miscellaneous Descriptions

Plants

Ridane (Rih - dane): A plant used to slow Talin's disease by increasing blood production through the bones.

Luel (Loo - el): A grass like plant used for disinfection and pain relief.

Terebinth (T - air - eh - bin - th): A rare tree with nearly impenetrable properties. It grows mostly in the land of Woodkin.

Lulac (Loo - lack): A yellow flower with roots used for calming stress.

False Ash: A tree with highly flammable bark that once lit causes dizziness leading to loss of consciousness.

Swiftfoot: A plant used for path-finding in Sher. This perennial is difficult to kill, and highly invasive when not in a controlled environment.

Moss-rose: Moss with rose-like flowers that is used for burns and skin-related issues.

Moss-camelia: Related to the Moss-rose, the little pink flowers have leaves good for tea, which soothes fear. It can also be made into an oil to prevent illness.

Moonlit Flower: Silver flowers which glow when the sun sets. Commonly used for lighting doorways and/or windows in Sher.

Bluemint: Yellow stalks with blue-green leaves. Its use is wide and extensive, though often the stalks are made into a salve, and applied to healing wounds.

Descriptions

Abba (Awe - bah): The Phoenix title for Elohim who is the creator of the world, and the Rideon.

Rideon (Rid - eon): The source of magic and power in the world, part of Elohim or Abba.

Kirsco (Ker - sco): A robe that splits into four separate pieces that drape down to the knees. Usually made from a lightweight fabric such as cotton.

Draels (Dr - ales): Like water droplets in appearance, draels cover the skin of Tear Ivirians, holding extra water inside them, as their bodies need more water to survive.

Ivira (Iv - ear - ah): Female noun or gender distinction for the ivirian.

Iviro (Iv - ear - oh): Male noun or gender distinction for the ivirian.

Ivirian Orders

Growth Order: Ivirians with the ability to manipulate plants and dirt. Though the most common, they have a second additional skill to feel vibrations in the ground. These ivirians must be on the ground to utilize their power.

Purge Order: These ivirians manipulate and generate fire, though they can only do so with suitable fuel, such as lumber, plants, or even themselves. Their skin is fairly fire-resistant, the strength of which varies between ivirians. Some Purge Ivirians have the secondary skill to melt and manipulate molten metal.

Tear Order: From the weather to the water in a creature, Tear Ivirians manipulate water of any form. Their second skill is a way of healing, using imbued water to sort out injuries. They must have access to water in order to use their power.

Gale Order: The most powerful and terrifying of the ivirians, their power is over the wind and air. All they need to access this gift is breath in their lungs. Their second skill allows the ivirian to summon and manipulate lightning.

Made in the USA
Middletown, DE
13 December 2024